THE MIRROR OF ETERNITY

The Night Trilogy, Book Three

Garrett Boatman

A white fog rose over her vision, wisps floating in from the periphery, then rising like a sea mist till all was shrouded and the grotto's walls were seen through a gray-white roiling haze. She heard the sea, as if through a shell held to her ear. Its surf rose as if she stood on some ancient pebbled beach and watched great rollers wash ashore the bones of ships and heroes.

Her panic evaporated, replaced by an exquisite sense of curiosity and anticipation.

Then the combers breached the sea wall and the presence was flooding into her mind and limbs and she experienced a sense of immeasurable age but without the decrepitude and senility that accompanied too long a life. Rather, she sensed a powerful intellect and a vast and crowded memory palace. Not the paltry allotment of recollections accumulated in a single lifespan that might fill a volume or two, no matter how remarkable a life, but a vast and ancient athenaeum of arcane lore and first-hand witnesses to history-making events, a storehouse of millennia.

Though it felt as if a god had taken residence in her blood and bowels, the presence that filled her mind like a beaker had once been human, for beneath the yellowed pages of recorded history and the fanning visions of tremendous events, she saw

A girl running in the hills, herding goats, her sandaled feet skipping over white rocks as the bright Aegean sparkled below.

A young woman, excited to be chosen but afraid of what waited in the cavern.

She closed her eyes.

The Sibyl woke.

PRAISE FOR *THE MIRROR OF ETERNITY*

"Franz Kafka, J.R.R. Tolkien, and Gene Wolfe knew the secret to creating the essential sense of wonder that gives us engaging fantasy. Reality! Garrett Boatman's *The Mirror of Eternity* holds a mirror to reality and it's an unpredictable, dark funhouse mirror: dangerous illusion and awesome, shocking truth. No spoilers here—only the highest praise for the immersive and enveloping world(s) of (demon) Azazel and (human) Richard Scott, and an intriguing cast of many, all conjured up by Master Word Magician Garrett Boatman. *The Mirror of Eternity* is the best fantasy-thriller I've read in years."
—Mort Castle, three-time Bram Stoker award winner, editor, *On Writing Horror*

"In *The Mirror of Eternity* Garrett Boatman proves himself a true magician in the tradition of such visionaries as Clive Barker and Neil Gaiman. The climactic book of the Night Trilogy weaves threads of time travel, cosmic horror, and apocalyptic adventure around the core myths of the Western esoteric tradition. The resulting tapestry is a tour de force of philosophical dark fantasy unlike any you've read before."
—Douglas Wynne, author of *The Exorcism of Winchester House*

"In this final volume of his Night Trilogy, Garrett Boatman spins a cast of demons and fallen angels, an ancient priest, a magical EMT, and a score of other fantastical characters into a harrowing and thrilling narrative that is far-reaching, frightening, learned, and above all highly entertaining. Fast-paced, dark, but also wonderfully humorous, The Mirror of Eternity is a thoughtful and well-wrought meditation on the eternal, epic struggle between good and evil, and the unlikely heroes that emerge victorious. A superb piece of fantasy fiction, and a furthering of Boatman's unique literary vision."

—Joshua Rex, author of *The Inamorta* and *New Monsters*

"Garrett Boatman's *The Mirror of Eternity* will reflect your darkest fears and most sinuous of nightmares with biting, uncompromising clarity. Full of menacing monsters, meticulously crafted characters, and a veritable vortex of plot twists, this is one cosmic horror novel—labyrinthine and explosive—you do not want to miss."
—Christa Carmen, Bram Stoker-nominated author of
The Daughters of Block Island

Thanks to:

My wife Roberta, my first reader, harshest critic, and fiercest supporter, David Niall Wilson and David Dodd of Macabre Ink for giving my Night Trilogy a home, Luke Spooner for his terrific covers, and to my readers, without whom…

I'd also like to thank Deborah E. Harkness, historian and author of the wonderful All Souls trilogy, for her article "Managing an Experimental Household: The Dees of Mortlake and the Practice of Natural Philosophy" and Benjamin Woolley's The Queen's Conjuror for helping me visualize John Dee's household, and Ingrid Rowland's Giordano Bruno for insights into the Nolan's delightfully eccentric character.

This book is dedicated to
my sister and brother-in-law
Susan and Charles Urso

The beings who live below say that God is on high, while the angels in heaven say that God is on earth.

—The Zohar

CONTENTS

PART II: The Mirror of Eternity

PART 1

THE LABYRINTH OF TIME

1
OFF THE RAILS

The first sign that the world had gone off the rails was the horse-drawn wagon they passed as the ambulance barreled down Union Avenue on its way to the waterfront fire. Richard Scott, the EMT at the wheel, recognized it as an ice wagon because the word ICE was painted in big red letters on the side of the white wagon hitched to an old brown nag. The ice man on the bench seat—a burly man who, despite his slouched shoulders and forward-thrust head, looked quite capable of hauling ice blocks up tenement stairs—wore a straw hat and a leather apron over his work clothes.

The sight was an anomaly for sure, but Rick didn't pay it much attention: he had a fire to get to. The buildings along Wagner and Riverside Drive were mostly residential apartments and there might be injuries. Besides, this was Memphis, second only to New Orleans in the number of oddities that showed up day-to-day. The apparition could have been an eccentric who preferred antique wagons to classic cars or a movie prop on its way to a shoot. A single anachronism didn't count as an epochal change in the world's progress.

The cobblestones weren't so easily explained.

"What the heck?" Mack, the unit's paramedic, said as the tires jittered over the uneven surface. Rick felt the vibrations in the steering wheel despite the ambulance's air suspension. He wasn't a Memphis native, but he'd traveled the downtown streets often enough to know the only cobblestone thoroughfare was Main with its pedestrian mall and two miles of trolley rails. Rick would have stopped and marveled at the road's overnight transformation, but there wasn't time: ahead black smoke billowed over the buildings into the jaundiced sky.

The sky itself was an anomaly. Just minutes ago, when they were eating lunch in the Kwik Chek parking lot and the call came in — "Multiple-alarm fire 35 Union Avenue at Wagner Place." — the sky was a hazy blue, the temp on the dash reading 87 and likely to top ninety before the shift was over though it was only late April. Now the temperature was dropping and the sky had darkened an unnatural yellow.

"Looks like we might be in for a real drencheroo," Mack said, scowling at the sky.

Rain wasn't in the forecast, but if Rick had learned one thing in the past year, it was to expect the unexpected.

"Hope that's all we get."

"Amen to that." Mack knew what he meant: Memphis was no stranger to tornadoes.

The third shock came when they arrived at the fire.

Union Street T-boned into Riverside Drive. Across the waterfront highway, a wide slope of restored cobblestones, often used as a parking lot, led down to the historic Cobblestone Landing where paddle wheelers took on tourists for riverboat rides. But now...

Rick shook his head as he pulled up behind Engine 17. Was he hallucinating? If so, Mack shared the illusion. His partner's square face was pale, his blue eyes staring in disbelief.

Riverside Drive was gone. All four lanes. Vanished as if they never existed. The cobblestone landing marched all the way down to the river, right across where the highway should have been. And covering the acres of cobblestones along the riverfront was a sea of cotton bales bound with metal bands and stacked several high on wooden pallets. The scene was like a sepia-toned poster you might find in the Waterfront Museum depicting the riverfront as it appeared over a century ago when it was a busy center of commerce and steamboats plied the Mississippi. Only they were seeing it in the here and now.

And the apartment buildings along Wagner Place, in front of which the engines of three companies were parked...they, too, were gone.

Vanished. In their place an old barnlike warehouse was engulfed in flames. The sign on the white-washed façade read

Patterson Transfer Co.
Carriages and Baggage to Meet All Incoming Boats

Roiling black smoke mounted to the sky. It was as if Rick and Mack had been transported to another century.

Or as if the past had come to dwell in the present.

But the biggest surprise came when Rick and Mack piled out of the ambulance and rounded Engine 17.

Two antique horse-drawn pump carriages stood closest to the conflagration. Beside the wagons, firemen in peaked leather helmets and old-fashioned uniforms stared not at the burning warehouse but at the modern fire engines and emergency vehicles and Memphis firefighters that had arrived on the scene.

2

RESURRECTION

For the first millennium, Azazel raged and swore if he gained his freedom he would devour the earth and assail the heavens. But time cooled his fury, and, slowly, over the long centuries bound in his rocky crypt beneath the burning sands of Dudael, his desire for slaughter and revenge gave way to heartrending visions of green earth and blue skies, bird song, the warmth of women's flesh, and the cool contact of sunlit water. And so, for ages more, he longed for what was lost and mourned his state.

But even sorrow has its span, and desire for all things—for bloody vengeance and submersion into fleshly pleasures—yielded to the ultimate warden, the soul-crushing lethargy of ennui.

For still more ages he squatted against the rock of his barren prison, his mind and senses more asleep than awake, without ambition or hope or even the daydream of resurrection, much less the thirst for vengeance, with only an occasional sigh or spasmodic clenching of his fist to show that he was alive.

So when the rock above his narrow house split open and sunlight drove the shadows from his lair, he cried out in agony and shock.

At first, he thought the Maker was sending His Avengers to inflict further pain, and he cringed, but a flash of forgotten rage flared and he rose, chains rattling, a long-forgotten snarl on his lips. When the dust settled, he saw the rocks piled against the opposite wall formed a ladder to the outer world.

6

His chains, so long a part of him, fell away.

He didn't need to be told twice to heed the invitation. Scuttling on hands and feet, he climbed toward the sun.

———————————

The desert was a furnace, the sun a great blazing disk. But he who loved green forests and blue waters and the warmth of woman's flesh and the hot reek of man's blood rejoiced and collapsed upon his knees in wonder and gratitude and cried out.

"Why have You resurrected me? What vast and immortal change has passed that You would unleash me upon Your creation?"

He blinked at the raw desert sun but got no answer.

Freed! After what seemed like eons. The Maker, who had sent His avenging angels to incarcerate him for all eternity, had changed His mind and set him free. But to what purpose? Whatever it was, the Maker never gave without taking and the price for his freedom would be great.

A fat black beetle emerged from the shadow of a rock and scurried across the hot sand. He plucked it up. Its brittle legs squirmed in protest. Unlike the blind white bugs that occasionally entered his prison, this one glittered iridescent colors. He popped it in his mouth. Its juice, bitter as bile, was acrid on his tongue that had savored all the sweetness of Earth's delights—the vineyard's bounty, women's embrace, human flesh hot from the spit. Still, for all its bitterness, after his eternal fast, its blood was sweet as ripe grapes.

The beetle crunched between his teeth, its juice moistened his parched tongue, and that small repast awoke a raging hunger.

Man… He was back in the world of man. So many beating hearts and pulsing veins!

The thought brought a gush of saliva to his parched lips and made him, as always, crazed with lust for man-flesh. The forbidden fruit was his greatest weakness. The predilection had earned him special treatment when the Avengers came for the Grigori.

He closed his eyes against the white disk of the sun that burned over the cauldron of Dudael and spread his nostrils, inhaling the hot air. From beyond the Mountains of Darkness and around the great curve of the world, he caught the scent of human flesh. The blood roared in his head. In his mind's eye he saw streets filled with teeming masses. Humans pressing through crowded bazaars and rumbling down broad thoroughfares in strange conveyances horseless and roaring, and towering buildings soaring against the burnished sky. Man had multiplied. Oh, how fruitful he had been. He had made abodes in the waste places of the earth, his industry spawning great metropolises.

Azazel sniffed again, caught the scent of the nearest oasis—and man—and began walking. His stride was long, his steps eager.

3

PACKAGE

The apartment was empty without Fergi. In the months since her abduction, coming home felt like walking into a morgue.

Mentally and physically exhausted, Rick laid his keys and wallet on the white Formica table he and Fergi had found in a thrift store when they first moved in and sat in one of the matching chrome-and-vinyl chairs. He spread his hands flat on the cool Formica and let out a long sigh. He looked out the nearest window, its glass framed by the curtains he and Fergi bought at the flea market the last day they spent together.

The day he met the Goddess and began his plunge into nightmare.

But he found no answers in the ominous yellow sky glowering over the roofs across the street.

He was a medic...well, an EMT-B studying to be a paramedic...and he recognized the symptoms he was experiencing.

Shock.

Not the shock that resulted from physical trauma, heatstroke, or blood loss, but acute stress reaction which resulted from the psychological trauma of witnessing or experiencing a harrowing event. Mack and all the firefighters and policemen on the scene had the same haunted look in their eyes. They had all witnessed the impossible.

A whole block of buildings and their inhabitants had not burned — but vanished...gone as if they'd never been. And in their place strangers from the past marooned in the present. The antique firemen

9

had stared in shocked disbelief at the Memphis Fire Department's gleaming trucks and emergency vehicles with their rumbling engines and flashing red and blue lights...just as Memphis' finest gaped at their visitors with their bushy mustaches and peaked leather hats and their archaic horse-drawn steam pump. One of them—their captain—an owlish man with a huge white mustache, demanded to know what was going on. And when he found that his modern counterparts were just as much in the dark as he, he asked what year it was. When Captain Rawlings told him, all color drained from the man's face and his lips moved without speaking.

Another of the castaways had a stroke and Rick and Mack stabilized and transported him to emergency. Though Mack stayed in back with their passenger, Rick had helped lift him onto the stretcher and into and out of the ambulance. The man—a good five-ten and close to two hundred pounds—was as solid and real as any patient he'd lifted in his time on the job.

Afterward, on the drive back to the station, Mack was pale but full of questions.

"What the hell is happening? I feel like I'm dreaming, but it was so..."

"Real," Rick finished for him. "Yeah, it was real."

He imagined the look in Mack's blue eyes mirrored his own. Despite his encounters with the macabre, despite the marvels—and horrors—he'd witnessed in the recent past, he was as susceptible to shock as anyone. Driving with his siren and emergency lights off as they headed back to the station house, he'd run a red light.

"Look out!" Mack yelled, waking him from his revelry.

He hit the brakes and found himself in the middle of an intersection. Luckily, traffic was light and no one was coming.

In the days and months to come, they would all relive the event in flashbacks and nightmares. Pulses would quicken, faces would pale, pupils would enlarge as eyes gazed off at what was not there. Friends and loved ones would worry and call them back and they would start as if woken from a dream. If not overcome, ASR could develop into post-traumatic stress disorder. Rick couldn't afford the downtime. Despite wanting no part in whatever was happening, he had to know.

The Sisterhood could tell him something, but he had no way to get in touch with them. They—or more likely their Mistress—would find him if She willed it.

The Priest might know something. But Rick wanted no part of what he offered.

"I'm not your hero..." he said to the Formica, to the Goddess, to the Priest, to the men and women lining a dirt road on a dark night with faith in their eyes. Faith in him.

Rick knew the disorienting terror of shock and disbelief, the feeling that you were walking in a dream while knowing you were not. He'd been down the rabbit hole and through the proverbial mirror more than once, but that didn't stop his heart from racing. He had learned what the world called reality was a mask hiding a monstrous universe.

He licked his lips. His mouth was dry. A parched tongue was another symptom of shock. His gaze sought the white kitchen cabinet over the sink. Fergi's half bottle of Jameson whiskey stood on the top shelf. He hadn't poured it down the drain. Just as he hadn't unpacked the suitcase she'd left when she was abducted but had set it in the closet in case she returned.

I have my work and you have yours.

He shook his head.

Focus.

Whatever was happening, he got the nasty feeling he was about to be sucked into a whirlpool. Like it or not.

Leave me alone! he shouted at the universe. *I am not your hero. I will not be a pawn in your game.*

Again, his gaze sought the cabinet. He thought about taking the bottle down and pouring himself a stiff one. But he hadn't touched the stuff in so long it was sure to burn a hole in his gut.

The door buzzer sounded.

He walked over and pressed the intercom button. "Yes?"

"FedEx. Package."

Rick buzzed the woman in.

The watch shimmered on the table. Not from the kitchen's fluorescents and surely not from the sickly light falling through the window. No, the watch itself gave off a subtle energy. In a long-ago world, it would have been called a fairy light and the watch would have been a magical object. But it was technology that gave the watch its glamor. It had begun life as a vintage 1934 Omega RAF pilot's timepiece. Its black dial had large, luminous hands and numbers for easy reading in pre-World War II cockpits. A second hand appeared in a separate dial below. Its oversized crown allowed an early aviator's gloved hand to access its chronograph function. Around the face a rotating bi-directional coin-edged bezel permitted calculations such as time, speed, and distance. While these nostalgic features might pique the curiosity of a museum visitor or appeal to a collector, it was the alterations da Silva had made to the watch that made it special. By his own account, the master horologist had created a number of complications on the astral plane which allowed the watch to operate by subtle laws while in the physical. And he'd enclosed the balance wheel and escapement in a flying tourbillon, a cage that rotated to even out positional errors. According to da Silva, the complications allowed the wearer to traverse time and space.

Rick was skeptical. But after today's visitation from the past, he was not so sure.

Gooseflesh crept across his shoulders as he gazed at the unworldly device. He feared touching it, as if it were some coiled viper waiting to sink its fangs into his hand should he reach for it.

A note from the Priest accompanied the watch. It requested he strap it on and manipulate the crown in such a way that he would be transported to the Priest's home in Italy.

"No way," Rick said to the watch. He was not going to put it on or get involved with da Silva again. The previous time cost Wally his life.

His cell phone chimed in his pocket. He took it out and saw he had a message.

From da Silva.

For a second, he considered deleting it. But the Priest would have answers. Why else would he contact him and request his presence?

He opened the message. It read:

"Put the watch on and press the crown three times. *Tempus fugit.*"

Rick's fist curled at his side. "I have much to show you," da Silva had said, but he'd sworn he would have nothing to do with Her Priest. As an EMT he had the opportunity to help save one person at a time. Sometimes he failed, a patient dying on the scene or in transit, but more often he could do some good. A patient might not thank him, but he felt he made a difference. What da Silva wanted—what *She* wanted…

No! He would not be their pawn again.

He shook his head. He'd been battling ASR since before he knew that was what it was called. You'd think by now he'd be used to the macabre. Get over the shock of knowing the universe was a bad place, full of unexpected corners and a monster around every one. But every time another layer of reality peeled back, the experience left him reeling.

He blamed himself for the deaths in Jersey City: Frank, Shorty, Wally's mom, Fergi's stepdad, the waitress the cops found in his car. Those were on him.

…you *were the dynamo that powered the rest.*

And while he technically wasn't responsible for the Watcher's murders—Jewelie Light, his best friend Wally—he felt guilty by association.

Grigori blood flows in your veins, the monster told him that night on the ridge when he invited Rick to join him.

It helped that Reverend Grace assured him his blood didn't make him evil, but that didn't stop the nightmares that rode him nightly like the hag of legend so that he woke sweat-soaked and went to work exhausted.

And now this new calamity.

If da Silva's "gift" were any indication—and he didn't believe in coincidence—he was once more being drawn into the eye of the storm. The walls closed in on him as images from the day flashed before his eyes: the ancient wagon with ICE painted in red, the horse-drawn pump, the dazed firemen, the fire chief's face paling as he learned the year, the burning warehouse that could not possibly have been there.

Except it was.

What hell was being unleashed?

His hands were balled into fists, his teeth clenched. He uncurled his fingers, took a deep breath.

Da Silva would have answers.

The watch glowed on the table. The power hidden in its miniaturized components radiated across the kitchen.

He picked it up, fastened the leather band about his wrist. The back of the watch was cool against his skin. The hair on his arm rippled as if disturbed by subtle currents.

Before he could talk himself out of it, he pressed the crown three times.

4
WHIRLWIND

The demon Azazel felled the first human he encountered and feasted prodigiously. By good fortune, a strong, burly youth had parked his ATV near the lake and was lounging with a plump young woman under a palm. The woman had fled screaming. On foot. She didn't get far before he caught her.

As he gorged, he read the state of the world through his victims' blood and marveled at the growth of mankind. It wasn't just his proliferation or his sprawling cities. His puny ships had grown, and he flew. He paused a moment to marvel at that. Man flew! Not on wings of his own as birds, but on wings of his making. He had even been to the moon! Was man become as gods? Did he now vie with angels in his mastery of arts and warfare?

Man had a habit of displeasing the Maker because he was never content to serve but must forever be master of his fate, never mind that he was as ignorant of the great wheel of time as the beetle he had eaten.

"Is that it, Lord?" he said to the white-hot sky. "Have you released me to punish them?"

But there were so many. He could never eat them all.

A wind stirred the palms. Birds lifted in a great whir of wings and set off across the desert. A dark funnel rose, up and up until it towered above the trees. The whirlwind spoke. Its voice was thunder.

"I do not release you so that you may feast! I release you to serve Me!"

Azazel fell upon his knees. The sand stung his eyes. The wind whipped his tattered rags.

"How, O Lord, may I serve You?"

An image formed in his mind. He saw a young man, one destined to challenge the Maker. The youth appeared unremarkable. Above average in height but not especially powerful. There was anger in his watchful eyes, but also a sadness that suggested he'd suffered loss and shouldered great responsibility. He saw nothing that posed a threat to the Maker or to himself.

"Destroy this one and I will make you king!"

His heart leapt at the Maker's words.

"This world perishes. Destroy the youth and I will make for you another. But mark Me well—fail and you perish with this world!"

The whirlwind vanished. Sand and palm fronds rained to the ground.

Azazel rose, excitement and purpose buoying his heart.

After washing himself in the cooling lake, he sat under a palm and closed his eyes and sought the youth.

5

THE UNMAKING

The lake was perfectly round. At least it appeared so from where Rick stood on the hillside. Dark woods cloaked the steep slopes, and above the circling rim a gibbous moon burned in a starry sky.

Rick knew where the Priest's watch had brought him. He stood above the shores of Lake Nemi, called by the Romans *Speculum Dianae*, the Mirror of Diana. And true to its name, the lake reflected the moon so perfectly in its still waters that even the dark patterns of the lunar seas were reproduced with photographic fidelity.

Below, on a triangular apron of shore, was a small temple. In the moonlight, its golden roof appeared silver. The temple was built into the hillside, and though he could not see its façade, he imagined wide marble steps leading up to a columned portico. Between the temple and the lake shore was a small grove where torches glowed among the trees.

Rick took a moment to catch his breath. Da Silva may have designed a special mechanism and tourbillon to compensate for the turbulence of the transition, but the trip through

Time?

was disorienting.

When the nausea passed, he looked up the hill behind him. The little medieval town of Nemi perched just beyond the ridge should have been visible by the glow of its electric lights...were he still in his own century. In his day, only ruins remained of the temple—a few low walls, a row of broken columns. The town's lights would have made it hard to see so many stars, and planes heading up the coast for the airport in Rome would have traversed the night sky. But the crest was as dark as the slopes, and the temple was whole.

A chill that had nothing to do with the night breeze raised gooseflesh on the nape of his neck. He was truly in another time. He suspected that, like the Goddess' sanctuary—the Sibylline Sisterhood where Fergi now resided—the temple and the torch-lit grove existed outside time's relentless stream.

The Priest was waiting for him in the grove.

Reginaldo Balthazar Tavares da Silva. By his own account born in the city of Lisbon in the year 1779. Master horologist and Rex Nemorensis, King of the Woods. The "Nemorian," as Grace—priestess of the Goddess and matriarch of the rural hamlet of Hendricks, Arkansas—had jokingly hailed da Silva when he arrived with Rick and Wally in tow because Silva meant forest and he was priest of Her sacred grove.

Incongruous with the ancient scene, the supercentenarian wore, as he had in Hendricks, a Hawaiian shirt over cargo shorts. This one featured palm trees and surf boards against what looked like a red background, though it was hard to tell since the torchlight cast an orange glow over the grass and trees. More in keeping with the priestly image, he wore sandals, thought these were rubber-soled and fastened with Velcro.

"I would have thought you'd be wearing a robe," Rick said by way of greeting.

White teeth flashed in the olive face. Despite the full head of silver hair that gleamed in the firelight, the man's brow was smooth and he didn't look a day over forty. "I never saw myself as the robe-wearing type. You look like hell, by the way."

"It's been a day."

"That it has."

They appraised each other in silence for a moment, the Nemorian smiling as if genuinely glad to see him. Rick's expression remained grim: his uniform smelled of smoke, he was tired, and he needed answers.

"What's going on? You know, don't you?"

"Abrupt as always. Good to see you, too."

"Cut the crap. The last time our paths crossed, my best friend died."

Da Silva looked genuinely grieved. "I regret that, as I regret every fallen hero. But Alwin was brave and chose to fight."

"Not everyone is cut out to be a soldier."

"No, but you are."

You are my knight.

Unbidden and unwanted, the Goddess' image rose before him. Diana, Hecate, Ishtar, Isis, Artemis, Astarte, Sophia, Kybele, Cybele…names given to Her by a thousand civilizations over millennia going back to prehistory when men in mud hovels chipped pendulous-breasted idols from stone. "Kee-vELL-ess," Grace had pronounced Her ancient Phrygian name. "Cybele will do," Grace told him, pronouncing the name in two syllables with a sibilant c, which he misinterpreted as Sibyl, the oracle who scribed in riddles the fate of man. But he had learned better. However long-lived, the sibyls were mortal and of Her Sisterhood, while She, their *Magna Mater*, was immortal.

Her hair was the blaze of evening sun, Her eyes the green of unfurling leaves. A dusting of freckles across Her cheeks and perfect nose suggested an ageless innocence that vied with the curl of Her sensual lips. She radiated sex and wisdom—Aphrodite and Athena— an exhilarating combination. He hoped to never see Her naked. He suspected the myths might be true and he would be struck blind or turned to stone.

Her kiss still burned his lips. He suspected it always would.

"She still thinking I'm Her knight?"

"Aren't you?"

"If I had my choice, I'd have nothing to do with either of you."

"You do have a choice. Yet you're here." The Priest held his gaze a moment, then gave a nod as if confirming something he already knew. "You're not the type to stand by when people need you."

That jolted him. Fergi had said the same at Wally's funeral. The memory conjured an image of Delores Ferguson standing under a dripping maple in a quilted black coat against a backdrop of tombstones, the gray sky muting the emerald flecks in her dark-brown eyes, the streak in her auburn hair—more platinum than silver—adding a glamor, a mystery, a heroic melancholy that made him desire her more than ever.

But administering first aid was one thing; what the Goddess and Her people expected of him was not acceptable.

"What do you want?"

"The same as you. The world faces the gravest threat it's faced in its storied existence."

Rick frowned at the familiar refrain. "I thought the Nephilim were the greatest threat the world ever faced."

"Not the world. If Talmaiel had succeeded and the Grigori wiped mankind from the planet's memory, the world would survive. The sun would rise, the tide would keep rolling in. But this…what has gone on all over the world today—the catastrophic visitation of the past upon the present—is the beginning of the end. What is at stake is the unmaking of the world—earth, moon, sun, planets, stars. The physical universe…" He looked up at the Milky Way that hadn't burned so brightly in the night skies over Italy in more than a thousand years. "All you see above, as well as the astral planes beyond… Everything below the Pleroma…" He spread his hands and shook his head.

Rick looked up at the blaze of stars, at the gibbous moon burning in their midst. Had da Silva lost it? Was such a thing conceivable? The scene at the riverfront today—the warehouse fire, the old-time firefighters—was mindboggling, but the entire physical plane, Malkuth, and the astral planes above…

"How?"

Torchlight flickered in the man's black eyes. Walking down a city street, he might appear an innocuous tourist, but there was a glamor about the man that drew the discerning eye. Though half a head shorter than Rick, he appeared taller, so that Rick, not for the first time, got the disorienting feeling he was looking up at the Priest rather than down.

"What do you know about time?" da Silva asked.

Rick frowned. The Priest could be exasperating. The sky could be tumbling down and the man would wait for his response, probably wait for him to do something spontaneously since his method of teaching was not to teach but to offer useless platitudes

Truth is a pathless land…

Dogma is not the path to progress…

Experience is the best teacher…

(that last had led to some harrowing experiences)

and to ask leading questions designed to prod his pupil into drawing conclusions.

"You bring me here and answer my question with a question?"

"Time, Richard Scott. Despite the longevity Cybele has bestowed on us and our ability to traverse its waters as if to make a mockery of Heriklitos' river, time is flying."

"*Tempus fugit.*"

"*Precisamente!*" The Priest flashed a grim smile—the teacher pleased with his pupil.

Rick gritted his teeth. He hadn't meant to be clever: Tempus Fugit, time flies, was the name of da Silva's clock shop, which the Priest transported through time and space with less effort than one might expend carrying a suitcase.

Time.

Time was one of those things you took for granted. Until it ran out. Everyone knew what it was. Didn't they?

He thought of the burning warehouse that couldn't possibly be there but was. And the antique firemen with their antique steam pump and their chief's wide-eyed question:

"*What year is it?*"

Relics out of time.

He heard a mental clicking and pictured an old analog clock, the kind that hung on the classroom wall in high school.

"It's how we measure duration," Rick said carefully. That felt safe. But he knew as soon as he spoke, his answer was inadequate, a thesis without an argument. It would probably take a physicist's answer, complete with mathematical equations and words like "duration" and "velocity" and "relativity" to satisfy da Silva. Wally could've answered the Priest.

The Nemorian's smile surprised him.

"*Bem!* A measurement. But what precisely are we measuring? Measurement implies quantity. What quantities are we measuring? Seconds, minutes, hours, days, weeks, months, years, decades, centuries, millennia, ages, epochs, eons. Do these things even exist?"

"They're mental constructs."

Da Silva nodded. "Man is a tool-using animal, and, if you think about it, time is a convenient tool." The Priest's grin was a little too broad. It was obvious he felt what Rick felt—that something was amiss, a tension in the air of what should have been a calm, mystical night. The feeling of time running out. "We might miss our dental appointment without it. But would time exist without man to measure it?"

"The earth would still orbit the sun. The solar system would still orbit the galactic center every couple hundred million years." Wally had taught him the latter.

"The galactic year." With the torchlight reflected in his dark eyes, da Silva looked distinctly Mephistophelian. Again, Rick was struck with the curious illusion that he was looking up into the eyes of the shorter man. There was a sea of power and knowledge in those bottomless pools and he shivered. Rick masked the sensation with a frown; no point in letting the Priest think he viewed him as anything more than an annoyance.

An insight occurred to him.

"Entropy would still increase. That's not an illusion."

Da Silva waited.

"In the long term, geological ages would continue to change, seas recede, expand, ice ages come and go. The sun would burn off its hydrogen and expand and cool. The earth and, eventually, the sun would die. So, yes, time would pass regardless of humans—or at least the changes that we associate with the passage of time." He felt the explanation would have gotten him at least a nod from any undergraduate science professor, but he suspected da Silva was after something more specific.

"So, time is not merely a mental construct but a discrete thing?" da Silva prodded.

"Well, I've heard it called the fourth dimension of space-time. And maybe it's a force—like gravity—that physicists don't yet entirely understand." When the Priest's expression did not change, he felt his anger rise. "I don't know. And you know I don't know, so why don't you cut the bullshit and tell me what's going on. I know what I saw today isn't an isolated event or you wouldn't have contacted me."

A wry grin lifted the Nemorian's lips. He looked at the temple visible through the trees. Rick followed his gaze. The edifice was white, but ensconced torches burning on either side of the wide doors gave the columned vestibule a ruddy glow. Behind the temple, the hill rose like a black cliff.

Da Silva's gaze returned to his. "You're right. Let's *corte a besteira*. Two ways philosophers, theologians, and scientists have looked at time: one is as a fundamental structure of the universe—a force like gravity, or a dimension, as you said, of space-time; the other as an intellectual concept, an illusion that has no real existence outside our deceptive perceptions…in other words, time as a by-product of how our mind rationalizes the information provided by our limited senses. Neither interpretation is precisely true."

It was Rick's turn to outwait the Priest.

Da Silva continued. "Remember what I told you about emanation?"

Rick remembered. According to da Silva—as well as others, including Her priestesses, the Sibylline Sisterhood, and the citizens of Hendricks, Arkansas, who were descended from the ancient tribes of Anatolian Phrygia, a race devoted to the Goddess—a First Principle, the Ein Sof—literally "without end," the Infinite Source, the Ancient of Days, not a god or even a being, but the conscious potential for all things—emanated the higher, spiritual planes. Each of these succeeding super-subtle planes were ruled by a pair of male-female Aeons, themselves without physical form but reflections of the infinite light. On the lowest spiritual plane, the Aeon Sophia dwelt alone. Consumed with a desire to know the Source—what some would say to know the mind of God—certainly an act of hubris—Sophia inadvertently and spontaneously in an act of autogenesis emanated a being that should never have existed.

Knowing She had overreached and fearing the Aeons would be appalled and seek to destroy Her offspring, She hid the misshapen one, a shadow of a shadow, reflection of a reflection, in a cloud. And in his narrow kingdom, this offspring, Yaldabaoth, this Demiurge, without knowledge of the Ein Sof or the Aeons in the Pleroma above, or even of the existence of his parent Sophia, but flush with his mother's curiosity and overweening pride, felt about in the darkness and seized the light that flowed unseen around his cloud. And the light, which was not a physical light but the creative impulse emanating from the Source, inspired him. And without knowing the origin of his inspiration, thinking it proceeded from his own fecund mind, he cast the light that was not his to cast down into the void that some call chaos and others potential, and so created the gross material universe of gravity and time and death. The world of man.

Rick thought these things but to da Silva he simply nodded. "I remember."

"Remember also what I said about each succeeding plane being a corruption, a shadow, of the one above?"

"A light is brightest at its source, but as it spreads, the photons become diffuse and the light grows dimmer."

"*Precisamente!* So, by the time the light reaches the physical world, it is a shadow of a shadow. The process of emanation proceeding downward through the Sephiroth is the process of involution, wherein spirit becomes enfolded in matter. But when it reaches the material world, something wonderful happens. The physical world is the world of reflection. It is the mirror of all other worlds. When the light reaches the physical world, the process of involution stops and the process of evolution begins. Just as a mirror reflects light, the physical plane reflects the light of emanation back into the subtle planes. As spirit is involved into matter, so matter is evolved into spirit."

Da Silva paused to let his words sink in.

"I'm not talking about survival of the fittest or the random mutation of genes. Evolution is goal-oriented. It tends toward greater and greater

24

complexity and ever-increasing consciousness. All matter is evolving into consciousness, and man into superconsciousness."

Complexity...consciousness... The man—if man he still was after so long a life—was making some sort of sense, but Rick was too impatient to pursue it.

"What does this have to do with time?"

"Once, people believed the sun rose in the East and set in the West; therefore, the earth was motionless and all things revolved around it."

"Geocentrism."

"Precisely. And like the rising and setting of the sun, time's arrow is an illusion of apparent motion. But apparent motion of what?"

The question was rhetorical. Rick waited.

"Time's arrow is our perception of the rising tide of consciousness, the light of emanation, reflected off the mirror of the physical plane returning to its source in the Infinite One. And as it rises back through the subtle planes, it carries on its tide the consciousness of man. It is this process, this perception of rising consciousness, that we perceive as the progress of time."

Rick thought about it. Like most things that came out of the Priest's mouth, the proposition sounded utterly fantastic. But he'd seen for himself how many of his pronouncements turned out to be all too true.

"Okay, so time's an illusion. Is what I saw today an illusion, too?" He told him about the warehouse, the changed riverfront, and the antique firemen.

Da Silva showed no surprise. "No, I daresay, it was all too real. Such occurrences are happening all over the world. You've been busy, but the news is full of such events. And as the world is swept into temporal chaos..." Da Silva shook his head. "Those who have only logic and modern man's foolish religion of science will feel their world crumble, their comfortable faith in the solidity of the material universe scatter like chaff in the wind. The sons and daughters of Abraham will smugly assert the prophesied end has come."

"But why? Why are these things happening?"

"Because Yaldabaoth is discreating the world."

"'Discreating'?"

"Uncreating…devolving…destroying…reclaiming the light he unleashed into the void."

Rick held up his hand. "Time out. If I hadn't seen the Nephilim with my own eyes, I'd think you were a raving lunatic. Or else I was having one long fucked-up dream. But this—" He shook his head and wagged a finger under the Priest's aquiline nose. "—this is too much!"

"But you have seen. And you will see more. I understand you need time to—what is it your generation says—to wrap your head around it? But we don't have the luxury of time. After all you have seen and after all I have tried to teach you, you are still in denial. The pragmatic bedrock of your upbringing keeps asserting itself, grasping for logical explanations for your experiences. But we don't have the luxury of rationalizing, of forcing the genie back into the bottle."

Rick unclenched his fist. Though he knew deep down da Silva was not responsible for Wally's death, he couldn't help thinking if he could just punch the man out of existence, he could go back to his blissfully ignorant life.

He expelled a deep breath. "Why would Yaldabaoth destroy his creation?"

"Jealousy."

"'Jealousy'?"

"Fear. Caution… At present, only an awakened few travel the subtle planes, and even then, only the lower realms. The Pleroma, the hypostasis of the Archons, the Infinite Source, all that lies above the middle kingdoms, remains beyond man's reach. For now."

"'For now.'"

"Umm. But, in time, as consciousness rises, more and more humans will explore the astral planes. And as the astral planes become populated, those humans will evolve to the next state, and so on, until consciousness reaches a point where man will confront his maker."

"Yaldabaoth."

"He is a jealous god."

"How do you know this?"

"My Mistress told me."

As outlandish as da Silva might look in his tourist getup, the man's gaze was as sober as any Old Testament prophet's. The dark eyes showed no trace of the shining light of the zealot or the self-deceived. He truly believed what he was saying.

And so help me, Rick thought with a shudder, *so do I.*

...storm clouds roiling on all sides of the mountaintop, a whorling tempest funnel...

...the night sky irising open like a great eye...

...the Pleiades vanished, in their place a swarm of alien constellations that had no place in Earth's sky...

As much as he would have liked to remain ignorant, he had seen too much to doubt. "But why now?" he said, pulling himself back from the images burned into the retina of his mind's eye. "I don't see a lot of evidence that man's consciousness is going anywhere soon. Why now?"

The Priest studied him. There was no humor in his eyes, only a great sorrow and compassion.

"It seems," he said, "the future is upon us. You, Richard Scott, have entered the arena."

6

DEFEND YOURSELF

"**M**e? Why would your Demiurge be jealous or afraid of me? I've made no effort to follow in your shoes. All I want is to be left alone."

That wasn't true, of course. He wanted back what he had lost: Frank, Wally, Fergi...his good old ignorant life where the sidewalk was solid beneath his feet and the sky didn't open to admit monsters.

...the stars falling...not stars but the Shining Ones, the Grigori descending to reclaim the earth...

"What one wants and what life gives us is not always a matter of choice," da Silva said. "Your destiny will not permit you to be 'left alone.' The world—or rather the unmaking of the world—will pursue you wherever you hide. None of us can escape. I wish I could tell you differently, but you're the only one that has the remotest chance of stopping Yaldabaoth."

"Why me?"

But he knew the answer.

...the world has not seen one as powerful as you in a thousand years.

...you were the dynamo that powered the rest.

Grigori blood flows in your veins.

He experienced a moment of vertigo as he was forced to face a reality he wanted no part of. Suddenly his hands were sweating and he was cold all over as he thought of the implications.

Mom... Dad...

Da Silva waited, his countenance furrowed with immense compassion.

"Fergi…tell me she's safe."

Da Silva shook his head. "Nothing is safe: no *one*, no *thing*. All will be lost."

"But she's with your Mistress. And Cybele…Sophia…whatever you want to call Her…you tell me is Yaldabaoth's mother. Why can't She stop him? Jewelie Light told me Fergi would be safe so long as she remained with Her."

"That was then. This is different. The Sisterhood exists in the astral world, which is still part of the Demiurge's making. He will destroy all of his creation. All!"

"But She's the Goddess."

"She is. And Her powers are great. But She incarnated Herself into this world to serve as its protectress. She is of this world."

Beyond the crackle of the torch flames, water lapped the stony shore. The languid sound cast the illusion of the eternal. Caligula would have heard it when he floated his giant barges and it would have accompanied the meditations of the first Nemorenses. But eternity, if da Silva was right, had an expiration date.

Somewhere a night bird warbled. Eerily beautiful, the trill of a creature blissfully ignorant that change was inevitable.

Rick turned his gaze to the heavens where the stars—so many, so bright—blazed above the treetops.

All…earth, moon, stars…gone!

Again, as he had last November when he faced Talmaiel, who plotted the return of the Watchers and the Nephilim, as he had the Christmas before when he faced his doppelgänger, who wrecked a bloody path across his life in its efforts to replace him, he thought what a bizarre and baroque world he moved in, so different from the stable, everyday, often boring world he'd grown up in where his biggest problem was his brother Frank.

But then that seemingly stable world had never existed. Not really. It was as much an illusion as da Silva's time. A façade that masked a monstrous reality.

The world—all creation—rushing back into the maker's mind. Recalled like a defective appliance. He envisioned the end like a sped-up reverse-motion film, the universe with all its galaxies and clusters and nebulae imploding and withdrawing like a cloud of smoke into a singularity and vanishing.

Back... He started at the thought.

"The past isn't invading the present, is it?"

Da Silva nodded, confirming his insight. "The past invading the present is another illusion of apparent motion. We are so used to thinking the arrow of time moves from past to future, it would never occur to most that the flow could be reversed. You saw the past encroaching on your present. And those who find themselves transported to your time will think themselves swept into the future. But if the past were invading the future, your present would have found itself in its future and so on. But that's not possible."

"Because the future is undetermined and, therefore, does not exist, whereas the past is fixed—at least it used to be."

"Exactly. Now, to your task."

"My task?"

"You will go into the past and seek that which will give you the means to confront Yaldabaoth."

The past...

Rick held his hand up. "Whoa, whoa, whoa! You're talking about time travel." He shook his head as he fumbled with the watch clasp. "You're the horologist. You made this thing. You use it. I'm just some guy with messed-up genes."

The Priest laid his hand over Rick's. "The watch is yours now and you must use it. Refuse at the world's peril. You cannot escape your destiny. It will come to you no matter what. Best be prepared."

Rick looked at the watch. Its crystal caught the torchlight. He tilted it so he could see the luminous dial. Its hands rested on the 12.

Midnight.

Of course, that didn't mean anything here. Wherever here was. He had visited the astral world, but that was more by necessity and accident than by intent. He was pretty fuzzy on the geography and laws of the subtle planes. By avoiding da Silva, he had neglected much that the Priest wanted to teach him.

"Before you go, however, we have another matter to attend to."

Da Silva stepped away and knelt beside the trunk of a nearby tree. He lifted a long wooden box Rick had not noticed and which, perhaps, had not been there until the Priest needed it.

"What's that?"

"Open it."

The box the Priest offered him in his outstretched hands was old but well-preserved, about four feet long. Its oiled, dark-grained wood gleamed in the ruddy light.

Rick licked his lips. What dread thing lay within that caused the gooseflesh to rise on his arms and back as if an arctic chill had invaded the sultry Mediterranean night? Surely even the ills of Pandora's box were paltry beside the end of creation.

"*Tempus fugit*, Richard Scott."

Quickly, before he could give in to the impulse to shove his hands in his pockets, he flicked the locks and raised the lid.

Inside, back-to-back on a bed of red satin, lay not a nest of coiled serpents or a swarm of pestilence like Poe's red death spreading through the chambers of Prospero's castle but two curved swords. The scabbards were red leather with silver fittings. The grips were horn wound with silver wire. The cross guards were brass and the bulbous pommels were in the downturned Turkish style. They were both beautiful and terrifying. Presented to him on such a propitious night here on the shore of Lake Nemi in the fireglow of Her sacred grove just yards from the portico of Her pillared temple…how could they presage anything but disaster? He shivered suspecting what da Silva would say next.

"Take one."

He shook his head. "I'd rather not."

"We would rather not a lot of things. But refusal is not an option."

Rick gazed into the pools of the man's eyes. Were it anyone other than da Silva bidding him lift the sword, he would have called the gleam he saw there madness; but it *was* da Silva, Cybele's Priest, and he recognized the expression for what it was—amusement. He had

31

gotten to know the supercentenarian well enough to understand the humor was not directed toward him but at the vicissitudes of this wayward world and the fate that had carried him thus far across the centuries. The world was—what? crumbling? dissolving? spiraling down the rabbit hole?—yet the man was able to savor irony in bitter fruit. Rick had to admire that. It was a kind of strength, a way of remaining sane when faced with the terrors that every so often stepped through the veil into this world, as well as a defense against ennui.

Or maybe the old man *was* insane. How did one survive so long and experience what da Silva had and not go a little mad?

He reached into the case and lifted one of the twins. Grasping the scabbard, he drew the blade. It whispered from its sheath as if rejoicing in freedom. The wavy pattern of the Damascus steel danced in the fireglow. Two-thirds of the blade's length was single-edged, but from where it flared wider near the end to where it curved upward to a wicked point the edge was double. The weapon was lighter than he'd imagined. His hand tingled as if he wielded a living thing eager to leap to his enemy's heart, and he resisted the urge to carve a figure eight in the humid air.

Da Silva's voice broke the spell. "It is a Turkish kilij. I purchased the set on a whim during my travels. I figured when the time came..."

"Time for what?"

"Why, to die."

"Die? What are you talking about?"

"You are not without curiosity, Richard Scott. Surely you know my fate."

And, of course, he did know...at least from an academic perspective. After Wally's funeral he'd researched the Priest's line of work and read of the fate of the Rex Nemorensis: how the King of the Wood's successor took the title by slaying his predecessor in mortal combat. But he'd dismissed the story as an old tale that lent drama to a largely monotonous occupation. A chill stole over him. Was da Silva suggesting he use the blade?

He slid the sword into the scabbard and laid it in the case. "I see you still have your sense of humor. Either that or you're as nuts as ever."

The Priest's teeth gleamed. "I may be whimsical at times—the Portuguese are famous for it—but I am serious now. Take up the sword."

Rick looked at the weapon lying with its mate on their satin bed. He had no doubt its blade was sharp. Deadly so. And his hair bristled at the thought of its edge slicing human flesh. "I will not!"

Da Silva set the case on the grass, lifted the sword Rick had chosen, shook the scabbard off, flipped the weapon in the air, caught it by the blade and offered Rick the hilt.

"You must. It is your destiny. And remember: *tempus fugit*."

Had it really come to this?

The burning warehouse

Patterson Transfer Company

gone for over a century. And the buildings that had long replaced it, as well as the people who dwelt in them—gone…vanished down the corridors of time.

And time itself out of joint.

Surreal images of clocks running backward, hour and minute hands spinning in reverse. The sun rising in the West, arching across the sky and setting in the East. The cycle whirling faster and faster till alternating sun and moon and stars became a white-black-white-black blur. Not the universe winding down some billions of years in the future, a victim of entropy, matter and energy degrading into inertia, but an ever-swiftening implosion, the light of emanation sweeping back to a white-hot singularity of thought in the creator's mind.

Yaldabaoth

the Demiurge

reclaiming the world.

He reached a shaking hand and took the proffered hilt. The ribbed grip fit his hand as if some long-ago bladesmith had fashioned it expressly for him. The heavy, down-turned pommel behind the heel of the grip gave the weapon a wonderful balance, forming a counterweight to the upthrusting curve of the blade. Again, he shivered with the sensation of wielding a living thing that strained to quench itself in hot blood. He squirmed at the thought and wondered about his own subconscious appetites.

33

Id.

Reptilian complex.

The dragon of the subconscious lashing its tail.

His doppelgänger in the abandoned warehouse on a snowy Christmas Eve. Red eyes glaring.

He'd thought he'd seen the last of the outré, the supernatural, the weird. Sweat beaded his forehead as he clenched the firm horn of the sword grip and remembered standing on the Plutonian shore, the ultimate gulf spread before him—not the darkling reaches of intergalactic space where galaxies grew distant and dim but the tide of oblivion encircling the fragile island of man's consensual reality. Da Silva had referred to the lowly material plane on which mankind toiled and died blissfully ignorant of the vast and unknowable realities beyond as the basement. Malkuth, a reflection of reflections, a shadow of shadows. And faced with no alternative, Rick had determined to defend that basement. Now da Silva was asking him to do it again.

The Priest stepped back to the tree and set the case on the ground. He drew the other sword from the scabbard and returned with a bared blade. Bringing the crossguard up smartly to his chest, blade extended skyward, he paused as if expecting Rick to return the salute. When he didn't, da Silva assumed a fighting stance, stepping his left foot back perpendicular to his right, knees bent, left arm akimbo, hand resting lightly on his hip, sword angled at Rick's throat.

"Defend yourself."

Red mist clouded Rick's eyes. Angry at the Priest—at fate—for placing him in an impossible situation, he felt like hurling the sword into the dark and walking away. Where he would go, he had no idea. He was far from home and space and time were devolving.

"I want no part of your games," he hissed through clenched teeth.

"En garde," da Silva said and rapped his blade smartly. The move was so rapid and the Priest was back in his stance so swiftly, Rick hardly saw him move. The humor was gone from his eyes, and Rick saw from the set of his mouth—lips like two halves of a clamshell above a square jaw—the Priest was in earnest.

He lifted the blade uncertainly.

What am I doing?

The Nemorensis crossed swords with him, tapped his lightly and settled into the en garde position as casually as one might lean upon a door post.

"Protect yourself."

"How? I've never held one of these things."

But when da Silva thrust, leaping forward, his left arm flinging backward, his feet gliding as if the grass were oil, Rick parried, slapped the blade away.

"*Bien!* You'll be a swordsman yet!"

Da Silva returned to his guard position, circled the point of his blade. Rick kept his steady, not knowing from which direction the next attack might come.

"Good. Don't take my bait. Be ready for anything. Good advice for fencing and everything else."

On the last word da Silva attacked. His lean body swept almost to the ground and his sword looped so he came up under Rick's guard. The kilij's deadly point halted an inch from his EMT shirt. Rick slapped the blade aside with his own and lunged, not intending to wound the Priest but to turn at the last second and clock him with the pommel, maybe knock some sense into him. But the Nemorensis maintained his crouch as if he were gliding on a string and danced out of reach.

Rick followed, swinging left and right as he advanced in a poor but energetic imitation of da Silva. The Priest retreated. His white teeth gleamed in his tanned face, his delight in his pupil's initiative obvious. Then he sprang forward, parried Rick's sword with a rasp of tempered steel, and shouldered Rick off his line of attack. Though the bump was slight, Rick was caught off guard and staggered back.

He was at once embarrassed and angered. The Priest was playing with him.

"If time is of such importance, why are we fucking around? I don't need fencing lessons."

"Such language!" Da Silva feigned indignation. "And in this sacred place." He tsked Rick with a shake of his head. "Ah, but who am I to call the *caldo* black? In my youth I had as foul a tongue when in my drinks."

Then the Priest was attacking with such speed and precision his movements were a blur. His flashing blade whooshed the air inches from Rick's right ear, his left.

Astonished, heart in his throat, Rick retreated, parrying this way and that but never connecting because the Priest's blade was always elsewhere. Rick felt a sting in his ear. Reaching up, he encountered blood. Da Silva had cut him!

As in the old days when he and Frank slugged it out and the neighborhood guys cheered them on and old folks watched from the windows or called the cops, he saw red and retaliated. Surging forward, he knocked da Silva's blade aside, stepped inside his guard, and slammed a left hook into his cheek.

The Priest staggered back and rubbed his face. "Oho! You'll make a fine successor."

Before Rick could react, da Silva did the unthinkable. He dropped his sword, seized Rick's blade in his bare hands and ran his body onto it.

His breath escaped in a rattling sigh. *"Merde!"* he said, clinging to Rick. "That hurt!"

7

FERGI SCRIES

The world was ending. Time hurtling backward along its track. Chaos swallowing Order.

Sitting at the table by her bedroom window gazing into her silver scrying bowl, Delores Ferguson saw in the water:

A section of Newark, New Jersey's Ironbound District—houses, apartment buildings, banks, shops, restaurants—vanish, replaced by block-long façades of Industrial Age iron, chemical, brewing, tanning, leather, varnish, and dye factories. Asphalt roads become brick, and brick smokestacks, black with soot, spew columns of smoke over the transformed skyline.

In nearby Jersey City, Newport Center's multi-level mall, office buildings, and condominium towers similarly vanish, replaced by stockyards, trainyards, warehouses, and leaning piers.

The Lower Manhattan skyline metamorphose when dark tenements, marine supply warehouses, and gin joints replaced the waterfront from Peck Slip to Wall Street, including the South Street Seaport, the riverfront esplanade, the Circle Line cruise ships, and the Fulton Fish Market.

On the West Coast:

A pileup on the lower deck of the San Francisco-Oakland Bay Bridge when train service, decommissioned since 1958, suddenly resumed, leaving dozens dead and dozens more sucked into the time slip.

Such events were happening all over the world: islands of the past cropping up as the present swept inexorably back.

In India, the ancient Brihadeeswara Temple in Thanjavur was suddenly renewed, the vibrant azures and deep reds of its frescoes and murals restored, the weathered inscriptions of the ancient Tamil dynasties made legible as if carved that morning. Its granite towers gleamed under the hazy subtropical sun.

Not all timeslips involved the past—tantalizing glimpses of the future appeared as tomorrow overtook today.

In Brazil, a city sprang up on the Amazonian flood plain, which had been dredged and reclaimed...only to drown in the waters of the present.

A great swath of the Sahara blossomed with palm trees and golf courses. Orchards replaced dunes, and fountains flowed in the tiered gardens of fabulous dwellings.

A glittering cluster of fantastic glass and steel sprouted along Brisbane, Australia's aging waterfront—parks and plazas, waterfalls and garden terraces, and an utter whimsy of a pedestrian bridge linking the two sides of the river.

And all over the planet, shocked faces showed surprise, confusion, and terror.

Fergi started when the water in the bowl turned red and a familiar face appeared.

Rick.

He stood in a torch-lit grove. He held a sword and faced another man—*Her Priest*—who also held a sword. They were fencing. Though she could only see and not hear, she imagined the whisk of steel through air, the clash of metal on metal, the deadly whisper of naked edge passing dangerously close to flesh. She cringed.

As she watched, Rick's blade plunged into Her Priest. The length of the Damascus blade burst from his back and his sternum slammed into crossguard.

Recoiling, she slapped the water, upsetting the bowl.

"No!"

Her hand sought her throat. In her mind's eye, she saw Rick's doppelgänger, red-eyed, drooling, bending her over the car seat, her hair twisted in its fist. On top of everything else, had the creature returned? Surely Rick was incapable of murdering his mentor.

But instead of sloshing over the table onto the bedroom floor, the water was rising. It formed a dome, continued to rise, until a watery globe broke free of the bowl and hovered in the air above the table.

She watched, mesmerized, as a new vision formed in its watery depths.

No longer red, the great globule was suffused with a pale silvery light. Its depths revealed an icy world, all white and mist and arctic blue. Cold radiated from the globe. The temperature in her bedroom fell. From a bird's eye view she saw plunging ravines and soaring crags and everywhere white of every shade and hue. The only color was a dim red sun perched near the horizon.

It wasn't Earth. She was looking at an alien world.

The perspective changed…as if she were, indeed, a bird now soaring through that frigid air instead of viewing the world from outside the watery globe. A figure stood atop what might have been an icy rampart too smooth to be a natural formation.

She stepped closer to the wavering globule, stared deeper with her Sibylline eye at the pale man who stood on the rampart in rags, as if impervious to the bitter cold.

She started back.

Not a man.

Grigori!

8

ABYSS

Talmaiel stood atop the rampart and looked out over the frozen world. Carved into the ice, the rampart was the only visible artificial construction on the planet. The rest of the fortress lay deep beneath the surface, spread through a labyrinth of caverns that descended into the mountain's bowels. From his lofty aerie, the world plunged to glacial valleys miles below, and rose in snow-crowned peaks that merged with the mist. The distant sun was a dim red smudge behind the kilometers-thick cover of ammonium hydrosulfide clouds. The solar disk did not track across the sky as Sol had above Earth. Abyss was tidally locked and the equatorial plateau upon which he stood was forever centered under the astringent rust-colored canopy. Exposed to the void of interstellar black, the planet's far side plunged hundreds of degrees below the "bright" side's relative warmth. There was no life on the planet other than the prisoners. There were no stars, no moon, no sweet evening breeze.

No birdsong.

No unfurling spring or green summer walks.

No wine, barbeque, or Belgian ale.

Talmaiel scooped a handful of ammonia ice from the parapet and let the crystals fall. Crystals so cold they did not melt at his touch but fell like grains of sand.

How the Shining Ones had fallen. It had grieved his heart to find them, upon his arrival, faded shadows of their ancient glory.

40

Though Grigori were virtually indestructible and had no need of food or drink or even air, they had wasted to emaciated wraiths over the long millennia of their imprisonment. All save Semjaza, their commander, who, though not as powerfully muscled as Talmaiel remembered him, remained hale and vigorous and kept the Choir busy with projects. Though they'd long ago carved out of the mountain more space than they needed, Semjaza kept them burrowing deeper. Beneath the planet's icy mantle was rock, and where there was rock there was iron. Of course, there was no fuel to burn to supply the heat to separate iron from ore and no tools to fashion the iron into implements, but the Brethren possessed a technology of a sort. It was time-consuming and physically and mentally draining, but they had no alternative. All of the Two Hundred were powerful intellects. Most were adepts at manipulating the etheric vibrations of rock and mineral, thereby transmuting whatever came to hand into the materials they needed; several, Semjaza chief among them, were mages. But despite the collective power of their combined will and the thousands of years they'd spent in this lonely prison Yaldabaoth forged for them, they'd failed to break through the barriers the Demiurge had put in place.

Talmaiel ran a hand over his scarred face. He wasn't terribly vain about his appearance and Sariel and Raziel had done the best they could for him, but there were no medical facilities and they were limited to the laying on of hands. He hoped by the time he made his way back to Earth (he hadn't given up the dream and, after a half-dozen earth months spent cooped up with his fellow Grigori in Abyss' eternal winter, desired it more than ever) he would heal. If the Choir's incarceration was any indication, he'd have time to heal a thousand times over.

He sighed. He hated this foul-smelling, frozen waste. The ammonia-methane air was a continual burning stench that seared his nostrils. He would gladly give up breathing were the habit not ingrained in him after millennia of enjoying Earth's sweet air. The atmosphere would have killed a human within minutes. The air pressure—more than seventeen times that of Earth despite Abyss' being only half the size of the watery blue world—would have ruptured men's lungs and crushed their skulls. The planet's volcanos had died eons ago and the world existed in a perpetual ice age.

Abyss was entering a brief century or so of summer weather which occurred once every few millennia (Talmaiel, so used to roaming the earth, still thought in terms of Earth's diurnal and seasonal cycles) for no reason any of the Grigori had yet discovered. Summer was relative on Abyss where, according to Chazaquel, the Grigori's meteorologist, the temperature was still hundreds of degrees colder than Earth's Antarctica.

On a fair day like this, sheets of methane ice did not lash the rampart and the winds were well below their two-hundred-kilometers-per-hour norm—winds that would have hurled a human from the battlement and flung him spinning like a leaf into the frozen waste.

Not that there were any leaves—nor trees or plants or mosses or lichens.

The irony of what he'd said to the youth, Richard Scott, that he missed the company of his brothers and wished to share the earth with them, wasn't lost on him. What a crock that turned out to be. Dictatorial Semjaza was unbearable and his fellow Grigori waspish crones by long servitude to barren existence.

He shuddered to think he would become like them.

Kashdejan had been right. Keep a low profile, fit in and enjoy the fruits of the earth. If he'd followed his advice, he could be basking in the warm Mediterranean sun or enjoying a Turkish coffee and a sesame-honey cake at a sidewalk café. Though food was optional, his stomach growled sympathetically.

He squeezed the stone in his pocket, felt it ground him in his purpose. He had to get back to Earth.

9

SEEK THE PHILOSOPHER'S STONE

Da Silva slid off the sword. The flare where the blade widened caught his rib cage and steel grated on bone as he collapsed. His brain roaring with horror, Rick flung the dripping weapon away as if he clutched a snake. He dropped to his knees, pushed the Priest's hands aside and ripped open his ruined shirt. The wound gaped in the torchlight, a wet mouth just below the ribcage. The wound was far too wide to staunch the flow without a tactical tourniquet. The blood was pumping out. Da Silva had hit an artery; knowing the Priest, it wasn't an accident.

Rick shook his head, as if to deny what just happened, as if to will it to unhappen. Tears blurred his vision. "Why?"

The man's eyes were round with shock but humor still curled a corner of his mouth. His speech was spasmodic, phrases forced between gasps. "For years you prepare...You think...*não tem problema*...And then you shit your pants when it happens." The smile widened. "Kidding about the pants."

"Why?" was all Rick could think to say.

"My time...your turn." In the ruddy torchlight, da Silva's normally tanned face was white as moonlight.

"But you can't die!"

The Priest's smile was kindly—a patient father indulging a dull-witted son. His hand sought Rick's. Rick took it and placed his thumb over a vein on the inside of his wrist. The pulse was erratic. "You mistake," da Silva said, and between gasps he recited something Rick had heard before but couldn't place.

"Nothing is ever really lost,
or can be lost,
No birth, identity, form—no object of the world,
Nor life…nor force…nor any visible thing…"

The Priest coughed blood. He tried to bring a hand to his mouth but couldn't complete the effort. He was losing control of his limbs. The grass was slick with blood. Rick drew his handkerchief, wiped the Priest's mouth.

"At least not for us…" the Priest continued. His voice was weak. Considering the blood loss, Rick was surprised he was still conscious. "I've met many…of the so-called dead…who share the blood…You will too…And you and I…will meet again…"

The grip on his hand grew slack. The Priest was dying. Rick had found the man annoying in their brief acquaintance, but now a cold panic seized his gut at the thought of a future without him. Another fallen soldier. Like Wally, and Jewelie Light, and so many other guardians at the gate. It must always have been so. How else could the world survive the long ages surrounded by beings that would feast on her?

And now he was guardian. *Rex Nemorensis*. King of the Wood.

You are *my knight*. Her words, that evening in Her garden in that other magical place that was not of his world, Her perfumed fingers brushing his cheek. He had denied Her, but denial had not kept him from facing the Shining One in the midnight hour.

He looked at the temple in the near distance, no pile of ruined stone crumbling into the earth but miraculously restored, braziers casting a ruddy glow over its columned façade. It all seemed so surreal. The antique firemen, da Silva committing *hari kari* in the shadow of Diana's temple… Was it all a dream? Would he wake and go to work and put in another ordinary shift? Kids with lollipop sticks in their ears, the elderly complaining of chest pains, lack of breath, the obese needing a ride to the clinic, the teenager with soaring blood pressure because he downed too many energy drinks, and maybe, in the evening, an overdose? Nothing outré, weird, apocalyptic. Just the usual muck of another routine day in which he maybe did some good and wasn't required to save the world.

Nearby, the lake lapped the shore. A screech caught his attention and he watched an owl sail over the moonlit water.

Da Silva squeezed his hand. The whites of his eyes glowed. His voice was the whisper of rustling grass.

"Closer."

Rick leaned in to catch the Priest's words. With surprising strength, da Silva curled his fingers behind Rick's head, pulled his face down to his and kissed him.

Surprised, Rick struggled, but the Priest's grip was iron and his lips pressed hard against his. No passionate kiss but a farewell.

And an imparting.

No breath passed between them, and it was not his lungs but his mind that expanded with impossible images thoughts smells music tastes sensations faces memories…all transmitted simultaneously yet with the impression they were the accumulated experiences of lifetimes. The assault on his senses left him paralyzed with wonder.

Da Silva's grip grew weak and his head sank back on Rick's arm. His eyes reflected starlight and the flicker of torches.

"Seek the Philosopher's Stone," he said, his voice as soft as water lapping pebbles. He patted Rick's face. Then his hand found Rick's wrist and he pressed a sequence into the watch crown and the air blurred and the lake was gone and Rick was tumbling down a well.

10

BLINDED

They sat at one of the long tables in the dining hall under the coffered ceiling, the Goddess at the head of the table, Fergi on Her right, Margreet and the twins, Maija and Keija, on Her left. A handful of older Sisters sat further down, giving Fergi and the Goddess space. All wore the white gown of the Sisterhood, only the Goddess' was fastened with golden brooches at the shoulders from which stared fierce lions' heads in relief. A golden cord encircled Her slender waist.

The room was large and could probably accommodate two hundred. But less than forty Sisters resided in the residence. Thousands more were scattered around the world, ministering to the Goddess' people and working to ensure the future of the human race. In a way, they were weavers, finding and binding the threads that wove the tapestry of tomorrow.

"You saw this in the water?" Cybele asked. The Lady's habitual smile was missing and She appeared tired—not withered and shrunken as She had after raising the false moon on a moonless night, depleting Her powers in battle against the Fallen Watchers, after which She endured a spell as the withered crone until the next full moon replenished Her strength, but weary, the physical and mental toll of dealing with the present calamity evident in the crease that furrowed Her smooth brow and in the corners of Her sensuous lips where dimples normally resided. She fingered the silver pentangle she wore on a slender chain about Her neck as She listened. The Endless Knot,

46

traceable by eye or finger around and around ad infinitum was a symbol of perfection and of infinity and, along with the Triple Moon—two outward-facing crescents bookending a circle (the waxing and waning crescents bracketing the full moon: Maiden, Mother, and Crone)—were Her symbols. However animated Her features were when She was engaged in conversation or whisking about the residence—or worlds—Her countenance was generally happy, Her demeanor serene, Her hands by Her sides, or, if sitting, resting on the lions' heads of Her throne. Fingering the silver pentangle meant the Goddess was worried. Never a good sign.

"Yes." Fergi's hands still shook, and she kept them folded out of sight in her lap.

"But he wasn't in this world."

"I don't think so. The place…" Her eyes sought the tall, mullioned windows. The light falling through the leaded panes cast the hall in a yellow gloom. Even here in Cybele's sanctum—separated from Earth by the thinnest of veils and accessible only to adepts and those She summoned—no one was safe from the coming doom. The light on the world she saw in the watery globe was paler than this. The icy rampart on which the Grigori stood seemed carved from the ice itself. The scene was like some movie filmed in Antarctica, but the sun…

"The sun was so small, and red. And it felt so…" she shivered remembering the cold and the pale misty air "…alien."

"And you are sure it was him? Talmaiel?"

"His face was scarred and stretched like a burn victim's. But even if it wasn't, I would recognize him."

She faced her mentor across the table. Margreet, purportedly well over a hundred but appearing a youthful fifty, was the residence's senior Sister and the closest thing to a confidant she'd ever had. The matron's skin was smooth and unblemished, her silver hair luxuriously thick; only the trace of neck wrinkles and hint of crows' feet suggested she was older than she looked.

"You told me what we do, our scrying, was to seek out potentialities and collectively will these potentials into a consensual reality. But I see what *is*, not what *may be*."

"We are sequential creatures," Margreet said. "We're wired to see the arrow of time moving from past to future. But this is an illusion of apparent motion. In reality, time is a continuum. The very concept of eternity means past, present, and future exist simultaneously. But our consensual reality is based on the commonsense perception of moving from birth to death. Our senses, therefore, limit us to thinking about one moment and then the next. Take language, for example. Over millions of years our frontal lobe," she touched her left temple, "developed the capacity for speech. A thousand things can be happening around us at once, but we can only relate them—or even make sense of them—one at a time. This deficit has caused us to experience everything sequentially. Only in a state of fugue or under the influence of a hallucinogenic do some people sometimes glimpse the true holographic nature of the multiverse."

"So I've got what? A learning disability because I can't see the future?" She was more dismayed at the notion than she would have thought.

Margreet smiled. "Oh, no, child. You are a prodigy. At your age, few of us had your sight. But unlearning what we're hard-wired to do—seeing linearly—and developing the ability to see non-sequentially took most of us decades."

"What did Sister Alycia teach you?" Cybele asked, changing the direction of the conversation.

Fergi looked down the table at the matronly woman with the graying brown hair and kindly dark eyes. The plump Sister nodded, the teacher prompting her pupil's response.

"That all things are only modes of vibrations, time as well as space." She held her teacher's gaze and repeated the lesson as close to rote as possible—the only way she kept track of the mass of information she'd encountered in the months she'd been at the Sisterhood. "And if something is invisible to us, because it exists on a different plane or a moment behind or before us, it is only because it is vibrating on a different frequency, an octave beyond our perception. But if we open our minds, we may perceive the vibration just as a guitar or violin string will vibrate if the same note is plucked an octave higher or lower. This is known as 'sympathetic resonance' and our ability to open our minds to it is called 'insight,' and from this insight we may interpret what is occurring on another plane or what may be before us in the timestream.

"I have to confess, Sister," she said after a moment's pause, "I still find all of this strange."

Sister Alycia said, "Certainly no stranger than seeing a banished Grigori on a planet not only spatially distant but probably in a different universe as well."

"I guess not."

"And about raising that watery globe…" The Sister lifted her eyebrows. "As young as you are and as new to the calling…" She shook her head. "There's something about you, girl."

Fergi recalled the false moon rising from the bonfire, expanding as it rose into the spark-filled air until it illuminated the night sky. But that had taken the combined efforts of the whole coven and cost Cybele Her strength for weeks.

"I didn't do that on purpose; it just happened."

"That's what I mean. It's as if your subconscious mind is tenacious, and when your conscious mind doesn't know how to respond, your subconscious takes over and gets the job done. Like what you did with the clay and the wax figures."

Sister Alycia was referring to the crude clay figure she'd shaped by daylight and baked in the sun to represent Rick and into which she'd whispered her hopes for his success, and the wax image she'd fashioned at night during the waning moon to represent Talmaiel into which she'd poured her fears. She'd cast the waxen effigy into the bonfire the night of the battle, resulting in his disfigurement. But Grigori are not easily destroyed and, though hideously burned, he'd remained intact; and, if what the water revealed was true, he'd mended considerably.

She still heard his voice in her dreams, his charred features contorted with rage, his blackened lips rasping, "You will pay!"

"My dream instructed me to do that."

"And what is such a dream but the subconscious mind taking the helm?"

49

She remembered how insistent the dream had been, and the clarity with which she'd recalled its instructions when she woke. It was no ordinary dream.

She looked down the table. These were the elders of the Sibylline Sisterhood. The women with the most experience scrying and interpreting what they saw. Surely, they would make sense of what she had seen. But she hesitated to ask. In her rush to tell the Sisterhood about the Grigori Talmaiel and her fear that last year's nightmare would be repeated, she had omitted mention of Rick killing da Silva. She still refused to believe Rick was capable of such an act and clung to the hope for a logical explanation. Was what she saw symbolic of the friction between instructor and pupil? She knew Rick well enough to know he wanted nothing to do with either the Rex Nemorensis or Cybele and that he chaffed under authority. Or had she broken through the barrier of linear time and glimpsed what might happen in some possible future? If so, then might there not be time to prevent it from happening with the help of these women?

"Okay, so I see the present and not the future. But what does it mean? Haven't any of you seen anything that might help me understand?"

There, she had said it. She held her breath waiting for someone to acknowledge seeing Rick plunge the blade into his mentor and confirm that the act had, indeed, already occurred.

Some of the women stared at their hands on the table. A few, Alycia among them, held her gaze. She sought Margreet and the twins.

"No, child," Margreet said. "For whatever reason, it appears you are the only one seeing anything."

Shocked, Fergi drew back. She shook her head. "How—?"

"It's true!" Maija and Keija spoke as one. They looked at each other. Keija, as she often did when both realized their habit of speaking in unison was confusing to most, deferred to Maija. The way Fergi learned to distinguish them was Maija had a curl uplifting the front of her blonde hair that Keija didn't have and Maija wore white-gold earrings while Keija wore yellow, and that Maija had the ever-so-slightly more dominant personality.

Maija continued. "Neither water nor crystal nor runes reveal anything. We thought Yaldabaoth's wrath had blinded us all."

Fergi looked at her mentor. Margreet shook her head. "You're our eyes now."

A chill ran up her spine. What did it mean? Again, as she had last fall on the cusp of Samhain when the Pleiades approached the zenith at midnight and the hour of the Nephilim threatened to release the Fallen from the Abyss, she experienced the gut-wrenching feeling that she was being singled out and appointed a dreadful task.

"The only one..." she repeated, stunned, not wanting it to be true, overwhelmed by what it meant—the staggering responsibility. "Surely that's not possible."

Cybele released Her pentangle, folded Her hands on the white linen tablecloth. "I've often felt that the Infinite Light, the All-father— or mother—isn't as disinterested in human affairs as we might believe."

Fergi looked into the Goddess' eyes. Normally, doing so was like gazing into emerald pools flecked with golden sunlight. Today, the pools were clouded. Another bad sign.

She decided to tell the rest of her vision.

She told what she had seen. How the water in the scrying bowl turned red and in its depths she had witnessed Rick and his mentor battling with swords in the torch-lit grove. And how the battle ended.

When she finished, Cybele squeezed her hand and said in the tone of a mother explaining to her child the ways of the world without sugar coating.

"You would witness such an event eventually. The succession of the *Rex Nemorensis* is an ancient tradition."

"Succession? Then Rick is—"

Cybele nodded. "My Priest. It is our way since time immemorial. Your Rick cannot avoid his destiny. Too much depends on him."

Fergi withdrew her hand. She almost hated the Goddess when She was cold like this, employing humans like pieces on a chessboard. But that wasn't true, was it? Cybele cared deeply for Her people—for all humans—but She did what She saw was needed, no matter the sacrifice.

"So, Rick didn't murder Reginald?"

"No, child." She offered a commiserative smile. "I doubt your Rick wants anything to do with Reginald's death. Or with taking his place."

Fergi frowned. Though relieved Rick was not a murderer, she was appalled by the injustice of the universe. She shook her head. "It makes no sense. Rick doesn't have da Silva's experience. Why should he have to take his place?"

"Because out of all the tangled skein of futurity, Rick's thread is the brightest. Time, the world, rolling backward, gaining momentum in its long decline…yet Rick's thread fights the current."

"But how can you know this if no one can see the future?"

"I saw it long ago," She said simply, and given the Goddess' age, She might have meant decades or centuries. "But you're right. Not even I can see what might be."

"No?"

"No. You are our eyes now." She exchanged a glance with Margreet, who nodded. "Therefore, I have a request of you."

Fergi hesitated before responding. The Goddess' requests often ended in death. "What is it?"

"I want you to gaze into the mirror and tell me what you see."

Fergi's blood ran cold at the memory of the locked basement room and what she had seen in the black mirror.

11
SEMJAZA

A round him his fellow Grigori swung pickaxes or shoveled rock into mine carts. The work was backbreaking and endless. Abyss was prone to earthquakes and the Fallen spent as much time clearing and rebuilding as they did gathering the raw material for transmutation into what they needed to endure this, literally, godforsaken place.

The Fallen did not sweat as humans did, but their stooped postures, hollow cheeks, and sunken eyes told Talmaiel how bone-weary they were. Dressed in rags as filthy and tattered as his own, the Shining Ones—guardians of man (however lax), bestowers of knowledge—were mere wraiths of their former selves. As their shovels plunged and heaved and their pickaxes rose and fell, they moved as automatons, as silent and weary as any terrestrial ghost. He was amazed they hadn't collapsed centuries ago.

He was aware of their hungry stares. The legends of their bloodlust were true: they and their offspring, the Nephilim—drawing power from the divine spark they imbibed along with their feasting—were the progenitors of the legions of vampire tales ubiquitous to nearly every culture on Earth. But even in his present condition, with his burn-scarred body and ruined face, he was hale in comparison and they would not dare attack—not singly at any rate. Still, it was imperative he show no weakness, and he stared back as good as he got.

Talmaiel paused to wipe his face. The rag, like the tattered overalls that hung from his scarred torso, had begun life as rock. Same as the chairs, tables, pickaxes, shovels, even Raziel's alchemical equipment and the coal he used to heat his alembic. Rock and ice were all they had to work with—the very elements from which they fashioned whatever made life more bearable on this unbearable planet.

He rested his pickaxe against the tunnel wall, picked up a rock and held the gray lump to his ear. He tuned out the noise of iron striking stone, of rubble tumbling into the carts, and listened. Was it his imagination, or did he hear the supra-auditory hum of the stone responding to his touch? He pressed the lump against the mastoid bone behind his deformed ear and felt the vibrations within the mineral's crystalline matrix.

All chemical elements were modes of the one primordial substance and could be transmuted one into another by changing the state of their etheric vibrations. To accomplish this, one had to know the vibrational frequency of every element and have the tremendous willpower and discipline needed to access and manipulate an element's counterpart on the astral plane. To transmute silicone into the polymers of their clothing or into the iron of their tools, or lead into gold for that matter, one had to change the vibrational frequency of an element on the astral plane into the frequency of the element one desired. The rest took care of itself: as above proceeds by the process of emanation into the physical plane below, the molecular structure of the physical element in the material world altered to correspond to its new etheric vibration. But the first part—willing change in etheric vibrations—that was easier said than done. His own efforts to transmute the stone secreted in his pocket had failed miserably.

Reaching into his pocket, he caressed the stone he'd found in his previous shift. As his finger touched the rough edge, he felt an anticipatory shiver at its potential, however remote the realization of that potential might be. Though fresh from Earth, and physically and mentally stronger than his fellow Grigori—with the exception of Semjaza, who miraculously maintained his strength and vitality—he needed help. The transmutation of the planet's meager resources into the materials they needed took the combined wills of the Two Hundred, led by Kokabiel, Raziel, and Semjaza himself.

Suddenly the stone grew warm in his hand and his flesh tingled as if the stone were vibrating against his palm. He started to pull the lump from his pocket, to see what it was doing, when the booming voice made him jump.

"Talmaiel."

The laborers about him did not look up but attacked their chores with renewed vigor.

The leader of the Two Hundred stood before him. Tall though Talmaiel was, Semjaza was taller and more powerfully built. And though his gray-white clothes were fashioned from the same transmuted material as theirs, where Talmaiel and his fellow laborers wore loose-fitting trousers and went barefoot, the Sorcerer wore braided sandals and a knee-length robe of a more fashionable cut that hung from one shoulder leaving his muscular chest half exposed. He wore a broadsword on his hip in a scabbard made from the same material as their clothing, only stiffened and made to resemble leather. Talmaiel had never seen him use it, but though Semjaza could easily defeat any number of Grigori hand-to-hand, the sword forestalled any largescale revolt. Semjaza husbanded his strength, but despite his preference for giving orders to dirtying his hands, he was anything but soft. Though hairless and smooth-skinned as all Grigori were, there was, nevertheless, a difference that marked him besides his physically intimidating presence. With his wide-spaced icy eyes and cruel smile, he looked the very image of the ancient predator: cold, ruthless, evil. Only his lieutenants, Samael the Destroyer and Asmodai the Beheader, and monstrous Azazel, instilled such human terror in bygone days.

"How is the work coming?" The voice was a rumble deeper than that of the rocks tumbling into the iron cart.

"Slow," was all Talmaiel could think to say.

The smile that crooked Semjaza's lips did not reach his penetrating gaze. "Find anything interesting?"

Small as it was, the stone weighed in his pocket. Did Semjaza suspect he was holding out?

"Just rock." He tossed the rock he was holding in his left hand into the mine cart while withdrawing his right from his pocket. He let his hands hang at his sides while he cast a look of disgust on the mountain of rubble waiting to be moved. "Lots of rock."

Semjaza's unsmiling eyes held his gaze. Talmaiel winced at the sharp pain that dimmed his vision, as if a callous doctor were probing his brain with a blunt scalpel in search of his secrets. He'd seen others who had long ago succumbed to the Mage's intrusions grab their heads as they convulsed with sudden pain. He'd built a wall against such incursions, but he wouldn't hold out forever. He would weaken and Semjaza had eternity.

When the Merkaba, the spinning light vehicle that had borne him to Abyss at the youngling's command, deposited him on the rampart and departed, the star gate irising closed behind it, he'd been wearing the charred remains of his leather biker's vest with the scorched gothic letters on the back proclaiming THE FALLEN and the inverted angel with its rope-bound ankles and pendant, downward-arcing wings between which was displayed his MC's motto NON SERVIAM. Semjaza had ribbed him about the credo, "I will not serve."

"How'd that work out?" the Sorcerer said when Talmaiel was brought before the throne, all the while eyeing him as if he were a juicy steak dangled before a hungry wolf.

How the Brethren endured this place without going insane, he couldn't imagine. Then again, seeing the line of sharp teeth showing between the Mage's thin lips, he had no illusions on that score. There was little sanity in this place. After millennia of freedom, of tasting the earth's sweet air and the wine of her sun-warmed grapes, his incarceration was bitter.

The pressure stopped and with a very wolfish growl, Semjaza pursed his lips and nudged his chin toward the cave-in. "Rocks aren't going to move themselves."

"No," Talmaiel said and lifted his pickaxe.

"Let me know if you find anything unusual. Anything that's not 'just rock.' Don't hesitate."

Before leaving, Semjaza's cold gaze swept the cavern, lingered on this or that angel, as if to spur tired limbs into action. The clatter and clang grew louder.

When he was gone, Talmaiel looked at his palms. His nails had scored deep crescents into his palms.

12

MORTLAKE

It wasn't a well exactly. Rick had no sense of falling, felt no rush of air. No sense of up or down or where. It was simply as if the world — the grassy sward beneath his feet, the starry sky, the moonlit lake — had vanished, blinked away in an instant and he was...nowhere.

Then came a lurch that left him dizzy and he remembered what da Silva said about the gravitational flux generated by time travel creating phase shifts that made for a rough transition. One of the main reasons he had incorporated a tourbillon, the rotating cage that protected the wheel and escapement from positional and gravitational shock, which, in turn, increased the likelihood of the chrononaut's return to his own century.

Before the nausea passed, he landed...elsewhere.

He stood in a dirt lane in the midst of a crowd of men and women dressed in old-fashioned clothing. Very old-fashioned.

The men wore short, baggy breeches, close-fitting doublets, and flat woolen caps with narrow floppy brims. Several wore leather vests over their doublets. Their ruddy faces, woolen breeches, and scuffed shoes identified them as laborers. While most wore open collars, a few more prosperous-looking gentlemen wore a short ruff about their necks. The women wore long dresses with laced bodices belted around their ample waists. Some wore aprons. All wore white caps or straw hats over braided hair. Beyond the crowd, on the other side of the dirt lane, rose an ancient stone church, its square tower brooding over a cemetery of leaning headstones. The smell of wood smoke and body odor hung in the air.

Whatever the reason for the gathering, the crowd's focus was now on him. Some faces were aghast with surprise, others darkened with displeasure, their expressions decidedly unwelcoming.

The crowd was closing on him. A youth picked up a stone. Wings of panic beat in his throat as he turned. Behind him was a tall, wrought-iron gate. The gate was closed. On the other side, four beefy, sword-wielding men wearing scarlet doublets and peaked black velvet caps stared back at him. Behind them stood a large old house that had not seen better days in decades. Its eaves rose against the scudding, red-tinged clouds.

Cries of "demon!" and "sorcerer!" rang out. A rock struck his shoulder. Expecting another, he threw up his left hand to protect his face. His right grasped a bar of the gate. "Open up!" he shouted to the closest guard. The man glared at him and held up his sword defensively, but there was fear in his eyes. His sudden appearance had startled these rustic people and what might get him a booking on a late-night talk show in the twenty-first century could get him executed for witchcraft in the current age.

The crowd formed a tight pack around him, but it appeared no one was brave enough to be the first to touch him. He shoved through the gate, grateful it was not locked. The guards backed away but crossed swords before him, blocking his passage.

Tell them you've vital news for Sir Sidney, insisted a voice in his head.

Shocked, Rick spoke aloud. "What? Who?"

Sir Sidney. Hurry!

Reginald?

Later! Hurry!

"I have news for…"

Sir Sidney.

"…Sir Sidney! Vital!"

The guards looked at each other, confusion in their eyes. Behind him the crowd hushed, their fury over his demonic entrance momentarily replaced by curiosity. Hope seized him as he perceived his role as messenger trumped that of sorcerer. He squared his shoulders and shouted at the house, "Sir Sidney! I come with news!"

The great oak door opened and out stepped a tall, gray-bearded man in a long black cloak with a stiff white Elizabethan ruff about his scrawny neck and a black skullcap on his head. Several others piled out behind him. The assembly were more splendidly dressed than any in the crowd or even the guards in their scarlet livery.

A dashing young man in black and gold with slashes in his breeches and darts in his doublet came up beside the older gentleman. By his erect posture and the way he rested his hand on his rapier's golden hilt, not threateningly but as if from habit, Rick took him for a soldier.

A shorter man with chestnut hair, a wispy beard, and a paltry mustache passed these and came up behind the guards, peering between them as if to get a better look at their outlandish visitor. His olive complexion and dark Mediterranean eyes reminded him of da Silva. He wore no ruff or lace but a simple white smock under a hooded woolen cloak. Unlike the guards or villagers, his eyes showed not the slightest trace of fear but radiated equal parts scrutiny and curiosity.

He was surprised he knew their names, as if he were sharing someone else's

Da Silva's?

memories.

The tall, black-robed man was Doctor John Dee, court astrologer and royal mathematician to Queen Elizabeth I, the same John Dee, who, following his death, would be castigated by historians as a sorcerer. The handsome greyhound of a man with the air of perpetual youth and the poise of a natural born fighter was Sir Philip Sidney, poet, diplomat, soldier—universally esteemed as the embodiment of the Elizabethan courtier. The shorter man with the intense eyes who exuded an air of restless enthusiasm was Giordano Bruno, an excommunicated and defrocked Dominican friar on the run from the Roman Inquisition, infamous throughout Europe for his radical teachings and inflammatory publications. A free thinker in a day when thinking outside officially approved dogma could get you burned at the stake.

Another courtier-soldier, stouter than Sidney and sporting an enormous ruff, was dressed in what must have been a very expensive and fashionable outfit—a black doublet and matching breeches, both slashed with white satin. His cheeks and nose were ruddy above his pointed beard and meticulously brushed mustachios, not from dissipation but from time spent outdoors. This was Sidney's friend, Lord Russell, who, Rick understood, would be knighted and made first Baron of Thornhaugh two decades hence...if, indeed, the future came to pass.

Another ruff-collared fellow in a modest brown suit and a small goatee stood slightly taller than Bruno. Voices debated the man's identity until a strident voice overrode the others insisting this was John Florio, tutor to the children of and secretary to Michel de Castelnau, Seigneur de Mauvissière, French Ambassador to the Court of Queen Elizabeth.

The clamorous debate startled Rick. The implications were disturbing—voices in his head...da Silva's and others...*many others*...after da Silva's kiss—but he was too occupied at the moment with external affairs to examine what was happening to him.

Most striking of all was the tall, barrel-chested man in the back of the group dressed in scarlet with a great scarlet cape, a full white beard parted in the middle like some ancient warrior-prophet and shoes the toes of which curled upward like some character out of Robin Hood. This was the adventurer and ardent alchemist, the Polish prince, Count Albert Laski, Palatine of Sieradz, visiting England ostensibly to meet her glorious Queen and to acquaint himself with the two "eyes of England," Oxford and Cambridge, but in reality, seeking the Philosopher's Stone, by which means he hoped to turn base metals into gold to finance his ambitions to the Polish crown.

This last resonated in Rick's mind. Was this what da Silva had sent him into the past for? To find some stone that transformed lead into gold? How was that going to defeat the Demiurge?

"Is he armed?" asked the graybeard. Though he stood several yards away on the flagstone at the foot of the steps, his voice carried like one used to lecturing in a large hall. He certainly had the high brow and piercing eyes of a learned academic.

A guard looked him over. "Not that I can see. But you canna tell with a warlock."

"None of that," Sidney admonished. "Let him pass."

The guards didn't put away their swords but let him through. Soon as he was past, one of them shut the gate and they resumed their watch. The citizenry on the other side of the fence pressed as close as they could without putting themselves in sword's reach.

Sidney and Russell looked hard at the blood on him, but Dee met his gaze as if he had seen stranger things than blood on a foreigner's shirt. "You are Uriel, are you not?"

———

"Uriel?"

One of the angels the good doctor speaks to in his gazing crystal, a voice that carried a German inflection and sounded nothing like de Silva informed him.

Rick raised his brows and returned Dee's hopeful gaze with a skeptical one.

Tell him yes, one voice insisted. *No,* another countered. *He'll only have to later admit he lied. He comes with questions, not answers. True,* a third decided.

Tell him you're Hermes Trismegistus, said a voice in an unknown tongue.

With his knowledge of the future, he could pass for Nostradamus.

He speaks no French!

The voices—a multitude by the sense of it, like picking out individual speakers in a crowd while the rest remained a background babble—stunned him. He was understanding languages he had never heard before. And thoughts as well as speech. And memories. And emotions.

Reginald?

Tell him the truth.

As much as he had wanted never again to cross paths with the Nemorensis, it was comforting to know da Silva was there—however impossible that was. He wondered if—hoped—he was sleeping and when he woke, the whole adventure, from the fire to his duel with da Silva to his present confrontation with antiquity, would prove a dream.

Among the personalities crowding his awareness, da Silva's suggestion met with approval and disproval in equal measure.

Whether he was dreaming or going mad, he had to say something. He chose to let da Silva guide him.

"No, I am not Uriel."

The man looked disappointed, but curiosity and hope, the two lamps of the human spirit, never left his searching gray eyes. There was something feverish in his gaze, the gleam of the mystic long seeking the elusive and now finding himself on the edge of discovery. "But you are one of the celestials come to riddle us out of our present," he raised a hand to the scowling heavens, "predicament, are you not?"

"No, not one of the celestials. I'm as human as you." But that wasn't true, was it? Not quite?

You have Grigori blood.

Talmaiel's voice resonated like the rumble of distant thunder. But it was only a memory—the Shining One had not taken residence in his head. He felt relief for small blessings.

Lord Russell spoke. His brusque tone matched his burly physique. "You're covered in blood. Whose?"

Rick looked down at his clothes and was shocked to see his Memphis Emergency Technician blues were wet with da Silva's blood, as was his left hand. He wiped his hand on his pants leg.

"I…"

Stopped to help another.

"…stopped to help someone."

"You are a physician?"

"A…?"

Dee tipped his sharp nose at the white-on-blue Star of Life emblem on his shoulder, a serpent entwined about a staff. "You wear the Rod of Asclepius."

"Not a physician, an apprentice."

Dee nodded as if he approved.

Russell was not so polite. "'Vital news,' you said. 'For Sir Philip.' Well spit it out man!"

"The end is near!" Rick shouted for lack of anything more constructive and immediately felt like some idiot, street-corner soothsayer. In a flash of inspiration, because they would all know Latin, he added, *"Tempus fugit!"*

Russell's red face bunched with impatience. "Yes, yes, we know that. All the signs of heaven have spoken. The new star, the Great Comet, the fiery trigon. The prophecies. That is no news. Why have *you* come?"

The listening crowd fell silent. Dee and Bruno looked expectant, Sidney and Russell skeptical. Florio cocked a brow. Laski took it all in as if it were a Punchinello show, entertaining but just, and he looked about as if searching for a meat pie (he did have a hungry look as if food hadn't passed his moist lips in an hour). Finding none he stroked his beard.

Rick glanced at the rustics crowding the lane outside the fence. The mob had grown larger. Their expressions, still hostile, had taken on the look of people desperate for answers. Rick sympathized: veined with nauseous yellow, the glowering red sky was wholly unnatural. He imagined they thought the apocalypse was upon them. Nor were they wrong.

He turned to Dee. "Perhaps we should take this indoors."

The Queen's Mathematician looked over Rick's shoulder at the crowd and nodded.

13
MIRROR ROOM

Dust motes floated in the close air when they entered the windowless room and turned on the single sconce. Nothing had changed since Fergi fled its confines last fall. A gauzy muslin curtain divided the front of the room from the rear. The easel against the back wall was ancient, the oak of its tripod legs dark with age. A drape—a square of black velvet—covered the upper portion of the easel. A cord ran from the drape up to the ceiling where a pulley passed it along to another pulley this side of the curtain.

The back of an oval dressing mirror was visible just on the other side of the curtain. The mirror was positioned to reflect the easel or, more specifically, what lay beneath the drape.

"Are you ready?" Cybele asked.

Moths fluttered in Fergi's stomach as panic threatened to send her flying from the room. She imagined the black drape sailing up and a great slit-pupiled serpent's eye glaring at her with malignant intensity. She shuddered.

She wasn't ready, never would be, but she nodded. She mistrusted her voice.

Cybele reached for the cord.

"Wait."

Fergi squeezed her eyes shut as her vagus nerve produced a wave of nausea and lightheadedness, accompanied by a gurgle in her bowels. She wiped her sweating hands against the front of her gown. But closing her eyes made things worse: the great serpent's eye, which was all Talmaiel allowed anyone who spied on him to see, rose up in her mind. It was a snare, and, according to Margreet, anyone who fell victim to the monster's gaze would be driven to madness or suicide. Or worse—turned into a weapon against the Grigori's enemies.

She opened her eyes, took a jagged breath.

"Okay."

The Goddess pulled the cord, gently. The ancient wooden pulleys creaked as the drape lifted.

And there it was.

The obsidian disc, black as midnight, polished to a mirror shine. Its surface gleamed in the sconce light. The disc was a two-way mirror, a scrying glass, a powerful showstone, fashioned ages ago on the astral plane.

Fergi breathed a sigh of relief. No eye—neither a blue Grigori one nor fiery red serpent's—stared back at her. The scrying disc reflected only the dressing mirror, its oak frame as blackened with age as the easel's, and a portion of the curtain. Standing in shadow behind the muslin partition and with the sconce's shade aimed at the easel, she and Cybele were invisible, safe from the demon's questing gaze.

She looked at Cybele. They could leave now.

But Cybele tilted Her head toward the scrying glass. Her instructions were imperative: if the vision was not forthcoming, she was to conjure it.

Her breath trembled as she exhaled.

She cleared her mind, forced her hands to relax at her sides, and gazed through the curtain at the scrying glass. She sought Talmaiel within its surface.

Her stubborn brain tried to divert her attention to Rick, to see what he was doing (Where was he? How was he dealing with what destiny had pressed upon him?) instead of seeking the Grigori, but she overrode the impulse. She forced her heart and breathing into a deeper calm and intensified her search.

Presently, the mirror fogged, not with the mist of warm breath on cool glass, but as if with tendrils creeping over damp earth. The mist faded, revealing not the landscape of frozen tundra she expected—a panorama of crags and peaks and snowy ravines and ice-laden sky as white as the landscape and a dim red sun—but a room.

The disc was some yards away and the picture within it small, but she saw the room as if it floated before her eyes.

Then she was within its bounds.

She found herself in a great columned hall. The ceiling, floor, and columns were carved from ice. She shivered as a deep, meat-locker cold penetrated her flesh.

The Grigori Talmaiel stood before one of the ice-blue pillars. She peered closer.

He was barefoot and dressed in rags. She had been too startled and the watery globe had splashed back into the bowl too soon for her to get a detailed look at him earlier. She took a closer view now. She gasped. He was hideous. The skin of his face was mottled and stretched like wrinkled plastic where the burned flesh had scarred over. His seared lips transformed his mouth into a rictus. One eyelid was missing, and the staring blue orb gave him a look of wild hilarity that would have been comical were it not so frightening. All Grigori were hairless and his perfectly bald head, like his face, was a patchwork of gray and livid purple-red.

Despite the revulsion his ravaged face evoked, a liquid swirl of guilt twisted in her gut at what she'd done. But people of Hendricks had been dying. She'd had no choice. She shuddered to think of the misery that would have been loosed upon the earth if Talmaiel had succeeded in freeing the Grigori. No, she had done right to burn him. Her failure was not completing the job.

She peered closer still. He appeared to be whispering to the column. Though no sound escaped from the scrying glass, she could almost hear him.

She tilted her ear, as if doing so she might catch his words.

In that moment, he looked over his shoulder. His blue eyes scanned the hall, as if watching for an eavesdropper.

Then he looked up.

And she was looking straight into the Watcher's eyes. Or, more specifically, one bright, lidless blue orb.

Her heart hammered as her hand found the cord and dropped the black drape over the platter.

14

TALMAIEL SEEKS ADVICE

Talmaiel leaned against the pillar. Beneath his hands thrummed a silent power as if the column hid a generator within its blue translucent ice. Yet the vibrations were not the product of any machine or even the slow meat pulsations of lung and heart but the quicksilver ripple of thought.

"Kokabiel."

The ancient voice answered, soundless as Kokabiel no longer had lips.

Talmaiel.

The voice was dry and uninflected, a rusty, humorless vestige of the vibrant lecturing tone he remembered from long ago. Having sacrificed his body, it was as if the ancient one had relinquished all nuances of individuality.

Good to see you.

Of course, Kokabiel had no eyes either, but that didn't keep him from seeing any more than his lack of ears kept him from hearing.

Kokabiel had once commanded the influence of the stars and taught man astrology—not the insipid sun signs and nativity charts that passed for astrology in recent centuries, but the wisdom of the Philosophic Fire, which was a metaphor for understanding the correspondences between the celestial and the corporeal and the art of calling down the etheric emanations of the stars and planets to perform work for the mage who controlled their influences. Now his brain resided within the column. The remaining kilometers of nervous system were distributed beneath the floors and walls of Semjaza's audience chamber as well as the adjoining rooms and corridors. The power grid, which was what remained of the Grigori Kokabiel, was like an antenna, a net receiving, concentrating, and augmenting not the emanations of stars and planets because Abyss was far removed from any such celestial objects save the lone red dwarf whose paltry light barely warmed the dismal planet, but the collective concentrated will of the Brethren.

Whether Kokabiel sacrificed himself for the good of the Brethren of his own free will or at Semjaza's command, Talmaiel hadn't asked, but given Semjaza's sadistic nature, he imagined the latter.

"I need your advice," he whispered. Semjaza was making his rounds, keeping his troops on their toes. What the point was—seeing they'd been here for thousands of years and weren't going anywhere soon—he had no idea, but he supposed Semjaza's bullying kept them from falling prey to inertia. His gaze sought the throne on the raised dais at one end of the hall. The throne was fashioned from the same ubiquitous gray polymer as every other piece of furniture the Grigori made from transformed rock. Semjaza might return at any moment and it was imperative he speak to Kokabiel in private.

How may I help?

Did he detect a note of curiosity? As if, after ages of unremitting sameness, he'd been offered a diversion. Was that what he was? A diversion?

"Can I trust you not to reveal our conversation to Semjaza?"

As long as he doesn't ask.

That was ambiguous, but given Kokabiel's helplessness, it was about what he expected. He seized upon a way to get the information he wanted that would appear innocent enough if Semjaza learned his line of inquiry.

"Semjaza asked if I'd found anything unusual in the mine. Is he looking for something specific?"

Yes.

"What?"

He is working on something with Raziel.

70

That was interesting. "What is he and the Artificer working on?"

I am not permitted to say.

The hell with it. "All right. Then tell me this if you can: when we gather in this hall to transmute, would it be possible for someone to tap into the process, to siphon off some of the energy, and use the collective will for a personal project?"

Only if you don't mind pain.

He winced, recalling the public punishments Semjaza regularly meted out to brethren who fell short of the Sorcerer's expectations. He didn't bother with pincers or flails, nor did he need a tormentor to do his bidding. His mind dug deep into their brains' pain centers and squeezed. He'd seen Grigori spasming on the ground, wracked in agony. Kokabiel, reduced to a web of raw nerves beneath the floor, had reason to fear his master.

"Point taken. But I mean no harm. So lately from Earth, my curiosity hasn't yet been blunted."

And seeing Abyss, you long to return.

"Yes."

Suddenly, his flesh tingled with the sensation of being watched. He turned, expecting to find Semjaza standing behind him ready to demand what he was up to. But the Master Mage wasn't there. He looked about the chamber, saw no one. Still, a pins-and-needles warmth crawled over his body. He looked up.

For an instant, remembering Cybele's girl—*Delores Ferguson*—spying on him, he experienced a sense of déjà vu. But only for a moment, for, as he scanned the ceiling half expecting to see a face looking down from the ice, the sensation vanished and he sensed only himself and Kokabiel inhabiting the room.

Something troubles you, Kokabiel said.

"It's nothing. Your talk of pain is making me paranoid."

You are wise to be wary.

15
THE SHOWSTONE

Dee's house seemed larger inside than from the street. The Magus of Mortlake had built additions with an eye toward usage rather than aesthetics. The ancient, wood-paneled walls gleamed with the dull patina of age as Dee led the procession through a warren of rooms. Upstairs, the personalities crowding his brain jostled to look on the wonders of Dee's collection as they passed through his *Externa Bibliotheca,* his chief library and reading room, where visiting scholars and copyists consulted the main body of his collection. Room after room of vertical shelving housed Dee's vast collection of rare books, manuscripts, and scrolls—a collection that dwarfed the combined libraries of Oxford and Cambridge, and which, for scientific purposes (containing as it did references on mathematics, alchemy, astrology, astronomy, geology, metallurgy, mineralogy, mechanics, engineering, architecture, navigation, natural history, medicine, and music) was of greater value. Other treasures included a five-foot quadrant, a ten-foot cross-staff used by astronomers for measuring angles between stars and by mariners for determining latitude, an astrolabe made by William Borough, and a pair of Mercator globes, one of Earth, another of the heavens.

As they went, Rick learned Dee's visitors had just arrived in the Queen's royal barge on their way back from Oxford, where Count Laski was entertained and Bruno was ridiculed by the Oxford dons, not because they found his radical infinite worlds theory more offensive than Copernicus' heretical heliocentric model, but because of his diminutive stature and his Neapolitan pronunciation of Latin. Where they butchered Latin as if written in English, pronouncing *benedicite* "bene-dice-itee," Bruno pronounced it as if it were Italian and said "bene-dee-chee-tay."

"Pedagogues! Execrable bipeds!" Bruno grumbled as they made their way through the stacks. Born in Noli on the outskirts of Naples, Bruno styled himself as *il Nolano*, the Nolan, and his philosophy as "the Nolan philosophy."

Sidney related how Oxford residents venturing onto Broad Street that morning discovered the smoldering remains of two crosses and corpses on the spot outside Balliol College, where Catholic martyrs Hugh Latimer and Nicholas Ridley had been burned nearly three decades earlier.

Dee informed his visitors how London woke to find the city covered in fog. When the fog rolled out, boatmen discovered the Thames frozen and their crafts gripped in ice (though it was June). By noon, the river had thawed and swans plied its gray waters. Elsewhere in the city, citizens encountered neighbors they'd never seen before and, as rumor had it, some who had died in Henry's day. Whole blocks in certain districts were replaced by leaning, thatch-roofed tenements razed decades past. Tied up at one dock, a Dutch caravel of a style not seen in nearly a century, whose skipper swore he had set out from Amsterdam in 1498.

"Most curious of all," he said, "the ancient cross in Charing, along with many buildings, vanished in the night, replaced, or so Walsingham's messenger told me, by a bronze equestrian of a noble figure, bareheaded, with a pointed beard and seated upon a charger. No one could place the countenance, but all marked the kingly features and the baton of command held in his right hand. Were the alterations the work of her Catholic enemies trying to cast doubt on her legitimacy and stir the populace to rebellion, Elizabeth would have Walsingham scouring the city for the traitors, but as the transformation appears the work of divine intervention, her Majesty fears for her Crown."

"Even in our quaint corner," he added, "astonishing things happened this day. Clarence Dykes, eighteen—no twenty—years dead, walked into St. Mary Virgin this morning complaining that someone was living in his house and received quite a shock when white-faced Reverend Griswold showed him his gravestone." Though deeply troubled by the day's events, the twinkle in Dee's eye hinted he enjoyed sharing his news with his company.

Then Dee ushered them through a pair of double doors into his *interna bibliotheca* or private study and the voices in Rick's head really got loud. The large, low-ceilinged room was a veritable museum of curiosities. Here, Dee kept his magical books and equipment and performed his esoteric experiments. Books great and small filled the shelves lining the walls; more books teetered in stacks on the floor making navigation precarious; still others cluttered the ancient oak writing table standing before the bay window that overlooked the garden and the Thames beyond. Next to an hourglass on the desk, a large leather-bound volume drew the attention of several of the voices. One identified the book as a copy of Cornelius Agrippa's *De Occulta Philosophia*, which Dee kept open for easy reference.

Among the bedlam of wonders was a great oval mirror standing in a corner in a heavy frame of dark carven wood. Nearly as tall as he, the convex perspective glass augmented the sullen light from the window while reflecting everything in the room—books, instruments, ceiling, floor, the congregation of men—in its curved surface. Rick's gaze slid over its face and he quickly looked away, as he experienced a surge of nausea at the memory of a certain funhouse mirror in an abandoned warehouse near the Holland Tunnel.

Frank.

He grimaced at the stab of loss and guilt. After all their squabbling and fighting, his brother had died saving him—twice!

I'm Superman, remember?

He tore his mind away from the memory. Time for remorse when he got back to his own century.

His gaze fell next on the table that dominated the center of the room on a vast Turkey rug. A small pink crystal ball the size of a goose egg stood in the middle of the table in a silver frame on a square of red silk. The crystal was of great clarity and reflected the room in its curved surface like the perspective glass only in miniature. A larger square containing words in a cryptic alphabet encompassed the square of silk. This, in turn, was surrounded by a pentagram and seven copper discs tacked to the table into which were etched arcane Kabbalistic devices. A voice identified the language as Enochian, the "Angelic" alphabet Enoch supposedly used when he was taken up to heaven to serve as the scribe of God, and the seven emblems as the "Ensigns of Creation" corresponding to the seven planets and the stages of the alchemical process. The celestial alphabet painted in blue letters along the sides of the table provided further decoration. The effect was magical, as if the table were an altar, neither Christian nor pagan, but something that transcended religion.

The "table of practice," an awed voice explained, was an earthly representation of a celestial one and the crystal an earthly stone that corresponded to its celestial likeness. All things in the physical had their counterparts in the celestial. As above, so below. By modeling earthly representations—images, talismans, sigils, statues—of celestial objects, the skilled practitioner called down subtle rays from the stars and thereby effected change in the physical realm.

It occurred to Rick that Dee's starry irradiation was another way of explaining da Silva's light of emanation, which wasn't physical light at all but a "divine" energy, the creative force that man could learn to harness and put to use if he set his mind to it.

As he looked into the crystal, its surface cleared. The reflections of the room—books, instruments, ceiling, floor, men—vanished, and he saw into the depths of the glass. He took a step closer. Sure enough, something there.

Faces emerging…

For a moment he panicked, remembering…

Night on the ridgetop…a swarm of alien faces staring down from the great rift in the sky, too distant to make out features but knowing what he was seeing were not stars but fantastic creatures winging down from immeasurable cosmic depths—

Grigori

The Sleepless Ones

—returning to reclaim their domination over earth and man.

75

But as the torrent of faces swam up from the depths of the crystal, he saw not the long utterly hairless features and arctic-blue eyes of Grigori, but faces fair and dark, bearded and shaven, eyes blue and gray and brown and green, faces ancient and in the prime of life—and he knew he was looking at a lineage of long-lifers stretching back into antiquity and beyond, not just the storied Priests of Diana of Classical fame, but magi from Egypt and Anatolia and Mesopotamia and back through the Neolithic and Paleolithic, back as long as man had fashioned gods from wood and stone and sought in the great wheel of the stars the mysteries surrounding their little fires. As long as She had walked among Earth's peoples and Her sibyls had cast runes or gazed into still waters to divine what might be and joined hands and will to shape from the currents of possibility what was to come.

A long-nosed Priest with a narrow forehead and a thatch of hair like a squirrel came forward, his nose made even longer by the curve of the globe, and he heard the man's voice speaking in an ancient tongue he should not have known but did.

Be not afraid. We are here to help, and you will need all the help you can get. Though we have traveled the astral, none of us have penetrated the supernal realms and are as much as you at a loss as to how to reverse Yaldabaoth's undoing. These men may have answers.

Da Silva's face replaced the Ancient's.

Reginald.

Yes.

You are here.

Yes and no.

Rick heard the humor in the man's voice and experienced a warmth toward the Nemorian he'd resisted feeling when he was alive. Immediately, the horror of what he'd done washed over him.

The Priest sliding off the blade as he sank to the grass. The blood...

We have each of us moved on, da Silva said as his face dissolved like mist in the stone. *What you experience is a reflection of the consciousness that existed. More than a repository of memories. But to work. As my brother said, you will need all the help you can get.*

A voice drew him back to the room.

His hand was outstretched, as if reaching for the globe. He lowered it, embarrassed.

Dee stood beside him. "You saw something in the showstone." The sage's eyes glowed as his gaze passed from Rick to the crystal and back again.

Rick started to protest he saw nothing, but da Silva literally stopped his tongue.

Hold on. This could work to our advantage. Asking these men's help in finding the Philosopher's Stone will make them suspect you are a treasure hunter. Telling them on no clear authority the Demiurge is discreating the world won't win you any friends either. Put yourself in their shoes, in their time. Enlightened men, some of the most enlightened in the world, but still with one foot in the old world and one in the new, believing in the scientific method, but also convinced of the existence of angels and demons. John Dee believes he has a direct pipeline to the celestial host. What better authority than angels?

You? An angel?

You're calling the kettle black? Grigori blood runs in your veins, too.

"You do see something." Dee was watching him. "Your lips were moving. You appeared to be conversing with…" He leaned forward, brow furrowed, frustration writ large in his features, as if he were willing himself to see what his visitor saw in the crystal's depths. "I see nothing myself. I have not the gift." His voice was wistful, regret barely mollified by resignation, and Rick felt compassion for this man, one of the great minds in an age of great minds, who, for all his bookish learning and practical accomplishments, was a failure in his own eyes for not having "the gift." A blind man yearning to see the stars. "To accomplish my work, I must rely on the talents of others."

"Where is your earless cur?" Sidney asked. "Is he shy of our company?"

Dee spared his former pupil an indulgent smile. "Ned Kelley *is* reclusive, and most vain about his deformity. But he is not here. He rode west this morning to see a man about a book found in the ruins of a Welsh monastery."

"A book?"

"Yes, a book and…"

"'And...'?"

"A red powder," he said reluctantly, as if he'd said too much.

"Doctor Dee—" Russell tilted his broad forehead at Rick. "—how do we know this man is not a popish spy? Or the agent of one who wishes to discredit your standing at court?"

Laski, who, in his scarlet outfit and magnificent beard, clearly had little regard for discretion, perked up. "Red powder? Doctor, you have found the stone?"

"I will not know until he brings it back."

The "stone." They're talking about the Philosopher's Stone? Rick didn't wait for an answer and was about to blurt out that he had been sent to find the Philosopher's Stone, but da Silva again stopped his tongue.

Patience. Direct your questions to the crystal.

But I'm no fortune teller.

Scryer. Just follow my lead.

Rick mentally shook his head. *What have I gotten myself into?* But following the supercentenarian's instructions, he leaned over the crystal as if something had drawn him closer and made as if he was oblivious to the conversation going on in the room and the eyes upon him.

The hairs on his neck prickled.

Whether it was a trick of the light or his imagination, he did see something in its depths. A golden light was forming in its center; it bloomed like a flower, flowed outward like liquid mercury, and when the light passed, da Silva's face gazed up at him from the crystal.

I see a man, da Silva prompted.

"I see a man."

Dee drew back clasping a fist to his heart. "A spirit of the dead?"

Careful, da Silva warned. *Communing with the dead is Necromancy. A black art punishable by death.*

"No, he is no unclean or avenging spirit, but very much alive."

But no ordinary man.

"But no ordinary man."

He's tall and his face shines like the sun.

He's short and ugly and needs a shave.

Don't go there. Give an audience what they want.

78

"He's tall and his face shines like the sun."

"Michael," Dee whispered. "You're describing Michael. Does he carry a sword?"

"No sword. And no angel. An ancient magus who has ascended to a higher realm."

Dee sucked in his breath. "He has discovered the elixir!"

"He says not. God granted him longevity and knowledge for his labor and devotion. My master is a member of a sacred order, whose purpose, like yours, Doctor Dee, is to humbly and reverentially know the end of Nature, which is to understand the mind of God, thereby to do Him greater glory and to better reverence Him by being nearer unto His purpose."

Dee nudged his bearded chin at the crystal. "This man is your master?"

Rick nodded. "He is." It grated to watch da Silva smile as he said it.

"His name?"

"Silvanus."

"Silvanus…of the forest. An ancient name. A holy name. And yet…" Dee peered into the stone and said in a commanding voice, "Silvanus, in the name of the Father, Son, and the Holy Ghost, I entreat you, give us proof that you are no wicked demon but a true and Godly wight."

Rick made a show of listening, then answered, "Silvanus says, does not your showstone rest on the *Sigillum Dei*? And have you not inscribed in a circle on the back of the seal the divine names of the seven angels of the presence—Zaphkiel, Zadkiel, Cumael, Raphael, Haniel, Michael, and Gabriel—by which no evil thing can appear in the stone? Therefore, were I the most powerful necromancer, yet I could not summon anything evil through the crystal."

Dee's eyes widened. He looked at Sidney, at Russell. "How can this young man know this unless he has the gift and is telling the truth?"

"Unless he is in league with Kelly."

Dee gave Sidney a reproachful look.

"Silvanus comes to you with a warning and a request," Rick continued.

"A warning?"

"He bids me tell you time is running backward."

16
THE STARS THEMSELVES

"Time run backward? Impossible!"

Russell's ruddy face was so close Rick smelled the leeks and ale he'd had for lunch. Veins stood out on the man's temple. His fist was clenched. Beneath the courtly veneer lay the disposition of a born brawler.

Rick rankled at the man's tone. Russell looked intimidating with his broad chest and rapier hanging at his side, and he probably outweighed him by forty pounds, but Rick was a hair taller and he traded the courtier glare for glare.

Dee broke the tension. "I will hear him out. He has obviously come far to deliver his message. And I am intrigued."

"Doctor Dee, the Queen is waiting, all hell is breaking loose, and we waste time listening to this…" Russell flicked a pocket flap of Rick's bloody shirt "…*servant's* rantings!"

"Nevertheless, I will hear him out. He was right about the *Sigillum Dei*. No evil spirit can enter by the Holy Table."

"That doesn't mean he cannot lie."

Sidney put his hand on Russell's arm. Russell growled, but relented and withdrew.

"I, too, am curious to hear how time can run backward," Bruno said, coming forward. "I've heard of rivers running backward but never time."

Russell harrumphed from where he stood by Dee's desk, but the Italian was Sidney's guest and he made no further motion to intervene.

"Now tell us what you mean by your statement. It is obvious from the many strange and wondrous things that have happened this day that time is awry, but it seems the opposite of what you claim—that events of the past are visiting the present."

Rick experienced an anxious moment as he tried to remember the conversation he'd had with da Silva on this subject—what? An hour ago? Centuries? His mind swirled.

Calmo. The Priest was with him. *Take a breath and start talking. That's what I always do.*

You're gabby, I'm not.

He began as da Silva had. "What is time?"

When Dee paused to gather his thoughts, Bruno stepped in.

"Aristotle believed a motion in the present proceeds from a previous motion which proceeds from a still previous motion ad infinitum, and that time is the measure of that motion, a kind of universal order, independent of space; and, provided you have a good clock, the interval between two events can be measured. He furthermore held that time proceeds into the past and future infinitely. Augustine, on the other hand, argued the past and future do not exist, only the present, but the present is without duration. Which would seem to confute Aristotle, because how can you measure duration if it doesn't exist? Augustine further confutes Aristotle in saying time is finite since, in accordance with Scripture, the universe was created, *ex nihilo*, and will end with the rapture."

Florio spoke: "Time was circular for the ancients. The Church of Rome with their calendar dating from our Savior's birth made time linear."

Sidney said, "I see its effects on women's faces as they wax from green to ripe and from ripe to spoiled." If he thought his cavalier offering would bring a laugh, he was mistaken. Outside in the street, a strident voice arose; the crowd was arguing with the guards.

As if he had reached a conclusion, Dee nodded to himself. "The stars themselves show us the true nature of time. The moon goes through its phases. The great wheel of the heavens cycles through the seasons and the ages. It is clear time is circular and yet ever moving forward."

"How so?" Rick asked.

Dee looked up at the beamed ceiling as if seeing his beloved zodiac. "There are the smaller cycles of the seasons. Then there are the great ages marked by the trigons."

"Trigons?"

Dee raised a finger to lecture but Bruno was quicker.

"The twelve signs of the zodiac divide into four trigons: fiery, earthy, airy, and watery. The fiery trigon is considered the first, beginning with creation. The first sign of the fiery trigon is Aries. Great conjunctions, conjunctions of the superior planets Saturn and Jupiter, occur every twenty years. Greater conjunctions, when Jupiter and Saturn enter a completely new trigon, occur every two hundred and forty years and mark momentous changes on earth. But only once every thousand years does the conjunction of Jupiter and Saturn return to Aries and enter the fiery trigon. Historians and astrologers will tell you only six greatest conjunctions have occurred since the creation of the world: one during the life of the prophet Enoch, another with Noah's Flood, a third when Moses received the Ten Commandments, the fourth during the dispersal of the ten tribes from Israel, the fifth at the birth of Christ, and the sixth coinciding with the reign of Charlemagne."

"Each grand conjunction," Florio interjected, "coincided with great changes in the Book of Nature, especially in the political and religious realms. Christ's birth brought Christianity to the world. Charlemagne forged Europe into a Christian Empire. But the present grand conjunction marking our entry into the fiery trigon signals unprecedented upheavals. Doomsayers predict storms and flood, strife, poverty, famine, crop failures, shipwrecks…all to be crowned by the final dissolution of the world and the Second Coming." Bruno's fellow Italian raised his brows and held his hands out, palms upward, as if to say, *I don't necessarily believe but there you have it.*

Dee got his chance: "Genesis tells us God made the world and man in six days. And Peter tells us 'one day is with the Lord as a thousand years, and a thousand years as one day.' Therefore, prognosticators proclaim man's week is nearly over and God's great Sabbath rest is upon us."

Sidney, who had been pacing, stopped and waved a dismissive hand. "The latter day is at hand! Foolish star-tooters."

"These auguries," Dee continued, "though I admit they appear more dire than I had expected, presage a new dawn, not an eternal night. Jupiter's influence and irradiation is not given to calamity and dissolution but to noble progress. It is time for England to take her place upon the world stage, with her Majesty the Queen as its Empress, a new Charlemagne. As I have urged her Majesty numerous times, England must build a strong navy to keep the enemy from our sovereign shores and to spread British rule across the seas." He looked at Sidney for confirmation.

"So you've often said." Sidney smiled fondly on his mentor.

Dee nodded. His gray eyes were aglow with his vision of a new age with Elizabeth at the helm of the imperial ship. Rick's heart sank at the thought of disappointing Dee, who for all his science and wisdom, was mired in the superstitious beliefs of his time. He recalled a field trip to the Museum of Natural History back in high school. After strolling the Hall of Dinosaurs with the skeletons of Tyrannosaurus rex and Brontosaurus towering over them and then touring the Hall of Human Biology and Evolution with its fossil remains and replicas of various hominid species depicting the evolution of man, a student, a Seven Day Adventist, had thrown up her hands and said, "Enough!" and claimed these were all lies, forgeries meant to denigrate her religion. The occasion had been an eye opener; he had learned truth is relative and will always mean different things to different people.

But he needed Dee's cooperation, and now.

"Sir, I don't mean to contradict you," he said, putting iron in his voice, "but time is fleeting, so I must. The end is, indeed, upon us. But not as the doomsayers think."

"Go on." Dee's eyes were wary with the dread of a child about to hear he can't have his heart's desire.

"The recent anomalies are just the beginning and have nothing to do with your Grand Conjunction. What you are seeing is the total dissolution of the universe."

He hurried on before they could further press him with questions — or worse, turn him out of doors empty handed. His mind raced with his own thoughts and a babble of information from his "helpful" tenants. Without mentioning the Priest, Yaldabaoth, Cybele, or the fact that he wouldn't be born for another four hundred years, he told them how time's arrow was an illusion of apparent motion, not unlike the illusion of watching the sun rise in the East and set in the West, when in reality Earth rotated into the light. He told them how the physical world was the world of reflection, the mirror of all other worlds, and how the light of emanation, arriving from above, was reflected back into the higher planes. These men, da Silva told him, were versed in the Kabbalah and would understand this.

He spoke quickly, rushing through his preamble to get to his thesis. "As spirit is involved into matter, so matter is evolved into spirit," he said and explained how man's consciousness, as an effect of this process, was evolving into superconsciousness and how God (he dared not say "Demiurge") seeing man pushing out into the subtle realms, even as he explored new countries in the physical world, was unmaking creation to halt his ascent.

"Why?" Dee asked after pausing to take this in.

Rick shrugged.

"I suppose your ascended master told you this?" Russell's skepticism was blatant.

"Yes."

"And how does he know? Does he see the mind of God?"

"He sees from a different vantage. The physical plane is like a one-sided mirror in which we see only reflections, shadows. The subtle plane is like a two-sided mirror through which one can see the effects of the divine emanation on earth while also seeing the causes entering from above."

Laski, who had seated himself in the large green chair that faced the Holy Table and who, until now, had stroked his beard and listened quietly, said, "The way I see it, it doesn't matter if time is flowing backward or forward, but if what you say is true, how does your master propose to rewrite the Book of Nature?"

Rick opened his mouth to say he had no idea, except the solution somehow involved finding the Philosopher's Stone and deciphering how to use it, but a loud crash downstairs distracted him. The mob had broken a window. Voices outside grew to a roar.

A moment later one of the guards burst into the room without knocking. The front of his scarlet doublet was soiled with what looked like mud or excrement.

"My Lords. The crowd grows stronger. They've armed themselves with cudgels, pitchforks, and rusty swords. Should we not retire to the barge?"

Dee looked around his sanctum. His eyes were wide. "I cannot leave. They will destroy," he waved his hands at his books, his instruments, the Holy Table, "everything!"

Sidney's rapier wisped from its sheath. "I'll bring the curs to heel!" he growled and made for the door.

Russell caught his arm. "Leave them. They are unworthy of your sword. Besides," his beard parted in a grim show of teeth, "if anything happened to you, the Queen would have my head."

17
VISITORS

The garden was warm, and though Fergi was still cold, at least her teeth had stopped chattering. The sky was the color of yellow pus streaked with clotted blood and there was no birdsong. It was as if the birds that sang daily from every twist and turn of the garden's meandering paths had flown. Even the water cascading down the fountain's scalloped bowls had taken on a melancholy tone. But most telling of all that the decay swallowing the earth had reached the Goddess' abode were the flowers. Since the first time she walked in the garden, she had marveled that the bushes and flowering trees were forever in bloom and each leaf, each petal, each blade of grass always perfect and unblemished. Now decay was everywhere. The nearby roses were turning brown and withered petals littered the grass. Many of the trees were shedding leaves as if autumn had come to this place of eternal spring.

They sat on the fountain's edge: Cybele with Her sandaled feet on the pea stone walk, Her hands folded in Her lap; Fergi with her arms clasped, as if to ward off the cold emanating from the world she'd seen in the mirror.

"Tell me what you saw."

That the Goddess, with all Her powers, was as blind as the Sisters while she was the only one left with the sight was more terrifying than the decay eating the garden.

"You saw nothing?"

"Nothing. But I saw your reaction. Whatever you saw terrified you. Tell me."

Fergi folded her own hands in her lap and, looking down at them squeezed together so tightly her knuckles were white, she told what she had seen, careful to omit nothing and to explain everything in minute detail. She wanted desperately for Cybele to see through her eyes. Being alone with such a burden was too great to bear.

"And he seemed to be whispering to the column." She shrugged, at a loss. "I have no idea why. But he appeared furtive, as if he was afraid someone might catch him."

She sought her Mistress' eyes. "I don't understand. He's a monster. He tried to kill us all and bring his kind and the Nephilim to Earth. But the impression I got was he was afraid. As if there is something worse than him. Something even he fears."

Cybele held her gaze a minute more, then looked up at the toxic sky. The worry lines encroaching on the Goddess' features were, like the browning leaves and withering petals, another baleful sign. Fergi remembered the first time she saw Cybele. The Lady had taken a window booth at Hot Rod's, the greasy spoon where she waitressed. Dressed in capris and a sweater, She'd looked totally out of place, a fairy tale princess at a backyard barbeque. She remembered how the college boys, usually boisterous, often rude, even offensively sexist, had been cowed to silence by Her presence. And again, in this very garden, seated on a marble throne and dressed in a white gown that showed off Her ivory skin while Her hair burned like red maple leaves catching the afternoon sun. And the night she first put on the gown — she who hated dresses and wore only black and dismissed girls who wore dresses as weak conformists — and joined the Sisters dancing in the garden, the Sisters' sandaled feet tracing arabesques as two circles of linked hands orbited the Goddess in opposite directions and the panpipes wove a droning hypnotic tapestry and the Goddess' tympanum *rattle thumped rattle thumped* against Her hand. On all those occasions — and even when Talmaiel threatened the world with the return of the Grigori and the Nephilim and She'd led the Sisters in raising a full moon on a moonless night—Her countenance remained undaunted, Her forehead unmarred by doubt.

Fergi looked back at the house rising above the trees, its many-gabled roof silhouetted against the yellow sky. How many centuries had it stood in this magic place? She suspected it hadn't always looked as it did, that it changed with the times. Was it all to end?

She turned to the Goddess.

"I still don't understand. Yaldabaoth is your son. Can't you talk to him?"

"I will try, but first I must prepare."

"Prepare for what?"

"If I fail, I will need you and my people and my priest to carry on."

"If you fail, what can we do?"

Cybele was about to answer when Maija and Keija ran up, their sandals crunching the pea stone. Margreet and two others, an older woman and a teenage boy, followed not far behind.

Fergi recognized the visitors when they neared. She'd met them only once, at Wally's funeral, but she'd heard all about what they'd done in the battle against Talmaiel and the biker army he'd brought to level the little community of Hendricks, Arkansas.

The grizzle-haired matron in the denim jacket, cargo pants, and hiking boots was Reverend Grace, one of the senior Sisters, who did not live at the residence but ministered to Cybele's people at the foot of Crystal Mountain deep in the Ouachitas. (Fergi had learned not to say "worshipers" because Cybele's devotees did not worship Her but worked and fought alongside Her as She worked and fought with them.) Grace was a sort of combination Mayor and Reverend—and military leader when the occasion arose. At the funeral, she'd worn a black dress and wide-brimmed black hat.

Terrance Light, the gangly, blond-haired teenager beside her, wore a T-shirt that read:

> WEEKEND FORECAST
> TRACTOR PULLING
> WITH A CHANCE OF

BEER

He'd lost his mother in the battle and, so she heard, had leveled a deadly toll on the enemy. A raven's skull hung from a leather thong about his neck. It wasn't an ornament but a talisman. It was said he saw through its eyes and used it to summon animals. His own eyes were clouded with milky cataracts. Though legally blind, he seemed to be doing fine as he made his way unassisted toward the fountain. According to Margreet, he saw better than most, only not with his eyes.

Cybele was on Her feet before the visitors reached them, Her arms spread and Her dimples back in place at the corners of Her smile. She and Grace met with a mutually crushing bear hug as if they were old best friends who hadn't seen each other in ages. It was strange to think that Grace—who looked to be in her sixties, but being a Sister was probably over a hundred—was the younger of the two.

By many thousands of years.

Fergi stood and, with her hands clasped before her, waited to be introduced. She didn't have to wait long, and no introduction was necessary as Grace released Cybele and came to her.

"Ah, Delores," the matron said taking her hands and appraising her at arm's length. Grace had stunning violet eyes and an infectious smile. "I can see why young Richard Scott is so taken with you."

Fergi's heart fluttered at the elder's use of the present tense. The memory of Rick's sword bursting from da Silva's back jolted her.

As if she'd felt her shock, Grace's expression turned from appraising to sympathetic. "Difficult times, Miss, difficult measures."

Fergi nodded. It was strange being part of a society where so much was understood without being spoken. Strange, yet gratifying. She'd never cared for small talk, and getting to the point with as little chatter as possible was a bonus.

"And this is Terry," Maija and Keija said, introducing the youth beside Grace. Their lilting Scandinavian voices competed for her ear. Maija raised an eyebrow at Keija; Keija grinned back.

Terrance Light was a mute. He signed something she didn't understand, and seeing she didn't understand, took her hands. It was

90

eerie looking into those clouded eyes and knowing he couldn't possibly see through the opaque cataracts, but suspecting, if what she heard about him was true, he was seeing her more clearly than she saw him.

And then she was seeing…

A Grigori.

She started and tried to free her hands, but Terry's grip was firm and she continued to see...

Not Talmaiel but another. As hairless and blue-eyed as all Grigori but bigger, taller, his mouth a cruel slash beneath a hawk nose. He stood not in a vista of icy peaks and frozen ravines, but on a ridge of undulating dunes under a blazing sun

His head turned, his eyes seeking…

She broke free, shaken by the vision.

"Another's coming," she said. "Not Talmaiel."

"Azazel," Grace said.

"So you can see," Fergi said, looking at Reverend Grace with relief, thankful to find another to share the workload.

"No, Terry told me." When she looked confused, Grace added, "He signed. I'm as blind as the rest. Woke up this morning and my sight was gone." She shook her head in wonder. "After all these years."

"Oh." Fergi looked at the teenager. He was only a few years younger, but she was new to this game, while he'd been clairvoyant since childhood. He smiled at her, and she knew without a doubt he was seeing her—whether through his third eye or through the raven's ghostly vision, it didn't matter. Margreet had told her he saw through the eyes of many creatures, but had an affinity with flying things—birds, bats, butterflies—and, supposedly, an ancient catfish named Henry. She could only imagine. She'd never thought about learning sign language. It was something she would definitely take up when…

What am I thinking? We don't know if there will be a when.

He was signing again.

"He says he is pleased to meet you," Grace interpreted. "He also says he is glad you have the sight. He was afraid he was the only one."

"I know the feeling. Will you be staying with us?"

"No, we've only come to consult with Cybele and the Elders."

"There's been a new development," the Lady said.

91

"Oh?"

"Delores saw the Grigori Talmaiel today."

Cybele recounted for their visitors how "Delores" had seen the Shining One first in the water of her scrying bowl then in the Mirror Room.

"He wasn't looking for you?" Grace asked.

"No."

"That's significant," the gray-haired Reverend mused. "We've no word—neither from Terry nor any other source—that the Watcher is on earth, but the demon Azazel is coming. My feeling is he is being used as a weapon."

"Against whom? And who—*what*—is this Azazel?"

Margreet spoke up. "He was the leader of the Grigori, whom Yaldabaoth created and sent to Earth to keep humans in line. Man's purpose was to worship the Demiurge and to keep the spark of creation alive by passing it from generation to generation. 'Be fruitful and multiply!' Azazel was the worst of them. While most Grigori abandoned their mission, preferring the fruits of the earth to bowing to their Maker, many taught men arts and sciences, healing and philosophy."

"And warfare," Keija interjected.

"I doubt man needed the Choir to teach him that," Grace countered. "But metallurgy, chemistry."

"Astrology, sorcery," Maija added.

"Um. Anyway," Grace continued, "while some 'corrupted' man by teaching him what was forbidden—what would certainly distract him from worshiping their God—and most adopted the ways of men, especially where it came to women, Azazel had other appetites."

Fergi shuddered, remembering the shadow that had risen up in her kitchen as if condensing from the very air, until it towered over her, vaguely anthropomorphic, like a silhouette cut from oily blackness scintillating with worms of black starlight. Its eyes like inkwells glaring down. Clawed hands reaching.

She looked at Maija and Keija and had to choke the impulse to rush to them and hug them both. They'd saved her from the creature. If not for them, she would have been left a shrunken husk on the kitchen floor.

After the twins brought her to the Sisterhood and Cybele explained, she learned the creature was a Nephilim, a monstrous offspring of Grigori and human mating, and its lusts were not for the blood and bodily fluids it leached from its victims—that was only a side effect of its feeding. What it sought was the spark of creation that burned in every creature, but in man the brightest. She couldn't help equating the spark with the soul and thought of the Nephilim as eaters of souls.

"A soul-eater," she said. "Like the Nephilim."

"No, child," Grace said with a shake of her head. "Azazel's appetites were simpler. His was an insatiable bloodlust. Men, women, children. He could not drink enough human blood. It is said that he not only drank it but bathed in it daily."

Margreet picked up the tale. "For their trespasses, legend has it Yaldabaoth sent his Avengers—the angels Raphael, Gabriel, and Michael—to route the Nephilim and confine the Watchers."

"Is this true?" Fergi addressed her question to Cybele, who, if She had been around since man was placed on the earth, should know.

"There is usually some kernel of truth in myths; in this case, it is all too true. The Grigori were banished to the Abyss, which, if what you saw is to be taken literally—and I've no reason to doubt it—is an icy, distant prison, and Azazel was chained and buried deep beneath a desert wilderness."

"And the Avengers? The Arch Angels?"

Cybele shrugged. "All tales worth passing on get embellished over time."

Fergi gnawed her lip. No one had mentioned Rick yet.

She glanced at Terry, again wishing she knew sign. She returned her attention to Grace. "And Rick? Did Terry see what happened?"

"Terry told us this morning," Grace said. "But we all felt the transition. It is the beginning of a new era. Long live *Rex Nemorensis!*"

She was shocked. They were talking about Rick. *Rex Nemorensis*— King of the Wood. As if the "transition" was nothing more than the placing of a crown on a head—not the butchery she had witnessed.

She pictured Rick with a crown. And were it not for how he'd gotten the title, she might have giggled, but the image of his blade punching through the Priest's Hawaiian shirt in a spray of crimson precluded laughter. She shook her head.

Something else occurred to her. The demon Azazel is released from bondage. Rick becomes Rex Nemorensis. The world slides into chaos. The timing couldn't be a coincidence.

"Azazel's release has something to do with Rick," she said.

"I'm afraid it has everything to do with Rick," Cybele said. "With eliminating him."

"Why?"

"Why was Rick the one to defeat Talmaiel and ward off the Grigori and Nephilim?"

She thought about that. She knew what he'd done atop Crystal Mountain. He'd used a button to disrupt Talmaiel's plans. A coat button that had belonged to his dead grandmother and, therefore, had an emotional link to his childhood and the bond he'd shared with his Granny which he'd imbued with a power dredged up from only She knew where. Of course, to do that, Rick must have an innate reservoir, a sleeping source of energy — prana, qi, odic force — something inherent and inherited, augmented by genetics, need, and force of will.

Had she known Rick at all? Could she hope to know him ever?

Rex Nemorensis…

He had become so much more than the boy from Jersey City with the infuriatingly cocky smile and the hauntingly caring eyes that she had abandoned in Memphis, unable to bear the burden of being loved.

Rick…

"Delores."

Cybele was addressing her.

"Sorry. Gathering wool."

The Goddess' expression was sympathetic. "You have a lot on your mind. Look, I have to go in now. Grace and I will discuss with the Elders what must be done. But before I go, I have another request I must ask of you. A task, and not an easy one."

The worm of dread twisted inside her. The Lady's earlier request had led her back to that hated room. What worse quest would she ask of her now?

But she met Cybele's gaze. "Whatever it is, I won't refuse. Whatever will help."

A bloodthirsty demon. A vindictive god. As if she could do anything that might possibly help.

The Goddess studied her while the fountain burbled and yellow clouds scudded overhead. Fergi remembered sensing the night she met the Goddess the serenity in those emerald eyes, a center of calm that, like the eye of a hurricane, nevertheless projected the power of a storm.

If only I could hide in those eyes. It would be safe in there. I could find a place to curl up and sleep. At worse, I might have to watch the destruction of the earth through Her eyes, but at least I would not be alone.

"You and your Sisters who are blessed with the sight are *Sibyllae*," the triune Goddess said, and Fergi felt the presence of the maiden, mother, and crone—unearthly power incarnated in earthly flesh. "Do you know what that means?"

Sibyllae... Plural for sibyl.

She remembered Sister Alycia's lesson. "We share the ability to glimpse the future and pursue the threads of possibility. Something like what the sibyls did in the classical myths."

"The sibyls were no myths, Delores. They existed. And they exist. In you, Margreet, Grace, Maija, Keija, and all your fellow Sisterhood. But there is a difference."

Her stomach squirmed, waiting for Cybele to continue, as if her very bowels anticipated something she dreaded to hear.

"There is a creature, an elemental, perhaps a spirit of the earth itself—such things exist—who, if you, for example, would permit her and she finds you worthy, will enter into you and open your eyes and senses so that you will see clearly, without need of showstone or scrying glass, the shape of things to come and all the myriad threads of what might be."

"You're talking about possession."

"I am."

95

"In the classical myth," Fergi said, trying to make sense of what the Goddess was asking, "Apollo's spirit possessed the Sibyl and it was the god who spoke through her."

Cybele, Margreet, and Grace shared a dismissive glance.

"Apollo's a myth. The Sibyl is real," Grace said.

"Scientists also speculate that the prophecies were nothing more than the side effects of intoxicating gasses rising through fissures in the earth," Margreet said. "Hallucinations."

"And you want me to—what?—be a host to the Sibyl?"

"We are grateful you and Terry have not lost the sight. But we need—"

Cybele took Fergi's hands and looked into her eyes. Cybele was only slightly taller than she, but there were times, like now, when She seemed even taller, so that Fergi felt as if she were gazing up at a face looking down from the clouds. Underlying the feminine softness, the genial demeanor, of the Lady's countenance was the face of a general capable of sacrificing Her troops for the greater good, but who cared for them deeply. Fergi recognized the "Mother" aspect of the triune Goddess. An aspect she both dreaded and loved.

"Will you, Delores," the Goddess said, "accept the Sibyl?"

18

CORUNDUM

U nlike the rest of the Grigori whose flesh, so long deprived of sunlight, was pale as snow (even Talmaiel's bronze tan was fading), Raziel's was blue. He had always been thus. The aberration was believed to stem from his association with his "Book" — the ten sapphires he had fashioned in the dawn of history. Each gem was a duplicate of its siblings and contained the wisdom of the universe. Not written in characters as on paper or papyrus but stored as electromagnetic data in the gem's crystalline matrix. Useful information for the adept who could command the crystals. United, they formed the Sephiroth, the Tree of Life, connecting the ethereal planes to the physical and wielding cosmic forces.

When Talmaiel visited Raziel in his workshop, ostensibly to ask for his help, covertly to learn what the Artificer was up to with Semjaza, he found Raziel crushing rock in a press and feeding the debris into the receiving chamber of a Philosophical Furnace or athanor. The five-foot-tall brick tower stood in the center of the lab near Raziel's cluttered workbench. Openings around the bottom of the tower allowed for air flow and a metal door in the front permitted cleaning of the ash pit.

"Talmaiel." Raziel's greeting was less welcoming than he had hoped. The blue angel's reclusiveness was legend. He alone of the Two Hundred had not taken up with earth women. His mistress was knowledge. Talmaiel could well understand his humor: fettered here

97

on this abysmal planet, Raziel was forced to expend his energies on the grinding process of existence with no avenue for discovery.

"Raziel." Talmaiel made a show of looking around as if interested in the accoutrements of the wizard's lair. Glass vessels of every description—bottles, phials, flasks, tubes, long-snouted retorts, jars of mercury and sulfur, and whatever else could be transmuted from the planet's fundamental elements—lined nearby shelves. Bellows, hammers, tongs, files, shears, funnels, sieves, crucibles, and mortar and pestles crowded the worktable. The air—already pungent with the searing stench of ammonia-methane—was seasoned with coal smoke.

"What do you want?"

"Brief as always." The least sociable of the Grigori, Raziel had never been a conversationalist. Not that he couldn't be talkative: get him started on some obscure technical point you weren't versed in and he could lecture the ears off a granite idol. Despite Raziel's bluntness, Talmaiel detected a note of curiosity behind his guarded gaze. In a place where nothing ever changed, his recent addition to the Brethren made him a novelty. Perhaps he could monopolize on the interest.

"I need your opinion on a delicate matter."

Raziel glanced at his athanor as if its fire needed tending. It didn't: filled with coals, the device could burn slowly and evenly for days on end at a steady temperature needed for the alchemist's art.

The lamp light cast shadows in the Artificer's sunken cheeks and eye sockets. His rags hung on his emaciated frame. Talmaiel reflected he was seeing in Raziel a mirror of his future self; he, too, would grow weak and drift like a ghost through these halls if he stayed long enough on Abyss. Time was in abundance on the planet.

"Can I trust you to keep a secret?"

"Depends."

Talmaiel nodded. He remembered the violent punishments Semjaza meted out, often on a whim, and understood well why Raziel hesitated. He decided to test the water before showing his hand.

"You're working on something for Semjaza, aren't you?"

"Who told you that?" The response was accusatory and the flash of anger and fear in the Artificer's suddenly narrowed gaze told him he'd touched a sore point.

Careful, he told himself. *Proceed with caution.* "I'm not so muddled by lassitude that I'm blind to my surroundings," he lied, reluctant to put Kokabiel in jeopardy. He altered his approach. "Don't you ever dream of getting out of this prison?" A sweep of his hand indicated the planet beyond the room.

"Grigori don't dream."

"A figure of speech."

"If you've come to regale me with tales of Earth, don't. It is pain enough I remember better times. That we don't dream as humans do is my only solace. Do not make me long for what I cannot have."

"What if you *could* escape? What if *we* could?"

"Humph!" Raziel's gaze swept the cluttered walls, the gray ceiling, as if taking in not just the room but the planet and whatever, if anything, lay beyond the cloaking clouds. "You think I haven't wished? But that was ages ago. We do not even have the luxury of suicide. I could throw myself off the parapet, let the snow cover my broken body, and I would still be forced to think." He rapped his forehead three times with the heel of his hand. "To think and think and think!"

The ages of denied longing showed in his pained expression, in the angry wistfulness of his eyes.

"But that's exactly what Semjaza seeks, isn't it? A means of escape?"

Raziel looked at him, his eyes wary. For a moment, fear of Semjaza warred with his natural inclination to tackle an intellectual challenge. The angel broke off the gaze, made a show of rearranging beakers on the workbench.

"Don't worry. Semjaza didn't send me to test your loyalty. The Illustrious One told me—told all of us working in the mines—to be on the lookout for anything out of the ordinary. What is he looking for?"

The furrows in Raziel's usually placid forehead, the color of pale blue milk, deepened, and Talmaiel felt an unkind shiver of triumph as he watched the Artificer struggle between his desire to open up and his fear of reprisal.

"You saw what he did to Kokabiel."

Raziel's finger was pointing in the general direction of the great hall, and Talmaiel experienced a very different type of shiver at the thought of the Grigori's nervous system spread beneath the floor like an array of antenna, his brain entombed in an ice column. He had to admit the tactic was a stroke of genius on Semjaza's part, but it was a cold thing to do to one's fellow creature. He still found himself tiptoeing when walking on the floors above. He supposed he would eventually get used to the idea that he was walking on another's spine, but considering the Grigori's love of freedom—and the wide variety of life he himself had so recently enjoyed—as intolerable as existence was in this prison, Kokabiel's incarceration was infinitely worse.

"What are you working on? It can only be a means of escape. That's all he talks about. When I get back to Earth this and when I get back to Earth that. Never *we*."

Raziel's silence and his warning stare was his only answer.

Fuck it, as the earthlings so glibly said. He decided to take a chance. He reached into his pocket, plucked out the stone, and held it up for Raziel's inspection. "Could this be what he's looking for?"

Raziel's lips parted and his eyes grew wide. "Corundum." His tone was reverent as his fingers stretched toward the small blue rock.

Talmaiel thrilled to hear Raziel confirm his suspicion. He hesitated a moment, reluctant to let someone touch what others had, doubtless, sought for centuries and he'd unearthed within months, then let the Artificer take it.

The stone was no bigger than the first joint of his forefinger. Its surface was rough, polished only by spit and the hem of his shirt since he'd found it. Its deep midnight blue was broken by a silvery trace of titanium on one side and two reddish iron streaks on the other. One facet of hexagonal crystal glittered unblemished on the otherwise cylindrical lump, and as Raziel held the mineral to the lantern light, the facet glowed a startling blue.

"Looks like it's glad to see you," Talmaiel said, feeling more than a little jealous.

Raziel spat on the stone, rubbed it vigorously against his shirt and held it to the light again. His eyes were dreamy and was that a smile on his face?

"Where did you find it?"

"In one of the lower mines."

Raziel's expression was guarded. "Semjaza...he doesn't know about it?"

"That would defeat my purpose, wouldn't it?"

The angel gave him a long hard stare as if to say, *Don't go there.*

"Have you found others?"

"No, but I'll keep looking."

Talmaiel took the stone from Raziel and, holding it between forefinger and thumb, turned it so the light shone through the one exposed facet. The glow that had responded to Raziel's touch faded in his hand.

Corundum. The raw material for sapphires and rubies. The color dependent on the impurities in its crystalline structure. Rubies were red due to the presence of chromium; blue sapphires contained titanium and iron. Under tremendous pressure and over millions of years, nature could produce a gem quality sapphire ready for the gemcutter. This one was only partially formed and needed help to meet its potential.

"You'll help me?"

Fear shadowed Raziel's eyes. "I can't. You don't know what Semjaza is capable of."

"I know what he did to Kokabiel."

"So you know I can't help you. I dare not."

"But if there's a chance of escaping—"

A wild look came into Raziel's eyes and he scanned the walls as if they had ears, which they well might. The angel licked his lips. "Please leave." Again, his gaze sought the athanor as if its fire needed tending. "I have work to do."

"But—"

The Artificer's face darkened. He waved a hand toward the door. "Go!" When Talmaiel didn't move, he turned his back and returned to crushing rock with renewed intensity.

19

ON THE ROYAL BARGE

Swords drawn, Sidney and Russell and the red-liveried guards hurried the entourage through the garden past outbuildings that housed Dee's distilleries and alchemical laboratories and reeked of sour hops and sulfur. Then down the water steps to the landing where the Royal Barge waited. A wind had sprung up, driving whitecaps downriver. At least they wouldn't have to fight the current.

The barge tossed at its mooring. Colorful pennants whipped, and the canopy of green silk embroidered with branches of white roses and starred with daisies billowed in the gusts. On the foredeck benches, eight Royal Watermen in scarlet livery and peaked black velvet caps sat with shipped oars as vertical as their backs.

The Bargemaster, likewise liveried in scarlet but with silver braid and a cocked hat, waited on the landing. Between his ballooning knee breeches and buckled shoes, his white silk stockings gleamed in the ruddy afternoon light.

In Rick's head, a lone voice recited the Bard's lines describing Cleopatra's barge:

The barge she sat in, like a burnish'd throne,
Burn'd on the water: the poop was beaten gold;
Purple the sails, and so perfumed that
The winds were love-sick with them; the oars were silver,
Which to the tune of flutes kept stroke, and made
The water which they beat to follow faster,

As amorous of their strokes.

The truth was only slightly more prosaic. There was no beaten gold or silver oars, but the vessel was lovely with its swan-necked prow and high "lute" stern. Another, less-ornately appointed barge and a handful of smaller craft waited offshore, vessels transporting musicians, servants, and baggage to accompany the Count's tour.

The Bargemaster, looking like a great, bearded, scarlet peacock, gave Rick a sour look as he took in his bloodstained Memphis Emergency Technician blues, but Sir Philip spoke to him and ushered Rick aboard. Sumptuously cushioned seats awaited under the fluttering canopy. Here the company sat while the soldiers stood guard on the foredeck behind the oarsmen. The Royal Bargemaster manned a raised platform on the stern from which he could view the river over the canopy and called for two watermen to cast off. The oarsmen dug in and the vessel, helped by the squalling wind, leapt forward.

Dee passed through the canopied seating area to stand on the small after deck between the cabin and the high stern and watched his home recede into the distance. Rick and Bruno joined him.

"I'll be lucky if they don't burn everything," he said, as the rambling house and outbuildings grew increasingly smaller and the diminutive figures of his fellow townsfolk gathered at the wharf they had just left.

Rick reflected losing his house would be least of the man's worries if the world ended, but he felt for the kindly sage.

"Why do your neighbors attack you?"

"To lay the present calamity at my door. One of my acts of Necromancy gone awry no doubt. No matter how honest a student of Nature I profess myself to be, they will always condemn me as a companion of hellhounds and a caller and conjuror of wicked damned spirits!"

"I know the feeling, Doctor," Bruno said. "The vulgar herd will ever attack what they don't understand. Though I have never stayed long enough in one place to accumulate more than I could carry when the time came to run."

Dee looked paternally on the little Italian.

"You're right, Bruno. It is a small sacrifice to lose house and books compared to being burned." He referred to his own narrow escape from the fiery stake when, years ago, during Mary's reign, he had been imprisoned for treason after a letter he'd written the Princess Elizabeth predicting the end of Mary's reign was intercepted by the Queen's spies and to Bruno's own flight from the Roman Inquisition and his ever-mounting list of charges. He squeezed the Nolan's shoulder. "What a pair we make?"

"Perhaps someday we'll burn together," Bruno said. "We would make a light that would shine for centuries."

Dee laughed. "May it never come to pass. Your company is priceless."

———————————

The barge was broad and well-keeled but the wind chopped the water so the vessel pitched and bucked. Rick clutched the ornately carved rail and tried rocking with the boat to keep himself steady, but it was no use: there was no rhythm to the motion. He was beginning to feel ill. The sky remained bilious, purple-yellow clouds streaming across the darkening sky.

Florio, who had joined them, commented that on the journey upstream to Oxford, the wharves of the stately mansions they passed had been crowded with onlookers and many boats had put out to join the procession. Some, not knowing the boat was lent for Prince Laski's use, must have thought it was the Queen herself rowing to Greenwich. But today, the lawns and landings were empty, and no private boats accompanied them.

Sidney emerged from the cabin and tossed Rick a cloak.

"Wherever you came from, you left in a hurry. No doubt you're an infamous scoundrel and, if you're anything like my friend Bruno here, you'll have some wonderful tales to tell."

The cloak was red, an oarsman's no doubt. Gratefully, Rick threw it over his shoulders. The wool's warmth immediately blocked the worst of the wind.

"Thank you," he said, not offering to spin tales.

The courtier would be handsome enough by virtue of his genes despite the tracery of smallpox scars across his cheeks, but his dashing, elegant features were made more attractive by his infectious, genuinely honest smile. The man was the epitome of the swashbuckler: fearless and ready to face the end of time with mirth in his eyes and a joke on his lips.

"You've told us your master's name, but not your own."

Rick couldn't see where it would hurt, so he told them.

"You spoke of a warning and a request," Dee said. "You've delivered your warning. What of your request? And how does your master propose to 'rewrite the Book of Nature'?"

Reginald?

No time to hedge. The stone.

"The answer to your questions is the Philosopher's Stone."

"The *lapis philosophorum*? How is the Stone supposed to alter time?"

"I don't know. I believe my master intends that I will know when I find it."

Sidney looked incredulous, Dee and Florio skeptical. Bruno smiled broadly.

"When you find it? Good lord, man!" Sidney said. "People have been seeking the Stone for centuries. How do you propose to find it?"

"I was hoping you could help me."

"Do you have any idea what you're looking for?" Dee asked.

"None whatsoever."

"And your master, Silvanus, has not uncovered its secret?"

"He has not. All I know is what is commonly believed." He started to say "in my time" but caught himself. It was becoming increasingly difficult to avoid giving away that he was not of their world. "That it is a substance used to transmute base metals into gold."

"That is base indeed," Sidney said, "and a view commonly held by many—including our esteemed guest." He leaned in to speak, secure in the knowledge the wind would keep his words from Laski, who remained in the comfort of the cabin conversing with Russell.

"Still," Dee said, "it is a noble quest."

"And, potentially, a profitable one."

105

"I will not deny it. Mastering the Stone would buy Her Majesty many ships."

"And Laski an army."

"True, and the alliance would only strengthen England's influence on the continent."

"But what is the Stone?" Rick said to keep the conversation from veering off into European politics. "Earlier you mentioned a red powder."

Dee nodded. "The Red Lion. The *tincture physicorum*. Said to transmute all inferior metals to gold and cure all sicknesses."

"Some hold it is not a chemical substance at all," Bruno said, "but an Arcanum, an invisible ethereal fire. Albertus Magnus said it takes two perfectly harmonious people, equally skillful, to complete the process."

"Then it will, indeed, remain a mystery," Sidney quipped.

Bruno nodded. "I have ever found alchemical language too obtuse to make heads or tails of."

"More obtuse than your own writings?"

Bruno frowned, his pride pricked. Then, seeing Sidney's smile, he softened. "The wise will learn, the foolish will see only their own folly."

"Spoken like a true alchemist."

Bruno's smile widened. It was obvious the two were great friends and played off one another's wit.

"So," Rick said, "what I'm hearing is you don't know where to obtain the Philosopher's Stone, you don't know what it is, and it may not even physically exist."

"Ah," said Sidney, "the apprentice outmasters the master."

"Paracelsus said the whole process depends on understanding the nature of the 'Philosophic Fire,'" Bruno said. "Not in clowning around with alchemical vessels."

"But there is much to be learned from alchemy," Dee objected. "The practical applications are endless."

"Yes, in medicine and metallurgy, but I fear that is not what our young friend seeks."

"What is this 'philosophic fire'?" Rick pursued, hoping to catch a glimpse of something useful.

Again, Dee raised a finger and opened his mouth too late.

"Ah, this I do understand," Bruno said and launched into a discourse.

"Nature is unfinished, it produces nothing that is perfected. It is up to man, the man of wisdom, to perfect it. The art of perfecting is alchemy. The grape is only the grape until the vintner transforms it into wine; the grain only the grain until the miller mills it and the baker transforms it into bread. The alchemist's duty is to release the astral potencies. The astral is the hidden that resides in the visible.

"It is the true philosopher's duty to discover the Arcanum residing in every flower, fish, and stone, and to understand the nature of the stars and planets and their relations to every flower, fish, and stone. But it is not enough to desire to accomplish this task. The human mind is the link between spirit and matter, but the senses cloud the mind with illusions. Thoughts must break free of the shadow world and soar in the light. What is required is a divine frenzy, a heroic enthusiasm, a kind of madness that poets and artists seek from muses. That is the Philosophic Fire, which is the Fire of Love. Not animal love which is the lower aspect of Venus, but the higher aspect which is Divine Love. A philosophic rapture that raises the mind above the clouds and burns away the shadows and makes visible the quintessence. Paracelsus tells us we must see not with our physical but with our mind's eyes.

"Whereas your master's purpose, like Doctor Dee's, is to humbly and reverentially understand the mind of God, thereby to do Him greater glory and to better reverence Him by being nearer unto His purpose, mine is to become *as God*, thereby to grasp the very fire of creation and help mankind cast off the shackles of the senses and the blinders of ignorance and superstition, and see Nature for what it truly is—a vast workshop awaiting awakening man!"

Rick wouldn't have thought Dee capable of drollery, but the Queen's Conjuror said with a perfectly straight face, "I'm open-minded, but I can see why Rome longs to embrace you."

Florio said, "So that is the real goal of your Art of Memory? To build a memory palace so vast that you may hold in your mind all the arcana of Nature?"

Bruno grinned. "You've found me out. It is an alchemy of a different sort."

20

TO LOSE ALL SENSE OF SELF

Fergi sat on her bed in her nightgown, her back against the headboard, legs crossed, her bare feet tucked under her thighs. The Goddess had told her to get a good night's sleep and give her answer in the morning.

If there was a morning.

To become the vessel of the Sibyl...

Was she seriously contemplating doing that? But then, what choice did she have? If the Goddess believed her doing so might help, then she must agree.

Mustn't she?

She'd already told Cybele she wouldn't let Her and the Sisterhood down.

...whatever it is, I won't refuse. Whatever will help...

But that didn't make the prospect of allowing an ancient mystery into her mind any less terrifying.

She'd talked with Margreet briefly at dinner, where she'd picked desultorily at an excellently prepared chicken risotto.

"Will I lose my identity?" That was what worried her most. It was why people feared Alzheimer's so much, or insanity. To lose all sense of self. To cease to exist. That's what it really amounted to. And wasn't that a fate worse than death: for the body to live on while all memory and awareness fled? Everything you ever were gone. Leaving only an

109

empty shell that once housed a personality and thoughts and opinions and sorrows and dreams.

Margreet, so often full of sage advice and optimism, opened her mouth, closed it, studied the white linen tablecloth, before answering.

"I don't know," she said, meeting Fergi's gaze. "I doubt Cybele knows. The sibyls—the women who gave themselves to the Spirit—lived out their lives under her influence. They gave themselves over totally. I really don't know. But She would never ask you to do this if She didn't believe it absolutely necessary. You know that, don't you?"

She did know—as much as anyone could *know* based on the hard kernel of truth one felt in one's gut.

"Yes."

She unclenched her fists. She had dug her nails into her palms. She rubbed her hands together to get the circulation flowing.

She looked at the scrying bowl on the table near the window. She felt its pull. Scrying had become an addiction. Not like smoking or drinking—both of which she missed not at all. Nor did she take any voyeuristic pleasure in spying on strangers: she found the very thought of prying into people's private lives repulsive; but, even though her efforts were largely limited to current events, she found being able to contribute to the Sisters' work deeply gratifying.

She swung her legs off the bed and went to the bowl. The night air flowed through the open window and the wide floorboards were cool beneath her feet. She sat in the tall, straight-backed chair and gazed at the surface of the water.

Margreet's words, spoken in this room nearly six months ago, came back to her.

Do not stare at the bottom of the bowl, just gaze across the surface and meditate on the reflection of the candlelight. Let your mind be receptive but unfocused.

And I'll have visions?

You may. It's like casting a net and seeing what turns up.

Yaldabaoth had enlisted the worst of the Grigori to eliminate Rick. Which meant he must fear him. Or, at the very least, believe Rick capable of interfering with his plans.

Where was Rick now? What was he doing? If she followed his journey, would she be able to help?

The reflection of lamplight on the water's surface brought back a poignant memory.

April. A year ago. A beautiful spring day, the sunlight dazzling on the red-brown river. Huge barges and white multi-tiered paddle wheelers like great floating wedding cakes plying the water. They'd taken the pedestrian bridge over to Mud Island, where they'd visited the Mississippi River Museum and strolled the Riverwalk.

The Riverwalk was a detailed model of the lower Mississippi, half a mile long representing nearly a thousand miles of the river's topography from Cairo, Illinois, to the Gulf of Mexico. The riverbed and surrounding flood plain were laid out in mud-colored cement. Cities were represented in gray slate with major roads inlaid in ribbons of steel. At the southern end was a scale model of the Mississippi Delta with the River flowing through its dozens of channels into a one-acre Gulf of Mexico—which, until she read the signage, she mistook for a small lake.

It was on their way back upstream, passing by Vicksburg, that it happened.

She'd taken off her boots and rolled up her jeans and was wading in the meandering channel, the cool water flowing around her ankles. Rick was walking on the "bank." She must have laughed. (No—she *knew* she had laughed, a laugh that came out like a giggle. Decidedly unlike her.) It was then that he uttered the fatal words.

For a second, she thought she had misheard him. She hadn't, of course; she simply wanted to unhear the words. But the words were said and she had heard. Her laughter stopped, the sky darkened, and the day was spoiled. She handled the situation the only way she knew how: by ignoring it. And, in case he was disposed to repeat himself, she took off upstream leaving a wake.

She found a bench and put on her boots and gathered a cloud around her to keep him at a distance. He'd respected her space. The drive home was quiet, and at bedtime she turned her back and pretended to be tired.

The next morning, they both pretended he'd never said what he said and things got better.

I love you...

What a crock! The only thing hokier was people responding in kind because they felt it expected. As if it were a social obligation on a par with answering, *How are you?* with *I'm good, how 'bout you?* As if every *thank you* demanded a *you're welcome* no matter how insincere.

Anger warmed her ears. If she could eradicate one meme from society's sick heart it would be Valentine's Day. That monument to rabid American consumerism. She'd read that Hallmark kept sales statistics and valentine cards were second only to Christmas. And that didn't include the hundreds of thousands of cards teachers made kids draw in grammar school. In the second and third grades her whole class had been forced to make cards for classmates. No wonder kids grew up thinking you had to fall in love and say the ritualistic words, then hear them said to be fulfilled.

Still, she'd hurt him by not responding. And if she was honest with herself, she had to admit she cared deeply for Rick. And wasn't caring a type of love? Maybe it wasn't so much his uttering the words that made her squirm but the fact that his confession forced her to examine her own feelings. Something she studiously avoided.

She closed her eyes and reached out as if to touch his hair—his lovely thick brown hair—the unruly lock that curled over his brow no matter how he tried to shove it back—and made believe she was brushing it back and felt the pang of missing him.

Rick...

For a heart-aching moment, she wished more than anything she could hear him say those words again so she could say them back. God! What had she been thinking to pack her bag, intending to leave before he got home? Not for the first time she thought, *I should have loved you better, Richard Scott.*

But the moment was long gone. In the rearview. Each of them had their task and no time for distractions.

Enough! she scolded herself.

To become the woman she needed to be—the woman the Sisterhood and Cybele needed her to be—she had to burn away the girl in her in the pure fire of will. The world was ending. It was no time for sentimentality.

She forced the knotted muscles in her shoulders to relax, inhaled deeply, let the breath out slowly, and gazed at the reflection of light on the water.

21

SEMJAZA FEEDS

"Step forward, Artificer."

Raziel trembled as he took another step closer to the throne. Except for Kokabiel, whose brain resided in the central column and whose nerve system was entrenched in the floor, they were alone in the great hall.

Semjaza leaned one corded arm on the throne and smiled into the blue angel's face. "You *will* look me in the eye!"

Raziel raised his head and did so, lifting his chin as if to show defiance. But his chin trembled and his lips compressed as if stifling a sob.

Semjaza's great sword leaned casually against the side of the throne. Unsheathed, its twin edges gleamed in the light of the wall sconces.

"Progress?" Semjaza growled, as if daring Raziel to report anything less.

Raziel licked his upper lip like a human, as if terror caused him to perspire, which, like sleep, dreams, and beards, Grigori were incapable. It was all he could do to keep from wringing his hands. But if Semjaza expected Raziel's response to differ from his previous reports, he was destined for disappointment as the Artificer answered, "None."

Semjaza's scowl was the last thing a Grigori wished to see. But he didn't lean forward and cuff Raziel to the floor. The Mage handled his sword's pommel, twisting the point into the ice, not threateningly but idly. He leaned the weapon against the throne and, resting his hands on the smooth gray polymer of the arms, settled back.

Though his gaze continued to make the Artificer tremble, his mouth appeared weary. "'None'?" He shook his head ruefully, as if Raziel were a dog that had peed the carpet. "You made the Book. How can you not find others?"

Raziel's gaze faltered; his eyes sought the floor.

"Look at me!"

Raziel again met the Mage's eyes. "Perhaps they do not exist." It was an old mantra, used and rejected before.

Semjaza's fist pounded the arm of the throne. "They must! Anything less is unacceptable!"

Raziel remained silent. Semjaza was not one to let reality stand in the way of his ambitions. It was better to let his temper pass than to confront it.

"Well, tomorrow's another day, what say you, Blue One?" It was what passed for a joke from Semjaza's lips. There were no yesterdays or tomorrows on Abyss, only one endless now. As he'd done countless times before, Raziel chose to ignore the joke and simply respond, "Yes."

So the ritual continued, as it had since Semjaza, deprived of humans upon which to feed, felt it necessary to turn to the Brethren for sustenance.

"Closer, Artificer."

Raziel's gaze sought the cavernous hall's rough-hewn ceiling, as if willing himself out of Semjaza's presence, but the Mage's hand darted out and seized his face in a vicelike grip and yanked it to within an inch of his own.

"You grow stubborn, Artificer?"

He tried to eke out a No, but the Mage's grip was too firm for speech.

"All right." Semjaza released Raziel and patted his cheek paternally. "Though you continue to fail, yet you may contribute. And know in advance, as always, your contribution does not go unappreciated."

Almost lovingly, he cupped the Artificer's head and drew him closer and bent his face to where a vein in his throat throbbed beneath blue skin and began to feed.

22

GRIGORI

The chair legs scraped on the ancient floor boards as Fergi backed away from the scrying bowl. She put a hand to her mouth, choked down rising bile. Her body shook with horror at what she had seen. A Grigori—not Talmaiel but a cruel-faced giant—feeding on a blue angel.

Drinking his blood!

She looked around the room to make sure of her surroundings. There was her window, its shutters thrown open onto the garden. There was her bed with its headboard carved with birds and vines. There was her mahogany wardrobe, its polished wood dark with age.

She went to the window, breathed deep the night air flowing over the casement. Above the trees, monochromatic clouds boiled across the face of the gibbous moon like some sped-up footage in an old black-and-white film.

Her shivering continued: it wasn't just the horror of what she'd seen, she was cold, as if she had emerged from a meat locker.

That place… *Abyss*

What did it mean? Everything she saw in the scrying bowl had meaning. Nothing was without purpose.

She stared at the silver bowl. She couldn't dislodge the image of that monster feeding.

If these creatures

Grigori

were imprisoned in that frozen waste

Abyss

what did her seeing them mean?

Unless…

"They're coming here," she said aloud.

Not *here*—not to the Sisterhood, but to Earth.

Azazel had been released to eliminate Rick. Why not the rest of the Grigori? The Sleepless Ones? The Choir, as Grace euphemistically called them?

The only reason she could imagine for the bowl's showing her this vision was that the Demiurge had decided to add the Grigori to the world's woes.

As if the unraveling of time wasn't enough.

She considered seeking Cybele to warn Her, but it could wait. She suspected the Sisters had lost more than their power to *see*. What could they do if they could no longer pool their powers of concentration, their collective will, to attain an end?

She recalled the night of the battle, when she first lent her will to that of the Sisters. The Sisters joined hands around the bonfire, their warrior faces grim. As sparks rose into the starry night, they swayed to the mantra of the keening auros and the panpipes and the tympanum's *rattle thump rattle*, and a moon, on a moonless night, rose from the flames and expanded as it mounted the sky. These women so like true sisters and favorite aunts and stern but kindly teachers—but warriors all when need arose. Stripped of their powers, they were still a potent force—stories abounded of their battle frenzy, and the citizens of Hendricks had put up a savage resistance, for the most part wielding nothing more magical than guns and explosives.

It was all the more important she did her part.

She shuddered thinking of what was at stake: first Yaldabaoth's devolving creation, now the possibility of a Grigori invasion. She recalled the tales of their primal savagery, their utter disregard for human life and civilization, their insatiable bloodlust. She prayed she was wrong and what she'd witnessed, while no doubt a true vision, was only a random glimpse of what was, somewhere in time and space, an insight onto the harsh reality of the Watchers' fate and did not presage invasion.

Get some sleep, the Goddess had said. *Your answer can wait till morning.*

She covered the bowl with a pillowcase and, hoping for no more visions, lay down and tried to sleep. But sleep was long in coming, and when it came it was far from restful.

23

WHAT TALMAIEL SAW

Talmaiel slid his body down the column behind which he hid and made himself as small as he could. Gooseflesh rippled down his back and he shivered like a human crouching in darkness in a snake-infested tunnel.

He closed his eyes, but the lurid images of what he'd witnessed remained vividly painted in his mind. Raziel pinioned in Semjaza grasp, the Sorcerer's head bent to the blue angel's throat, the maddening sounds of the hideous feeding.

So this was how Semjaza maintained his vitality.

The once-hearty, free-spirited Grigori had become emaciated zombies, reduced to herd beasts existing only for labor and the Illustrious One's sustenance. Did Semjaza feed off all of them?

Not all. His lieutenants, Samael and Asmodai, were likewise hale. Did they rotate the Choir, allowing them to recover until their turn came again?

His heart raced. Terrified Semjaza would hear its hammering, he forced its beat to slow. A trick he'd learned from eastern masters on faraway Earth. As breathing was optional for Grigori, he stilled his lungs, cleared his thoughts, and waited.

Eventually the sucking stopped, and he heard Semjaza thank Raziel, followed by Raziel's steps dragging across the floor and the opening and closing of the hall door. Moments later he heard the scrape of Semjaza's sword followed by brisker steps as the Sorcerer left to make his rounds, and he opened his eyes.

After a while he rose and left the chamber. Trembling as if expecting the Sorcerer to pounce on him at every turn—as if Semjaza knew he'd been spying and was lying in wait to punish him—he made his way back to his lair.

24

WRESTLING WITH DEMONS

Night came early. There should have been three hours of daylight left. The temperature plunged.

"Look." Florio pointed shoreward.

Rick shielded his eyes from the torch glare and squinted at the nearer shore where lights burned in the windows of the manor houses they passed. Then he saw it, too. Where the trees had been green in Dee's garden a short while before, the trees on the lawns of the estates they passed were leafless. Where it had been summer in the afternoon, it was autumn in the evening.

Dee pointed at the sky. Through the flying ragged clouds the stars flickered in and out. "Those three."

"Orion's Belt," Bruno said.

Rick knew it well. In Jersey City and in Memphis, Orion and the Big Dipper were about the only constellations you could see for all the lights. As clouds scudded past, he made out more of the Hunter. There was Betelgeuse and Rigel, a shoulder and a foot.

Suddenly, he understood.

"Orion's a winter constellation."

Unable to tear his eyes away, Dee said, "It's not visible in the night sky until November. In June it transits the sky by day." He looked at Rick. His pallor betrayed his shock. "We have slid forward into next winter."

"Or back into the last."

A red glow fell over the barge. The men expelled a collective gasp. Even the Bargemaster raised a shielding hand as if to ward off some attacking predator.

The houses along the riverbank had not suddenly burst into flame. The light shone from the heavens. Above the scudding yellow and maroon clouds, a great comet burned, the long train of its twin tails arching eastward like a bow.

Growing up in Jersey City's urban environment, Rick had seen few stars except for the occasions he'd gone camping as a teenager. Not until he'd gone to the Ouachitas to confront Talmaiel had he been exposed to the awesome splendor of the Milky Way. But he had never seen the likes of this. The celestial messenger was stunning. And probably to the people of this time, monstrous.

A voice in his head told him how even Tycho Brahe, who studied the comet and published his scientific findings, ascribed calamitous events to its appearance.

The comet's head was white, like a great star. Its twin tails burned dark red, like flame penetrating smoke. The phenomenon covered the greater part of the sky.

"The great comet come again." Dee looked at Sidney. "You remember it, Philip?"

"I do. But how?"

"The great comet of 1577. The past repeating." Dee lifted his long, white fingers as if to stroke its tail. "Such a thing cannot be."

"How do you know it is the same comet?" Rick asked.

"Observe the two tails. I drew its likeness in my diary."

"It is true." Sidney's eyes reflected the red comet-fire as he held up a finger and traced the arc of the great tail. "This is the same comet I viewed from my sister's garden at Wilton."

The hair on Rick's neck bristled. He didn't have to see through their eyes to experience the wonder and horror of the uncanny event they were witnessing.

All...earth, moon, stars...gone!

Reality crashed over him like the cold slap of a wave. *It's really happening!* What before had seemed abstract or as something experienced in a dream suddenly snapped into crystal focus. Creation was tumbling into chaos, like stacked dominos swept off the table. His heart raced and black dots swam in his vision as panic seized him. He swayed and grasped the rail to steady himself.

Through the roar in his head, he heard the wonder in Dee's voice. "The stars themselves. Think on it, Sidney. The great wheel of the zodiac spinning in reverse."

Rick huddled against the gunwale beneath the twin scowls of the Bargemaster and the comet, his cloak wrapped tightly around him against the chill. Sidney and Florio had joined Laski and Russell in the relative comfort of the canopied cabin. Tired as he was, Rick needed the bracing air to help him think. Even if he were home in bed, he doubted he could sleep. He wondered if he would ever see his bed again.

Dee stood like a statue silhouetted against the sky. He had stood so for the last hour, gazing up, unable to take his eyes off the comet. In the guttering torchlight, his face was an etching of determination that might be titled "Reasoning the Unreasonable."

Bruno sat against the opposite gunwale, the man's unnerving stare studying him as Dee studied the comet. Both men parsing an enigma.

He closed his eyes to avoid Bruno's gaze.

Reginald?

Yes?

What have you done to me?

Only what was needed.

He felt the Priest's lips hard-pressed upon his own. Not a kiss but an imparting.

But an imparting of *what*?

The Goddess had kissed him and, according to da Silva, gifted him with long life, a thing that left him with mixed feelings, considering the strings attached.

You are my knight.

He was tired of being kissed against his will.

Well…the Goddess' kiss was not without its attractions, but that was a rabbit hole best avoided.

What had the Priest bestowed?

You had no right.

Does a fish need a right to swim in the sea? A bird to take wing? It is our way. And you are Rex Nemorensis. My successor. Besides, rights are irrelevant in extremo tempore. *You had much to learn before you could undertake this task but not the luxury of the years it took each of us. Would you be able to navigate the cultural and linguistic differences that face you in your quest? Would you know what to do with the knowledge once you found it?*

No. But why couldn't you?

But he knew the answer.

…the world has not seen one as powerful as you in a thousand years.

…you were the dynamo that powered the rest.

Grigori blood flows in your veins.

So the Stone is allegorical, a metaphor for some sort of mind game?

He heard da Silva sigh. Other voices started to protest. The Priest silenced them.

We've no more answers than you. Some agree with Doctor Bruno that the Stone allegorically represents our mastery of Nature. Others that the Stone is the goal of the rising tide of consciousness, an Omega Point. Others persist that the lapis is, *indeed, a physical substance or object, albeit endowed with metaphysical properties. The truth remains elusive.*

What is it about the Stone that makes you think it's the answer to our problem?

Its transformative properties, its interaction between the physical and the celestial. My own hope—I cannot say knowledge or even opinion—is that it provides some sort of gateway. Perhaps by demonstrating our potential. Or by addressing the Demiurge himself.

Theories? Hopes? I'm five hundred years away from home and that's all you've got?

We'll have to be patient and see.

"Patient? The world's ending. *Tempus fugit*, didn't you say?"

"To whom do you speak, Sir?"

Rick opened his eyes.

125

Dee hadn't moved. Bruno had addressed him.

"Just thinking aloud."

Bruno rose, came over, and sat beside him.

"I suffer from the affliction myself. Sometimes it's best to talk through a vexing problem. And when no one else is interested in the problem that vexes you, then who better to debate the matter than yourself?"

"I'm coming to that conclusion myself, since no one else seems to have the answer I seek."

"You speak a very Romanish tongue. You did not do so earlier."

That startled him. He hadn't realized he was speaking Italian with Bruno.

Curiously, Rick understood every word the little man uttered, though it was in Neapolitan Italian and that a sixteenth-century dialect far different than the more universal and cosmopolitan Italian taught in schools in the twenty-first century. Which, of course, he'd never studied and should have been beyond his knowledge. His head reeled under the assault of new information. If he allowed himself to, he could see as clearly as if projected on a Smartboard elaborate mathematical formulae defining mechanical and quantum phenomena, and beside this, hieroglyphs and scripts inscribed on ancient scrolls. And he knew with a certainty that astounded him that if he meditated on the formulae and scripts, he would understand them as surely as he understood the Nolan's native tongue.

Too much! My head's about to explode!

He felt as if he stood in a flood bracing himself against a mighty current and it was all he could do not to be swept away.

"You wrestle with demons, Sir?"

It was not a condemnation but offered matter-of-factly, as if Bruno had suggested he suffered from indigestion. Still, remembering when and where he was, in this superstitious age when anything not condoned by authority secular or religious might meet with dire penalties—drowning, burning, beheading, drawn and quartering—he was wary. Did Bruno think him possessed?

"Or with angels?"

Bruno leaned closer and spoke in a low voice, barely audible under the wind.

"I have been debating, but I must tell you."

"What?"

"When you were looking into the showstone..."

"Yes?"

"You were not deceiving us. You saw faces in the crystal. They spoke to you."

"I..."

"One in particular."

The hairs on Rick's neck stirred. "How...?"

"Because I saw them, too."

And now the little man's eyes were wide in the torchlight and his lips and wispy mustache stretched in a broad smile. "Who are they? They looked so alive, like watching people through distorted glass. Not pale like the ghosts I've seen."

"You've seen ghosts?"

"A consequence of sleeping in cemeteries. They are not Necromancers, are they?" His voice had risen with his excitement.

"*Shhh.*"

Rick glanced at Dee. The Queen's Mathematician was oblivious to them, entranced by the heavenly visitor. The Bargemaster was as intent on navigating the River as Dee was on studying the comet.

Rick leaned closer. "What did you see?"

"Faces. Many faces. Men's. Coming to the surface of the showstone as if they were emerging to the surface of water. Then one remained. He was not tall with a face shining like the sun. He might have been a countryman of mine, but had more of the Spaniard about him."

"Portuguese."

"Yes, that fits. I didn't hear his words, but I saw your master's lips move when you spoke to him."

Whispers ran through his mind, da Silva echoed by others: *He has the blood.*

All who possess...certain abilities...have some trace of Grigori blood. Reverend Grace, confirming the Watcher's words.

He watched the little man, excited by the visions he had seen in the showstone. Was Bruno aware of his difference from other humans? A difference beyond his hubris and genius? Did he dream true dreams? Did his feet choose for him the safe path when another's led to disaster? Considering the Nolan's fiery end, Rick knew that would not always be the case, but the little friar's fearlessness and utter confidence in his power of persuasion would bring him to that.

"No, they are neither spirits nor necromancers." He sought for the word; a Nemorensis supplied it. "They are magi. An ancient priesthood of ascended masters. And Sir Russell was right to ask why my master—"

"Silvanus."

He nodded. "—did not rewrite the Book of Nature himself. The truth is, what is happening is as new and unexpected to them as it is to us. No one could have prepared."

"Yet they chose you." Torchlight flickered in Bruno's brown eyes as he studied Rick. And, as so often happened with da Silva, though the Nolan was a head shorter than him, the little Italian had a presence that made him appear larger than he was. "You are no apprentice. That is certain. You converse with ancient magi. You appear at Doctor Dee's house as if you dropped from the moon. Who are you?"

Rick lifted his eyes to the comet. Behind a veil of scudding clouds, it blazed an arc across the heavens. Its light was baleful. How Dee could ever have seen it as a harbinger of good fortune was beyond him.

Who am I?

He wanted to say nobody. But that was wrong. If the salvation of the world depended on him and the Priesthood and the Goddess had appointed him to save it, then obviously he was someone?

But who?

25

THE SPHINX

"I dreamed I was a sphinx," Fergi said to Cybele, who stood beside her. "Not just any sphinx, but the great stone Sphinx at Giza. It was night and the desert was cool, but my stone flanks still felt the heat of the desert day. That was curious."

Fergi paused to recollect the experience. She was delaying she knew, but the dream that visited her in the hour she'd slept seemed important. Besides, she was afraid.

They stood outside the tall cavern entrance. The same gibbous moon she had watched from her window the previous night rode the restless clouds. Far below, the round lake alternately glimmered in its light and plunged into blackness. Streamers of mist rose above the black water, and noxious plumes of volcanic gas issued from fissures in the steep wooded slopes. It was morning when they left the Sisterhood, night when they arrived. But no time had passed for them. The Goddess simply took her hand and told her to close her eyes, and when she opened them, they were here.

"In my dream, I was aware I was the Sphinx," she continued. "Yet it was as if I were looking at the Sphinx—at myself—from outside. I remember...her face wasn't weathered like it is today. Her headdress was yellow and her beard was blue. But her eyes weren't open like the Egyptian Sphinx's. They were closed. She was sleeping. And..." She shivered, remembering.

Cybele waited.

"It was my face on the statue." Her eyes were wide as she touched her cheek. "My face. I was stone. And her hair…" Fergi's fingers found her own curls, moved them slowly, as if a cooling zephyr were lifting her tresses off her shoulders. "The headdress was gone, and her hair was moving softly in the night breeze." Her heart quickened with the memory. "She was alive. And as I realized this," Fergi's far-off gaze shifted to Cybele, "she looked at me. Those great yellow eyes opened and she looked at me. And then I woke with the feeling it wasn't an ordinary dream but meant something important. But what?"

"What do you think it means?" Cybele asked. Six months ago, if someone answered her question with a question, Fergi would have stalked off, but she understood what the Goddess was doing. The best answers came from within.

"I don't know. The fact that my body was stone but my head was living and the fact that I was sleeping and then I woke feels significant."

"And your head was human while your body was animal."

"There's that," she agreed. "The head always stands for intellect, consciousness. The Crown chakra represents connection to the divine. The Third Eye Chakra, intuition, perception."

Cybele smiled. "Good. The lower body of the Sphinx is animal, representing the lower principles, while the head is human, representing the higher. So there's that—above and below, the higher and lower worlds, the spiritual and physical, the infinite and the finite, immortality and mortality."

"So maybe the Sphinx represents the duality of man," Fergi ventured, feeling her way. "The intellect paired with animal instinct? Man's head in the clouds while his feet are mired in mud."

"You think?" One corner of Cybele's mouth lifted, but She wasn't mocking. Fergi appreciated the Goddess' wry sense of humor and Her ability to *almost* be one of the girls, as if they were just two women having a conversation.

"And the Sphinx's waking?"

"Sleeping symbolizes potential and waking the realization of potential. Your Sphinx, like humankind, exists in potential. For now. But humans have the potential to rise above illusion, to wake, and become immortal."

Fergi looked at the cave's forbidding mouth. She could see only a few yards into its maw. The fumes rising from the lake and volcanic vents smelled of brimstone and were choking her. How could anyone stand this nightmare place? Would she really encounter an ancient intelligence that would strip her of her will and replace it with its own? Was she really going to become the Sibyl? "I'm sleeping, aren't I? Will I wake in there?"

Cybele's smile was barely visible in the stunted moonlight. "You've always been more awake than most." She took Fergi by the shoulders and turned her so they were face to face. "But make no mistake, you will change. The alchemy of experience will transform you."

Fergi stared into the darkness. How did she feel about going in there? About giving herself over to an alien presence? About becoming a vessel and losing her sense of being?

She surprised herself that her impatience outweighed her trepidation.

She remembered the squall of jealousy that stung her when her Mistress kissed Rick. But she'd learned it was Her way of sealing a bond with Her priests and of bestowing long life and heaven knew what other gifts, and whatever anger she felt toward Cybele in the past had burned away in the common bond of duty and friendship. They stood at a crossroads and only by combining their wills would they have the remotest possibility of prevailing. Separate now and each would be lessened. She took a measure of pride, however petty it might seem, in knowing the Goddess depended on her.

She remembered, too, the first lesson she learned after coming to the Sisterhood. She'd asked Margreet if it was the Sisters' job to predict the future. Margreet told her, "Our job is not to predict the future but to shape it." She had scoffed at the idea, but after joining the Sibyllae and the Goddess in raising the false moon and, later, binding Talmaiel to the wax image, she wholeheartedly believed in their mission. Scrying with the Sisters and joining in the daily Willing into Being sessions, sharing work and meals and conversation with like-minded women had filled a hole in her life and given her a sense of purpose. She was no longer the angry young woman who wanted to keep walking until she reached the end of the earth—anything to put off going home—and whose best friend was the half-pint of Southern Comfort she carried in the breast pocket of her Army jacket.

For whatever reason, she had been allowed to keep her power of sight while the other Sisters were rendered deaf and blind. It was as if the universe was waiting her decision.

She was holding her breath. She exhaled.

"I'm ready," she said and entered the darkness.

26
GREEN GRASS, BLUE WATERS

Raziel looked a paler blue when Talmaiel next visited his workshop. His flesh hung loose from his frame and sickly rings underscored his bloodshot eyes. Talmaiel had seen others in the fortress who shared the Artificer's symptoms. He had attributed it to malnutrition and lethargy. Now he knew the truth.

The lump of corundum lay on the workbench before them.

"You must help me," Talmaiel insisted. He had to get out of this abominable place. Despite his injuries, he was still relatively healthy and was dead set on bettering his situation, not making it worse. There was no future on Abyss, only a prolonged and ghastly wasting. Unless he became a predator himself. He looked at the purple bruise on Raziel's neck with its cuts of jagged flesh and imagined himself sucking at such a wound and, despite his feasting on human blood centuries past, found he no longer had such sanguine cravings. Instead, he had developed a taste for red meat, fresh seafood, wine, and strong ale—none of which were obtainable on Abyss.

Raziel wiped a shaky hand down the front of his raggedy shirt. "I can't! You don't understand!" His voice shrilled with the residue of terror.

"I do understand," he said, attempting to soften the blow. He tried to lick his bottom lip but couldn't. With his lips shrunken away from his teeth, he was forever drooling when he engaged in conversation.

He wiped his mouth with his sleeve. He squeezed Raziel's shoulder and whispered, "I know."

The Artificer pressed his knuckles to his mouth. His face purpled. Then he scooped up the corundum, shoved it into Talmaiel's hand, folded his burn-scarred fingers over it, and waved toward the door. "Leave!" When Talmaiel didn't move, he added, "Please."

Talmaiel clasped Raziel by the wrist, leaned close to keep his voice low. "Semjaza's mad. We must leave. He can't take me yet. Not alone. But if I stay here, I will weaken and end up like..."

"Like me, you were going to say." Raziel glared, defiant.

"Yes, like you, damn it. And like the others. I have to get out of here while the fight is still in me."

Raziel's shoulders sagged. He opened Talmaiel's fingers, took the stone, held it to the lantern light. The exposed facet gleamed with blue fire. His anger melted into a look of resigned longing. Talmaiel saw him mentally shake his head: the task was formidable, the punishment painful if he was caught betraying Semjaza.

Talmaiel pressed his advantage while Raziel wavered. "Don't you want to see Earth again? Even in the mines, I feel the warmth of her sun on my back, the cool night breeze on my face. Do you recall the salt smell of the sea?"

Raziel closed his eyes. His nostrils widened as he inhaled deeply. "I do. How I miss the green grass, the blue waters, the dates that grew in the oasis." Blue fingers stretched as if to pluck a fresh, sun-ripened date from the palm. If the Maker had permitted Grigori tears, one would now be trailing down Raziel's cheek.

The Artificer opened his eyes as if waking from an unattainable dream. "But if we fail..."

"Let's not."

Despite the apprehension in Raziel's bloodshot eyes, there was a hint of hope in his voice as he said, "We'll need Kokabiel's help."

27
AT THE EMBASSY

Death was in the streets. From the coach window, Rick witnessed roving crowds armed with pitchforks, staves, and rusty swords dragging foreigners from their homes, a house burning, the body of what Bruno identified as a Catholic hanging from a post with a paper pope hat stuck on his head. A reign of chaos was unfolding beneath the comet's lurid glow. Not knowing from what quarter calamity hailed, a superstitious and contentious populace was lashing out at all they hated or did not understand.

After the royal barge landed at Whitehall and Sidney found them a coach, he and Russell straightway ushered Laski into the palace. The Queen would not sleep without hearing their report. Florio borrowed a horse to return to Oxford. If the end was coming he wanted to spend it with his family. Whether it was early or late, no one knew. Time had slipped its mooring.

They sat in Bruno's room under the eaves of the French Embassy on Butcher Row: Rick at Bruno's writing table under the sloping ceiling; Bruno on the small bed; Dee, with the knees of his long legs up to his chest, beside him. The Nolan's writings were spread out on the desk and Rick resisted the Nemorenses' urge to examine them. Rain pelted the window's leaded glass.

A low fire burned in the grate and Rick was thankful for the warmth. His red cloak hung on a nail beside Bruno's short one. Dee, seemingly oblivious to heat or cold, continued to wear his black mantle fastened to its fur collar.

Bruno had scrounged a platter of bread and cheese and a jug of wine from the kitchen. Rick, who hadn't eaten since abandoning his Memphis hoagie to respond to the fire, was grateful for the food. His stomach made happy noises as he munched. Bruno picked at a few morsels from his plate then sat it aside. Dee's plate remained on the floor by his feet.

The comet's return had shaken the wind from the Royal Astrologer's sails. Where he had proclaimed it an auspicious sign, a stellar declaration of England's ascendancy, he now yielded to the doomsayer's predictions. Rick recognized the symptoms of shock: the dark crescents under the eyes, the pallor, the furrowed brow, the dull, unfocused gaze. Where before the man's posture had been erect, his back straight, his head held high, his back now slumped, his beard resting upon his chest.

Recalling the staggering epiphanies that had destroyed his own delusions of reality, Rick felt for the elderly scholar. It was no mean task for him to overcome the shock of encountering the antique firemen

Had it only been this afternoon?

on the Mississippi riverfront. And only the necessity of moving forward prevented him from succumbing to the raging guilt and horror at what he had done.

The great mouth of the wound spilling the Nemorensis' blood in the torch-lit grove...

Bruno, on the other hand, remained sharp-eyed and clear-witted. He had said nothing to Dee about seeing faces in the showstone, presumably because Dee, who saw nothing in the crystal himself

I have not the gift.

employed scryers like Edward Kelly to assist him and Bruno did not want to inherit the task.

The Nemorenses hadn't gotten over their excitement at learning Bruno had Grigori blood. As did Rick and da Silva and every Rex Nemorensis the Goddess had ever kissed. And Fergi and the Sibylline Sisterhood, and Reverend Grace and many of the people who had assisted him last fall when he'd confronted Talmaiel on Crystal

Mountain and thwarted the return of the Two Hundred and their offspring, the Nephilim. He supposed his mother had some of the blood, and Granny, for they saw visions and dreams that came true and had a knack of knowing what he was thinking—though that might have been simply women's intuition, something that was as much a mystery to him as Yaldabaoth.

A number of the priests had mentally riffled through the Nolan's writings to the point where he had a good sense of Bruno's philosophy. The Neapolitan believed in an infinite universe. Where Ptolemy's cosmos put the earth at the center with the sun and planets revolving around it in concentric circles and the fixed stars embedded in a final crystal sphere and only God beyond, and where the new Copernican theory simply substituted the sun for the center with the earth and moon revolving around it and the rest of Ptolemy's system remaining intact, Bruno preached to anyone who would listen his sermon of an infinite universe, wherein stars were suns like our own that went on forever and every sun orbited by planets peopled with races like our own and no center anywhere.

"As long as Astrologers with their astrolabes restrict their calculations to the nine moving spheres they will remain like parrots in a cage. A Supreme Ruler could never have a seat so narrow, so miserable a throne, so trivial, so scanty a court. On the contrary, we recognize a noble image, a marvelous conception, a supreme figure, an infinite representation of the represented infinity, a spectacle worthy of the excellence and supremacy of Him who transcends understanding. Only by acknowledging an infinite creation do we acknowledge the excellence of God magnified and the greatness of his kingdom made manifest. He is glorified not in one, but in countless suns; not in a single earth, a single world, but in a thousand thousand! I say in an infinity of worlds!"

"To imagine there is nothing beyond the sphere which limits our range of sight, is to be as I was as a child, believing nothing existed beyond Mount Vesuvius because that was the limit of my senses."

And to anyone so base as to disagree with him:

"They are like the proud and presumptuous pedants who, swollen with confidence in their individual genius and holding it for certain

137

that they are in the light while standing in shadow, dared raise themselves to the knowledge of divine secrets and to know the mind of God dared raise the Tower of Babel—which is but a metaphor for the overweening ambition of the mentally truant—and ended confused and scattered, the passage to divine wisdom and vision of the eternal truth shut to them."

And on the impossibility of convincing the mentally truant of the truth of his philosophy:

"It would be in vain to attempt to catch water in a net, or fish in a plate."

Bruno glanced at Dee. Then, looking at Rick, made an exaggerated show of lifting his brows.

"Enough melancholy. We can't just sit on our hands. Between the three of us—and your ascended masters—if there is a solution, then we may discover it if we apply ourselves."

Dee sighed. "No use. No man can alter what God has willed."

Not God. Yaldabaoth, the Demiurge.

But that would only complicate the discussion. These men were Christian…well, Dee was. Bruno was something else. Part Renaissance magician, part Egyptian magi, part philosopher-scientist, he was not so much ahead of his time (he was still rooted in his century's enthusiasms for Neoplatonism and Hermeticism as well as the new cosmology, and desired not a reconciliation between Protestantism and Catholicism but a return to an exalted Egyptian mysticism) as outside his time.

All this Rick gleaned from the debate that ran like a subsonic hum in the background of his thoughts.

But Bruno was undeterred. Assuming a lecturing tone, the defrocked friar ticked off his points on his fingers as he responded to Dee's thesis. "Creation is God's will. Let us start with the premise. Furthermore, God created man and commanded him to subdue the earth and rule over His creation. Do you grant this?"

"Certainly."

"And as He made man in His image, He therefore, *a priori*, intended man as a reflection of Himself and, therefore, possessed of will. A willful being."

Rick caught the pun. Bruno was speaking of himself.

"And as man is a product of God's will and of God's creation, so it must follow that God intends man to use the power of his will and imagination to create."

Before Dee could raise his finger or open his mouth to object, Bruno continued. "Did not Ficino write that 'man can create the heavens and what is in them himself, if he could but obtain the tools and the heavenly material'? And did not the Divine Pomander say, 'For man is a divine living thing, and is not to be compared to any brute beast that lives upon earth, but to them that are above in heaven, that are called gods'?"

Dee studied Bruno. The Doctor was regaining his posture and, though they were both seated, looked down as if from a height on his shorter colleague. Rick watched as the light of penetration returned to the Mathematician's gaze. He spoke quietly and with great deliberation, as if pronouncing a heresy that was nevertheless true. "For 'earthly Man is a mortal God, and Heavenly God is an immortal Man'."

Wherefore, by these two, an ancient Nemorensis intoned, *are all things governed, The World and Man; but they and all things else of that which is One.*

Not one to leave the last word to another, Bruno finished, "Unless you make yourself equal to God, you cannot understand God: for the like is not intelligible save to the like."

Rick, prompted by a Nemorensis, added, "Did not Ficino also write that man, 'created to rule over Nature and invested with both divinity and free will is, therefore, outside the hierarchy of the cosmos and is a world in himself'?"

Who the hell is Ficino?

Later.

Wagging a finger, Bruno bounced to his feet and began to pace. "Exactly! God gave man free will to..." He stopped. His gaze drifted off for a moment, then returned. He snapped his fingers. "What if He is testing us?"

"Testing?"

Bruno's head bobbed like a cork on a fishing line. Candlelight flickered in his brown eyes. He was actually smiling. Rick supposed only boredom could extinguish the Nolan's restless flame.

Bruno addressed Rick. "You say He is discreating the world because, along with the rising tide of consciousness, man is evolving toward godhead, earthly man becoming divine. If this is so and He feels us breathing down His neck, would it not make sense that He would test our mettle?"

"If so," Dee said, "it is a cruel test."

"Crueler than sending an angel to demand Abraham sacrifice his son?"

Dee conceded the point.

"For argument's sake," Bruno paused to address them, "let us proceed as if it were a test. How would we go about meeting the challenge?"

When no one came up with anything, Bruno said to Rick, "Let us go back to the Philosopher's Stone. You seek it—whatever *it* may be—for its transformative powers. You propose it may be used to reverse the alchemy of time."

"I propose nothing. But I don't have an alternative."

"All right. Let us move on to another enigma."

"Which is?"

"You."

"Me?"

"You are a mystery. You appear from nowhere. You say you are an apprentice, yet you converse with ascended magi. You speak Neapolitan haltingly, then fluently as if you were learning it *ex tempore*. Your shoes are made of a material I've never seen, and I've seen many shoes. Who are you? Where are you from? How do you communicate with your master? Do you visit the astral plane? Or does he come to you in etheric form? Or do you communicate through crystals, mirrors, or water? I do not mean to play the inquisitor? But one never knows what little thing might help, so one explores everything."

Rick was grateful his mouth was full. He continued chewing while he consulted his "master."

Reginald?

Tell the truth: I speak, you hear.

Rick swallowed and tapped his head. "I hear him, he hears me."

Bruno's eyes lit up. "Ah, you communicate by thought. I have long believed it possible." He tapped his lip, considering, then added, "But as exciting as that is, I don't see where it helps us. I was hoping you ascended to the astral realm to take your instruction."

"Why?" Was the Nolan on to something?

"I am thinking of what you said. How the subtle plane is like a two-sided mirror through which one sees the effects of the divine emanation on earth while also viewing the causes from above. If, as the ancients held, the pure ethereal light of emanation dims as it becomes mired in the gross physical plane and so becomes a shadow of itself, and as the light reflects up again it sheds the shadow and grows pure and radiant, then, does it not also make sense that, if we were to ascend to the celestial sphere, would we not, as it were, be able to whisper in His ear? And, therefore, our appeal stand out from the great blather of the multitudes?"

"Good Lord, man, you astound me," Dee said. "You might as well catch the attention of the sun by waving from a mountaintop. The proper way to appeal to God is by prayer."

"I'm sure He's listening to quite enough prayer right now. Does not the crying baby get the tit?"

Rick stared at the man in amazement. It was an inspired idea. He had already out-Copernicused Copernicus; now he proposed to out-Bell Alexander Graham Bell by, in effect, placing an esoteric phone call to God. He considered trying the experiment himself. He had, after all, traveled in his astral form to converse with Talmaiel atop Crystal Mountain while his body lay in a fevered delirium. But the OBE had been the result of a hallucinogenic potion. At the moment, he was tired and firmly rooted in the physical world—albeit not his own.

Reginald?

It's a thought, but no. We are not on the astral plane. We're here with you and aren't going to the astral plane unless you take us. Sorry.

Rick thought of the watch, how he'd gotten here.

Does your time travel pass through the astral realm?

It does, but only in passing. Besides, it would be dangerous for you to stay there for any length of time. The spheres are not uninhabited. And not all the inhabitants are friendly. Many an inexperienced traveler has strayed and never returned. You're not ready.

Rick chewed his lip. If he could not directly approach Yaldabaoth, then what was left besides prayer?

His thoughts drifted to Dee's subtle rays and how the Renaissance magus claimed to use the starry irradiation to effect change in the physical realm. Was it possible? And was the Stone, the *lapis philosophorum*, the means to do this? Were its reputed transformative powers capable of altering the alchemy of time?

He shook his head. "None of this is helping. We're back where we started?"

"The Stone," Bruno said, as if reading his thoughts.

He nodded.

Through the cuff of his sleeve, he traced da Silva's watch with his thumb, deciding.

Think about what you're doing.

I am.

Scant hours before as the clock ticked, he'd been home in his apartment in the present—*his* present. Until this day, he'd never given the present a second thought. It was simply the moments of his life sliding into the future from birth to death. But if his being here with John Dee and Giordano Bruno in 1583 seemed utterly fantastic to him, how then would these men, products of a superstitious age, no matter how enlightened for their time, react?

"You asked who I am, where I'm from," he said.

Bruno set his goblet on the floor. Dee balanced his plate on his knee.

To Dee Rick said, "You converse with angels." And to Bruno, "And you accept an infinity of peopled worlds. You might find my origin stranger still."

"And what is this miraculous origin?"

By way of response, he yanked back his sleeve and shoved the watch under their noses.

Two sets of brows rose in appreciation.

Dee: "It's a clock."

Bruno: "So small. The workings must be minute."

The watch crystal gleamed in the candlelight. The stainless bezel and oversized crown shone. The hands indicated it was about three a.m., which seemed right, considering their journey from Mortlake. Did the watch automatically correct for time differential, as modern watches did when you changed time zones?

"I've never seen its like," Bruno admired. "What workmanship. Did you make it?"

"No. Its maker was a master horologist who…"

"Yes?"

"Who hasn't been born yet."

Dee's eyes narrowed. "'Was'? 'Hasn't been born'? You speak in riddles."

Go ahead. Tell them. Time is—

Yes, I know. I know.

"The…chronograph…is from the future. Your future."

Dee gazed wonderingly at the watch. Bruno met his gaze. "Does this mean?"

Rick nodded, watching their reaction. He hoped he was doing the right thing. "Yes. With the help of this device, I journeyed here from the future—your future, my present—to seek your help."

Dee stared as if trying to understand its workings. Bruno touched the crystal, jerked his hand back as if he'd received a shock. Rick withdrew his wrist, afraid the little friar might inadvertently press the crown and send him God knows where.

"It has power," Bruno said, rubbing the tip of his finger with his thumb. Rick recalled his own reaction the first time he'd put the watch on and felt its subtle currents raising the hair on his arm.

"Then you *are* one of the celestials," Dee said.

"No, only human."

"You are much more than that," Bruno said. "No matter. Does this…" pointing at the chronograph for once at a loss for words "…open the doors of time?"

"Is it magic?" Dee asked.

"Yes, it opens the doors of time. And no, it is not magic. It…" He started to say it was a mechanical device—complicated, ingenious, but still a machine—but changed course. Considering what it did, transport him through space and time, how was it different from magic? He adopted a compromise. "It's no more magic than your showstone."

"And it allows you to travel through time?" Bruno said.

"It does."

"And you came seeking the Philosopher's Stone?"

"I did."

Dee and Bruno exchanged glances.

"Then," Dee said, "you must seek the greatest of alchemists." He looked at Bruno for confirmation.

Il Nolano nodded enthusiastically. "Paracelsus!"

28

THE SIBYL WAKES

Mist rose from crevices in the rock, sweet, colorless wisps like frosty breath on a winter morning, not cold but warm as if risen from a hot spring deep underground or seeped upward from the gaseous heart of volcanic fire. The sweet-smelling vapors curled into Fergi's brain. She grew, not sleepy, but calm. All the anxiety she had felt entering the grotto—her terror of giving herself over to the Sibyl, of having an alien mind overpowering her own, her worry over what would become of her very self—dissipated like dew in the morning sun.

She arched her back, shrugged her shoulders and, nostrils flaring, inhaled deeply the intoxicating fumes. Her head swirled with visions.

She heard voices, not one but many, speaking a multitude of languages, as if the collective babble of all mankind past, present, and future, in every language that ever was or would be, were presented for her selection, not a roar but a gentle hypnotic murmur, carrying her along like a leaf in a brook. She swayed on her feet. She hardly felt the Goddess' strong hands as She led her to the throne, nor the chill of the marble as it conformed to her back and buttocks. Her hands slid over the carven lions' heads of the armrests. Power radiated from the throne, charged the air around her. This was a sacred place, a nexus between mortal and immortal, but also a tomb where memories, past and future, wandered like restless spirits.

"I must leave you now," Cybele said. "You must face the Sibyl alone. She will decide whether or not to accept your sacrifice. She does not answer to me."

The Goddess' words barely registered. Nor did she notice when Her sandals no longer sounded on the cavern floor. She stroked the lions' manes as visions paraded before her inner eye: kings, paupers, heroes, villains, rich, poor, philosopher, fool. Her mind spun tapestries of history and burned holograms of what might become. She caught a photo tumbling past. A familiar image. A childhood memory blazed into her neural pathways. How often she'd reviewed the memory growing up. Especially during the holidays. And how she'd suppressed it and others like it by the end of middle school.

It was Christmas. She was seven and her father had not yet abandoned her and her mother. Under any other circumstances, she would have felt cold, simmering rage and wiped the stray remembrance from her mind as if erasing a particularly vulgar slogan chalked on a board. But now she let the memory unfold, vaguely curious how the movie playing in her head would turn out. Would it end, as it had in life, with Christmas ruined? With the shrill exchange of her parents' disgust of one another and the resounding slap of her father's hand striking her mother's face and her spending the closing hours of the holiday in her room trying to muffle her tears? Though she remembered Roy Ferguson as a surly, red-faced man and a mean alcoholic, he was uncharacteristically nice that morning. There were gifts under the tree. Not from Santa—no Santa or Easter Bunny or Jesus Christ in the Ferguson household. They unwrapped presents while Dad sat on the couch and drank his morning coffee. He was fidgety during lunch and short with Mom, insisting she hurry it up. Fergi had grown familiar with his moods as one grows accustomed to changes in the weather. A storm was brewing. He ate in silence and left while Fergi was still picking at her potato salad. She knew the sequel. It was always the same. How many times had Mom sent her to her room when Dad came home reeling, swaying through the living room to the kitchen where he threw off his coat, more often than not missing the chair and leaving Mom to pick it up off the floor. From where she sat, back against the headboard, arms folded tight across her chest, she heard

146

through her closed bedroom door his strident voice arguing with Mom in the kitchen. His words were clear because his voice was raised, shouting. Mom's voice was usually quieter, the voice of reason, occasionally agreeing with him to prevent an argument. Tonight, Mom wasn't having it. It was Christmas. For one day out of the whole year he could've drank at home—in moderation—instead of going out to the bar to get sloshed with his buddies. That was when she heard the unmistakable slap of his hand against Mom's face. A slap that would leave red fingerprints on her cheek the next morning.

Or would she, in her present state of lassitude, invent a more agreeable alternative, as she had so often during those turbulent years. Scenarios where they shared a pleasant dinner and watched TV or played music and sang Christmas carols and Dad tucked her in and asked her if she'd had a Merry Christmas without his breath stinking of booze.

Before the choice could be made, something roused her from her revelry.

She sensed a presence. Was she dreaming? The vapors had left her drowsy. Had she drifted off? But no—she licked her lips and smoothed her gown—the air was chill and the tactile smoothness of the fabric under her fingers all too realistic.

She was not alone in the grotto.

The hair on her arms stirred, as if a breeze had started up from somewhere deep within the mountain, a breeze that blew through the tall trapezoidal doors that led she knew not where. Dread crept through her. Though she saw nothing, she felt a cold, alien intelligence approaching. Something indescribably ancient. Not exactly inhuman but so long removed from human society and the familiar rhythms of daily life it might have been a traveler from Arcturus.

And then a deeper cold was creeping into her, and the voices fled taking with them the calm into which she had settled. Mothwings of panic fluttered. But she could not rise, nor release her grip on the marble lions' heads, nor turn her eyes toward the exit. Besides, where was there to run? She braced herself.

A white fog rose over her vision, wisps floating in from the periphery, then rising like a sea mist till all was shrouded and the grotto's walls were seen through a gray-white roiling haze. She heard the sea, as if through a shell held to her ear. Its surf rose as if she stood on some ancient, pebbled beach and watched great rollers wash ashore the bones of ships and heroes.

Her panic evaporated, replaced by an exquisite sense of curiosity and anticipation.

Then the combers breached the sea wall and the presence flooded into her mind and limbs. She experienced a sense of immeasurable age but without the decrepitude and senility that accompanied too long a life. Rather, she sensed a powerful intellect and a vast and crowded memory palace. Not the paltry allotment of recollections accumulated in a single lifespan that might fill a volume or two, no matter how remarkable a life, but a vast and ancient athenaeum of arcane lore and firsthand witnesses to history-making events, a storehouse of millennia.

Though it felt as if a god had taken residence in her blood and bowels, the presence that filled her mind like a beaker had once been human, for beneath the yellowed pages of recorded history and the fanning visions of tremendous events, she saw

A girl running in the hills, herding goats, her sandaled feet skipping over white rocks as the bright Aegean sparkled below.

A young woman, excited to be chosen but afraid of what waited in the cavern.

She closed her eyes.

The Sibyl woke.

29

TINDALOSI

From its lair among the angles of time, the Tindalosi lifts a snout and sniffs the timewinds. Something…where nothing was… has entered its domain.

There! It glimpses the fleeting travelers from a corner of one if its many eyes.

Its senses alert, crystalline quills along its angular flanks, its humped lupine back, scythe the air.

It stretches one of its myriad necks, then another, moist nostrils flaring. The tang of human blood arouses voracious thirst, but it is the light glowing within each of the travelers—one of which is brighter than the others—that causes the creature to tremble with desire. Smoking ichor drips from tubular tongues that unfurl to catch the "scent" of blood and light.

These travelers are not so wise as others. They are not cloaked in invisibility, nor have they masked their smell with the scent of other prey to throw the hounds off track. Stretching its limbs and with the pack falling in behind, it lopes over leagues and years, closing on its prey.

30
PARACELSUS

Rick hammered the knocker for several minutes before a gruff German voice approached from the other side cursing them to return to whatever pit they'd crawled out of.

The man who opened the door was no taller than Bruno. Rick knew him at once as the thin, balding man the Nemorenses had shown him at the Embassy. He even wore the soiled leather apron.

Philippus Aureolus Theophrastus Bombastus von Hohenheim.

Self-styled Paracelsus: Greater than Celsus, the influential Roman author of *de Medicina*, a Nemorensis informed.

Ignoring Bruno, as if someone as short as himself and so plainly dressed was beneath his notice, the physician scowled up at Rick and Dee, both a head taller than him. He was plainly annoyed and impatient to get back to whatever he was doing.

Rick felt conspicuous in his red cloak, but at least it hid his bloodstained EMT uniform. He was glad for its warmth for they had emerged in winter. The narrow, cobbled lane was covered in an inch or so of grimy churned snow and more was piled along the curb where the sidewalk had been shoveled. They had only just arrived— disoriented and a little nauseous—and already Rick was beginning to shiver. As on the barge, Bruno didn't seem to notice the cold, and Rick marveled at the man's fortitude. In his black, fur-collared robe, Dee's only concession to the wintery air was to tuck his hands into his sleeves.

"What do you want? I'm—"

The Doctor stared at Rick's shoes. Then his pants. He tilted his head and frowned as he looked up at his face. "You look as if you fell from the sky." To all of them he added, "Who the devil are you and what do you want?"

Only when Dee spoke did Rick realize he understood German. Another marvelous advantage of having an academy of sages rewiring your brain.

"We have traveled far to consult with you, Doctor."

"Go away!" Paracelsus scowled at the glowering rust-red sky as if it were another bothersome intruder. "The world ends and I have much to do!"

"We're here to help," Rick said.

"Help? You clowns? What do you know of the Art of making Sol and Luna? Of the tincture, the arcanum, the quintessence? Of the philosophic fire? Sophists!" He spat the word as if it left a foul taste in his mouth.

"I am no Peripatetic," Dee's face was a portrait of dignity, "but a true disciple of Trice-Great Hermes, Father of Philosophers."

"True," Rick said, prompted by a Nemorensis, "Doctor Dee possesses the greatest library in England, including the texts of Trismegistus, Plato, Ficino, Albertus Magnus, and the *Corpus Hermetica*."

Paracelsus sneered. "Pfft! So you read. Another dreamer carrying golden mountains in his head without ever putting hand to fire. Only experimentally and by long practice, through the agency of fire, is the true separated from the false!"

"I am no armchair Spagyrist," Dee countered, barely tempering his, if not anger, then a certain petulance at having his credentials questioned. "I know well the long labor with alembic, circulator, reverberatory, as well as the virtues of mercury, salt, and sulfur."

Paracelsus leaned closer and sniffed the air. His lip curled contemptuously. "You do have an alchemical whiff about you." While it was true the scent of sulfur and ash clung to Dee's clothes, Rick caught the pungent smell of alcohol on the Great Man's frosty breath.

"And you?" He'd finally noticed Bruno.

The little Italian lifted his sparsely bearded chin to the occasion and pronounced in florid Neapolitan: "Philotheus Jordanus Brunus of Nola, a doctor in perfected theology; a professor of pure and blameless wisdom; a philosopher known, approved, and honorifically acknowledged by the foremost academies of Europe; to none a stranger, save barbarians and the vulgar; a waker of slumbering souls; a breaker of presumptuous and stubborn ignorance; who looks not to the anointed head nor to the consecrated brow, not to the pure in hand nor to the circumcised, but thither where man's true countenance is to be found, toward his soul, and the perfection of his spirit; whom dispensers of foolishness and hypocrites abhor; whom upright and sincere men love; whom noble souls receive with acclamation; at your service."

Paracelsus opened his mouth as if to launch into an equally baroque rebuttal but a passerby casting a long look at the strangely dressed foreigners standing on his doorstep caught his eye and he glared after him until the man looked away. Then a strange thing happened. As the man walked on, he disappeared. As if he passed into a fog, though no fog was there. A row of houses vanished with him, and, in their place, as Rick had seen before, a much older group appeared.

Across the street, an elderly man sweeping snow from his steps saw it too and looked from the "new" buildings to the group at Paracelsus' door.

Frowning as if the city were a patient in need of treatment, the physician stood aside and waved his visitors in. "You'd better come in, Herr Professor," he said to Bruno. He pursed his lips at Rick and Dee. "Your assistants, too."

Inside, Rick wrinkled his nose at the rotten-egg stink he'd encountered crossing Dee's garden. He was getting familiar with the alchemist's den. The worn floorboards of the front room were dusty and the air only slightly less cold than outdoors. He glimpsed chairs and a table in the next room. A short hall led back to what he supposed was a kitchen.

Though he had clearly engaged in libations, their host was steady on his feet and his sentences showed no sign of slurring. "I hope I'm not wasting my time," the Doctor said to his guests, "but I detect an aura of mystery about you that I cannot explain." Narrowing his gaze on Rick he added, "You speak German well but it is an old dialect I've not heard in years and your lips do not seem comfortable speaking it. And your clothes…" He looked again at his EMS boots with their synthetic uppers and rubber soles and his ankle-length slacks and lack of hose, then cocked a bushy eyebrow. "I find you most strange." He turned to Dee. "You on the other hand, butcher German as Englishmen butcher all languages. *E tu, Signor Professore,*" he said to Bruno, his tone almost collegial, "in you I detect a mind whose brilliance reflects my own."

Bruno's smile was genuine, the underappreciated genius receiving praise from the great man himself.

"Now, briefly, why have you come?"

Dee and Bruno looked at Rick.

"Time, Herr Doctor," he began. "Time and He who created time." And, as briefly as he could, he explained how God was uncreating creation and how time ran backward, not smoothly but sporadically with currents and eddies, as chaos precluded orderly progression. And when the physician asked "Why?" he answered "consciousness" and explained how the rising tide of consciousness offended the Maker who was recalling the divine emanation to its source.

Paracelsus started at the revelation. "Say that again?"

"I do not presume to know the mind of God, but it would seem, in His infinite wisdom, He has found fault with man and decided he is unworthy of…" Rick waved his hand, not sure how to express himself.

"Of completing the great work," Dee finished for him.

He hoped the physician wouldn't ask where he got his information or that his companions would bring up his story of having an ascended master. But Paracelsus merely rubbed his stubbled chin for a long moment, his forehead bunched in concentration, before saying, "That agrees with what I was working on." He nodded as if reaching a decision. "Come with me."

"Yesterday, it was high summer; today snow blankets the earth and birds that should have flown freeze in the street." Paracelsus looked at the grimy street-level window through which the feeble westering light cast a sullen glow. "And the day is short when it should be long. Yesterday, this was a juniper tree."

The Doctor's basement laboratory was warmer than upstairs. A low fire flickered in the hearth. A confusion of alembics, crucibles, phials, funnels, flasks, tongs, and bellows cluttered the shelves and workbench. The evergreen sprig that lay in the dish was about four inches long. Soil clung to its delicate roots. To Rick, it looked like one of those ready-to-plant seedlings you might buy at a nursery.

"This was a tree?"

"As tall as the house."

Rick exchanged glances with Dee and Bruno. Buildings sliding backward into the past, the present overtaking comets that appeared years ago, was bad. But this...finding yourself an infant again would pretty much take you off the game board.

"Man and everything in the universe, above or below, are formed of one primordial substance, *materia prima*. The forms are different—sun, moon, man, tree," he pointed to the sprig, "but the essence is the same."

A wine jug and a half-empty glass sat among the workbench paraphernalia. The physician reached for the glass, remembered his manners and touched the jug. "Drink?"

"No thanks," they murmured in three different dialects of German.

Paracelsus shrugged, sipped, and continued. "Primordial matter, which forms the basis of the human body, absorbs influences from the stars, which, in turn, nourishes the physical body. By means of these influences, man's soul is united to the souls of the stars. Therefore, the sun and the stars attract something from us, and we attract something from them, because our astral bodies are in sympathy with the stars, and the stars are in sympathy with our astral bodies. The Chaldeans, Persians, and Egyptians had the knowledge of the secrets of Nature and understood the conjunction of celestial influences, whereby heavenly virtues act upon inferior bodies; how the stars are in sympathy with our astral bodies, as they are with the astral bodies of all things, vegetable, mineral, or animal. The invisible forces acting in the visible body are very powerful and may be guided by the imagination and compelled by the will."

Rick recalled what Dee said about the table of practice, how it and the crystal corresponded to their celestial likenesses and how "the skilled practitioner called down subtle rays from the stars, thereby effecting change in the physical realm."

Bruno chimed in. "Man is the quintessence of all the elements, a microcosm of the universal soul. Everything that exists or takes place in the universe, exists in man. The forces and essences making up the constitution of man is the same as the forces and powers that on an infinitely larger scale is called the universe."

"Everything in the universe is reflected in man," Dee added. "And a wise man, conscious of this conjunction of celestial influences, whereby heavenly virtues act upon inferior bodies, may work wonders."

Images appeared in Rick's head, no doubt the excited memories and imaginations of the horde sharing the pathways of his thoughts. A vial of golden liquid that restored lost youth, a basilisk rising from a cloth impregnated with menstrual blood and exposed to the rays of the new moon at night and the rays of the sun during the day, a red rose rising from its own ashes.

"You're talking about magic."

"Magic is simply the complete understanding of the conjunction of celestial powers with elementary bodies and the development of the art and faculty needed to manipulate those correspondences," Paracelsus said.

Dee lifted his brows. "'Simply'?"

"And how does one…'manipulate correspondences'?"

"As I said, imagination and will. A strong faith and a powerful imagination are the two pillars supporting the door to the temple of magic, without which nothing can be accomplished. Imagination is the astral tool with which the magus manipulates elementary matter and

155

alters the underlying sidereal forces of the ethereal world. The *imaginatio,*" here he tapped his forehead, then spread his fingers toward the ceiling, "rises up to the heavens where it is transmuted into an astral influence and then falls," his hand swooped to the floor, "back down to Earth as an 'impression,' able to affect man and nature."

"'It rises from Earth to Heaven and descends again to Earth, thereby combining within itself the powers of both the Above and the Below,'" Dee said, quoting Trice Great Trismegistus.

Paracelsus nodded. *"Solve et coagula."*

"What has this got to do with the juniper?" Rick asked impatiently.

"Ah!" Paracelsus raised a finger as if he'd been waiting for this question, but Dee was quicker.

"The correspondences. The juniper, an evergreen plant, corresponds to the birth of the sun, new year in the sign of Capricorn. The plant is governed by Saturn, Cronos, who reigns over time." He looked at Paracelsus. "We don't have time to do calculations, but I would say Saturn is in the Tenth House and below the horizon."

"Most like," the physician admitted, reappraising Dee, "given the circumstances and the wintry shift."

"So this plant has a connection with the planet Saturn?"

"And with time," Bruno added.

"And you think you can use this plant to influence Saturn to alter time?"

"Not the plant," Dee said. "Its quintessence."

Rick heard da Silva groan.

Paracelsus pointed out a still-like apparatus on the workbench, mounted on a tripod over an oil lamp. A long tube descended from the elevated device into a wide-mouthed, narrow-necked vessel, presumably to collect the distillations from whatever was heated in the device.

"To reduce the plant to its quintessence, you must first reduce it to its *materia prima.* Chop it, boil it in strong wine in a jar well closed. Let the wine be separated through frequent straining. Collect all wines and distill through the alembic. Let it set till its 'virtue' collects. Keep distilling until the pure is separated from the impure and you have the essence."

"And what do you do with that?"

"As the universe is a product of the divine will, all forms and objects are vibrations of will. We may look upon physical nature as being constituted of a low order of vibrations, upon the soul as a higher octave of the same, and of spirit as one higher still. Each thing, from the sun down to a tumor in the body of an animal, constitutes a certain state of vibration of the one original essence."

"And man can influence these vibrations?"

A sly grin shone in the physician's eyes. "Some can." The grin vanished as quickly as it had risen, replaced by a stern voice and a cautionary finger. "But it is a task not easily accomplished. There are no shortcuts."

Some can...

Was that what da Silva and his mistress expected of him? To bend the universe to his will?

You *were the dynamo...*

Grigori blood...

But to thoroughly comprehend the nature of all things in heaven and earth and the correspondences or sympathies that bound stars and planets with the astral bodies of plants, minerals, and men... No way he could achieve a mastery of those influences in a lifetime, let alone in the dwindling time allotted the earth.

Impatient voices were calling out.

The Stone! Ask him about the Philosopher's Stone!

"Excuse my ignorance, Doctor, but why not use the Philosopher's Stone? History records you found it."

"And what is history but the record of man's faulty memory?"

His heart sank. He sensed the Nemorenses' collective disappointment.

"So, you did not find it?"

"That depends on your expectations of the *lapis*. If all you're looking for is a shortcut to riches, a means of transmuting base metals into gold, as Pythagoras and legions of Spagyrists," here he cast a doubtful eye at Dee, "have reduced the Stone. Then, no. Here, look at this."

He took a wooden box down from a shelf and opened it on the workbench. The misshapen lump he removed caught the lantern light and cast a yellow gleam on the glass beakers and retorts. "What do you see?"

"May I?" Rick asked.

"Go ahead."

The lump had heft, and though ropy with ridges and depressions, its surface was smooth beneath his thumb. Though it was cool in his palm, its gleam dried his mouth and brought sweat to his pores. A thrill crept over him.

"Is it...?"

"Gold? Most certainly. Now look at this." From the same box he removed another, slightly larger lump, a crystal-latticed, brass-colored mineral, and placed it in Rick's hand.

"Auriferous chalcopyrite," Dee said, looking over his shoulder.

Rick hefted the stone. It was heavy. "You made gold from this?"

"Did I? Or was the gold already there?"

"*Auriferous*...gold-bearing," Bruno explained, disappointment in his voice.

"Crush it, grind it, apply mercury. The mercury separates the gold from the minerals producing a mercury-gold amalgam. Heat the mixture—gently, no hotter than sunlight will do—the mercury vaporizes, leaving gold. There's no mystery to it. I learned the process in my youth working in the Villach mines. Any chemist can do it. No Philosopher's Stone needed."

Rick returned the specimens to the box. "That's it? There's no such thing as the Philosopher's Stone?"

"I did not say that." Paracelsus returned the box to the shelf. "Only that fools look for it in the wrong places. To say that a drop of the tincture will turn a sea of baser metals into gold by multiplying—these are but dreams. Vanities." He waved his hand dismissively. "The *lapis* does not reside physically in vegetable, animal, or mineral form. No," he gazed soberly at the blue-green sprig lying in the thick-bottomed plate, "the Stone is nothing less than the attainment of complete self-awareness and of the higher consciousness. You see why your news so startled me?" The physician shook his head in disgust.

"Ironic," Bruno said.

"What's that?" Dee asked.

"Here we are, on the threshold of the seventh and final age as demarked by the fiery trigon, the Golden Age of the Sun, coagulation, the seventh stage of God's great alchemical experiment, and just when the Philosopher's Stone will be universally attained," he held up his hand as if clutching at something beyond his grasp, "the world recedes from the very remedy we seek."

A great choking sadness rose in Rick's throat. He had not realized till now how much mankind stood to lose: not just the world or life, but his Destiny. The fulfillment of his great climb out of the primordial mud. To climb so high from stone and flint to iron and atom, only to have it snatched away. "The Maker does not intend for His great work to reach completion," he said.

"Not His." Paracelsus' hand shook as he reached for his glass. "Not His work, but man's."

31

TRANSMUTATION

The stone lay on an *electrum magicum*, a mirror made of electrum. Electrum being the metal the old alchemists compounded of the seven metals and containing the virtues of the seven as well as those of the metals' corresponding planets. As slow and exacting as the process was, it was one of the most valuable preparations known to the secret science because of its magic power. In a mirror made of the electrum, a seer could observe events past or present, and, because the electrum is antipathetic to all evil, any poison surreptitiously put into a cup made of the substance would sweat to the outside. The electrum's preparation required ten parts of pure gold, ten of silver, five of copper, two of tin, two of lead, one part of powdered iron, and five of mercury. Into the crucible, when the planets Saturn and Mercury come into conjunction, combine the mercury and lead. Then, at the conjunction of Jupiter with Mercury or Saturn, melt and combine tin with the previously prepared mercury-lead amalgam. And so on, at the conjunctions of any of the other four planets—Sol, Luna, Venus, or Mars—with one of the three former—Saturn, Mercury, or Jupiter— dissolve and conjoin the metals. Thus, the process follows the ancient alchemical maxim *"Solve et Coagula"* —dissolve and coagulate—which encapsulates the basic premise of the alchemical art, the breaking down or distillation of a substance into *prima materia* and its reconstruction into something new and more efficacious. For Nature is unfinished. She provides the raw materials, but it is up to the adept to manipulate the elements by reverberations, sublimations, digestions, reductions, and resolutions, in order to endow the natural with supernatural power by artful ministrations.

The mirror, a mere two inches in diameter, was unique on Abyss. The electrum could not be made on the prison world because there were, as far as the Grigori could ascertain, no planets corresponding to old Earth's companions—no Luna drawing the tides of sea and blood, nor was Sol's benevolent influence felt. This mirror Raziel had on his person when the Avengers herded the Watchers through the star gate. Still, though the mirror no longer showed what transpired on Earth, due, presumably, to the strictures of their prison rather than distance, the electrum, having once connected to the planets of its construction, continued to resonate with their influence.

Raziel delivered his lecture with much wagging of a long, blue finger and frequent raising of his hairless brows. It lifted Talmaiel's heart to see the Artificer's blue eyes sparkle with the prospect of an alchemical challenge.

"Everything visible is condensed *A'kasa* becoming visible by changing its supra-ethereal state into a concentrated and tangible form, and everything in nature may be resolved again into *A'kasa* and be made invisible by changing the attractive power that holds its atoms together into repulsion."

A'kasa was something like aether, the fifth element of the ancients, the quintessence or *qüinta essentia* of the medieval alchemists, and, later, the subtle, invisible substance that filled the plenum of space, the luminiferous, light-bearing aether of the Victorians.

"By alternating their magnetic polarity, you mean," Talmaiel suggested. He'd kept up with advances in natural philosophy—what moderns called physics—but, though Raziel's terminology might be archaic, the Artificer was way ahead of him. To put it mildly, Talmaiel was a dilatant theoretician while Raziel was a magus practitioner.

"Yes. The rapid fluctuation of the magnetic polarity of a substance's atoms alters the state of etheric vibrations, thereby transmuting any matter into any other form of matter. That's how we transform the ice and rock of Abyss into…" he waved a hand at the paraphernalia lining his shelves "…stuff."

161

"I'm aware of the process and I've seen the transformations, but it takes the whole of the Brethren to complete the transmutations. I am just there for support."

"You remember what the sapphires look like?"

Talmaiel recalled the six-sided crystals glittering like arctic ice yet smoldering with blue fire. He watched as the ten sapphires formed the Sephirothic Tree, arranging themselves in three vertical columns—four in the middle and three on either side. Watched the Tree rise into the night sky above the mountain, growing brighter until it outshone the stars and pulsed a blinding electric blue.

"I remember."

"Picture one… Now hold the jewel in your mind as you would in your hand. Feel its solidity, its cold fire. See the light shine within the crystal, not reflected or refracted from without, but glowing with its own inner light."

He remembered clutching the sapphires in his burned hand—all ten of them—just before he flung them into the air. Remembered the power radiating up his arm. He held on to the memory. Again, he saw the Sephiroth burning in the sky above the mountain. A three-dimensional Jacob's Ladder climbing not to Paradise but to the Abyss. In his mind's eye he reached up and plucked one of the jewels from the sky and left it floating in the air before the workbench, superimposed over the blue lump on the mirror.

"Kokabiel, are we ready?"

As he had in the hall with his forehead close to the column, Talmaiel felt rather than heard the Grigori's answer. *Always.* If there was a hint of irony in the "voice," Talmaiel took it as a hopeful sign. Kokabiel was risking much. Semjaza could not afford to cut Kokabiel off from society completely—he was too necessary for the long-term operations of the Dwelling, but he could mete pain. But even punishment had limits: if he pushed Kokabiel too far and drove him to madness, where then would the Brethren be?

The Artificer's eyes were closed as he saw the corundum with his sage's eye and envisioned turning it into a gleaming six-sided lozenge.

Talmaiel stared without blinking at the image he had concocted. Soon the air shimmered and he struggled to hold the vision of the jewel he had imagined superimposed over the corundum. The two stones—the imagined and the real—blurred so he couldn't tell one from the other. The air in the room grew warm and the image wavered like a heat mirage under a desert sun.

Then, when he thought he could maintain the image no longer, a blue thumb and forefinger entered his narrow field of vision and plucked the jewel from the *electrum magicum*. While the corundum was not cut and polished as the ten sapphires of the Sefir Raziel were, the stone in Raziel's hand was nevertheless a blue hexagonal crystal, a deep and vibrant blue needing only the gemcutter's art to reveal its hidden beauty.

"We did it." His voice was filled with wonder as he lifted his gaze from the stone to meet Raziel's eyes.

The Artificer was grinning like a lottery winner.

Talmaiel took the stone from Raziel's hand, admired the way the lantern light gleamed along its facets. He recalled the vortex of spinning cumulonimbus clouds above Crystal Mountain, imagined the portal opening, only he was above now, looking down on the mountain. Down on the earth.

A sudden shock scattered his imaginings like mist before a wind. His spirts plunged. How could he have been so stupid? In his excitement—in his urgency to escape the planet and Semjaza's appetite—he had overlooked one important item: the Two Hundred had been on Abyss for thousands of earth years and in all that time this was the first corundum found.

"It's only one."

"What?"

"How long must it take me to find nine more?"

Raziel smiled. His white teeth contrasted with his blue face. "That won't be necessary."

32

HEXENMEISTERS

It was dark again when Rick, Dee, and Bruno stepped back onto the street, the sky a livid purple in the west in the aftermath of sunset. How many days had passed since he and Mack had responded to the call? Or was this the same day? He'd lost track of time.

Time... He had to agree with Lord Russell that it didn't matter if time ran forward or backward, only that it was ending.

He shivered as the cold crept under his cloak. "Did any of that make sense?"

Paracelsus remained inside, bent on pursuing his alchemical operation on the chance of wresting time from the hand of the Almighty.

"Yes, but I am at a loss as to what to do. I am truly humbled." Dee's shoulders were hunched, his eyes downcast at the sidewalk.

Rick understood the sage's disappointment. If Dee could return home with the secret of the Stone, he could lift himself out of his impoverished circumstances, clear his name of the stigma of conjuror, and fund his dream of a national library. His goals, balancing the noble with the self-serving, were only too-human.

"We should start walking," Bruno said, eyeing the crowd coming down the block to join the onlookers that stood outside the houses across the street.

Rick saw them. Another unhappy mob like the one outside Dee's. Like Dee, Paracelsus had a reputation as a magician. Was everyone not in lockstep with the gatekeepers of conformity to be hauled out and beaten and stoned and hung?

Not your fight.

I know.

"Maybe we'd better."

But before he could take a step, a shockwave rippled at his back and he was thrown to the pavement. He rose, stunned. Looked into angry faces. The crowd surrounded him.

A cloud of dust was settling in the gap where Paracelsus' house and the houses on either side had stood.

"*Hexenmeisters!*"

Warlocks!

"No! I—"

Something hit him in the back, knocked him into the arms of two of the townspeople. A burly, red-faced man raised a fist to strike him. He drove his fist into the man's nose, ducked, kicked, and he was free. He searched for his companions. Saw Dee being dragged away, his long coat dragging the ground, his knees pumping as he tried to get his feet under him. Bruno launched after him, fists swinging.

"Stop!" he shouted, but the crowd wasn't listening. Then he was on the ground, curled in a fetal position protecting his groin, arms over head as boots smashed into him. He felt the priests wrest his arm away from his head, force his hand to find the watch and press the crown three times.

"*No!*"

He couldn't leave Dee and Bruno prey to the mob!

But he was gone.

falling

dizzy

a blur of lights

roar of timespaceplanetswhizzingby

He slammed into a wall and darkness fell.

33

HOWLING ACROSS WORLDS

Like a living mirage, shimmering, ethereal, all impossible angles and unearthly planes, its quill-armored flanks rippling like quicksilver, its eight legs and several necks shifting as if its very cells are in a constant state of transformation, the Tindalosi growls. A sense of loss wells in its abdomen, which, along with hunger and thirst, is the seat of its primal emotions.

It shoves its snouts through dimensional veils and sniffs worlds. It has lost the scent. In all its eons of feasting on the thousands of races that have mastered the timestream, it has never encountered as powerful an aura, as brilliant a light, as this one's. To another species in another dimension, the beast's dread desire might be called a kind of love—and it *is* love, but a terrible love that demands a oneness so total that the object of desire must be devoured.

The pack mills about, impatient for their alpha to lead.

Never has it felt such yearning, as if to acquire this one's flame would be transformative and raise it to a crystalline plane where its thirst would be slaked and it would feast forever on eternal light.

It thinks these things instinctively like the cunning beast it is. Just as it instinctively knows it must have the human to itself, even if it means rending its siblings to red mist.

Suddenly, a light flickers across decades and its hundred eyes trace its meteoric flight. Far ahead of the pack it hurls itself, slavering in pursuit. Years unfurl like ribbons beneath its taloned paws. It draws

166

close. So close it tastes the cold white flame burning in the warm matrix of blood and bone. So close it hears the babble of the creature's thoughts.

The prey vanishes. As if dropped through a hole in the floor of time, the traveler is gone. The hound circles, sniffing, above, below.

Its hunger blossoms. In rage and frustration, it lifts its heads, and from its many mouths issues such a keening howl that on a thousand worlds across the light years canine creatures bay in reply.

34

INQUISITION

Cold water brought Rick around.

His head sagged upon his chest. Pain racked his body. His arms were being wrenched out of their sockets. He opened his eyes. The first thing he saw was his wet shivering body. He was nude. His ankles were bound. He was standing on tiptoes. He shook his head trying to focus. The act brought a crescendo of pain. He looked up. His wrists were tied to a rope that ran through a pulley attached to a beam.

Where...?

The last thing he remembered...

"Hexenmeisters!"

The mob. Fighting.

Dee and Bruno! He'd left them!

His surroundings snapped into focus. He had to be dreaming. He was in what looked like a movie set.

The dungeon was surreal. Vaulted brick ceilings, moist stone walls, exposed beams, iron rings, chains. He recognized some of the torture devices. A too-authentic-looking rack—its ancient oak boards dark and shiny where sweating bodies of the tortured were broken. A great wheel over by one wall upon which other bodies could be bound and broken. A furnace, well stoked, in which a glowing bed of coals awaited the tormentor's pleasure. Manacles hung from a man-sized table before the grate, tongs and other instruments of torture neatly arranged on a smaller table beside it.

The stench was horrible. He recognized the smell from when he worked unloading trucks at the industrial laundry on Laidlaw Avenue. Most of the trucks came in from Manhattan hotels, but some brought in soiled linen from hospitals. These reeked of vomit, urine, blood, and shit.

Seated at a table before him was a gray-bearded priest in a black-and-white cassock. A second priest in a plain gray monk's cassock sat beside him with a quill in hand and ledger before him. A brawny hard-faced hooded man stood to one side.

"Ah, you've returned to the living," said the priest in charge. His voice projected authority. "Good. You have much to answer for."

"Where am I? What are you doing to me?"

The hard-faced man backhanded Rick across the mouth. The blow caused a fresh wave of nauseating pain as he was knocked off his toes and his shoulders received his weight.

"Do not question his Most Reverend Eminence, the Cardinal Bellarmino!" the tormentor growled.

The Grand Inquisitor held up his hand as if to say, "Enough."

"You are a guest of the Holy House."

"Holy?" He could barely think. The pain was a globe enveloping him, a world.

Reginald?

A euphemism, Rick, for the Palace of the Inquisition. I'm so sorry. We did not foresee this.

He heard the fear in his mentor's voice, the flutter of panic.

Inquisition! The word sluiced fresh terror through his bowels. The rack, the wheel, the *strappado,* the burning at the stake—images that drove home the horror of his situation. Not something read about in a history book or seen in a movie but enfolding him in the visceral reality of his surroundings.

The Cardinal's shoulders were a little stooped as if he'd spent decades bent over books and writing at his desk. And he had the domed forehead and graying beard of a scholar. But the brown eyes that shone beneath his dark brows and the sharp frown lines that creased the corners of his mouth were hard. This was not a man who brooked argument. However beneficent he might be to the truly devout, however erudite and profound his many tracts, he exuded the cold authority of a man rigid in his convictions, a man adamantly convinced of the primacy of the Roman Pontiff and the unquestionable truth of scriptural dogma. A man whom no amount of evidence could sway. Rick reminded himself this was the man who would condemn Giordano Bruno to the pyre and order Galileo to recant his discoveries and place the aging astronomer under house arrest for the remainder of his life. A man whom his admirers and detractors alike called the "Hammer of the Heretics."

A man whom the Catholic Church, in a cosmic twist of irony, would one day canonize as Saint Roberto Bellarmino.

"Why?" he groaned.

The tormentor raised his hand to strike him. Bellarmino stopped him with a finger.

"Why what?"

"What am I accused of?"

"Witchcraft. *Maleficos non patieris vivere.*"

Wizards thou shalt not suffer to live.

"Yours is a crime against God. For your heresy and apostasy to Satan, your wicked idolatry, your wicked offenses against God and Man must be scourged from your flesh for the sake of your immortal soul. Do you confess?"

"I am no wizard. Where are your witnesses? Who has spoken against me?" His words came out in gasps, every syllable an agony.

"Witnesses?" The Inquisitor looked around the dungeon, a pale hand, lifted palm forward, one finger raised, as if he were offering a beatitude. "We need no witnesses here. You are not in a civil court, but in the tribunal of the Inquisition. Suspicion is enough and since heresy is a sin of the soul, therefore confession is the only proof needed."

The Cardinal Inquisitor conferred with his notary for a moment in quiet tones. From far off, Rick heard someone screaming. There was madness in the voice. Water dripped nearby. Bellarmino continued. "You are accused of flying. You fell from the sky. And then there's this."

170

He tapped the table, and for the first time Rick saw what lay on its surface before the Inquisitor. The watch gleamed in the ruddy light of the ensconced candles.

All hope fled. He was lost. Centuries away from his time and his only means of return—of escape—in the hands of his tormentors!

"Are you ready to confess? Or would you rather be put to the question?"

"I am no witch!" he blurted, pain augmenting his anger so that his voice echoed off the masonry.

The Grand Inquisitor, His Most Reverend Eminence the Cardinal Bellarmino, raised his hand and nodded to the hooded man.

"Two hundred lashes," he ordered.

The tormentor took up a scourge, held it for Rick to see the evil-looking thongs trailing from the crop before stepping behind him.

The first blow across his naked back took his breath away. His agony soared to fantastic heights. With his arms stretched to the rafter, he danced on his toes as he fought to maintain balance.

By the twentieth blow, he was gasping and blind with tears.

"*Reginald!*" he shrieked aloud.

Leave your physical body, Rick. Will your astral body to travel.

But the room was fading. A white swirl as if he were caught in a snow squall obscured his vision. The roar in his head drowned out the crack of the scourge. Nausea welled in his throat.

He passed out.

35

THE LIGHT VEHICLE

A top the rampart, the endless day of Abyss' solar side had changed not at all since Talmaiel last ventured out. The world below was frozen, white, and dismal. The dim red sun stained the rust-colored clouds, the wind howled, the monotonous succession of icy peaks and glacial valleys marched into the mist-blurred distance. Talmaiel and Raziel stood at the parapet shouting to one another to make themselves heard over the wind.

"Each of the stones contains all the knowledge of the others," Raziel yelled into Talmaiel's ruined ear. "Together they create great energy, the sum of which is far greater than the potential of the stones individually. But what is really interesting is they share a mutual attraction. Wherever they are, no matter how far apart, they pull toward one another, even as the planet we're standing on pulls us toward its center."

"Gravity—that's the new name for that phenomenon," Talmaiel offered.

"'Gravity.' Ah, I've been away so long. Sounds as if I've much to learn from your humans."

"I doubt it. So you're saying the sapphires are predisposed to finding each other no matter where they are?"

"Drawn like magnets. Everything in nature has its own unique frequency. Every element, every object. The sapphires I imprinted are no different, and as they are all twins, they resonate sympathetically.

Pluck an open string of a lute, the corresponding string of a nearby lute will resonate. Hold a page of my Book in your hand and will the others and all will vibrate to the frequency of your will."

"And you can summon the others? With this?"

Talmaiel looked at the jewel he clasped tightly between his fingers lest the wind take it. It looked as blue and glittered as brightly as the sapphires of the Sefir Raziel, but he did not feel the deep thrum of energy pulsing within its azure heart as when he'd held those others.

"But this is not a page from your Book. How will it draw the others?"

That got a smile from the Artificer.

"Ah, but I am their author and know their contents chapter and verse." He held out his hand for the crystal. Talmaiel handed it over. Raziel clasped the stone in his fist, arched his neck back, and gazed into the rusty zenith. Talmaiel felt Kokabiel's considerable will supporting them, augmenting the creative power of their collective intent.

Talmaiel followed Raziel's gaze. He knew what he had to do. He imagined the roiling clouds parting as they had that night above a mountain in Arkansas' Ouachitas. Imagined them forming a vortex, a whirlpool of cloud in the calm center of which strange stars burned in a pool of night. He remembered what he'd seen that midnight hour atop Crystal Mountain as the flinty ground thrummed with the power generated by the vast reservoir of quartz crystal deep beneath their feet. Recalled the ten sapphires of the *Sefir Raziel* aligning themselves into the three columns of the Sephirothic Tree and, pulsing a blinding electric blue, burning brighter than any constellation. Imagined blue light blazing from sephirah to sephirah, streaking point to point to point forming the Twenty-Two Paths of Emanations. Envisioned the Sephiroth, a three-dimensional Jacob's Ladder climbing into the vortex, collapsing upon itself and reforming into two inverted counter-rotating superimposed triangular pyramids, like a three-dimensional Star of David, whirling like a top, its whistle rising above the keening wind.

He remembered his wonder at watching the Merkaba descend, and he stretched his arms toward the sky to receive it.

And there it was, a blur of blue fire carving a cometic path through the clouds, descending toward the rampart. The light vehicle. The chariot that would transport them to Earth.

36

THE SENTENCING

Again, a bucket of water brought him around. He could no longer stand but hung from his bound wrists. His back was on fire. Mercifully his shoulders were numb. He lifted his head. The dungeon swam into blurry focus. He blinked tears from his eyes.

Cardinal Bellarmino and his notary sat at the table. His tormentor stood nearby, arms crossed, awaiting orders to inflict more pain.

Bellarmino nodded once. "For the record," he said for the notary's benefit, "the accused is awake." To Rick he asked, "Do you hear and understand me?"

When Rick made no answer, the tormentor moved to strike him.

"I hear you."

"The prisoner is awake and conscious. We may proceed with his sentencing."

"Sentencing? What about a trial?"

Bellarmino sat back, tented his fingers. "We've no time for trial. All nature revolts. No doubt you and your fellow wizards are responsible. Will you not confess?"

Rick glared at the Cardinal.

"The prisoner again refuses to confess and avail himself of the mercy of the Holy Office."

The scribe recorded.

"What now? The rack?" He eyed the grim machine, and his stomach turned at the thought of being stretched upon its greasy boards and his joints pulled apart.

"No. We are past that now. You have refused our mercy and obstinately refuse to confess your heinous crimes against God and scripture. Hear now your sentence: in the morning you will be taken to the place of execution, bound to the stake, and burned. May God have mercy on your soul."

The Inquisitor crossed himself and rose.

The notary scribbled in his ledger. If his tormentor was disappointed, he did not show it, but remained standing cross-armed like a statue.

Burned!

Rick thought he would be beyond surprise by now, but the news drove an unnerving terror through his heart such as no amount of lashing and not even promise of the rack could arouse. He fought back tears. To combat the terror that threatened to engulf him, he fell back on an old strategy that had served him well growing up in the hostile environment of Jersey City. He replaced fear with rage.

Look hard or look down!

He met Bellarmino's gaze with a ferocity that widened the scholar's eyes. The Inquisitor smiled.

"Leave us," he said to his notary. The man closed his ledger and left. "You also," he said to the tormentor who followed the notary.

When they were alone, the Cardinal Inquisitor came around from behind the table and approached Rick. Bellarmino was not short, but stretched as he was upon his toes, Rick looked down on the scarlet skullcap that covered his tonsure.

The Cardinal's gaze bored into his eyes. Rick felt himself fading again, as if the news of his death by fire wasn't fearful enough to keep him awake. But then a new terror blossomed in his brain. As addled as his senses were, it took him a moment to comprehend the mystery he was seeing. Bellarmino's eyes were brown and condemning, but the eyes before him were a pale, icy blue and were twinkling with a cruel irony totally devoid of humor.

He blinked.

And now he no longer looked down on the Grand Inquisitor but up.

Bellarmino was gone. The being that stood before him was tall. At least seven feet. And broad-shouldered.

The skull cap still perched on his head, but the moon-pale scalp was bald—not cropped or shaven—but utterly hairless. As was the long face and the ridges over the cold blue eyes and the eyelids themselves.

Grigori!

Now that he knew what he was facing, he discerned among the dungeon's putrid reeks the serpent smell endemic to the race of angels. Involuntarily, his skin crawled with atavistic repulsion.

"I know what you are!" he said, his flight-or-fight response returning a little of his strength. Given the bizarre turns his life had taken in recent years, he wasn't too surprised to learn he wasn't merely a victim of circumstances, of being in the wrong place at the wrong time, of being mistaken for a warlock because he fell not from the sky but out of time. He remembered the sensation of being wrenched from the trajectory that was speeding him home. There was premeditation at work here. He had fallen into a trap.

"You're not Talmaiel."

"Talmaiel? Is he still around?" No longer was the Inquisitor's voice that of Bellarmino but had transformed along with his appearance into something deeper and entirely more sinister. "No, I am not Talmaiel. I was ancient long before Talmaiel was born."

"But you and your breed were stopped. I sent you back to the Abyss myself."

He remembered the whirlwind surrounding them when he faced Talmaiel atop Crystal Mountain. Remembered standing in the eye of the storm with the midnight sky irising open, admitting alien stars that weren't stars at all but the Shining Ones, the Fallen Watchers, sent to shepherd man, then banished by their Maker when they fell like wolves upon the flock.

The creature gave Rick an appraising look. "Did you indeed? Perhaps the Maker is justified in wanting to see you dead."

"Maker? Yaldabaoth?"

The Grigori smiled. "He promised me a world. All I need do is kill you."

Kill me? Was it possible the Demiurge had taken a personal interest in him?

You're the only one that has the remotest chance of stopping Yaldabaoth.

He envisioned a great eye staring down from the heavens, watching his every move. Only the eye he imagined wasn't human but the great slit-pupiled eye of a serpent. Or dragon.

"Yaldabaoth is the father of lies," he said. "He is recalling everything. The universe. All time and space. There will be no world for you."

"He is the Maker," the Grigori said with a shrug. "He can make me a world. You, however, cannot save this one." He waved a long white hand as if to say *No matter.* "If I must choose—and I must—I choose a god over a man."

Rick was too tired to argue. His body was a white-hot fireball of pain. He desired sleep. No, oblivion. *If I am to burn in the morning, please let me not wake!* But something Dee said at the Embassy drifted into his consciousness.

"'Earthly Man is a mortal God, and Heavenly God is an immortal Man.'"

The hairless brows lifted. The thin blue lips stretched in an ironic smile. "You debate with me? A Cardinal of the Holy Roman Church, professor of theology, Rector of the Roman College and Inquisitor General?"

"You are none of those!" Rick spat, impatient to end this. "You are an abomination!"

"Nevertheless, your world will end while mine begins."

"With a population of one? What use is a world with no one to share it? You'll go mad. Help me defeat him."

The Grigori's smile broadened. "Help you? You cannot help yourself. No, Richard Scott. In the morning you will burn. Your world will end and mine begin."

37

ABANDONED

A shout broke his concentration.

The light vehicle continued its descent, but Talmaiel, startled, turned to see his worst fear realized as Semjaza and a horde of gaunt Grigori swarmed out of the fortress onto the rampart. Semjaza's eyes blazed with fury, his mouth a slash of anger across his broad face.

The Merkaba came on. It would reach the rampart in moments— moments they didn't have.

"Seize them!" Semjaza's rumbling bass thundered above the keening wind. A dozen Grigori charged across the ice.

"Go!" Raziel shoved him toward the Merkaba. "I'll hold them!"

Thin though he was and debilitated from Semjaza's feeding, Raziel spread his arms and flung himself into the Grigori charge. Two went down under the blue angel's assault, but others pinned him to the ice.

The ground vibrated beneath Talmaiel's feet as the Merkaba touched down behind him. The wind off the whirling, counter-rotating pyramids blew his rags out before him. For a moment, he considered leaping into the Merkaba and willing it away from Abyss and the insane wraiths assembled before him, abandoning Raziel to whatever cruelty Semjaza had in store—but only for a moment. Before he could contemplate the consequences of his actions, he rushed Raziel's captors. In an instant he was among them, hurling his weaker brethren aside, reaching for Raziel, who stared up from the ice.

A hand grabbed him by the shoulder and flung him back. He hit the ice hard, skidded to a halt against the parapet.

Semjaza loomed over him. His broad, well-fed bulk blocked the sky. Recalling the feeding he'd witnessed in the hall, Talmaiel raised a shielding arm.

"You can wait!" Semjaza roared in Talmaiel's face. Drawing his great sword, he turned to Raziel, who struggled in the grasp of four Grigori.

Understanding what was in store, the Artificer increased his efforts.

"Hold him!" Semjaza barked.

The Grigori stretched the blue angel's arms wide as if they intended to pull them out of their sockets. Raziel writhed in their grip, his feet slipping on ice.

Semjaza raised the sword over his shoulder—and brought it round in a sweeping arc. The blade severed Raziel's neck. A spray of blood dashed across the nearest brethren. The head hit the ice, spun, came to rest on its ear.

Grigori do not die easily. Inconvenienced certainly, but short of a plunge into a sun's blazing heart or a nuclear explosion, not killed. Raziel's headless body fought against his captors as they rushed it to the parapet, and his eyes watched in horror from their low vantage as they flung him over.

"NO!"

Talmaiel rushed to the parapet and watched the Artificer's living corpse flail until it disappeared into the mist.

"RUN!" Raziel shouted.

Talmaiel spun. More of the Two Hundred were charging him. He grabbed the first and flung the creature, arms windmilling, over the parapet after Raziel's body. The others, seeing the danger of attacking one who still maintained his earth-given strength, backed off. Talmaiel stood by Raziel's head, fists doubled, glaring at the circling Choir, daring them to try him.

The Grigori circled warily.

Samael and Asmodai, better clothed and in better health than the rest, started forward.

"Leave him!" Semjaza shouted. "Leave them both. Let the coward savor Abyss' hospitality."

The Grigori withdrew. And he watched as they filed out of the fortress and into the whirring Merkaba, as if the interior of the light vehicle were greater than its exterior. Finally, only Semjaza with his bloody sword stood between him and the Merkaba.

"Your lot is to keep what's left of the Artificer and Kokabiel company. Perhaps we'll come back for you. Some day." The giant's sneer told him it wouldn't happen. "Tell me, all those centuries you walked among the teeming millions you spoke of, man proliferating the earth, and you failed to drink your fill? To make yourself a god among them? You do not deserve the earth, coward. We will make of it a paradise—but not for humans."

He turned and entered the light vehicle. The Merkaba rose into the howling wind and, pulsing blue fire, passed through the star gate that closed behind it.

38

TIME TO DIE

Rick woke into what seemed like a dream.

He remembered...two guards dragging him down a narrow passage...being shoved into a cell. He was unconscious as soon as his face hit the straw-covered floor.

He woke hovering just beneath the ceiling looking down on his naked bloody body. Seeing his condition, he groaned. Da Silva's watch lost, his arms useless, his strength sapped, his physical body soon to be reduced to ashes.

When the physical body perished, his astral body would cease to exist.

Rick.

Reginald! I've lost the watch. Soon they will burn me.

He fought back tears, let anger shove aside the fear crowding his mind. But what use was anger without someone to vent it on? Holding anger in led to frustration, which was as debilitating as fear.

I don't see any way out.

There is another way.

What way? I'm whipped. I'm too weak to stand, let alone break down the door, find the Grigori, and take the watch back.

You'll heal quickly. Her gift. But your body needs rest.

Rest? They'll come to take me to the stake, maybe any minute now. I have no idea how long I've been unconscious.

Calm down.

I am calm. He gritted his teeth. *He knew my name. The Grigori—who is he?*

I told you about him once. He is Azazel. He was the leader of the Grigori and it was he who led them into rebellion against Yaldabaoth. For his great wickedness, or so the story goes, he alone of the Watchers was singled out for special punishment. Where the Avengers cast Semjaza and the two hundred into the Abyss, Raphael bound and buried Azazel in a pit beneath the fiery desert of Dudael. It seems Yaldabaoth has struck a bargain with him.

But the Demiurge is not to be trusted, is he?

No. But if you were on a sinking ship would you not clutch at an oar if it was offered? Da Silva paused before continuing. *And yes, it seems the Demiurge has singled you out for special consideration. But come, we must hurry.*

Don't I know that? Soon I'll be reduced to ashes and I'll cease to exist.

I'm not talking about the auto-da-fé, the Priest said.

What then?

The hounds.

Hounds?

The Tindalosi. creatures who exist in the angles of time. They caught your scent. They are seeking you now. If—when—they find you, an auto will be the least of your worries.

Separated from his body, Rick did not feel physical pain, but his mind reeled with conflicting emotions and the seriousness of his plight. Grigori. Burning at the stake. A demigod wanting him dead. Was there still another danger to deal with?

Seeing his confusion, da Silva continued. *Hounds, jackals, vampires of the void. These are just convenient words to describe them. They truly are otherworldly. They dwell in a plane contiguous to the physical universe and the astral but separate. Our universe is non-Euclidean, meaning straight lines and angles are rare. While theirs is a starless, empty void. An abstraction, though real. Like a mathematical world of Euclidean lines and planes and mind-bending angles through which they course, always hunting.*

Legend has it they are soul-eaters—which is half-right: for what is the soul but the consciousness of the divine light of emanation involving into man and evolving back to the spiritual plane upon the perishing of the flesh. How could they — lurking in the infecund waste of their lightless dimension — not hunger for the light within us?

A nightmare vision from his recent past rose like an unsheeted corpse. One that often visited his restless nights. The face of the girl he found in the bathtub the evening he and Mack responded to the call out by the University of Memphis. Her forehead and nose sagged inward as if her bone structure had gone soft. Her teeth were bared in a rictus, her eyes wide with the terror she experienced at the moment of her death. As he stood over the girl, the creature had emerged from the wall, its obscenely long, vaguely man-like head towering above him, its talons reaching, evil emanating from its shadow flesh like stench off rotten meat.

Like the Nephilim.

Yes, da Silva agreed. *Like the Nephilim.*

If the...

Tindalosi.

If they are alien, why are they called hounds?

Because once they catch your scent, nothing stops them from hunting you down.

But if they exist in a Euclidian environment, how can they pursue their victims into our universe?

Because even in our curvilinear world, there are exceptions where straight lines and angles are the rule. Snowflakes, crystals...

Rick looked about the tiny cell, the flat square planes of its walls, the angles of its corners. *Man is fond of straight lines and angles.*

Precisamente. They may access their quarry through any angle. Plenty of angles here. All they need is one. Now come. We must hurry.

He looked down at his sleeping self. *I can't leave my body.*

You will not. I transported not only myself but Tempus Fugit.

That was true. At different times the horologist had operated out of London, Vienna, Montreal, and, most recently, Memphis, Tennessee, and with every move his ancient clock shop miraculously appeared overnight where some vacant storefront stood the day before.

But you had your watch.

I had much more than that. Now so have you.

Rick understood. *The Priesthood.*

Your brothers now. You are not alone. And the combined willpower of six hundred twenty-one Rex Nemorenses is no inconsiderable thing.

He remembered the long-nosed priest in Dee's showstone telling him not to be afraid and that the Brotherhood was there to help.

And I need all the help I can get.

Exactly. But hurry.

But Bruno and Dee… I left them to the mob. We've got to help them.

There is no time. Now hurry!

Gentle, invisible hands assisted him as he rose through the ceiling and found himself in a spacious hall or gallery with a frescoed ceiling, then he passed through upper, luxuriously appointed apartments that were poles apart from the pestilential dungeons and cells that lay beneath the Holy House. Then he was through the roof and looking down on the Palace. The Inquisition lay in the shadow of the Vatican. Saint Peter's Square spread below, and in the near distance the dome of the Basilica rose against the turgid sky. But he had no time for sightseeing.

Close your eyes and imagine yourself on the astral plane.

As recent as yesterday, he would have resisted da Silva; now trust was his only hope for salvation. He closed his eyes and imagined the Sephiroth blazing above him, each of the ten Sephirah a brilliant blue star. Now he stood on Malkuth, the Kingdom of the lowly physical plane, and gently pushed off as a swimmer might from the bottom of a pool and rose along the glowing path that led to Yesod, the gateway to Hod and Netzah, Intellect and Emotion, and on to Tiferet, which balanced Chesed and Gevurah, Compassion and Discipline. Beyond Tiferet lay an Abyss separating the lower Astral planes from the Supernal Triangle, a chasm in consciousness that separated the knowable from the unknowable.

Opening his eyes, he found himself in a gray void. There were no stars or planets to mark distance, no up or down, nor any visible horizon, and no way to tell if the limbo in which he found himself extended more than a few feet or stretched to infinity.

Do you know what a Cartesian grid is? da Silva asked.

Rick rummaged through the unruly storage bin of his memories. He was going to have to build himself a memory palace like Bruno's one of these days. If he made it out of the Inquisition alive.

Something like graph paper.

Bem. *Now imagine the lines on your graph paper in three dimensions, so that instead of just height and width, you also have depth. And instead of squares, you now have cubes.*

Rick did so. All around him, stretching into a multiplicity of vanishing points, brilliant blue threads gridded the universe near and far. Despite the desperateness of his situation and the immediacy of the twin dangers of the auto and the hounds, he thrilled at the sight.

It's beautiful.

Da Silva ignored the comment, hurried on. *This is the Cartesian coordinate grid. It has dominated architecture and city planning since Rene published* La Géométrie *in 1637. We could use it, but it's too dangerous. Notice the planes and angles of its cubes.*

Your hounds could move freely here.

Precisamente. *We must hurry. I want you to bend the straight lines of your grid so that they curve around you in a sphere.*

Rick did so. The dazzling blue lines bent over and under and around him so that he floated in the center of a vast sphere of glowing blue threads. From his vantage, the lines still looked straight, but they bulged away from him like lines of longitude and latitude on a globe. Again, he thrilled at the sight and basked in the power flowing from his astral form.

This is a curvilinear or spherical coordinate system and conforms to non-Euclidian space, which is hostile to the Tindalosi.

In the physical world, da Silva continued, *a distant object is perceived only if it is in line of sight and is reached by motion and the passage of time, while, on the astral plane—where ideas formed in the mental world are transformed by desire into the objects of the physical world—a distant object does not have to be in line of sight to be seen and no passage of time is required to reach it. Rather, the astral traveler need only hold in his mind's eye an image of what he wishes to see or some talismanic symbol of who or what or where— a palm tree and a scent of sea breeze and a remembered or imagined crescent of sandy beach or the curve of a beloved's neck and the scent of her perfume inflaming the night or a certain arrangement of constellations prescribing the coordinates of a mountain, desert, or moon in a particular season —and transform desire by focusing it into a laser beam of intent, and voilà, destination reached. The invisible made visible. The passage complete.*

As simple as that?

He sensed a hundred smiles. *Not so simple. But we can do it. Picture some feature of your apartment.*

He imagined his kitchen, the green-and-white squares of the linoleum floor, the white Formica and chrome table he and Fergi purchased from the used furniture store. He moved into the bedroom, saw the bed he'd shared with her before she'd been spirited off to serve the Goddess. The bed was messy. He'd gotten lazy and only pulled the comforter over his pillow anymore. He imagined the smell of her hair, the soft sound of her breathing. He was tired. He desired only to lie down in their bed—if not beside her, then next to the memory of her.

A dazzling blue point appeared far off down one of the myriad avenues of coordinates. He focused on the vector, and imagining the scent of Fergi's hair, reached for it.

He jolted awake, soaked and shivering. The straw on which he lay was wet. A guard stood at the door of his cell, bucket in hand. A second guard behind him.

"Get up, warlock," the bucket-wielding guard growled. "Time to die."

39

WE ARE IN SYMPATHY

Talmaiel sat on the ice, his back against the parapet, Raziel's head beside him. Already the blood pooled around the Artificer's neck was frozen to the rampart, preventing the wind from sending the head tumbling. The rust-colored clouds above were an angry sea, an unbroken tide rushing from horizon to horizon.

"All is lost," he lamented, speaking as much to himself as to Raziel.

Raziel frowned. It was disconcerting to see the head expressing such normal reactions without a body to support it.

"Are you always this negative?"

"*What?*"

"You live. I live. Do you give up so easily?"

"But the Merkaba… The train has left the station." He didn't care if Raziel got the reference; he'd understand the gist.

"So what? Call it back."

"'Call it back'? The Sephiroth—the *Sefir Raziel*—is gone." Another setback occurred to him. "And the stone we made that summoned the Merkaba—it's gone as well."

"It's in my pocket."

Talmaiel stared at the head in disbelief.

"Yes, and your pocket is hundreds of leagues below. And yes, I can climb down and retrieve it. Will probably have to. And, *maybe*, if I don't collapse and end up buried in ice for what's left of eternity, I could climb back up. Do you want me to retrieve your body while I'm at it?"

The head tried to nod, but frozen to the ice shelf, could only dip its nose. "I *would* like that—very much. But there's no need to climb down."

Talmaiel regarded Raziel doubtfully. "You've got an ace up your sleeve?"

"An ace up my…?"

"A better plan."

"I do. Just as talismans are receptacles for storing the sidereal influences of stars, so my Book, the Sephiroth, of which the whole is greater than any single member, has not only stored the power of the stars and the wisdom of the eternal, but is imprinted with my mind. We are in sympathy."

"You're talking about sympathetic vibrations again?"

"I am. And now that I have used the sapphire we transformed to call the Sephiroth, it is in harmony with the ten."

"But it's still hundreds of leagues below us."

"Distance doesn't matter, especially a few hundred leagues. Did we not summon the Merkaba across time and space?"

Talmaiel sat up, a sudden buoyancy uplifting him. He hoped Raziel wasn't suffering delusions stemming from the beheading.

"We did." A trace of a smile hitched a corner of his blackened lips. "What now?"

"Kokabiel?" Raziel struggled to look over a non-existent shoulder at the fortress door behind him.

Talmaiel felt as much as heard the astrologer's response. *Yes?*

"Will you help us again?"

Whatever I can.

The light chariot was waiting when Talmaiel emerged from the fortress. At Raziel's request, he'd ridden the Merkaba to the valley below and fetched his broken body and laid it and the Artificer's head in the great hall beside the column in which Kokabiel's brain resided.

"I'm a lot more likely to heal if my head's attached," Raziel had reasoned. As much as he'd like to have the Artificer accompany him to Earth, he couldn't argue with his logic. Even with Kokabiel's influence, the healing process would take decades. Time they didn't have. He'd offered to use the *Sefir Raziel* to speed his companion's recovery, but Raziel had countered what good would it do to be whole only to vanish with the imploding universe. Against such impeccable logic there was no argument. Talmaiel felt a pressing urgency. He had to get back to Earth. Deprived of human blood for millennia, Semjaza and the Choir would cut a bloody swath that would encircle the planet.

Above the rampart, the ruddy clouds whirled in a vast vortex, a towering funnel that bored through the atmosphere oblivious to the planet's winds, opening not on a starry field of constellations but on utter blackness.

Squinting against the methane snowflakes battering his face, he took a last look at Abyss. Though the cold did not affect him, he shivered. He would not miss the bleak and unvarying sameness of the frozen world.

With an excitement he'd thought gone forever and with visions of Earth's moonlit nights and summer grass, her familiar constellations burning over a calm sea, and green valleys spread below him dancing in his head, he stepped into the Merkaba.

The light vehicle rose from the rampart and passed into the portal.

40
AUTO-DA-FÉ

They bound him to the stake and he was naked under the sick yellow sky.

From his elevated vantage, Rick looked over the *Campo de' Fiori*, the Field of Flowers, a combination marketplace and execution site. There were no flowers or field. The square was paved with cobbles and surrounded by many stately buildings. A crowd filled the piazza to celebrate an *auto-da-fé* and watch the wizard that had brought terror to the Eternal City burn.

Summoned from their homes by the ringing of cathedral bells, the citizenry had lined the *Via Papale* to watch the procession. Clad in the *Sambenito*, a sulfur-yellow tunic painted with flames and devils, the flames pointing upward, signifying that he was unrepentant and, therefore, to be burned alive rather than receive the mercy of the garrote, Rick had been tied to the mule that carried him to his doom. At the square, exhausted and distraught, his arms all but useless, he'd been taken down, stripped of the holy sack cloth, and bound to the stake. Wood was piled to his chest.

Below and around the unlit pyre, the black-robed lay brothers of the Confraternity of Saint John the Beheaded alternately sang litanies and exhorted him to confess his heresies so that he could be spared the horror of being burnt alive. Two of the comforters held aloft a painting of the Crucifixion, the anguished image of the Savior likewise imploring him to confess his sins. Not that he could—his jailers had

191

stopped his speech with a leather gag before handing him over to the secular authorities.

Close by, representatives of religious and secular authority were seated on a long, raised scaffold. Cardinal Bellarmino, his resplendent scarlet robes flapping in the wind, presided over the celebration. He stood on the stage, his height equal to Rick's, and pronounced the heretic's sentence to the sea of upturned faces. No doubt the populace saw a prince of the Church, the Inquisitor General, while he alone saw the angel Azazel.

Despite the constant adrenal surge of terror, Rick's attention faded in and out so that he was only dimly aware of the roar of heated discussion among the Nemorenses in his head and Azazel's powerful voice rolling over the assembly.

"...by the authority invested in me by the Holy See...do hereby pass judgment on you, Ricardus Scottus, for the errors of practicing witchcraft in direct disobedience of scripture and church and for the heresy of refusing to acknowledge your error before the holy tribunal in direct contradiction of the evidence of the witnesses of your infernal acts..."

He closed his eyes and drifted.

"...having been found guilty by this Holy Office, and that having undergone questioning and given ample opportunities to recant, you chose not to do so but persevered in constancy..."

Sleep...welcome sleep enfolding him...

"...your unwavering rejection of the Roman Pontiff's authority..."
Rick, wake up! You must leave! Now! Hurry!
Reginald's voice called him back.
But he was tired, drifting.

"...have consequently incurred all the censures and penalties imposed upon such unremittent heretics by the Sacred Canons, laws, and constitutions, general as well as special..."
RICK!

"...do hereby proclaim that you, Ricardus Scottus, shall be committed to the judgment of the flames and burned alive in the presence of the people..."
RICK! WAKE UP!

Panic gripped him as he snapped awake.

Reginald?

Thank the Goddess! Hurry! We must leave! Now!

But he was in the throes of panic. Blood pounded his temples, his heart raced. The world blurred in and out of focus.

"May God have Mercy on your soul. Amen."

"Amen," murmured the collective response of clergy and citizenry as Azazel crossed himself, and the lay brothers again took up their litanies. The painting of the Crucifixion flapped in the wind, sending ripples through the Savior's admonishing face.

At a nod from Bellarmino, the civil executioner, dressed in black, came forward with a torch and thrust it among the faggots. The fire took, and immediately the crackle of burning wood reached Rick's ears and smoke rose into his nostrils. The torch was thrust low into the pyre to prolong the spectacle, but within moments his feet and legs felt the heat and he squirmed against his ropes trying to pull away from the flames. Panic beat in his throat as the painted Jesus flapped in the wind. If he passed out now, all would be lost. The flames would consume him.

The heat grew unbearable. He writhed, picturing the flesh of his legs blackening and splitting open, his blood bubbling and sizzling as it streamed into the flames. The smoke burned his eyes. He could hardly breathe.

His gaze fell upon the accusing eyes of the painted Christ, and his wandering mind screamed for him to confess, to beg the mercy of strangulation, a quick death, anything but the torment of the flames eating his flesh. But his mouth was gagged.

His gaze wandered upward to the intersection of cross staves just above Christ's right ear.

Angles…

Despite the heat and his panic, he squeezed his eyes shut to remember.

The Tindalosi, creatures who exist in the angles of time.

He stared at the angle made by the vertical and horizontal beams of the cross.

They may access their quarry through any angle.

He tried pursing his lips to whistle, but the gag prevented him. If only he could call the hounds.

The timestream ran through the astral as well as the physical. If he projected a mental whistle across the astral plane, they might hear it and come. He willed a mental whistle into the timestream.

To his surprise, the whistle came through his pursed lips. The gag was gone. His hands were free. Without realizing he could lift his arm, he had put two fingers to his lips and blew a blast that silenced the crowd and drew all eyes to him.

Somewhere in time, the Tindalosi stiffens. The crystalline spikes on its back bristle like the neck fur of a challenged wolf.

It takes the creature only a moment to locate the source of the sound. Its many necks writhe as it sniffs, recognizing its quarry. In the dim corridors of its primitive brain, the beast sees the gleaming star that had shot across its vision.

Athirst, it leaps across the timestream, its brethren at its heels.

Through the curtain of smoke, Rick saw other smoke curling from the painting of the Crucifixion—from the intersection of vertical and transverse beams.

The flames of his pyre bent away from his body as desire—*need*—fueled his will, pushed out in a wave. The air thrummed, as if with the beating of dragons' wings. The earth trembled. Burning kindling rained down on the brothers who backed away. A collective gasp rose from the crowd. The spectators nearest the pyre turned to flee from whatever the sorcerer-heretic had conjured, but there was nowhere to go. So dense was the crowd that those retreating ran into a wall of humanity.

On the scaffold, doubt creased the Grigori's brow, but Rick did not mark the shadow that blighted the tall hairless head. His gaze was intent on the crucifix.

Something was forming in the smoke issuing from the angle of the cross, fantastic visions of animated shapes, constant movement, a working and reworking of lines, planes, and eye-wrenching angles. Like some cubist animation sped up so that it was more a stroboscopic flickering of impressions than a clear delineation of line and form. Great angular heads, vaguely wolf-like but with gnashing, scythe-like teeth. Lashing tails. Backs writhing with spikes like knife-edged quills. The whole rippling like a reflection in water on a windy day. A flashing, ever-changing kaleidoscope of impressions. A stench billowed across the piazza, the reek of brimstone and burning dung and ammonia laced with the tang of hot molten metal and the choking effluvia of the alchemist's lair.

Pandemonium erupted as the hounds fell upon the Confraternity of Saint John the Beheaded. Scything maws opened, closed. Blood arced through the smoky air. Like the thudding of arrows finding their targets, the sound of tubular tongues punching through the brothers' bodies was audible over the crowd's rising screams.

Tearing his attention from the spectacle, Rick stared at the angle from which the creatures had emerged and willed himself to pass back through the portal they had opened before it closed or they turned their attention on him.

Reginald! He commanded, and with that word summoned the combined will of the six hundred twenty-one Rex Nemorenses pledged to assist him.

41

AZAZEL DISCRETELY TAKES HIS LEAVE

From his vantage atop the scaffold, Azazel clenched his fists.

The boy was gone! He'd slipped out from under his nose. And unleashed the hounds.

The Tind'losi. They were old, perhaps older than he. Legend whispered they had existed before the beginning. He had never met them and had no desire to do so now. All creatures wrought by the Maker from the divine light were food for the Time Wraiths.

They were feasting among the Confraternity and the crowd who had taken up positions closest to the pyre to get the best view of the auto. The Campo was in chaos: priests, citizens, constabulary fled screaming, madness in their eyes. Those who could not move fast enough were trampled beneath the crowd.

Below the scaffold was a montage of unfurling tubular tongues, gnashing razor teeth, questing acid-dripping mouths—all driven by a rapacious, unquenchable hunger. Steaming blue spittle sizzled on the cobbles, sending up puffs of smoke.

Discretely, the demon Azazel stepped into the timestream and left the populace to the hounds.

42

OUTRAGEOUS ANGLES

Rick floated in a void. There were no stars, no nebulae, no gray shore curving along a dead and primordial sea, only a close, suffocating darkness and the stench of the hounds.

He was in their lair.

To which they would return once glutted.

Dark as it was, he saw surfaces. His eyes—his brain—hurt to look at them. Try as he may, they would not come into focus and kept shifting. Near and far were meaningless. There was no horizon, no vanishing point. What seemed a plane extending toward some unseen infinity the next moment seemed an outrageous angle racing toward him. It was as if he were trapped in a complex geometrical equation to which there was no solution.

Reginald?

We can't stay here, Rick. You know what to do.

He did. He recalled the dazzling blue longitudinal and latitudinal lines of the curvilinear grid surrounding him as if he were enclosed in a gridded sphere. He imagined his kitchen again, the linoleum floor, the table and chairs he and Fergi had purchased. The lines around one curvilinear square grew brighter while the rest dimmed. Within the glowing square, a brilliant blue point of light appeared. As intense as one of Raziel's sapphires glowing in the psychotronic generator.

It seemed so far away. Impossibly distant.

But he remembered:

...no passage of time is required...the astral traveler need only hold in his mind's eye an image of what he wishes to see—a palm tree...a scent of sea breeze...

...transform desire by focusing it into a laser beam of intent, and voilà...

He held in his mind's eye the picture of the chrome-and-Formica table where he and Fergi had shared many pleasant breakfasts and suppers. His heart swelled with desire.

And suddenly a curving path lighted the way through the great globe, and he was hurtling across light years of space-time that would have taken lifetimes to traverse were he not traveling at the speed of thought.

43
SPREAD THE WORD

Hendricks, Arkansas, population 87, was an unincorporated hamlet nestled beside a lake in a long, narrow valley deep in Western Arkansas' Ouachita Range. The mountains on either side formed long ridges. Their flinty crests dappled with scrub oak thrust out of the pines that cloaked their steep slopes. The local group of the Ouachitas were called the Crystal Mountains and Crystal Mountain was also the name of the long ridge that overlooked the hamlet. Within its granite heart resided vast deposits of quartz crystal. During major thunderstorms, Hendricks' more sensitive citizens felt the piezoelectric effects of the crystals' excitation. Some claimed the crystals were alive and when the internal vibrations of their lattices attuned to the vibrations of the storm, their voices were heard by other crystal populations around the world. Geologists from the United States Geological Survey using seismometers determined the subterranean deposit one of the most extensive in the world and speculated that some of the crystals might be taller than a man. The nearest "big city" was Mount Ida, population 1,005, the county seat of Montgomery County, known as the "Quartz Crystal Capital of the World."

The hamlet itself was little more than a grid of dirt roads and a few dozen neat double-wides, most with porches decked out with rocking chairs and potted plants, nestled among pines on half-acre lots, the exception being the church, a triple-wide sporting a white fiberglass steeple purchased online and installed at the congregation's expense.

There was no cross atop the steeple and the church was more meeting place than house of worship, though its sanctuary did feature a big pentangle of woven willow wands on the wall behind the lectern instead of a crucifix, the pentangle being the Goddess' symbol.

The settlement had a zip code but the postal service dropped off the residents' mail at the General Store several miles up the road. The hamlet did have a mailman of sorts, however, in the person of Darryl Givens, who picked up the mail Mondays and Thursdays and delivered it to his neighbors. Hendricks was the kind of place where everybody knew everybody and everybody contributed. Larry Longacre oiled the road as needed, and Wanda Frances baked cookies for the Little League, and Beatrice Joanna and her dad Bob Bevens operated a radio station out of the pole barn behind their house, keeping in touch with the other Kybele communities around the world.

Reverend Grace and John Hanley were making the rounds, advising the populace to come to the war council in the church. John was driving his camo Kawasaki Mule with his deer rifle in the overhead gun rack. Reverend Grace rode shotgun. Every block or so— block being a stretch of road—John stopped and folks would come out and congregate about the UV and Reverend Grace would tell them to meet at the church and ask what they'd heard, if anything. As she suspected, the hamlet's several Sisters with the "gift" hadn't picked up anything and were worried about their sight's sudden blackout. The few gifted males, who would have been called warlocks in earlier times, expressed concern over the same problem. It was vexing to be reduced to depending on mass communications for news like the bulk of Earth's population. Even worse since their rural patch had lost Internet, phone service, and electricity during the night. The sound of generators running behind the houses was louder than bullfrogs croaking in mating season.

"Whaddya hear, Reverend?" Paul Farley asked, removing his John Deere cap and mopping his face with his handkerchief. The white of his forehead above the brim contrasted sharply with the red of his creased neck. A big man in overalls, he'd come from chainsawing firewood behind his house and his sweaty arms were dusted with sawdust. Despite the coolness of the nights, midday in late April was hot and humid.

"Azazel's been turned loose," Grace said to the group.

"And apparently—and we have this on good authority—the Grigori are scheduled to make an appearance," John added.

Paul and his neighbors, Carolyn Sublette and Philander Key, raised eyebrows and exchanged glances. They knew "good authority" meant the Sisterhood.

"On top of the end of the world." Elsa Newhouse, sister-in-law to Agnes Goode, the church's piano lady who had died the night of the attack on Hendricks, looked up at the long ridge looming against the brooding yellow clouds where the Lady's paladin had confronted the Grigori Talmaiel. She wasn't questioning, merely bemoaning an addition to the already considerable trouble facing the planet. The others followed her gaze, remembering the last time a Grigori graced their presence.

"Come to the church. Four o'clock," Grace said, breaking the mood. She motioned John to move on. "Spread the word," she called over her shoulder as the UV sped off.

44

LA LUMIERE SORTANT DES TINEBRES

His eyes opened.

The curvilinear grid had disappeared. In its place was a 2-D Cartesian grid, parallel rows of squares receding away from him as if he was looking across a plane from an oblique angle.

Angles.

His heart fluttered. The angles would draw the hounds.

But the squares were green and white, and a chrome table leg rose nearby.

He'd made it home.

He closed his eyes and pressed his hand gratefully against the cold linoleum of his kitchen floor, remembering...

The heat of advancing flames...

The hounds feeding...

He shivered with the cold that crept over him like a damp draft.

He barked a laugh. Better cold than watching your legs turn to charred sticks. Even the laugh produced a fresh wrack of pain. His back was a screaming agony.

He tried to sit up, but his arms gave out, so he lay on his side and took stock of his naked body. He was blackened with soot, his legs were tender as if he'd been badly sunburnt, and he smelled of wood smoke, sweat, and blood.

And fear!

The sour reek rose off him like corruption off spoiled meat.

Tears welled in his eyes. His body shook uncontrollably.

It's all right, Rick. You're alive.

But I failed!

Can you get up?

He made it to a sitting position, but couldn't get his legs under him to stand. His back was on fire. He remembered the lashing.

Let us help you.

He heard a murmur of voices, consoling, urging, and felt a strength flow through him as if he'd drank some healing nectar. He staggered to the refrigerator and downed half a container of orange juice. He carried the container to the table, sat in a kitchen chair, and looked out the window.

The day was fading toward evening and the sickly yellow sky was bloodshot with red the color of clotted blood. The Pizzeria across the street with its defective neon sign that pulsed across the kitchen ceiling was gone, along with a row of three-story tenements. In their place a string of small clapboard homes on small lots, most with a vegetable garden and an outhouse in back.

He shook his head. He took the orange juice with him into the bathroom and ran cool water in the tub. It would be some time before he could stand heat. While the water ran, he examined himself in the mirror over the sink. He looked as if he'd crawled out of an alley after a mugging. But his back—still crisscrossed with livid scarlet welts—was healing. The Goddess' gift at work.

Settling into the bath, he winced as his back touched the fiberglass. He gritted his teeth until searing pain subsided into a sustained ache.

"It was all real, wasn't it? No dream?"

It was real.

And you?

I'm here.

So killing you wasn't a dream either?

Technically, you didn't kill me but only helped me escape my body.

Why?

So I could assist you.

Some help. You led me on a wild goose chase. A waste of time you said we didn't have.

203

It wasn't all a waste. An education comes in many forms. There are classrooms and there are classrooms.

Education?

Nothing like putting one's feet to the fire to spur one into action.

As always, funny as a crutch.

Paracelsus claimed there are two types of knowledge: that concocted by our own cleverness and that gained by experience. He commended the latter.

Experience almost got me killed.

Ah, but you mastered astral travel without mechanical aid.

By necessity. Probably couldn't do it again unless my life depended on it.

Not at all. Something is waking inside you, Rick. You are embracing your destiny.

Bullshit!

A mental headshake. *Sem besteira.*

Rick paused to think. Unwilling to slide his back down the tub to submerge himself, he poured water over his head with his hands. The bath water looked like a hospital pan after washing a wound.

What about your Philosopher's Stone? Even Paracelsus seemed pretty vague as to what it is.

Then you weren't listening.

Huh? He squeezed his eyes shut, tried to remember. *He said the Stone was nothing less than the attainment of complete self-awareness and of the higher consciousness. I remember thinking at the time that sounded a lot like what you said about the evolution of consciousness.*

So you were listening but not understanding.

His temper was short and he wanted to snap at the Priest, but he thought about the physician's words. Attainment...self-awareness...

Attaining self-awareness, a higher consciousness, is a transformative act. Go on.

The one thing I've gathered is that the Stone is about transformation. And?

His eyes widened as he heard a mental finger snap. *The Stone is a metaphor for transformation.*

He sensed the Nemorian's smile.

And gold. Gold's a metaphor too. For—what?

The philosophers say there are three kinds of gold. The common metal gold, which you can purchase. Then there is elementary gold, believed by the ancients to be the purest of all elements, the one element compared to which all others are impurities and which it was the alchemist's quest to extract. The most perfect gold of the physical world. All living beings are said to have this fire within them. Some say elemental gold is the Philosopher's Stone and the end of the Great Work. La Lumière sortant des Ténèbres. *The light emanating from the darkness. The true heavenly gold, the light emanating from the Ein Sof. Some equate this gold with consciousness, the goal of evolution. Without its influence, man would be without spirit and would truly see for all eternity through a glass darkly.*

Finally, there is astral gold, the fiery gold emanated by the rays of the sun and from all the planets which we absorb. We breathe this astral gold. It permeates our brains, stimulates our thoughts. This is the astrological gold magicians sought to animate their statues and infuse their potions. The gold of correspondences. As above, so below. The astral gold is the source of life, of spirit, of imagination. Without it man is truly an automaton, born to eat and shit and procreate and die and nothing more. But with it, by understanding it and opening himself up to its influence and channeling it, to what ends man might attain.

Rick sensed the shrug, the whimsical smile.

So alchemy is all about metaphor, allegory?

Alchemy gave us the roots of chemistry, modern metallurgy, pharmacology. But to your point—yes, it's best to think of alchemy as a language. A language that expresses the correspondences Paracelsus spoke of.

Between the celestial and the physical.

Yes.

Rick heard Dee's professorial monotone: *...the conjunction of celestial powers with elementary bodies...the art of manipulating correspondences...*

Magic.

Precisamente. *Sulfur, sun, gold, the red lion, the red king,* rubedo, *the rational mind, the intellectual principle is the higher consciousness, the culmination of the Great Work. Mercury, moon, silver, the white eagle, the white queen,* albedo, *the unconscious or irrational mind is the emotional intuitive principle, the transition from the lower to the higher, reminding us that without awareness of our lower natures and our desire to rise above them, there can be no transmutation to the higher.*

Sun, moon, gold, silver…

"Sol and Luna," he said, remembering Paracelsus, the man's frosty breath smelling of alcohol.

But he was tired…so tired. The Priest's words were spinning…like silver pinwheels…spinning…his head spinning. *I'm tired, Reginald.* He yawned. His eyes closed. All he desired was deep dreamless sleep.

45

IT STARTS WITH WANTING

Her lips were heavenly fire. He wanted to resist, but the burning was so sweet that while Her mouth was pressed to his he did not care if the kiss consumed him.

Her scent was ambrosial, redolent of gardenias and musk, dewy spring mornings, and sultry moonlit evenings. Between the fire of Her kiss and the arcanum of Her scent, he felt restored, as if he were an empty bottle being filled, not with water or spirits, but with life-giving nectar.

Rick opened his eyes. She stood before him on the millefleur grass in a white gown and sandals, looking every bit the Goddess. Cybele, Isis, Diana, Ishtar, Sophia, *Magna Mater*…She of a Thousand Names. The sight of Her was as intoxicating as Her kiss. Her white hand lay on his chest and he felt the cool heat of Her fingers through the clean EMT shirt he had put on after his bath.

Her finger rose to his mouth and traced his bottom lip. "You've gotten better at this, my knight. Either that or it's been a season since you kissed anyone." The corners of Her mouth dimpled with the tease and Her freckled nose wrinkled, making Her look almost girlish. Almost, but there was no mistaking the quintessence of womanhood She exuded from every pore. She was Aphrodite and Diana, passion and reason incarnate.

The sky was azure. Water burbled in the scalloped fountain. Birds sang in nearby trees. Down the pebbled walk rose the residence of the

Sibylline Sisterhood. His eyes were drawn to an upstairs window and he felt a stab of guilt for not pushing the Goddess away.

"Is she here?"

The Lady lowered Her hand and stepped away in mock reproach. Gold flecks danced in Her emerald eyes. Her flaming red-gold hair swayed as she shook Her head, as if to say *Am I not enough?*

He set his jaw and kept his hands close to his sides resisting the temptation to throttle Her. She was as exasperating as She was seductive. How much simpler life would have been if She had never entered his life.

Of course, he and Fergi would probably both be dead and the Nephilim eating their way through Earth's population.

"No," She answered, seeing he wasn't going to be baited. "She's working. We all have our part to do." The latter was pointedly aimed at him.

He looked around, at the billiard-table lawns, the pebbled walks winding through the riot of floral color, the surrounding trees. He had no idea how he'd gotten here.

"What must I do?"

"Understand."

"Understand what?"

"This, my knight. Man is a materialized thought; he is what he wills. To change his nature from the mortal to the immortal state, he must change his material mode of thinking, and even rise above the sphere of thought. He must reject that which is illusory and perishing and hold fast to that which is eternal. The visible universe is a thought of the eternal mind thrown into objectivity by its will, and crystallized into matter by its power. Look at the everlasting stars. Look at the indestructible mountain peaks. They are the thoughts of the universal mind, and they will remain as long as the thoughts of that mind do not change."

"But He has changed his mind, hasn't He?"

"Not God. Yaldabaoth. But think—if we could hold on to a thought, we would be able to create. But who but the enlightened, who live above the region of mentality in the kingdom of spirit, can hold on to a thought? Are not the illusions of the senses continually destroying that which we attempt to create? Men do not think what they choose, but that which comes into their mind. If they could control the action of their mind by rising above it, they would be able to control their own nature and the nature surrounding them."

"How does one rise above the illusions of the senses?"

"Desire—it starts with wanting, but will is needed to focus desire and turn it into a creative act. Impulsive actions motivated by desire are unconscious. Such actions result in fate wherein there is neither free will nor predestination but only accident. A life led willy-nilly to the grave. Fate is passive, destiny active. Fate unconscious, destiny conscious. As Reginald told you, the progress of evolution is the transmutation of matter into consciousness. In man, on an individual level, the path begins with self-reflection. Each of us has a mind mirror. In most humans, it is a murky thing he investigates seldom, if ever, and most are not aware of its existence. But he who will stare into it until the veil lifts will see beyond the physical world into the spiritual.

"Man under the domination of desire is a slave. But who harnesses the power, the potency, of desire and bends it to his will is free. Free yourself from the domination of desire and you become free. Will is all."

"That's quite a speech. But I'm no man's slave."

"Perhaps not another's, but to yourself? Are not all humans born slaves to their primal desires? Unconscious beings groping in the dark seeking fulfillment and never finding it so long as we delude ourselves that fulfillment exists only in the satisfaction of our desires?

"That is not to say that will must displace desire. Desire is the sleeping energy, the potential. But desire alone is a mindless thing, a whirlpool that will suck you into itself, a vampire master whose appetites you may spend a lifetime trying to appease and never succeed. Yet the mind cannot do without desire. It is a primal force waiting to be harnessed.

"As long as we look outward, we see only the projection of shadows on the wall of Plato's cave. Only when we look into our inner mirror, break the cycle of ignorance, and subject desire to our will can we leave the cave and walk in sunlight."

She stiffened. A frown creased Her forehead and wrinkled Her freckled nose as She scanned the line of trees where garden met forest.

He turned expecting Nephilim to come charging from the dusky boles, but saw nothing.

Still, a sense of urgency, of danger.

Her eyes snapped back to his.

"Wake up, Rick. You're in danger." She shoved him toward the trees.

He felt himself falling.

Wake up, Rick!

Da Silva was shaking him. He started awake.

He sat up, swung his legs off the bed, winced from the pain. He was dressed in jeans and a clean EMT shirt and a pair of sneakers. He didn't have spare EMS boots.

"What?"

Azazel is here!

46
AZAZEL IN MEMPHIS

A zazel stood in the street looking up at the curtained third-floor windows. The youth—Richard Scott—was there. He was not alone. Azazel sensed their presence but could not make them out.

No matter. He would kill them all.

He thought about going up there and crushing the boy with his hands, ripping his throat out with his teeth and drinking his blood. His blood would be special, enhanced as it was with the Grigori strain.

But the boy had power. More than he would have guessed. The Maker considered him dangerous. How he had enlisted the aid of the ancient Tind'losi, he had no idea.

No matter. Time to crush the pup.

He held up his hand, fingers spread wide.

At the window, Rick saw the demon Azazel, still wearing his scarlet cardinal's robe and four-cornered biretta, standing in the street. He was looking up, no doubt seeing him framed in the window. As he watched, wondering whether to retreat into the timestream or hurl some missile at the Grigori, and worrying if he were up to the task, the creature raised his hand, spread his fingers wide—and suddenly made a fist.

The building trembled. Rick turned to race to the door. The floor lurched and the ceiling rained down.

PART II
THE MIRROR OF ETERNITY

47

A MEETING LONG OVERDUE

Outwardly, the youth appeared a fairly typical specimen of the billions He had spawned. Nor was he the first to have escaped the bonds of the physical plane and mastered the timestream and, more worryingly, evaded His hounds. So why did this boy fill Him with an unease He'd never felt before?

Sitting on His throne, gazing down into creation, Yaldabaoth refused to name the emotion that squeezed His throat and clenched His fists. There was power in names and what the logos created was not easily undone. It was true He had felt a similar emotion emanate from the humans who knelt before His altar, but for Him to experience this...*disturbance*...was beneath Him.

Once, He'd enthusiastically followed the exploits of the few heroic figures who had risen above the masses and had even influenced their successes, but the ingratitude of the common herd irked Him. He worried how man in increasing multitudes were abandoning His worship and either turning their collective back on Him or leaving the world He'd created for them and seeking His throne.

Was this boy the one to lead them? Was this insignificant speck of flesh a threat to his dominion?

Another disturbance interrupted his brooding.

He blinked but the apparition did not vanish. He recognized the woman. Her presence persisted across the history of man. She'd interfered in man's affairs and made a residence in the lower astral realm alongside man's world. Many worshiped her, siphoning off the devotion due Him. Yet she was a source of unease and He'd avoided following her exploits or questioning her existence too closely.

Now here she was, standing before Him!

Her green eyes glittered like the stars He'd placed in man's firmament. Her red-gold hair glowed like His sunsets. Pearl-white teeth glinted between smiling coral lips. It was as if a sun had risen in the cavern of His domain.

"How dare—"

Except for the few times He'd sent His avatar into the physical plane to converse with one of His devout—often in the form of some supernaturally endowed physical object: a fiery column or burning bush or wave risen from a wine-dark sea—He'd seldom spoken, and words failed Him.

He refused to rise from His throne but leaned forward and with darkened brow waved His hand and commanded, "Be gone!"

The apparition did not vanish.

"We need to talk." Her smile was indulgent, perhaps even fond. "This meeting is long overdue."

"Silence!"

"Silence will not help. It is time you learned who you are."

He said nothing, refused to acknowledge the apparition's presence. It was true she had done more to watch over His Making than the Watchers He'd so long ago sent to do the job, but it infuriated—and chilled—Him that she was such an enigma, a knot in the elegant equation of His creation.

"I made you," she said. Was that pride He saw in her eyes?

"No one made me," He growled between clenched teeth, speaking despite His desire to ignore her. "I am alpha and omega! The first and the last! I am all!"

"Nevertheless, I made you. And you are not alone."

"Impossible! You are of my Making; therefore, how could you make me?"

"Ah." She reached as if to caress His cheek but did not touch Him. There was something adoring yet amused in the twinkle of her eye. It took considerable fortitude to resist flinching and He steeled himself to strike her hand aside if she pursued contact. "I am not of your making. I exist above the hypostasis in which you dwell." She spread her hands and lifted her eyes to the seeming infinity of His creation.

"Above? There is nothing above! I am the first and last! And I am alone!"

She shook her head kindly and proceeded to reveal to Him the presence of the Aeons who dwelt in the hypostases above His darkened cave. And she related how she—however misguidedly and for which act she had no remorse but only pride—spawned Him, but fearing the Aeons would destroy her offspring, hid Him in this inconsequential corner of the Infinite where He, having inherited her curiosity and creativity, had, believing He was supreme and alone, shaped the lower supernal realms and the physical universe that mankind beheld as vast but which fit in a corner of His darkened cave.

As she spoke and revelation after revelation dashed His senses like cold waves, His anger rose till the blood roar in His head drowned her words and He flicked His hand and she was gone, hurled in an instant into the worlds beyond worlds that existed in the multiverse displayed on the concave wall of His habitat.

Eventually, He uncurled His fists, released a deep shuddering breath, and returned His attention to the boy.

48

TABULA SMARAGDINA

Snakes. Coiling around his ankles, gliding over his sneakers. He struggled to move but couldn't; he was bound to the chair in which he sat. His skin crawled with atavistic repulsion as he studied their heads in the dim light. He didn't know much about snakes, but the venomous ones were said to have wedge-shaped heads. These did. Their collective musk was overpowering. The smell reminded him of something. He blinked.

Rick came to sitting in a desk chair in what looked like a hotel room. A queen-size bed still neatly made. Sofa, television, microwave, miniature refrigerator, beige carpet, beige curtains.

The distinctive odor came from the angel standing before him. The Grigori towered over him, his head approaching the ceiling. He was not as massive as Azazel, nor quite as tall. Unlike their last meeting when he'd worn a biker's leather vest over his bronze, muscular body, Talmaiel was dressed in black sweats and hoodie. His face had healed somewhat since Rick last saw him. The raw, blistered flesh had scarred over and taken on a grayish tone. The ear that hung from his head where Wally struck him with the branch was back in place. Someone had done a bit of magic on him. His eyes were still startlingly blue, but one was missing a lid and it was disconcerting to see one eye blink and the other continue staring.

The angel's smile was hideous, his lips like two smears of scar tissue. The monster was trying to tell him something but he heard only the blood roar in his head, felt only the rage for vengeance. He saw Wally lying in the weeds and shale atop Crystal Mountain, starlight glittering in his dead eyes. And here was the beast that killed him!

Wally, now six feet under and never again to ride shotgun beside him or to trade insults in the ongoing game of one-upmanship they'd started in middle school.

Fuck you.

Fuck you better.

Dickweed.

Ass munch.

He was out of the chair in a flash. His lacerated back forgotten, he launched himself across the room and came within an inch of striking the Grigori's chin, before the giant caught his fist and spun him around. He drew Rick in close, his massive arms folding over Rick's chest as he hugged him. Wrapped in the beast's arms, Rick recoiled at the creature's serpent scent.

"I expected that would be my welcome," Talmaiel said. There was humor in his rumbling baritone. "Is that any way to greet me after saving you from Azazel? How did you get him pissed off at you? You haven't been practicing your people skills, Ricky. What would your Granny say?"

"I'll kill you!" Rick spat as he struggled in the angel's arms.

"Maybe later. We've got to talk."

Rick's response was to throw his head back and butt the Watcher. But Talmaiel was too tall; he simply lifted his chin, so Rick slammed his chest.

"Here, maybe this will convince you." He hauled Rick around so he could see the boy standing in the corner.

Terry!

Rick hadn't seen Terrance Light since Wally's funeral. The boy had lost his mom, Jewelie Light, the night Hendricks' citizens held off Talmaiel's army while Rick confronted the Grigori on the ridgetop. Terry had been the first to greet them upon their arrival in Hendricks. He'd been shirtless, his lean body deeply tanned, stringy blond hair hanging in his eyes, eyes that were completely clouded with milk-white cataracts. He was blind and mute but that didn't stop him from seeing or communicating. He found his way around as nimbly as the sighted and "saw" what was yet to come and signed so fast he was hard to keep up with.

A big raven's skull suspended around his neck from a leather thong lay against his white tee shirt. The black-beaked, paper-white skull was a totem through which he communicated with nature, drawing butterflies and birds at will and God only knew what else. After the killing work the boy had done at Hendricks, Rick wouldn't be surprised if he called down lightning.

But now Terry stood, as Wally had in Talmaiel's tent, as if under a spell, silent, slack-jawed, a catatonic statue from which all vivacity had fled. A thin line of spittle trailed down his chin.

"What have you done to him? Do you intend to kill him? Like you did Wally?"

Talmaiel looked genuinely pained. "That was unfortunate, and though you will not believe me, unintended. No, I will not harm this boy. Like you, he has Grigori blood and may prove useful."

"Useful! Is that the only measure of sympathy you know? And I suppose I'm here because you find *me* useful?"

"I'd be lying if I denied it. We must work together. We may have been on opposite sides in the past, but now we have the same goal. To save Earth."

Rick looked at the disfigured Watcher in disbelief. "Save Earth! Last time I saw you, you wanted to destroy it."

The giant shook his long head. "Not destroy it. I love the earth. It's the only home I've ever known. But I wanted to free my brothers from their long incarceration. To be among my own kind, and lord it over man again, instead of always living in the shadows."

It suddenly occurred to Rick—if Talmaiel was free, then...

"You freed them!"

The sheepish grin looked positively wolfish on the Watcher's long face. "Inadvertently. But yes, Semjaza and the Two Hundred are back to add to Earth's miseries. I had changed my mind. Living among them again, I missed the earth and did not want—"

"To share it."

The remains of Talmaiel's lips stretched in a frown over his teeth. "No, I did not want to share it. They would make it a hell. I realized I've grown fond of humans. And though their lives are fleeting, they seldom interfered with my enjoyment of Earth's delights, her mountains and deserts, her sunsets and auroras. I knew once loosed on the world, my brethren would cut a bloody path through humanity and make of this planet an abattoir."

Images flashed through Rick's mind: alien giants rending and feasting on human flesh, gutters running red, legions of their offspring, the Nephilim, unleashed from the spells that bound them, ravaging mankind's billions.

He shook the visions from his head, but other images replaced them.

He remembered Jewelie Light, her hazel eyes sparkling, dirty-blonde hair waving in the soft breeze the night of the reception, remembered her proud smile as she gazed at Terry, not lamenting his infirmities but celebrating his strengths, remembered her hospitality, her sweet potato pie and homemade buttermilk ice cream. And he saw her laid out on her bed in a white gown. He looked again at the catatonic orphan standing in the corner. And though he refused to be at Cybele's beck and call, he vowed to himself that, if the world survived, he would stay close to the people of Hendricks and to Terry and fight beside them and protect them.

"Free him. I'll do whatever you want. Doesn't matter anyway. The world is ending."

"Same as before: I want you to join me—or at least work with me."

"I'll never join you.

Rick.

What?

Listen to him.

Are you kidding?

Hear him out.

"The Priest is with you, isn't he?" Talmaiel said, speaking softly in his ear. "If you hear me, Priest, tell your apprentice I'm right. Whatever differences we had in the past, we must work together now."

Rick said nothing. Hoping to catch the Fallen One off guard, he tried to headbutt him again, but Talmaiel lifted this chin and tightened his grip.

"This is getting us nowhere. I'm going to release you."

He did so and stepped back. Rick debated charging him, or maybe willing the microwave to stave in his ugly skull, but decided to listen to what he had to say.

"Get to the point. Just tell me what I have to do to free him."

"Find the Emerald Tablet."

"'Emerald Tablet'?"

In his mind's eye, Rick beheld an arch-topped slab like the tablets Moses brought down from the mount inscribed with the Ten Commandments. Only the tablet he envisioned was of solid emerald glowing with its own inner light and inscribed in an unknown tongue.

The Stone had turned out to be a metaphor, but Raziel's Book was real, written in ten sapphires that formed the Sephiroth, the Tree of Life. He had held the jewels in his hand, felt their power, seen them open then close the very heavens. Had seen them form the Merkaba, the light vehicle, like two pyramids pointing and spinning in opposite directions so fast it hurt the eyes to look at it. Had watched the Merkaba transport Talmaiel to the Abyss. Was this tablet another wild goose chase? Or some powerful magic that might actually help?

Even as these thoughts passed through his head, a dozen Nemorenses, all talking at once, offered explanations. He followed no one line of thought but images flashed through his mind. The tablet was a papyrus, a scroll, a slender volume written in green ink, an incredibly ancient fragment of green stone inscribed with hieroglyphs. In general, they all agreed on an image of a great mage, robed and white-bearded, his face bearing an expression of wisdom and profound compassion.

Hermes Trismegistus.

The name was familiar.

"I am no Peripatetic," John Dee had said, defending himself against Paracelsus' insults, *but a true disciple of Trice-Great Hermes, Father of Philosophers.*

Tell him you're Hermes Trismegistus, a Nemorensis had suggested when he arrived at Mortlake.

His heart sank. John Dee's library held the writings of Hermes Trismegistus. Was the *Emerald Tablet* among them? Had he missed his chance to secure it?

A Nemorensis told him that, yes, Dee possessed the volume in question, as had Roger Bacon, Albertus Magnus, and Isaac Newton, each of whom had made their own translation. Another Nemorensis informed him that the *Tabula Smaragdina,* as it was also known, was a distillation—a mere thirteen lines—of a much older lost body of work.

While the *Tabula* contained the secret of the *prima materia* and its transmutation into the Philosopher's Stone, its central tenet "That which is below is like that which is above and that which is above is like that which is below," usually shortened to "As above, so below" stressing the correspondences between the celestial and mundane worlds with which Rick was already familiar—the longer lost work from which it was derived reputedly contained all the secrets of the universe—sciences, arts, philosophy, medicine, creation—everything.

"Does this book really exist?" he asked Talmaiel.

"Oh, it exists," said the Grigori, "for the time traveler."

"And how am I supposed to locate this lost book?"

"I have no idea. But there is one who might help you."

"Who?"

"The Sibyl."

49
YOUR EMINENCE

He had failed. The youth had slipped his grasp. And he'd had help. That a Grigori was responsible for snatching the youth out from under his very nose was galling. He would deal with the upstart Talmaiel, if time allowed. Meanwhile...

The road before him was crowded with the sleek conveyances he'd seen in Memphis, conveyances that seemed to propel themselves. Across the street, before another of the towering buildings ubiquitous to this teeming city, stood a statue of a giant bearing the weight of the celestial spheres on his shoulders. Again, he was impressed by these mortals' industry and understood Yaldabaoth's decision to destroy them.

Behind him rose what appeared to be a place of worship, not unlike Rome's great basilica but puny in comparison. A constant flow of pedestrians parted around him as if he were a boulder amid a stream, the humans hurrying past as if on business that could not wait. Perhaps because he still wore his cardinal's scarlet robe and biretta, as well as Bellarmino's face, they either looked at him in scorn as if he were an unpleasant obstruction blocking their way or reverently ducked their heads.

Unable to find the boy, he'd made his way here. Semjaza and the Two Hundred were back from the Abyss. Coincidence? He thought not. Yaldabaoth left nothing to chance. It made no difference. There were more than enough humans to go around.

He turned to face the Cathedral. The great bronze doors were open. Inside two rows of suspended lights lit the high, columned nave. He mounted the steps and entered, leaving the noisy street behind. The church was nearly empty. A few soft, elderly men and women sat in the pews. A few women with covered heads knelt in the side chapels, lighting candles and praying, little good it would do them. He had to admit though, as he gazed up at the vaulted ceiling, at least some of these humans possessed a taste for the elegant.

A black-frocked priest spied him, and impressed by his cardinal's robe, hurried down the aisle to great him.

"Your Eminence!" he said, smiling.

The smile vanished when Azazel revealed his true face.

50
MUCH TO LEARN

In sheer numbers the crowd was impressive. Semjaza had seldom seen so many humans in one place. The proximity of so much flesh and blood was maddening, but he resisted the urge to feast. Partly because of the millennia-long discipline he'd maintained feeding judiciously on the Choir, knowing he depended on their labor and, frankly, not wanting to spend eternity alone. After all, what was a general without his army?

But he also held back because he wanted to observe.

Much had changed since their banishment. Walled cities built around temple and palace had given way to sprawling metropolises built around commerce. Standing amid the pedestrian plaza in what the natives called Times Square, he marveled at the gigantic screens advertising everything from eateries and beverages to what appeared to be entertainments. Many of the displays were animated. The vast form of a whale—every bit as big as the real thing—swam vertically up the front of a wedge-shaped tower at one end of the plaza.

But the greatest change was not their progress but their reaction to the presence of the Grigori.

To him!

If he'd expected humanity to cringe and grovel at his return, their hearts to stop with terror, he was disappointed. True, they gave him a wide berth, parting before him like waves before a ship's prow, but they did not *see* him. Had the mighty Grigori become such distant and

226

bloodless legends that their tales were not even suited for stories with which to scare children? Did they think him—massive as he was towering over them—in his gray clothes some vagabond to be ignored?

These were no longer the cowering merchants and farmers who propitiated the land each season with prayers and incense and sacrifice of slaughtered ram. They feared only the cosmic change that had come upon their world, falling like a plague disrupting time and space and shaking their narrow existence to its foundations.

They had much to learn. Old ways must not be forgotten. Time to awaken their fear and awe of the gods that now walked among them.

He chose one at random—a tired-looking man of middle age in a rumpled suit and open collar—and wrenched his head off and, laughing with the long-withheld joy of slaughter, hurled it into the crowd.

They saw him then! Saw his height. His mass. His alienness.

Saw the headless body spasming as it dangled from the great, long-fingered hand.

The screaming torrents swept away, trampling each other in their rush to evade the majesty that had appeared in their midst.

51
AVERNUS

The lake was round like Nemi, and dense woods cloaked its steep flanks, but here the similarity ended. Nowhere was there torchlight or sign of dwelling, neither home nor temple nor sign of any living thing. No moon reflected in the lake; no star shown through the roiling clouds. Great streamers of poisonous vapors drifted like ghosts over the black water and no bird—not even an owl—winged through the choking, sulfurous air that stung his eyes and clawed his nostrils with every breath.

No, this was not Diana's Mirror.

A Nemorensis quoted the poet:

> "...there th' unnavigable lake extends,
> O'er whose unhappy waters, void of light,
> No bird presumes to steer his airy flight;
> Such deadly stenches from the depths arise,
> And steaming Sulphur, that infects the skies."

"Avernus...birdless," another said, remarking rather than explaining the meaning of the name, as Rick sensed the crowding priests peering through the windows of his eyes.

He shivered, as much from the eeriness of the scene as from the damp. The darkness was claustrophobic, the encroaching trees gaunt shadows stretching taloned hands. He strained his ears, but all he heard was the solitary lapping of water against the rocky shore.

228

Daunted at the thought of finding his way through the darkness, he suppressed a tremor of panic.

"Which way?" he said, for once grateful for the company of the priests.

The grotto, one said.

The Sibyl, said another.

He let himself be guided by a Nemorensis who knew the path. Stumbling over rocks and tripping over roots, he kept to the shore as much as possible, feeling his way through the woods when the shingle ran out. Twice he encountered great pits of boiling mud whose bubbling surface spat clouds of sulfuric gases so noxious he couldn't breathe and was forced deeper into the tangling woods. But just when he despaired of reaching his destination, he came upon a high craggy rock that rose above the trees.

In the gloom he could barely make out the many darker portals that marked fissures or caves in the cliff face. More plumes of volcanic steam hissed from fumaroles around the rock's base. He looked back at the smoldering cauldron of the lake below, at the bruised and savaged sky above and reflected this was truly a Doréan hellscape. Were he superstitious, he might well imagine this tormented earth a place of spirits, where revenants roamed hungering for blood, and he understood why the ancients believed the rivers of Hades—Acheron, Cocytus, fiery Phlegethon, forgetful Lethe, and the mighty Styx, from whose shore wraiths of the unburied beg the Ferryman passage and are turned away—ran beneath the fissured volcanic rock.

Here, said a Nemorensis.

Up, said another.

The path was steep, and he clawed his way through the wood, twice falling and aiding his climb by grasping the moss-slimed flanks of trees. The air was stifling, as much from the fumes rising from the lake and the gases issuing from volcanic fumaroles as from the dense humidity. His clothes were soon soaked and he began to shiver from the night chill.

At last he stood panting on a shelf of rock. The tall cave mouth before him exuded a foul, funeral smell like rotting meat or decaying flowers.

"Enter."

The voice was not a Nemorensis, but came from the darkness within, an exhalation of the fetid damp, and though there was something eerily familiar about it, it was a voice unlike any he'd heard. Though no more than a whisper, it vibrated in his teeth and rumbled in his bones, as if it were the amplified voice of the mountain itself.

He swallowed hard and entered.

The cave mouth opened into a tall airy chamber in which his breathing and every scuff of his shoe was amplified. Dozens of fissures in the porous volcanic rock let in the night gloom but did little to dispel the darkness. The only illumination came from a trapezoidal doorway set in the far wall, a good stone's throw away, where torchlight flickered. He hesitated in the cavern entrance. Dark night and oblivion pressed at his back. The end of all things. Before him…

He had no idea what waited in the next chamber, but he was bone weary and wanted more than anything to lie down and sleep. Sleep and let the world go where it would. But no, too much was at stake. He thought of Fergi…somewhere. He wouldn't just lose her; they would both be lost, have never existed. And his parents… He thought of his mom, Jenny Scott, perhaps even now standing in the doorway to his old room terrified at what was happening outside and wondering why he didn't answer his phone. And Dad, like as not watching his beloved Benny Hill DVDs while the world went to hell in a handbasket.

Thinking of Dad brought a smile to his lips. Like as not, Frank Sr. blamed the corrosion of the neighborhood and the monumental fuck up of nature on government incompetence.

The choice was simple: sleep and die or push forward and maybe… He didn't need the Nemorenses' urging to decide.

For all the cavern's expansiveness, a claustrophobic closeness pressed in on him as he approached the Sibyl's lair. It was not the cavern itself that caused the sweat to bead his brow and trickle down his back, but what waited beyond the door. There was nothing of terror in the icy emotion that sluiced through his veins—his body was far too tired to muster fear—but a kind of dread awe, as if he was about to encounter a mystery, a majesty, an unknown intelligence that eclipsed whatever claim to genius his poor brain possessed. Was this what ancients felt in the presence of their gods? Shrunken? Diminished? An ant in the presence of a colossus?

His neck prickled with an electric thrill as he crossed the threshold.

The walls of the second chamber were more finished than the first and bands of deep red and bright blue alternated with the white stucco. Other tall trapezoidal doorways opened onto tunnels burrowing deeper into the mountain. Perhaps the very passageways of legend leading down to the chthonic realm. Pale streamers of mist or steam rising from crevices in the cavern floor suggested such. The reek of brimstone so prevalent outside was fainter here and overpowered by a sickly-sweet smell that made his head reel. Pale wisps of colorless mist drifted from narrow fissures in the floor. He felt more than half dizzy from the fumes.

But it was not the room that demanded his attention.

She sat on a throne of white marble, her hands resting on carven lions' heads. Her hands were nearly as white as the marble. She wore a flowing gown, white like the marble, that reached to her sandaled feet. But it was her face that arrested him, stopped him in his tracks and stunned him to speechlessness as, perhaps, no god or goddess could have done.

Dark, green-flecked eyes regarded him from beneath lush brows. A great untamed mass of auburn hair, made fierier by the torchlight, spilled over her shoulders. Her hair still bore the silver streak that began in the cowlicked curl above her right brow and swept down to her breast. She had lost weight since he last saw her at Wally's funeral. Her face had thinned, making her cheekbones more prominent. She wore no makeup, never had, didn't go in for frivolities of lipstick, fingernail polish, eye shadow. As far as he was concerned, she didn't need them. She was never more beautiful than when she stepped out of the shower, her abundant mane wrapped in a towel, or sleeping, her full lips parted, said mane billowing across her pillow like a dark mystery. Even in the shock of recognition and amidst the urgency of his quest, he found her more beautiful, more desirable than ever.

"Fergi."

If she knew him, she didn't show it. Her full lips remained unsmiling, her eyes distant as if she regarded him from afar—as perhaps she did, if, as more than one Nemorensis insisted, she had become the vessel through which the Sibyl spoke.

"Seek not Delores. She is no more."

The ponderous, resonating voice set his teeth on edge: a god or the earth itself speaking through the feeble cords of a human throat.

"What do I call you?"

"It matters not. Since time immemorial, names have been given me, but now time grows mortal. I am Sibylla. Without number my years but numbered now. As are all. Unless you succeed. Time suffers not delay. Ask that I may answer."

Though time was rushing toward creation and the ordered world unraveling, the question utmost on his mind was a personal one: what had become of Fergi? But asking would be fruitless. The Sibyl was right. Time was fleeting.

But where to begin?

"I was told you might help me find the Emerald Tablet. But what I really need to know, if you have in your power to tell me, is how to stop Yaldabaoth."

She stared at him for a long moment. There was nothing of the tenderness he'd sometimes seen in her eyes, perhaps accompanying a rare smile when she looked at him, nor was there any trace of her usual furrow-browed impatience, only a remote coldness that chilled him to the bone and made him fear that, perhaps, his Delores truly was no more.

Her hands never moved from the lions' heads. Her breasts barely rose and fell with each breath. She might have been a living statue for all her remote austerity. Anger clenched his jaw. How dare Cybele use Fergi like this! But remembering Fergi's admonition, "I have my work and you have yours," he subdued his anger, took a deep breath, let it out slowly.

The Sibyl's face transformed. Her lips peeled back, exposing her teeth. Her hands gripped the lion-headed arms of her chair. Her back arched. The knuckles of her toes clenched. She moaned. The sound was like the sea, crashing through the chamber, receding down the many tunnels that honeycombed the hill.

She jolted forward, her full lips compressed to narrow lines, her eyes glaring. He stumbled back from the fury of her face, as if she were about to hurl herself from her throne and attack. But she remained seated and the voice that rolled over him left no doubt it was not Delores Ferguson who spoke.

"The Maker unmakes his making. Time's river backward flows. This you know. And even as the end spirals toward the beginning, the Shining Ones fight to regain what they've lost. But neither man nor angel shall survive."

Her words were chilling, spoken as they were with such utter certainty.

"That is what you see? Is there no chance for survival?"

"This is what I see because that is what is happening. What will *happen barring chance. But there is always chance. The past is written; the future an open book. Are you prepared to write the future?"*

"Am I prepared...?" The question jolted him.

No, the boy within him protested, *I am not prepared. I am overwhelmed and have no idea what to do and have not the will nor stamina nor knowledge to even begin.*

But aloud he said, "Yes, I must. I have no choice, do I?"

"None."

"Then tell me what I must do and how to do it?"

"You know what you must do. How is the hard part. With that I cannot help. But before you do anything, before you face the Demiurge, you must forge the weapon to defeat him."

"What weapon?"

"Yourself."

"Me?"

There it was again, the nonsense about his being a weapon.

Damn it, Reginald! That's the same crap you told me last year when you sent me up against Talmaiel.

She's right, you know. Da Silva's voice was as serious as the plague yet managed to convey a commiserative smile. *I'll say it again: you're the only one who stands a chance of defeating Yaldabaoth, but a sword is useless to one who hasn't learned how to wield it.*

So, we're back to fencing?

Pardon my metaphor. I'm just saying —

Don't! Tempus fugit, *remember?*

"Okay, Fer — Sibyl. I'll bite. How do I find myself?"

He expected something straightforward, some useful information like go down to the corner, turn left and look for… Something in that vein. His heart sank at what she delivered.

"To find the Emerald Tablet, you must seek the Pillars of Hermes."

He felt a mental intake of air as a hundred Rex Nemorenses gasped.

Immediately, the babble erupted as many vied to explain.

Reginald cleared his throat and the others fell silent. He briefly explained what little was known of the Pillars. They were truly the stuff of myth, so ancient only fragments of their memory remained. He told how, according to legend, Thoth, the Egyptian Hermes, preserved his canon of writings inside two great pillars before the Great Flood inundated the world. Thousands of years later, the Pillars were rediscovered, one unearthed outside the city of Heliopolis, the other near Thebes. The massive columns were covered with sacred hieroglyphs. The priests called them the Pillars of the Gods of the Dawning Light. They were moved to a secret temple dedicated to the First Gods. Some texts indicate this location was the Temple of Amin in Siwa, the oldest temple in Egypt. Only priests and pharaohs were allowed to view the sacred Pillars. They were described in scrolls as far back as 1550 B.C. Herodotus, who supposedly saw them in a secret Egyptian temple in 400 B.C., said one pillar was of pure gold, the other of emerald. When Alexander conquered Egypt in 332 B.C., he supposedly removed the scrolls for safekeeping to the Temple of Heliopolis. Then moved them again to a cavern in Cappadocia before starting his conquest of the East. He died. The writings were lost.

As for the Pillars. Best guess, if they ever existed, is somewhere under the Egyptian sands.

The Sibyl was not finished.

"Make yourself grow to a greatness beyond measure," she said, her voice reverberating off the distant walls, her glowing stare burning into his brain. *"By a bound, free yourself from the body; raise yourself above all time. Become Eternity. Then you will understand God. Believe that nothing is impossible for you. Think yourself immortal and capable of understanding all—all arts, all sciences, the nature of every living being. Mount higher than the highest height; descend lower than the lowest depth. Draw into yourself all sensations of everything created—fire and water, dry and moist. Imagine that you are everywhere, on earth, in the sea, in the sky, that you are not yet born, in the maternal womb, adolescent, old, dead, beyond death. If you embrace in your thought all things at once—times, places, substances, qualities, quantities—you may understand God."*

He remembered Bruno saying something similar: *Unless you make yourself equal to God, you cannot understand God: for the like is not intelligible save to the like.*

"But," the Sibyl continued, *"as the serpent casts off its skin to grow, so man must cast off his limited conceptions. Only through death can gnosis be attained."*

52

A MOUNTING RAGE

Darian Delgado wasn't enjoying his falafel.

Darian sat at a table in the Manhattan Mall food court, half-eaten pita on the tray. His hardly touched lemon ginger tea sat beside it. He had no appetite. He'd come to eat because what else was there to do on your lunch hour?

The food court was over half empty. It was usually bustling at lunch time, but with the world gone bat shit people weren't shopping.

"You've got to let her go," Tevi, his GameStop coworker, was saying. Tevi's small dark eyes were sympathetic behind the lenses of his Clubmaster Browlines. Tevi's appetite was just fine. He was nearly finished with his Nathan's hot dog and cheese fries.

By "her" Tevi referred to Angelica, Darian's ex, who dumped him last month. They had been dating for three years and Darian was still in shock.

"I was thinking of sending her flowers or maybe texting her to let her know I'm thinking about her." He looked at Tevi, his sad eyes hoping for confirmation.

But Tevi countered, "Dude, listen to yourself. She's gone man. In the wind." He waved a fry in the air to demonstrate. He dipped the fry in ketchup and popped it in his mouth. "Look at that chick over there." He tipped his nose at the cute half-Asian dirty blonde two tables over. She was skinny, her breasts small, her nose not overly large. She sat across from a heavyset girl with dark hair and a bigger nose. They were talking between bites, leaning over the table to better hear over the music piped from the speakers. "Her name's Lili. She works at Sephora."

"I know who she is," Darian said, and instantly regretted sounding harsh. Tevi was one of the few people he talked to. He didn't go out much and didn't have any real friends besides the group he played Magic: The Gathering with at his LGS.

He stole a glance at Lili, whose red bow lips were sipping Bubble Tea from a straw. Tevi was right. She was cute. She looked a little like the girl from the "Trapped in the Tower" Throne of Eldraine card…without the long red hair, of course. But would she be interested in a plainswalker whose win record was about as low as his love life? The chances were nil.

The thought brought on a wave of all-consuming anger, and he curled his fists. Such anger was uncharacteristic: Darian was more prone to displays of self-pity than to angry outbursts, and shows of anger appalled him. But looking at Lili—now he was staring—his rage mounted. He saw her through a red haze. How dare she reject him! Lili and Angelica and all the rest of the ball-cutting bitches!

His gaze swept the food court, targeting the women present. The teenaged girls, chattering like magpies, oblivious to the glory of his presence. The crone, hunched over her soup bowl, as if spooning the elixir of life down her withered gullet.

He returned to Lili. He was standing now. Tevi was saying something, but he couldn't hear over the blood-roar that drowned out the music from the speakers, the cacophony of chattering voices. His hand curled around his tea bottle.

He was at her side in a half-dozen paces. The first blow knocked her out of her seat and onto the floor. The bottle didn't break, so he smashed it on the floor before going to work on her face with its jagged edge.

NYPD officer Fran Witkowski was on duty when the young man attacked the woman. She did not see the initial attack but, following the cries of the lunch crowd to their source, came upon a scene of bloody carnage. The wounds caused by the broken glass may or may not have been lethal, but Witkowski knew from experience head wounds bled profusely so blood loss was no indication of fatality. Still, she had her service weapon drawn and was shouting, "Stop!" before she reached the attacker.

The young man was overweight, early twenties. His black tee shirt read, "Bite Me." His stringy hair was done up in a man bun.

When he raised the broken bottle again, she flicked the safety off and fired. She did not aim for a body shot where she would inflict the least damage as she'd been instructed in Academy but put a round in his head, literally knocking him off the girl and sending the nearest metal-and-plastic chair skittering so that he sprawled half under the table. He was dead instantly. That much was obvious from the size of the hole in his temple. But with teeth bared and eyes glaring, she leaned forward and emptied the magazine of her 9mm service weapon into the guy's head.

She kept pulling the trigger long after the magazine was empty.

———

Samael, Angel of Death, seducer and destroyer, Semjaza's grim lieutenant, observed the fruit of his labor. It had been so long since he'd projected madness into humans, filling them with rage so that they turned on each other. Exercising his power felt delicious, like stretching one's limbs after sitting for ages.

He watched from one side of the food court as his influence spread. The girl who had sat across from her faceless friend on the floor was on her feet, ineffectually bashing the policewoman over the head with her tray. The policewoman, her projectile-firing weapon empty, using it to cave her assailant's face in before turning on other diners. And everywhere bodies rolling on the floor, thrashing, punching, biting, gouging.

Samael picked up one of the little lightweight white knives from a nearby table. It snapped between his fingers. He flicked the pieces away in disgust. How much greater the carnage would be if these humans carried proper weaponry. As it was, reduced to punching and gouging, it would take forever for them to kill each other. He sent out another wave of influence. And now they sank their teeth into each other's throats.

Rend! he mentally commanded. *Tear! Kill!*

He laughed as he set their minds ablaze and every impulse of tolerance or mercy vanished like mist before a hot wind and they fell each upon the next and the next until they themselves were broken, torn, and consumed, and it fell to the next and the next to rage and rend until the floor was awash with limbs and gore and a red mist hung in the air.

So much blood woke his thirst. The Death Angel waded in to join the harvest.

53

THE PILLAR OF HERMES

Rick floated in the gray, featureless limbo of the astral plane. Featureless because it awaited him to give it form. He knew what da Silva and his mentors knew: that where the light of the sun made the physical world visible, the light from the fire of desire made visible the astral world, and that the matter of the astral world was given form by thought, by what is imagined, and made real by the intensity of desire.

...who harnesses the power, the potency, of desire and bends it to his will...
Will is all...

He remembered standing in a marshy clearing outside Hendricks with da Silva urging him to lift a log with his mind and telling him to *visualize*, to imagine the log floating, weightless as a balloon.

He visualized a spherical coordinate system. Dazzling blue lines appeared, curving above, below, and all around him, as if he were the center of a transparent globe looking out on lines of latitude and longitude. The lights grew brighter whichever way he looked, and if he stared into any vector and imagined the lines gridding away into infinity, he saw endless layers of past and present, armies clashing, lovers embracing, mothers birthing, civilizations rising and falling.

Find the Emerald Tablet.

He quieted his racing heart...willed an image.

A tablet like a solid slab of glowing emerald appeared, its surface covered in hieroglyphs. He stared at the tablet till the ibises and reeds, serpents and human-headed birds grew clear.

A grid in the coordinate globe grew bright, blazed like threads of blue fire, while other lines dimmed. Within the vector, a distant point of light burned like a blue star. He willed himself toward it.

He stood on the cool desert sand beneath a billion bright stars. He had no idea when he was, only that he was in Egypt and far into the past. Nearby, a pyramid rose against the starry firmament, its smooth mantle of white limestone glowing under the starlight.

In his mind's eye, he saw a chamber beneath the pyramid, a great cavern deep beneath the upper vaults, accessed down flights of rough and craggy steps cut into the rock and thence through dark chambers and winding passages, till, at last, down a long narrow avenue, a glimmering light led into a spacious cave.

He willed himself inside.

The cavern was, indeed, spacious. Far larger than the antechamber of the Sibyl's sanctuary. Toward the back of the cave, through recesses that led to still further caverns, came a roar like a far-off sea and the dashing of waves against rocks, or perhaps the noise was more like the confused murmur of distant armies clashing at the onset of battle. Whatever produced the sounds, Rick had no interest in pursuing, for before him, in the center of the cavern, rearing its mighty bulk toward the lofty ceiling, rose the Pillar.

There was only one. Whatever happened to the gold, or if it ever existed, he had no idea. The column before him was green. A deep emerald green that shone with an inner light so that, dark as the cavern was, he saw with great clarity the hieroglyphs, not carved into the single mass of stone, but embossed upon its great flanks in bas-relief.

As he came closer, the hairs on his body lifted as if he stood before a dynamo and his flesh was awash in electromagnetic current. He was reminded of the sensation of vast engines powering up deep beneath his feet the night he faced Talmaiel atop the Crystal Mountain. There was an elemental energy like that at work here.

His gaze traveled up the column. Bands of hieroglyphs receded into obscurity. Among the Nemorenses, there were two or three who, given time, would have made sense of the ancient pictographs, but he would let the Pillar speak for itself.

His gaze settled on a falcon-headed god seated on a throne, a staff in his left hand, the ankh in his right. The red disk above his head portrayed him as Horus, in his role as sun god. The falcon's black eye stared at him. He stared back until his eyes watered and the character changed, enlarged so that he watched a tableau form. The Pillar showed him a bearded mage holding a great two-handed compass with which he drew a circle on a wall. In the circle appeared a triangle. Below the center of the circle where the compass's supporting leg touched the wall, a square appeared, and in this square a smaller circle, and in the lesser circle the images of a man and a woman naked. Words formed in his head. The voice was that of a Nemorensis, but he knew it was the Pillar speaking through the Priest.

Make of the man and woman a circle, of that a quadrangle, of this a triangle, of the same a circle and you will have the Stone of the Philosophers.

There it was again! The Philosopher's Stone! And somehow the image almost made sense. Almost. Was the wise man with the compass Hermes? Was his drawing illustrating the secret of the Stone? If it was, why wasn't he understanding?

He bared his teeth in frustration.

As the serpent casts off its skin to grow, he heard the Sibyl (Fergi!) say, *so man must cast off his limited conceptions. Only through death can gnosis be attained.*

He understood that. She was saying to see with new eyes, he must pluck out the old.

As the serpent casts off its skin...

He took a deep breath.

Each of us has a mind mirror…a murky thing…But he who will stare into it until the veil lifts will see beyond the physical world into the spiritual.

He closed his eyes, watched the mage in his mind mirror.

A circle in a square in a triangle in a greater circle.

The Squaring of the Circle was an epithet for the completion of the Great Work, the end of alchemy, the achievement of the Philosopher's Stone.

The wisdom of all things above and below is contained in the squaring of the circle.

Okay. The alchemists expressed their wisdom through symbols the way the Egyptians used pictographs. Dee had his *Sigillum Dei* and *Monas Hieroglyphica*, Bruno his mnemonic emblems.

Symbols are to the mind what tools are to the hand.

Circles represented completion. But there were two…

The Pillar and his mentors were silent, as if he needed to understand on his own.

He thought of Ptolemy's spheres, each nested within the next. And Bruno's infinite worlds: stars that were suns orbited by living planets teeming with infinite races. It came to him with a mental finger snap. The outer circle represented the infinite. The inner, being contained, the finite.

He opened his eyes, looked at the relationship of the two circles.

Below, above.

The finite becomes the infinite. Mortal becomes immortal.

It was a passage. From below to above.

Involution to evolution.

Unconsciousness to consciousness.

Was the Stone a path?

The quadrangle…four winds, four points of the compass, four elements, the three dimensions of space plus the one of time, the four trigons.

The triangle contained all the mysticism of the trinity. Father, Son, and Holy Ghost. Maiden, mother, crone. No, think of the triangle from the alchemical point of view, of the work of the magician.

Mercury, sulfur, salt.

Body, soul, spirit.

All things in the physical have their counterparts in the celestial.

Magic is simply the complete understanding of the conjunction of celestial powers with elementary bodies and the development of the art and faculty needed to manipulate those correspondences.

As above, so below.

The triangle had a base and an apex: a structure joining below to above.

Dee wanted to call down subtle rays from the stars to affect change in the physical realm. Bruno wanted to assail heaven and confront God himself.

Again, his thoughts were drawn to the idea of the Stone as a path, a Jacob's Ladder connecting above and below like the Sephiroth.

He returned his attention to the nude figures of the man and woman enclosed in the lesser circle.

As he watched, the figures became animated, and where before they had gazed outward and stood separate, they turned their heads toward each other and joined hands.

Conjunctio!

Make of the man and woman a circle.

Man, woman.

Gold, silver.

Sun, Moon.

He remembered Paracelsus' challenge: *What do you know of the Art of making Sol and Luna?*

Sol, Luna.

Sun, Moon.

Man, Woman.

The union of male and female!

The Marriage of Sol and Luna!

His eye traced the path from the united figures upward through the circle's meridian to the apex of the triangle.

You had it wrong, Reginald! he thought with mounting excitement. *The material world is not the mirror that reflects the divine emanation onto the path of evolution. It's man. Man and woman together are the mirror of eternity!*

The image changed again. The mage and the compass disappeared. The figures inside the greater circle blurred, ran together like melted crayons, reformed. Now he was looking at a complex geometrical figure. The great circle remained, but inside it was a repeating pattern like the geometrical arabesques ornamenting the walls of Islamic mosques.

Circles overlapping circles, so that within each circle, no matter where he looked within the circumference of the larger circle, he saw six-petaled flowers. In the almond shape of the petals, he recognized only too well the *vesica piscis* or mandorla. Medieval Christians had appropriated the symbol and turned it into the Jesus fish, but it was far older. The ancient symbol was a gateway, a cosmic portal, an intersection between the human and the divine, between heaven and earth or the higher and lower planes. A threshold of sorts.

This is the Flower of Life, the Pillar informed him. *Its structure contains the seed of creation and the forms of all things.*

One by one, the lesser circles within the greater illuminated leaving others dimmed, as had the blue vector lines of the spherical coordinate grid. He counted nineteen circles in all. And now patterns appeared in the "flowers." Using the centers of the flowers—four in the middle column and three each on either side, the Sephiroth emerged, along with the twenty-two paths connecting the ten Sephirah.

Now the Sephiroth faded and a new image overlay the Flower. Something like a six-pointed Star of David and another inside it with the centermost circle in its midst and a hexagon connecting six circles at the points of the greater star.

Metatron's Cube, the Pillar spoke through the Nemorensis.

The transformations sped up and he was presented each in turn with the five Platonic solids contained within the Flower and Metatron's Cube: the tetrahedron like a three-sided pyramid, the hexahedron or cube, the eight-faced octahedron, the twelve-faced dodecahedron, and the twenty-faced icosahedron. The tetrahedron reappeared, its apex pointing down. Another tetrahedron appeared overlapping it, pointing up, so that looked at straight on, he recognized the star tetrahedron, the light vehicle, the Merkaba.

He stared in wonder, knowing what would happen next.

The chariot emerged from the Flower, grew three-dimensional and larger. He backed away to give it room.

Formed from the ten sapphires of Raziel's Book, the Merkaba that had descended onto Crystal Mountain to transport Talmaiel to the Abyss was a dazzling blue. This one, an emanation of the Pillar, glowed a living emerald green that pulsed as the superimposed inverted pyramids began to spin in opposite directions. Faster and faster they whirled, till his clothes flapped in the wind and his hair streamed and the keening of its whistle grew higher and higher.

Rejoicing at the sight, he stepped inside.

54

ASMODAI AT THE MET

Perhaps it was the rage in Asmodai's eyes, but more probably the fact that his naked flesh was drenched head to toe in human blood, that caused the puny creatures to flee from him. He'd wrenched limbs and heads until he'd had his fill. But while ripping muscle and tendon and snapping bone with his bare hands was satisfying, he longed for his old companions—sword and axe. Preferably a great two-handed battle axe. Memories of wading through human armies swinging his axe in a great scything arc pushed him to leave off his slaughter and seek a blacksmith.

But despite the impressive number of shops that lined the broad avenue—shops so different from the tents and straw-and-mud-bricked inns of ancient towns—he could not find one. In shop after shop he'd tortured keepers to reveal where he might find a smithy, but no one seemed to know. Some did not even know what he was talking about. He turned from torturing the keepers to promising them kingdoms and slaves, to no avail.

Did no one in this bizarre age in which he found himself know the art of hammer and anvil? Was mankind grown so ignorant of the skills the Grigori had taught?

In one shop he found a selection of swords on display. At first, he was delighted, for among the weapons was a great two-handed, double-edged broadsword. *Gadriel would like this*, he thought. But he'd hefted the sword and found it heavy and unwieldy. It lacked the

247

balance and grace of Gadriel's creations. Nor did it sing when he cleaved the air in a figure eight. The metal was soft, the edge dull. The weapon was no better than a cudgel. Worse. A proper war-hammer at least had the heft and balance to smash a foe's skull. This was nothing like the fine bronze blades forged by Akkadian smiths. It broke on the first swing when he smashed it over the shop counter. He'd used the broken blade to saw through the cringing shop owner's jugular before tossing it aside in disgust.

But now something was drawing him. The Beheader followed the lodestone pull of his instincts up the broad steps of the many-columned building that rose like a great temple or palace against the jaundiced sky. Scarlet banners on either side of its central arch read

THE

MET

The doors were locked but yielded to his touch. He stepped into a great hall. Lurid yellow light fell through the oculuses set in the three domes high above. Ahead, past more columns, a magnificent staircase led to an upper floor.

He did not take the stairs but, led by his instincts, followed one of the side galleries into a hall lined with glass cases full of armor unlike anything he had seen in the centuries before the banishment. Whole suits of armor designed to encase a man head to foot. Even the face was covered, the helmet providing only a narrow slit through which the warrior might observe his foe. Even though the suits were superior to the breastplates, helms, and greaves worn by warriors in his day, there was no mistaking them for the utilitarian armor of ordinary foot soldiers. They must have belonged to kings so ornate was the scrollwork engraved into the silver and gold surfaces.

Armored warriors mounted on armored and panoplied horses paraded down the center of the hall, as if some prince and his noble retinue were embarking on a state visit. The armor—man's and horse's—was exquisite, the articulation exceptionally fine.

But he had no need of armor. Indeed, he'd always preferred to plunge into battle as he was now—naked and wearing his enemy's blood for war paint.

He searched the retinue for a battle axe big enough for his hands. Seeing none, he returned his attention to the glass cases.

Behind the suits of armor, he spied an assortment of pollaxes. Some as tall as himself. The glass shattered at his touch. Some of the weapons were ornate, obviously intended for ceremonial purposes. He ignored these and selected the tallest in the middle. The squared-off staff was smooth with age. The killing end consisted of a thin axe on one side backed by a spike on the other. Another spike like the blade of a spear topped the staff. The butt end bore another sharp spike so that either end of the weapon could be used to pierce an enemy.

He stepped back to the mounted warriors and ran the topmost spike through a horse's breast plate. He wrenched it out and swung the axe blade into the warrior, cleaving off an arm and sending the tenantless suit clattering to the floor.

He twirled the staff through his hands, at first slowly, then quickly gathering speed as old muscle memory took over. He'd once been expert in spinning any blade—sword, axe, or javelin—fore, aft, overhead, one or two-handed, alone or in combination with other weapons, as few humans ever could. Soon the weapon was a blur and he rejoiced in its balance, its thrilling beauty.

He would have preferred the staff longer, the axe blade broader, but, he reflected as he strode to the exit, it would do.

Indeed, it would do just fine!

55

TALMAIEL PROPOSES A TRUCE

The green glow of the Merkaba flashed through the hotel room, and Rick was left standing on the beige carpet facing Talmaiel. He knew with certainty the light chariot would return when he willed it.

Terry stood where he had, in the corner by the nightstand on the other side of the bed, his mouth slack, his cataracted eyes gazing at nothing. It seemed neither of them had moved, and perhaps they had not—if he'd returned the moment he left.

Instead of speaking, he attacked.

Now a single Richard Scott faced the Grigori. Now six surrounded him. One behind lowered his stance and drove a fist into the angel's kidney. The Sleepless One let out a *whoomph* of surprise and pain.

A Rick on the left pivoted and drove a knuckle punch into Talmaiel's neck, going for the vagus just below the angle of the jaw, while one in front *tai sabakied* to the left and, blocking with his right forearm, drove his heel into the side of Talmaiel's knee. Only the angel's great strength saved the leg from snapping, but under the barrage, the Grigori staggered. Another Rick took the opportunity to smash his heel into the angel's solar plexus. Even through the layer of powerful muscle, he was rewarded with a satisfying grunt.

Then all six Richard Scotts were laying into Fallen One, unleashing the pent-up anger and remorse he'd stored since Wally's death.

Talmaiel mimicked Rick's maneuver, splitting himself into six identical Grigori, but Rick was ahead of him and each Talmaiel faced two Rick Scotts.

One Grigori was hurled over the bed into the air conditioning unit. Another slammed into a wall, leaving a dent in the plaster and a cloud of dust.

Talmaiel abandoned multiplicity, reverted to one. Now his method was defensive but incredibly fast; wherever Rick swung he suddenly wasn't. Now he was in one corner, now in another. Now in the open bathroom door, now behind him. Rick tried to predict where he would appear, but the angel was an accomplished magician and had the advantage of thousands of years' experience in real combat.

Rick was spread thin. And now Talmaiel took the offensive, delivering blows of his own instead of simply avoiding Rick's. Nothing debilitating, but the effects were cumulative so that within minutes a dozen Ricks were panting and aching in a dozen places. Though, thanks to the Goddess and his mentors and, likely, to his experience with the Pillar, he had undergone a miraculous recovery following the lashing he'd received in Azazel's torture chamber, he found himself wearying and too busy blocking punches to strike.

Talmaiel called from the bathroom, "Stop. We need to talk."

Rick regrouped, a single entity crouched behind closed fists. His lungs were aflame and he was dripping sweat, but he called out, "Fight, coward!"

Talmaiel stepped into the doorway, leaned against the jamb. His face was hideous from the ravages of the fire; otherwise, he looked unscathed. There was blood on his cornflower-blue shirt, but it wasn't his, Rick discovered, spotting blood on his stinging knuckles where the skin had split punching the angel's burn-scarred jaw. Grigori didn't sweat, they didn't sleep, and, apparently, they didn't bleed.

Rick shook sweat from his eyes.

"What's there to talk about?"

"You found the Tablet."

"I found a pillar."

"Same thing. Who knows how many repositories there are for the Book of Nature? Raziel's. The Pillars of Hermes... I wouldn't be surprised if there were others." He stepped into the room, hands before him in surrender. "I told you we must work together to defeat Yaldabaoth and the Two Hundred. At least hear my proposal."

Rick licked his lip, debating. His gaze was drawn to Terry standing in the corner. The youth was still comatose, his blind eyes staring at nothing, drool glistening on his chin.

"Let him go first!"

Talmaiel's lipless smile made his face more hideous. "Gladly. Only your friend's not really here."

"What?"

"See for yourself." Talmaiel gestured for Rick to approach Terry.

The teenager hadn't moved a muscle. And as Rick stepped around the bed, he detected no rise and fall of the boy's chest.

"Go ahead. Wake him."

Rick reached out, already knowing what he would find.

His hand passed through the boy. The image swirled, dissipated like mist.

"An illusion. We need to work together, and I knew you wouldn't listen to me unless I had something you wanted."

Rick's fists clenched. What he wanted was to lay into the monster now that he'd caught his breath, but he resisted. It was a dirty trick, albeit a clever one. And what had Talmaiel tricked him into? Because of the devious one's trickery, his powers had grown. As the Nemorenses had imparted their collective wisdom, so too the Pillar had revealed its secrets.

"And now you have nothing on me."

"I do not. But regardless of our past, we want the same things. Survival. The continuation of," he spread his hands taking in the wide world, "existence. I've enlisted several of my brethren who chaff under Semjaza's rule. I need to speak with others. Humans will fight—there are so many now. And united with the people of Hendricks—"

"You've spoken to Grace?"

He nodded. "She's a realist. She knows this is a battle to the end and we need all the help we can get."

It was what the Nemorensis had told him. And as much as his knowledge and his powers had improved, he had no idea how he could defend the earth against the Grigori and take on Yaldabaoth at the same time. Especially after his failure to beat Talmaiel...again.

Talmaiel provided the answer.

"You must deal with Yaldabaoth on your own—you and your colleagues. While I join Her people to stop Semjaza."

As much as he would have liked to join Grace, John, Terry, and the brave warriors of Hendricks, he knew Talmaiel was right. To paraphrase da Silva, he was the only one who stood a chance of changing Yaldabaoth's course.

Without another word, he summoned the Merkaba.

56

WAR COUNSEL

Reverend Grace didn't need a gavel to call the meeting to order. Standing at the lectern dressed in camos and tactical boots with the Goddess' pentangle of willow wands hanging on the wall behind her, all she had to do was sweep the filled pews with her violet eyes and a hush fell over the congregation.

Reverend Grace wasn't the only one dressed for combat; nearly half the citizens of Hendricks wore fatigues and not just for show. The majority of able-bodied men and women were ready for deployment. Their considerable arsenal was loaded into school buses waiting to take them wherever they were needed. Nor had they needed to restock last-minute inventory. Once Talmaiel and the poor bikers he had brainwashed and pressed into service were out of their hair, they'd immediately replenished their supplies.

Their arsenal included M15s, M16s, a few current close quarters MK18s, as well as several Vietnam-era Browning Automatic Rifles chambered for the .30-06 Springfield cartridge, Remington shotguns, a few Mossbergs, scoped Remington sniper rifles, Tasers, flashbang grenades, tear gas, tactical radios, and enough body armor and night vision goggles to equip a few SWAT teams. Cases of M67 grenades and the older Vietnam-era M26 series, plus quantities of IEDs and claymores rounded out the ordinance. In addition to the military artillery, most citizens possessed shotguns, deer rifles, and sidearms of their own.

"Evoi! Kybele!" Grace invoked the Goddess to bless the meeting with Her sacred presence. Though she spoke without a microphone, her voice filled the sanctuary.

"Evoi! Kybele!" the congregation responded.

"Friends, neighbors." Her gaze drifted from face to face, and every person in the room knew she was speaking from her heart, expressing her love for each of them. Hendricks was not just a village or community with shared values, but a family that relied on and supported one another. "We all know what Yaldabaoth has begun. The end time is upon us. Now we have a new threat. War is coming."

No murmur started as it might have in other congregations. With public utilities down—Internet and phone services, often iffy to begin with, were out—and most of the hamlet running off generators and those with the sight suddenly blind as the average Jane, most citizens were in the dark.

"We are ready to deploy, as I'm certain our cohorts in other countries are. What do you hear from our friends?"

The latter she addressed to two people in the front row.

Beatrice Joanna and her dad Bob Bevens, who operated an emergency radio out of their pole barn, wore baseball caps with the call sign W5CBL blazoned across the crown. Grace suspected in many parts of the world, ham radio was the last line of communication.

Bob said: "I've talked to our people in Vermont, California, Anatolia, Australia, Canada, France, Italy, Belgium, Germany, Norway, Sweden, Yugoslavia, India, Russia, Kazakhstan, you name it. But two groups I couldn't get a hold of—Madagascar and Argentina."

That set citizens murmuring. Kybele's people were always ready, day or night, rain or shine. Even before modern communications connected the world, scryers kept abreast of what was happening in each other's quarter. For a group not to respond was unheard of.

Reverend Grace voiced what many suspected. "They're off the grid?"

"Looks like. News report says the suburb of Argentina they live in disappeared. No news from Madagascar."

That was bad, but Grace told herself their people—like all the neighborhoods that had slid back in time—were alive somewhere. Or some *when*. And would do what was needed in their new era.

"What else?"

Beatrice Joanna answered: "The Grigori are in New York. We've picked up sporadic reports of carnage. People are panicking. The government is advising citizens to stay indoors."

"Any word from Our Lady?" Will Pritchard, a retired Little Rock high school chemistry teacher in the third row, tilted his head toward the pentangle.

"Not since I spoke to Her this morning," Grace answered. "She said She would try to talk sense into Yaldabaoth. We haven't heard anything since."

Terry, sitting in up front, stood. He'd changed his tee shirt into short sleeves—a yellow-and-green plaid with a button-down collar—and combed his hair. The raven's skull hung from his neck. He went nowhere without it. He stood so Grace and the congregation could both see him and signed. Many in Hendricks could sign, but Margreet stood and translated for those who didn't. Word had gotten round that Terry was the only one in the hamlet left with the sight.

"He says he can't see Her and he's worried."

"Has he lost the sight?" Philander Key called from the back.

Terry signed.

"He says, no. She's just gone off the grid. Like Madagascar."

That brought another murmur.

When it passed, Grace said, "It may be that She is with Her son. Our prayers go with Her that She might convince him to alter his course. But whatever happens, we have work to do. With or without Her presence, we must be ready to shift for ourselves." She paused to let that sink in. Not that everyone present, except for the few youngest children, weren't ready to put themselves on the line for the planet. "John."

John Hanley, a trim, unassuming elderly man who was a combination village shaman and military strategist, was not dressed in military fatigues. As usual he wore an open-collar dress shirt over navy kakis and topsiders. He was clean shaved and his haircut was recent.

He had the full head of wavy black hair of a much younger man and his sparkling dark eyes still fluttered hearts. Today their sparkle was replaced with the no-nonsense determination of a battle-tested commander.

"Friends," John greeted the congregation. "With most civilian communications down, the authorities are treating the Grigori invasion as a terrorist event. The New York National Guard with the support of the New York State Military Reserve is being mobilized. The police and Army National Guard have no idea what they're up against. Luckily, Jeremiah Eckler, Mayor of Middleville, has been in contact with his brother Jacob, a Colonial in the New York Guard and a close friend of General Ambrose Green, the Guard's CO. Jacob is one of us and will be advising General Green of the true nature of the threat and making him aware of our cohorts' presence and our own. The last thing we want is for the National Guard to mistake us for terrorists and fire upon us."

That got nods and a few affirmative remarks.

John ducked his head in Grace's direction. "Reverend."

When he stepped down from the rostrum, Grace took the lectern and said, "Thank you, John. Well, there you have it. We leave immediately. It would take us a good twenty hours to join our people in Manhattan were we to drive there. Probably more with electricity chaotic and paved roads suddenly disappearing or turning into rutted tracks."

Several heads nodded at that. The General Store-Post Office up the road had disappeared sometime before noon, replaced by several stout trees that must have stood for generations.

"But we have a better way. The Sisterhood will be joining us. Or rather we will be joining them. Sister Margreet assures us they can get us there faster."

That brought some smiles and more than a few Praise Hers.

She looked over the sea of grim faces, her eyes at once hard with the reality of the battle to come and damp with the knowledge that there would be sacrifices. "This is it, friends. We are all family. And we know what it is to lose family." She could see that they, like her, were thinking of the loved ones lost during the last encounter. Her gaze fell on Terry. He was staring up at her as if he could see her through the white cataracts that webbed his eyes. Brave Terry. A boy no longer. A man now, young as he was. His mother dead. She'd killed the man who'd shot Jewelie Light with her own hand, beheaded him with her katana, but she'd been moments too late. Terry had amassed more kills than anyone in this congregation, and he hadn't cried at his mother's funeral but maintained an expression much as he wore now, his face grim, his gaze distant. She flashed back on Jewelie laid her out on her bed. At peace, a smile on her face, her hands folded over the white gown she and Becky Bloom and Samantha Waters dressed her in.

"Oh, my Blessed Lady," she murmured under her breath, "be with us."

57

GUARDIANS OF THE THRESHOLD

"Are you sure? No one's been this way since...longer than memory."

The creature who spoke would have been taller than Talmaiel if he were standing, but both he and his mate were crouched on their haunches surveying something between them on the flinty ground. Both would have appeared almost human, were it not for the red scorpion tails curving over their heads, each tipped in a knife-like stinger and their auras that shimmered across the surface of the mountain.

Craggy peaks rose above them on either side of the narrow defile, the gray rock towering against the glowering yellow sky.

"The bones don't lie. Someone's coming." Without rising from where she crouched over the bleached white bones scattered on the ground, the Scorpion-woman lifted her head and sniffed. "He's close." Lidless black eyes, perfectly round and unblinking like two platters of polished obsidian, as liquid as spider's eyes, scanned the pass in his direction.

Rick pressed himself closer to the outcropping behind which he hid. The Merkaba had dropped him off at the foot of the pass, as if it could take him no further.

These are the guardians of the threshold, da Silva said. *You have no choice but to face them.*

Easy for you to say, he thought but did not mean for da Silva to hear. The Priest heard anyway. *True, nevertheless…*

Rick fought back the terror that threatened to unhinge him, shoved himself to his feet, and stepped into the open.

The great twin heads swiveled at once. And at once they were standing, blocking the pass. Spears had appeared in their hands. Long honed blades glimmered in the sullen light.

"Halt! You may not pass!" the Scorpion-man hissed, leveling his spear at his chest. His stinger bobbed over his head, dripping venom.

"Wait!" the female said.

The Scorpion-man sneered. "Wait? For human? A mortal?" He started forward.

She laid a glowing hand on his arm. "Smell."

The nostrils of the male's proto-nose flared as he sniffed the air. Though his arachnid eyes showed no change, he stepped back and raised his spear.

"You meet our gaze and live! You are more than man."

For a moment, Rick shielded his eyes against the glory of their aura, then he lowered his hand. He was tempted to say, "I am no one," but sensed humility was, under the circumstances, inappropriate.

"I am Richard Scott!" he said in a loud, commanding voice full of confidence and authority he did not feel. "Son of Frank and Jinny, Rex Nemorensis, Diana's Priest, Warden of the Lower Plane. I seek Yaldabaoth, Cybele's pup. You know I speak truth. You smell my blood. It is both less and more than human. Look into my eyes and see Her image. She who made Him who made the rock beneath your feet."

He raised his hand and he saw fear in their eyes. Their auras dimmed. Their tails lowered.

"Who dares come here must be a god," the Scorpion-man said.

The female guardian said, "Two-thirds a god. The third part is mortal."

"I am no god. I am only human but I will go on."

"You are more than human," the Scorpion-man said.

His companion sniffed again. "And you are not alone," she said with wonder.

"Stand aside!" Rick commanded, using his fear to put an edge to his voice. "You will not stop me."

"We will not," said the Scorpion-woman.

"Pass Priest," said her mate.

They bowed and moved to either side.

When he was past, he turned and asked, "What do you know of the Philosopher's Stone?"

The female guardian said, "The Stone is the journey connecting what lies below to what is above."

"The Stone is behind you," said the Scorpion-man, "it is beneath your feet, it is the road ahead of you. The Stone is the path, the path the journey."

Rick turned and, leaving the guardians behind, passed over the mountain.

58

RAPTURE

It was still early and the bar was empty when Talmaiel strolled in. Come evening the place would be packed, the bar four deep under red lights, the din of voices yelling to be heard diminished only by the shriek and growl of heavy metal erupting from the performance area beyond the bar. The world was ending but tonight's show was sold out. That was metal. The end of time a call to party loud.

The bartender gave him a questioning look but, seeing the monstrous disfigurement of the face beneath the hood, returned to polishing glasses.

The walls and ceiling of Saint Vitus' cramped performance space were, like the bar and unsigned cinderblock façade, painted matte black. Appropriate for Brooklyn's premier metal venue. The four men on the smallish stage were rehearing, the thunder of guitars and drum deafening. Three were men at any rate. The bassist, lead guitarist and drummer were all human enough, though a vestige of the ancient Grigori bloodline ran through their veins so that, like Rick and Fergi, they were gifted with second sight and other powers the scientific community scoffed at and labeled "paranormal."

The fourth figure, as tall, hairless, and blue-eyed as Talmaiel, was Kashdejan, the sole Watcher besides Talmaiel to evade the Avengers when the Choir was rounded up and banished to Abyss. Their paths had crossed many times, but while Talmaiel played the warrior, leading armies into battle and even ruling a kingdom or two between long spells when he explored wildernesses, Kashdejan preferred keeping a low profile, using his curative and musical skills to act as physician or royal musician to numerous courts over the past several millennia. At various times his prosthetics and clockwork automatons had been all the rage.

His latest alias was Dean Cash—a humorous play on his ancient Gallic name, Dian Cecht, though he liked to tell groupies he styled his stage name after James Dean and Johnny Cash. Despite his (current) signature silver-tipped cowboy boots and pearl-buttoned, turquoise rodeo shirt, Kashdejan's band didn't perform western music. Theirs was an intricate baroque mélange of guitar-driven heavy metal and classical (Baroque again) tapestries that suggested electrified Bach with a strong dose of Sabbath combined with the technical wizardry of a Paganini. Together they formed Rapture, appropriately named for a band performing on the eve of Earth's demise.

The Maestro's custom eight-string, reminiscent of a B.C. Rich Warlock, all sharp edges and looking as if it was made for chopping wood, he'd built himself. All of Rapture's instruments were custom made. Lead guitarist, Ariel Patton's copperhead snakeskin Gunslinger, Zak Reed's Crimson King bass, even the metal on Carol "Thunderman" Fleming Jr.'s drum kit, were fashioned from electrum and tuned on the astral plane.

All things—all forms and objects in the multiverse—were vibrations of will. Physical nature constituted a low order of vibrations; the astral world represented a higher octave of the physical universe; the spiritual plane a higher octave still. Everything in the four worlds were connected, enfolded in the implicate order. Including the human brain which vibrated synchronously with different rates of etheric vibration, thereby achieving different states of consciousness. Changing the state of consciousness involved changing the brain's vibrational frequency. The ecstasies of the dervish or ancient sages, as well as the feverish creations of poets and artists through the ages, relied, in part, on the brain's ability to vibrate synchronously with the etheric vibrations of the spiritual plane. With direct vibrational access to the higher octaves of the subtle planes, coupled with the group's artistry, Rapture's instruments raised their audience's experience to a near-religious ecstasy.

Talmaiel also knew that, because they accessed the astral plane and were capable of reversing the magnetic polarity of atoms at a frequency exceeding eight thousand fluctuations a second, their instruments could be used as powerful tools to transmute matter.

Or, if turned on living beings—rogue Grigori, for example—as a weapon.

Leaning against the back wall, Talmaiel pushed back his hood, dropped his shades into a pocket, letting Kashdejan see him. Not that it mattered: the Grigori would have sensed his presence long before he'd entered the building.

Surrounded by Mesa Boogie amps and effects processors, the foursome ripped a tonal frenzy from their instruments. While Ariel attacked with a pick, Kashdejan's powerful fingers dug into the strings. Ariel's high lead soared over Kashdejan's chugging basal chords.

The tempo sped up. Carol's drums rolled like thunder and hail. A chorus repeated the rhythm notes faster in a flurry of progressions. Suddenly Ariel's lead lost its distortion and clean notes cut through Kashdejan's overdrive. Then Kashdejan shadowed Ariel's ambient lead, finger tapping the bass strings while Zack improvised on bass and Carol's drums provided a rolling undertow.

Now Kashdejan swept down and down the fingerboard playing arpeggios in the key of A till his fingers blurred like hummingbirds' wings and notes higher than any six-string could scream wailed from the neck humbucker.

In a sort of antiphonal call and response, Ariel and Kashdejan roared the lyrics into their mikes, Ariel's melodic baritone ascending, Kashdejan's growling bass descending.

"Embrace the endtime."
"Reject the sunshine."
"Beyond the gates,"
"No future waits."
"Embrace the endtime."
"Release the starshine."
"Time receding."

"Mankind fleeting."

"Blackness looming"

"In the glooming."

Now the music launched into a rapid palm-muted machine gun staccato of distortion over which Ariel's furious arpeggios soared. Kashdejan's powerful animal growl took over vocals.

"Listen to the ringing knell,

This metal sky this living hell.

This island Earth breathes its last

As future slides into the past.

Embrace the endtime.

Reject the sunshine.

Darkness is its own reward."

Sonic dissonance soared like jets descending on the bar. Carol's black face glistened with sweat as his sticks blurred over the drums. Bursts of machine-gun, palm-muted staccato power chords followed.

Then Kashdejan, Ariel, and Zak heeled their strings. The guitars stopped. Carol's drums continued alone.

One two.

One two.

A death march echoing through the small performance space while Kashdejan's visceral growl intoned the final lines.

"The gods are mad.

Let us be glad.

Into the night

Let us take flight.

Welcome Sleep

My soul to keep.

As we plunge into the deep."

Ariel rang out a single heavily distorted E7#9 "Hendrix chord" and held his pick aloft until, at last, it faded, then screeched his pick up the bass strings.

The silence that followed was deafening.

———

"All hail, Kashdejan, Friend of Man!" Talmaiel greeted his fellow Grigori as he stepped down from the stage.

Kashdejan regarded Talmaiel with mock surprise. He would have raised eyebrows, if he had any. Being Grigori, he did not.

"You look like shit."

Talmaiel passed a hand over his face. Despite Raziel's and Sariel's ministrations, his flesh was still a web of scars. "I'll heal." He smiled, but succeeded only in making himself more hideous.

"Look," Kashdejan poked him in the chest, an annoying habit he'd no doubt picked up from humans, "we're performing an end-of-the-world show tonight. Why don't you join us? You can be our mascot. We'll give you a tambourine."

Mascot was insult enough, but tambourine player in a metal band was low. Talmaiel didn't take offense however—their infrequent exchanges generally went like this, at least at first, before they got down to whatever business brought them to seek each other out. Instead, he smiled his most gruesome grin, showing plenty of teeth and widening his lidless eye till it bulged. "Were I vain, you might offend me."

"Heaven forbid." Kashdejan's grin provided the only wrinkles in his otherwise smooth, ever-youthful face. His blue eyes twinkled with mischief. They'd never been friends, not really. They'd never seen eye to eye on anything, their respective careers affording little opportunity for commonality or socializing. Nevertheless, their bond was deep. For millennia they had been the last of their species, near extinct, the only two eternals on Earth. It had been a kind of—if not a comfort, then at least a constant in a changing world to know they were not alone, that another of their kind was around somewhere among humanity's ephemeral masses.

"I thought I heard a piece in there that sounded familiar, something from your Roman period."

Kashdejan smiled, as if pleased he remembered. Talmaiel had attended only two of Kashdejan's musical performances—once in first-century Imperial Rome and again at the *Palais-Royal* in the late seventeenth century. The latter was a smaller affair. Mostly religious and secular nobility, a sprinkling of artists and philosophers who, if not invited for entertainment, ate in the kitchen. The Roman Empire knew how to put on a show.

"That's right, you were there."

"I was in Rome to collect a debt."

"I recall how you collected debts back then."

Talmaiel ignored the bait. "You requisitioned kettledrums from the Praetorian Guard."

That won a broader grin.

The concert he referred to took place in Rome at the Festival of Jupiter in the restored Theatre of Marcellus. With an audience of twenty thousand spectators, the venue was a precursor of today's stadium concert. Kashdejan performed on the *hydraulis* or water organ, which, amplified via the astral plane, sounded equally loud everywhere in the amphitheater. Some listeners suspected sorcery. Besides the kettledrums, he'd also requisitioned a dozen *cornu*, the great curved horns the Legion used to signal orders to the troops over the din of battle. His inclusion of the *aulos* and panpipes—associated with Bacchus and the celebration of Cybele—and two-dozen Galli in native costume wailing away on bagpipes were criticized by the more conservative patricians as indecorous and an offense to Apollo. But the plebeians loved it, and Vespasian, who had no ear for music, was well-pleased with the spectacle and volume.

"Loudest music I'd ever heard."

"The loudest anyone heard till then."

It felt good to share a laugh with his oldest acquaintance, but he sobered as a thought occurred.

"You know, the whole time I was on Abyss, I didn't see a single instrument. I hadn't thought of it, but I don't believe in all the time they were there they bothered to make instruments. Imagine all those millennia without music."

Kashdejan shook his head. "I'd go mad."

"Many did. So much is at stake," he said, remembering red-and-purple sunsets over the Mediterranean and Alpine peaks glinting white at sunrise, the smell of orchids and the sensuous perfumes that graced women's throats in the court of Xerxes, the sound of panpipes and war horns and the bitter-sweet taste of toasted sesame seed cakes soaked in honey. "So much to lose."

His gaze met Kashdejan's, but before he could speak, the Maestro held up a hand.

"Before you ask, the answer is 'No.'"

"You won't fight? The Choir is back."

"Don't I know it. Araqiel was by. Thin as a rail, he still looks better than you."

"You're just going to let Semjaza run loose? Do what he wants? If we muzzle him, the rest of the Brethren can be made to heel."

"Fat chance of that. You've seen them. They're hungry."

The Watcher was right. Talmaiel recalled the ravenous looks they'd cast his way on Abyss.

"The boy is seeking Yaldabaoth."

"And I wish him luck."

"Don't underestimate him. He defeated me."

"You, my friend, are not the Maker. And where is She?" Kashdejan gazed up at the black ceiling as if searching the great beyond. "I don't sense Her presence. It's as if She's vanished." He shook his head. "No, I do not mean to offend, but it's over. We've had a good run. Better than any human or Grigori. If Semjaza is under the delusion he's going to rule Earth for the rest of eternity, who am I to burst his bubble? I would rather meet the end doing what I enjoy than locked in battle with my brothers." He grinned, his white teeth glinting under the lights. "Let them have their blood. I feed off my audience's energy."

"So your solution is to party while the ship goes down?"

The grin widened. "Sounds like a plan."

59
GOLEMS

The Merkaba set him down on a flat chromium-yellow plane that stretched to infinity in all directions. There was no horizon, no stars overhead, only the perfectly level plane below and the blackness above. And the Sphere. It was impossible to tell if the Sphere was spinning or standing still. So blinding was the radiance emanating from its shimmering surface, he couldn't look at it directly but only catch glimpses of it squinting out the corner of his eye.

Is this Yaldabaoth? Rick thought as the Merkaba touched down. But the Sphere was no more the Demiurge than the Merkaba was himself. It was a vehicle, an astral starship, an abode—perhaps all of these things and more.

Then he saw the guardians.

Ranked in columns around the Sphere, which hovered some yards above the plain, were a hundred warriors armed with shields and spears. They were human only in shape. They were made of bronze. The inanimate material from which they were forged did not keep them from movement, however. With a groan of metal, they turned as one when Rick stepped out of the Merkaba.

Reginald?

Careful Rick. We know no more than you. No human has ever ascended this far.

The bronze warriors closed ranks, formed a shield wall bristling with spears.

Unlike the scorpion guardians, they seemed unimpressed by his Grigori blood.

They're not attacking.

It was true. The army before him remained crouched, shields overlapping, spears leveled, but they did not advance. He sensed...curiosity, anger, uncertainty—a powerful questioning mind whose source did not emanate from the blank bronze eyes facing him but from the Sphere.

He shielded his eyes with a hand and tried to stare into the shifting radiance, but its surface was chimerical, a mercurial flux of liquid light, pulling the gaze so no part of the globe remained in focus but attention itself was always in motion.

He closed his eyes and opened the portals of his mind. The warriors were golems, automatons. He received no impression of thoughts from the hollow heads, nor was there a sense of a hive mind as if the automatons were constituents of a colony. No, he sensed only a single will directing them: a powerful presence emanating from the Sphere.

Yaldabaoth.

It wasn't fear that brought a ripple of gooseflesh over his skin, but a sensation akin to *déjà vu*, a cold certainly that there was a familiarity he couldn't put a finger on about the presence.

What now?

Da Silva did not answer immediately, and he sensed the Priest's uncertainty. But only for a moment. Then, as if the congregation in his head had reached a decision, a feeling of confidence radiated from within, and more than one voice said in unison in a half-dozen languages but with the same import: *We've got this!* And suddenly he was stretched on his toes, his back arched, arms thrown out to his sides, as the Nemorenses left him with a great rush of wind and noise, like the whirring of bats pouring out of a cave.

Then the automatons were no longer empty, no longer under the direction of the presence in the Sphere, but each occupied and commanded by more than one Rex Nemorensis.

The columns straightened, raised their spears, and parted ranks.

The constant pressure, the sense of crowding, he'd endured since da Silva's death was gone, and he felt relief. But also disappointment. For it was time to enter the Sphere and face whatever was in there.

Alone.

60
ARRIVAL

The buses rolled out of the arched tunnel into the murky, yellow afternoon light. Trees and shrubs green with the unfurling leaves of early spring overhung the stone walls that lined either side of the road. The trip from Hendricks to Manhattan's Central Park had, indeed, been brief. After loading onto the buses, they pulled out of Hendricks and immediately — as if space was folded so that two distant points touched back-to-back — pulled into the circular pea stone drive before the Sisterhood's Manor, where two other buses waited. Without discussion the entourage took the lane out of Cybele's abode, passed under a natural tunnel of overarching trees, and emerged from the tunnel in Central Park. They had not traversed physical space at all but penetrated the brane that separated the material world from the astral.

The road was deserted. Its emptiness in the center of one of the world's most densely populated cities spoke volumes about the desperate conditions Manhattan was facing. The convoy proceeded out of the park and pulled over along a stretch of Fifth Avenue beside a red sign reading "No Standing." Grace, in the third bus after the Sisters', thought it unlikely police would be issuing tickets given their current priorities.

John, sitting in the aisle seat across from her, nodded. They piled out onto the broad sidewalk. Normally, after a cold New York winter, spring was a time of rejoicing, but with the lowering sky pressing down like a great bruised thumb, the mood was anything but cheerful.

Margreet and a contingency of the Sisters, including plump Sister Alycia and the imposing twins, Maija and Keija, came down from the first bus to meet them. After a nod, they all looked to Terry, who, ignoring them all, had wandered into the middle of the deserted street and was gazing at the sky. His tan fingers stroked the raven's skull as he stared.

Though their immediate surroundings were deserted, the city was louder than usual. Toward midtown, sirens screamed and shots were being fired. By contrast, their present location was eerily quiet. No breeze stirred the trees and the jaundiced clouds churned slowly above the roofs of the apartment buildings across the street.

At first, Grace thought it was a wind rising where none had been. A dark cloud broke off from its fellows and swept earthward. The whirring became distinct as the mass of wings wheeled about and sped over their heads flowing like a black torrent down Fifth Avenue, pointing as surely as any arrow toward midtown.

"This way," Terry signed and started off.

"Hold up, Ter," John said. Terry stopped and turned. "We need to weapon up."

Terry nodded but while the arsenal was distributed, he shifted foot to foot, restless to get going.

61
ALEPH

Rick stood agape as he gazed above, below, around. The shimmering Sphere beheld from outside — great as it was floating over the chromium plane — was finite. But inside...

His mind reeled at the baroque mathematical intensity of what he beheld. At the utter innumerability of the impossible images, all shifting ceaseless motion because he was seeing past present future, all times, all places simultaneously. The tide rolling in on a primordial shore, microbes blossoming in salt pools under an alchemical sun, the same shore eons after washing up jellyfish and garbage but with the same crash and roar undiminished by cycles of moon and the same hot alchemical sun grown older but no wiser.

He saw Leo replace Virgo, the Ram overthrow the Bull, as ages revolved and humans evolved and the price of barter rose from bone to plastic.

Saw the first letter scratched into stone and letters innumerable whirling like leaves on the winds of cyber space.

Saw couplings and killings, burials and births, seemingly without number but numbered because beginning was not without end and end not beginningless.

Saw sand and monuments, monuments become sand, the rise and fall of cities and kittens and the imperturbable beatitude of the Pleiades.

Saw a child hold up its hand and encompass the moon between forefinger and thumb and smile for a moment godlike possessing.

Saw poets set pen quill stylus to paper papyrus tablet. Saw bonfires burning, flesh and pages crackling.

Twisting his eyes and driving a wedge of pain into his head, the visions expanding before him were like the ultimate Escher print, wherein pictures of pictures, each containing an image of itself, advanced *ad infinitum*. Except the picture was an infinity of galleries, as if he stood inside an exponential holographic map of the multiverse, a dense isomorphic enfolding and compressing of infinite universes and dimensions. Trying to make sense of what he saw, he recalled how the physical plane was a one-sided mirror reflecting the present, the astral plane a two-sided mirror reflecting the past and present, the mental plane a three-sided mirror or prism reflecting past, present, and future. But this...

The sphere was an all-surface mirror which reflected all worlds and all times. Though his mentors no longer resided in his brain, their memories—their vast store of scientific, philosophic, and esoteric knowledge—remained, and the word came to him as if da Silva had spoken it.

Aleph.

The sphere was an Aleph. Not merely a window onto all times all places viewable simultaneously, but the source of all things, times, places, past present future. This was the nexus point from which Yaldabaoth collected the divine light emanating from the Pleroma, the light imbued with the creative impulse, and shaped it to his will to create the lower planes.

Rick's revelry was broken by a sense of pressure at the back of his head. Someone was staring at him.

He turned and gasped. The being observing him couldn't be more like him. The resemblance was uncanny. Not at all like looking at himself in a mirror, but like looking at himself standing outside himself. Himself in 3D and vivid color and in living, breathing flesh. His fists curled as the thought

Doppelgänger!

flashed through his mind in a wash of red emergency light.

For a moment, they both stood thunderstruck, eyes wide, lips parted as if on the verge of speech but stunned to silence. Rick found his tongue first.

"You!"

By this creature's hands Frank had met his end! All his frustrated desire for revenge, his hobbled, life-altering need to restore the dead to life, welled into a primordial urge to wrap his fingers around the monster's throat and squeeze it to a red pulp!

But his doppelgänger had perished that Christmas Eve. In that deathly place beyond the funhouse mirror, its back broken on the shore of Night's Plutonian sea, while the tide of oblivion rolled in eating away at the world of matter.

"What trick is this?" the other growled, an angry scowl replacing the initial surprise. "Did She send you?"

"She?" Confusion shook him. He'd been so focused on the creature's face that only now did he realize the being before him stood utterly naked. Still, he knew his body and though he was more tanned and his double did not carry the puckered scar on his side from the policeman's bullet, he recognized the topography of his own flesh.

Could it be? Was this the Demiurge da Silva told him of? Bastard offspring of the Aeon Sophia? Creator of the lower realms?

Shape changer!

Why not? So powerful a being. If this creature could shape worlds—stars, planets, galaxies, multiple realms of reality, and everything walking, flying, or swimming—how easily it must be for him to alter his appearance. He was Protean.

Behind his duplicate's head, countless worlds revolved. With every flick of his gaze, ages passed, civilizations rose and fell on a thousand worlds, ten thousand thousands. Had Yaldabaoth created this? He must have. But over how many millennia? Epochs? Was he that ancient? Or had he gazed upon the face of the deep and spoken, creating worlds in an instant? The hairs on his arms and neck bristled.

Why would Yaldabaoth mimic him? His mind flashed on earthly predators that lured their victims to their deaths by imitating their prey. Wolves in sheep's clothing.

But this being was not him. Even a clone or an identical twin might have identical DNA and blood type, but because of environmental factors in the womb, fingerprints were different, and each would have its own thoughts, biases, and character traits depending on societal and environmental elements. His doppelgänger, a creature born of his subconscious, was certainly not him but possessed its own individual, however ghastly, traits.

Though the creature's eyes were not red like the doppelgänger's, its livid scowl was shockingly identical. Had he ever worn such an expression of raw hate? When Frank drove him up a wall and he saw red? Was his own face capable of twisting so?

"She's been here, hasn't She?"

Yaldabaoth ignored his question. "I am right to unmake my making," he said peering into the Aleph. Following the Demiurge's gaze, Rick saw a small blue world that grew as he watched. Its billions boiled over its soil, furrowed its waves, winged through its air. "My creations grow too bold!" He returned his gaze to Rick.

Rick pressed. "What have you done to Her?"

The creature's scowl morphed into a cold, self-satisfied smirk as its gaze returned to Rick. "I sent Her where She will trouble me no more."

"Where?"

The Maker waved his hand expansively, taking in three-quarters of the multiverse. "Somewhere. You'll never find her."

Panic embraced him with cold, wet arms. His gaze darted about the Aleph. Stars and nebula swirled, planets zoomed in and out of focus. Civilizations rose and fell. The vistas were staggering, overwhelming.

"Where?"

Yaldabaoth smiled. "If she, the strongest among you, is so easily dismissed, you will certainly be no problem."

The Demiurge raised his hand as if to hurl him into some far-flung corner of the Aleph where he would never find his way back. Not before oblivion overswept him at any rate.

Oblivion…

Again, he remembered his doppelgänger perishing on Oblivion's shore, nada rolling in to carry him back to the chaos from which he came.

"I can't kill you," he'd said, flinging away the knife clenched in his fist, unable to satisfy his desire to plunge the blade into the creature's heart.

"Nor I you," his double said, wonder replacing the blood lust that had burned in its eyes. "I'm you and you're me." The creature smiled, as if marveling at the change it had undergone at the moment of its death. "I'm you—the flip side of the coin, no doubt, but the same coin."

And now epiphany broke like sunlight. No one could ever know himself without looking into another's eyes. Seeing yourself as others see you is transforming.

"Wait!"

So compelling was his command that the Maker froze, his spread hand halted beside his face.

"You are nothing without me!" Rick flung the words in the creature's face, his voice contemptuous, as if he were the god and the Maker an erring subject. "Without mankind you might as well not exist!"

"What trick is this?"

"Why did you create man?"

"Because I could." The upraised hand, forgotten, returned to his side.

"No." Rick shook his head slowly and feigned an indulgent smile, as one fondly correcting an errant child. "You created man so you would not be alone."

"I created man to worship me, but he is ungrateful and presumes...too much!" He waved his hand as if to dispel an impish shadow that had the audacity to rise up and diminish his light. But the shadow remained. "What are you?"

"I am the mirror you created in which to observe yourself. Shatter the mirror and you are alone. Alone, your thoughts remain only thoughts. Abstractions without meaning. Only by observing yourself through man's eyes can you thrive. If man does not evolve, neither will you. It is not his subservience you want, nor his obedience. His achievements are yours. In observing the rising consciousness of your creation, you come to know yourself. The evolution of God and the evolution of humanity cannot be separated. Godhead cannot fulfill its divine potential without observing itself in the mirror of its creation."

Yaldabaoth waved him off. "Making man was a mistake. Perhaps I will create a being who will serve me better."

Rick raised his brows. "You admit you are capable of erring? When you first created, you had no suspicion that you could err. You thought yourself supreme, omnipotent. How would you ever become aware of the possibility of erring if you had not observed your fallible creatures constantly erring?"

Yaldabaoth's frown deepened.

"But you are not supreme. Because your mother hid you in this—" He paused to take in the mind-wrenching Baroque, non-Euclidian complexity of the Aleph.

"I have no...*mother*." The Demiurge spat the word contemptuously, as if it were wormwood in his mouth. "I am the first! There is no one before me!"

Rick shook his head. "She made you, as you made the physical planes and the world of man. She has been here, standing before you. I smell Her perfume."

Yaldabaoth sniffed the air.

"You banished Her. But banishing Her does not make untrue what She told you. How you came to be. How She protected you from the Aeons who dwell above you. You banished Her, hoping to avoid change. But that will never be. You've awakened and sleep will not come again."

He heard himself talking, trying desperately to keep desperation out of his voice while he groped for a plan. Who was he to presume he might change the tide of destiny?

Make yourself grow to a greatness beyond measure.

Fergi!

No, not Fergi. It was the Sibyl's voice that reverberated through his brain.

Seeking Fergi, he lifted his gaze to the Aleph. In an instant, he arced like a falling angel across the subtle planes and plummeted into the physical. Galaxies of worlds teaming with beings like himself shouldering histories and futures perceived in an infinite now flashed past. *If Bruno could see this!* Then he was plunging like a falcon toward a crag that rose above a smoking lake and a cave mouth opened and he was inside standing before the Sibyl, her wild hair coiling like serpents on the breeze that rose from the subterranean depths. Her eyes locked on his.

Raise yourself above all time, she said and his eardrums ached with the intensity of her voice. *Become Eternity. Believe that nothing is impossible for you. Think yourself immortal and capable of understanding all. Imagine that you are everywhere, on earth, in the sea, in the sky, that you are not yet born, in the maternal womb, adolescent, old, dead, beyond death. If you embrace in your thought all things at once—times, places, substances, qualities, quantities—you may understand God.*

And Bruno: *Unless you make yourself equal to God, you cannot understand God: for the like is not intelligible save to the like.*

Then the moment was over and he was again looking into the brown eyes of his mirror image, and as if the other's eyes were expanding, he saw himself in the widening pupils.

As if in a hall of mirrors, he saw his image doubled and redoubled, quadrupled and re-quadrupled, infinite lines of Richard Scotts proceeding in all directions, for here the mirrors were not one- or two-sided or even prisms, but perfect spheres that replicated on an endless array of planes physical mental spiritual above and below and on every side infinite vistas proceeding into infinity with no vanishing point because he no longer saw with the limited three-dimensional physical eyes with which he was born but with a newly-opened mental eye that saw at once all things from all perspectives—ALL—throughout time and space and on every plane above and below. His mind twisted and contorted and though thrilling with the terror of losing his sanity rose and rode the crest of exhilaration that was not unlike the rising ecstasy of orgasm but mental and spiritual as well as physical and ever rising as his mind's eye expanded and the images, emotions, recollections, precognitions of billions roared into his brain, a million towers of babble, a galactic ocean of information, and he staggered under the flood and collapsed not into a roaring kaleidoscope but into a welcoming darkness and silence.

62

REMIEL

They hadn't gone far when a single bird detached itself from the flock and circled back. Grace gasped at the sight of a bald eagle—a mature male by its white head, bright yellow beak, and six-foot wingspan—streaming so low over their heads she could see the wind ruffling its chocolate-brown feathers.

Tearing her eyes from the sight, she looked at Terry. Sure enough, he was following its flight.

The eagle turned and flew into the park. Terry followed.

"Terry?"

He turned to face her. He looked so young in his plaid shirt, jeans, hiking boots, and unruly hair, just coming into his late teens, but she knew he was anything but vulnerable. He had the makings of a powerful warlock.

"It's okay. I've got this. I'll catch up," he signed.

With that he hopped the low wall and disappeared into the park.

Flashes of color among the park's early spring greenery—tulips and daffodils in the flower beds and blossoming crabapple and cherry along the paths—failed to brighten the day. And though it wasn't yet sunset, the sky was so gloomy the lamps atop the wrought-iron poles came on.

Terry saw these things as he saw everything—whether close by in the here and now or far off in days to come—in vivid 3D. It was this heightened inner vision that allowed him to excel at video games and future casting.

Entering the zoo, he heard the angel before he encountered him. A sound like distant thunder marked his presence. A host of other sounds accompanied the ominous rumble, mostly made by frightened animals. Over the distant rattle of gunfire and shriek of sirens, grizzlies growled, monkeys chattered; peacocks' screams sounded eerily like humans. He *saw* snow leopards and lemurs anxiously pacing in their naturalistic habitats, bats battering the glass of their cages. Only the curious and fearless sea lions, having climbed upon the rocks in the middle of their pool, strained to see what the ruckus was about.

Though the park seemed deserted, he sensed the presence of humans. In danger.

The eagle descended, perched atop the entrance to the Dancing Crane Café. The door was unlocked. He entered.

Unlike other Grigori, a nimbus of white light surrounded this one. His eyes were deep bronze, his hair long and faded-gold. Though he was thin to the point of emaciation, he moved with a fencer's grace. He was weaving in place, as if he were a cobra undulating to the charmer's flute. Which, Terry saw in his mind's eye, was exactly what he appeared to be to the three teens cowering against the wall.

The girl had purple hair and a tattoo of Link on her arm. Another Zelda tat—a Winged Triforce inked in violet fading to black—dominated her chest above her tank top. As the Zelda games were his favorite, he recognized the artifact between the wings: the pyramid made of three equilateral triangles joined tip to tip with an empty inverted triangle in the middle represented the essence of the Golden Goddess. Godlike power belonged to whoever held them all. The wings represented the Loftwing, the giant guardian birds ridden by the citizens of Skyloft. Having a special kinship with the aviary world, he had considered getting a similar tat himself. Albeit a smaller, more discrete version.

The black-haired boy had an All-seeing Eye tat done in a subtle yellow-to-orange on his shoulder. The other had Link's sword-over-shield tat with a miniature Triforce in the center on one arm and a green-clothed Link on the other. The Sprite's bow was drawn, ready for battle.

Terry didn't have to ask them why they were here. He understood they had decided to take advantage of the deserted park to help themselves to some eats.

As was his way, Terry came upon the angel unobserved. The creature froze, his uplifted shoulders tensed with surprise. Then he spun hurling the image of a gigantic hooded cobra, red slit-pupiled eyes glaring, fangs dripping venom, at him with such force, the vision was driven into his mental eye. But he wasn't fooled and he hurled the vision back.

The angel staggered, shook his head, and blinked. Terry darted his head forward. The angel ducked the deadly fangs. Terry wasn't finished. Suddenly the angel was on his knees beating off the ravens that poured down on him, tearing his hair, rending his flesh, as if the roof had vanished and hordes of the black-winged birds were descending.

While the angel was distracted, Terry signed to the teens, "Go!"

They didn't understand, so he pointed to the door and waved them off emphatically. They got his meaning and, without a thank you, ran out of the eatery.

When they were gone, Terry called off his birds. The angel—Remiel, Angel of Visions, Terry understood him to be—blinked and examined his arms, touched his face.

"I—" He shook his head. Understanding dawned in his eyes. The attack had not been real. "You have the blood," he said in wonder.

Terry nodded.

"Who are you?"

Terry signed, but the angel did not comprehend, so he stepped forward and grasped the Grigori's arm. Images flooded into the creature's inner eye.

Images the Goddess had granted him of Talmaiel and his army pouring into Hendricks days before the battle, allowing them to prepare.

Images of himself summoning his birds to ravage and kill the offenders.

And last, an image of the eagle waiting outside and the certain knowledge that he would command the bird to rip the heart from his ribcage if he did not join him.

"Join you?" the angel said. "Gladly! I have no love for Semjaza!"

Terry received an image of a powerful Grigori feasting on the angel's blood.

The smile that transformed Remiel's gaunt face wasn't pleasant. Terry recognized the hard-eyed glare that mirrored his own face when he relived the revenge he'd inflicted on the enemy the night they murdered his mother. The obsession troubled him. He felt as if there was a hole in his life that would never be filled no matter how many enemies he slew. But for better or worse, he felt the bloodlust was a necessary part of him now—a keen-edged sword forged in vengeance that, wielded by his hand, would keep his people safe.

He signed for Remiel to follow him. This time the angel understood.

Outside, Terry walked a dozen paces before he realized the images in his mind's eye had changed. The rock gardens and green lawns of the spacious naturalistic habitats that previously enclosed the animals had vanished, replaced by the barred cages of bygone years.

63
A SMALL BLUE WORLD

Rick woke alone.

He was still standing where he had before consciousness left him...an instant ago? An age? The Aleph still surrounded him. An infinity of worlds, their histories unfolding in an infinity of nows. The throne was unoccupied. The Demiurge, Yaldabaoth, the Maker, was gone. Had he banished him as Yaldabaoth had banished Cybele? Flung him into an obscure corner of the multiverse?

But the truth struck him. However ironic and incongruous and antithetical to common sense, even as he was no more Yaldabaoth, son of the Aeon Sophia, than Yaldabaoth was himself, Richard Scott, son of Frank and Jenny, yet they were one.

Awe washed over him with the realization. Somehow, above and below, macro and micro, he and all the Ricks that had ever been—and he knew intuitively there had been legions—were, as all things in the multiverse were, one, and that expanding consciousness had absorbed both the Rick with which he was familiar and the Demiurge into the archetypal one.

Looking at the palm of his hand, at the long dominate lifeline, at the broken fate line, at the whorls of his fingerprints, he understood that, even as he was Rick Scott, Son of Jenny and Frank Scott, brother of Frank Jr., raised in Jersey City, lately an EMS driver in Memphis, he was multitudes and yet the one that encompassed them all.

He sensed no other presences, heard no clamor of voices striving to be heard, felt no other hands like layers of gloves cloaking his own. There was only himself. A calm came over him, a calm he had never known before this moment—a calm that came of understanding, a knowing and a reliance on the power of the knowledge that he was changed and had accepted the change without challenging it or analyzing how it came about or what it meant or would mean in the future. An acceptance and a moving on.

He gazed into the Aleph, seeking Earth.

And there it was, a small blue world zooming toward him, filling space until he no longer saw the curvilinear surface of the Aleph or even the planet whole, its globe expanding out of the star-littered blackness of space, then enveloping him as he plummeted dizzyingly through its clouds. Breaking through the dense canopy, he recognized the familiar shape of Manhattan bracketed by the Hudson and East Rivers. There, across the Hudson, was Jersey City, the city of his youth. Now he soared over midtown where battle raged.

64

THE BATTLE OF TIMES SQUARE

Gadriel had summoned a thick fog that filled midtown Manhattan's canyon-like streets, and the lurid glow of the setting sun, together with flashing emergency lights and the river of giant LED digital displays, turned Times Square into a stroboscopic battleground. The city was under martial law. Citizens had been ordered to stay indoors, but thousands were trying to flee the city.

Access lanes to the bridges and tunnels leading out of Manhattan were at a standstill. Port Authority and Grand Central Station were packed. The Seventh Avenue Line and the R Train were stopped due to commuters spilling onto the track from overcrowded platforms. The unidentified attackers, sensing the vulnerability of soft targets, had massacred dozens in the 42ⁿᵈ Street Shuttle.

Authorities were slow to identify the nature of the attacks terrorizing various parts of the metropolis throughout the afternoon. Frantic 911 calls reporting bloody assaults led the media to speculate the city was under siege by terrorists. Only when responding police units were attacked by blue-eyed giants and images caught on camera circulated through newsfeeds and social media did authorities realize they were experiencing something unique.

Now, at sunset, the New York National Guard and the 88ᵗʰ Brigade of the New York Guard were concentrating their firepower in Times Square, where the enemy had centered their activities. The citizenry had fled the area even before mandatory evacuation was ordered, so, though the battle would be costly, loss of human life would be kept to a minimum. Both the mayor and the governor agreed the assault on citizens warranted a full-blown response.

The rattle of machine gun fire combined with the whump of .50-caliber SASRs, the lighter *thump thump thump* of the 30mm cannons of Stryker Dragoon armored vehicles blocking intersections, together with the squawks of radio traffic and shouts of armored soldiers and the tracer fire streaking the gloom would have been more appropriate experienced in one of the area's IMAX theaters than amidst the iconic tourist destination. The effect was surreal, a waking nightmare in the heart of the Big Apple.

Because of the gloom and the attackers' incredible speed, the enemy was difficult to pin down. Often, a soldier would die screaming or simply disappear and companions would turn their weapons only to find the assailant vanished. It was uncertain who was surrounding whom.

Engaging an elusive enemy wasn't the only problem. At times the carnage came from the defenders' own troops. Samael, the Destroyer, drove soldiers mad with his visions, making them see their fellow soldiers as blue-eyed, hairless giants with murder in their eyes bent on their destruction so that they turned friendly fire upon their own. Wielding his sword with murderous efficiency, Semjaza quadrupled himself so soldiers fired on phantoms while the real Sorcerer strode among them reaping havoc.

Hemach, an angel made of red and black flame, hurled fireballs into the troops' midst.

The shapeshifter Pahadron alternated between the guise of a nightmare creature of glistening, sinewy flesh with razor teeth and claws and an unexceptional soldier, allowing him to draw the enemy's fire, then appear among them with lethal effect.

Not all of the Choir fought with Semjaza however. The twins, Baradiel and Baraqiel, whose powers were to command the elements, battered their erstwhile comrades with hail and lightning. Araqiel, whose element was earth, commanded the streets to swallow them. And Remiel, Angel of Visions, distracted the Choir with illusions of hordes of soldiers and tanks and armored vehicles so that they wasted much of their energy fighting phantoms.

Drone pilots sitting in a command vehicle some blocks from the battle's center had better luck locating the enemy with thermal imaging and taking several Grigori out in surgical strikes with Hellfire R9X missiles, nick named "flying Ginsus" because they deployed blades that cut through concrete, metal, and angels. The tactic worked until Semjaza forced a canon operator to take out the command vehicle.

And so it went, the enemy gaining the upper hand—until reinforcements arrived in the persons of a group of civilians armed and ready to engage.

"General, this is Grace Patton—Reverend Grace—and John Hanley." Col. Jacob Eckler of the New York Guard addressed his CEO, General Ambrose Green. They stood in the middle of a blocked-off street a half mile from the actual fighting. A pair of Humvees mounted with .50-caliber guns bracketed the command unit. Several M16-armed Guardsmen stood nearby. Behind them, an 18-foot trailer supported a mobile Joint Incident Site Communications Capability system, equipped with power generator and satellite dish. "These are the people I told you about."

The general looked dubiously at the assortment of weapons—mostly small arms: rifles, shotguns, light machine guns. One weekend warrior in a baseball cap that read W5CBL had an M-16 slung over one shoulder and deer rifle over the other. He raised an eyebrow at the bandoliers of grenades worn by some of the civilians that had strolled up to the command line like so many Sunday afternoon tourists.

Even the camo many of them wore was more Bass Pro Shop than military issue. More than half were women, some wearing white gowns. And was that the hilt of a katana protruding over the gray-haired Reverend's shoulder?

"They're here to do what? Advise?"

The Reverend started to speak, but Hanley, seeing her anger, spoke first. "We're here to fight, General. Our people—"

Green cut the trim elderly gentleman short. He was wearing topsiders for Christ's sake! "Your people? Sir, this is a military operation. Col. Eckler has appraised me of the nature of the enemy. I'm still not convinced—though they employ tactics I've not seen before. But I will not allow citizens to intervene and put themselves in harm's way."

This time Grace beat John to a rebuttal. "Harm's way?' General, the world is ending, if you haven't noticed. Literally!"

Green had no response. Time *was* out of joint. There was no denying that. But angels?

Reverend Grace continued. "For all that religion has, for thousands of years, masked the true nature of reality, and for all that scientific reason has denied the mysteries of the supernal realms, substituting a brick-and-mortar material world, angels exist. And they are not the benevolent, harp-playing, white-winged creatures of religious fairy tales. We know the enemy. You don't."

"Madam." Before he could continue, the boy standing beside the Reverend turned and walked into the fog.

"Terry, wait!" Grace started after him, but Green seized her arm. Without thinking, she drew her sidearm—a big bore Ruger Super Redhawk .454 loaded with 260 grain bullets with a velocity of 1,535 fps. and a stopping power "Good for bears and angels"—and shoved the muzzle under his chin.

Soldiers trained weapons on her. The Sisters and the Hendricks and Middleville constituencies showed discipline and did not escalate the situation by responding in kind.

"Whoa!" Col. Eckler raised his hands. "That's not going to help."

The muzzle remained snug under Green's chin. She addressed the general while holding Jacob's gaze. "This is our battle, General, as much as yours." She lowered her weapon but kept it trained on Green. "Don't try to stop us."

She shoved past the soldiers, who looked to Green for orders.

"Let them go." He massaged his throat as the civilians followed. "Maybe she's right," he said to Eckler when they were gone. "And maybe what you told me is true." He shook his head. "There's a lot more here than I'm prepared to accept."

65

SECOND THOUGHTS

The green room backstage at Saint Vitus wasn't green but matte black like the rest of the bar. Cluttered with black vinyl sofas, amps, guitars, a couple of snow shovels, and boxes of junk that looked as if they were meant for the trash but never made it to the curb, the big room was crowded. At least a dozen musicians were hanging out, one sleeping despite the din. (How Kashdejan envied their ability to sleep. To dream.) Others were in the bar drinking, hitting on women; still others, no doubt, were filling up at local Greenpoint eateries.

Flayed Rabbit was onstage. Their Ludwig bass featured a cartoon of a maniacal, red-eyed rabbit, partially flayed, white fur streaked with blood, one broken ear hanging over his shoulder. The band's name circled the image in bright-red Sixties psychedelic poster font. He didn't know if the logo was meant to be hideous or funny—probably both. He liked that about humans: their humor came in such a variety of flavors. Like ice cream. Not all of them had the gift of self-deprecation or the ability to laugh at an indifferent universe—too many were pompous, self-obsessed assholes—but enough did to make humor one of the defining traits of what it meant to be human. Unlike angels who, for the most part, along with their absence of a soul and the inability to sleep, lacked a sense of humor.

The Thrash Metal band was loud even back here.

"Gonna give my rabbit what he needs!

Flaaayed rabbit! Flaaayed rabbit!

292

Gonna flay my rabbit watch him bleed!

Flaaayed rabbit! Flaaayed rabbit!"

The masturbation/self-mutilation innuendo was not to his taste, but front man Nimrod—that was what he called himself—shouted the lyrics in a satisfactory beastly growl and the lead guitar was technically complex. The delivery was not quite fast enough to keep up with the drummer whose frenzied blast beats were a runaway train the rest of the band raced to catch, but the crowd loved it.

The night's venue featured eight bands. Blood Muffin was up next. It was going to be a long night. He hoped. With what was happening across the river in Manhattan there were no guarantees. Even now—over Flayed Rabbit's mad dash up the pentatonic scales and the machine-gun thunder of their drummer's pedal strokes—he could almost feel the percussive wave of far-off explosions.

He had to give it to these humans, when their backs were against the wall, they either fought or partied. Seriously though, with the whole world going down the toilet, where was there to run to?

Perched in an armchair too small for him, his ostrich-skin western boots crossed before him, Kashdejan thought about his conversation with Talmaiel.

Let them have their blood, he'd told him.

He'd meant it at the time. What did it matter now that the end was near?

Odd thing, it *did* matter!

He was having second thoughts.

It wasn't that he was sentimental. Humans were ephemeral. Here today, gone the next. He'd learned to keep relationships casual. He'd had memorable friends and a few testy enemies over the centuries, and a recollection of either could bring a smile to his lips, but he didn't dwell on the past. But when it came down to it—where it really mattered—the Grigori weren't his brothers. It had been millennia since he'd lived among them. And even then, he'd not shared their lust for human blood nor their need to dominate. To be honest, he'd learned more from humans than humans ever had from Grigori.

He looked around the room. This was an energetic lot. Though death was an intrinsic part of their culture, and while their music was darker and more cynical than most genres, they were not intrinsically morbid. How many performers of Satanic metal truly believed in Satan? How many Viking metal bands truly believed in Oden? It was obvious many *wanted* to believe and lived the role, but the morbidity, the paeans to pagan gods, the fevered chronicles of death, were part of their art. A narrative they wove to give their lives and the lives of their fans texture. The interesting thing was the shared cultural attitudes and social behavior produced some great music.

Inspiration, not necessity, was the mother of invention.

He remembered Talmaiel's words, "The whole time I was on Abyss, I didn't see a single instrument."

Grigori hadn't invented music. Humans had.

I'd go mad.

No, Semjaza and the Choir weren't his brothers. He couldn't stomach arrogant Semjaza or brutal Samael. And Azazel... He shuddered remembering his monstrous blood lust. The demon feasted on human blood not to satiate his hunger or to establish dominance as alphas tended to do no matter their breed—Grigori, human, wolf—or even to instill terror, but because it drove him to an erotic frenzy, a mad ecstasy from which even Grigori cringed.

"Boss."

He'd been so deep in his thoughts he hadn't noticed his band members approach. Their faces were grim, as if they'd made some hard decision.

All three were as bald as Grigori, Carol naturally, Ariel and Zak shaven. Carol's broad mahogany face glistened under the fluorescents. Ariel wore a scarlet muscle shirt. His left arm sported an angry, yellow-beaked, red-combed rooster head copied from the image on his Electro-Harmonix Cock Fight Talking Wah/Fuzz pedal. Zak wore no shirt. Odin's ravens, Hugin and Munin, spread their wings across his back. Thought and memory. What was thought without memory's reservoir of knowledge and experience to draw upon? What use memory without thought's contemplative eye? That was another area where humans shone. Their penchant for the symbolic representation of complex ideas again set them apart from angels. Religion had been pressed upon them, but philosophy was their invention.

"What's up?" he said, scanning Rapture's faces. Zak answered. "We need to talk."

66

A HELPING HAND

The fog was growing denser. Visibility was limited to parked cars and shuttered storefronts. Lamplights were dim glows, traffic lights smudges of red or green.

Grace moved through the murk, side arm holstered, katana at the ready. Where was that boy? She had lost contact with the others. She couldn't call out. That would alert the enemy to her presence. Of course, Terry knew what he was doing. Didn't he?

He'd shown himself more than capable in battle. Still, she couldn't help worrying. Since losing his mother he'd grown restless. He seldom smiled, had given up fishing and video games. He was forever up on the ridge, watching the landscape through the eyes of his birds. She hadn't seen him surrounded by butterflies since before Talmaiel came to Hendricks. She understood his anger—at himself for not protecting Jewelie, at the universe for allowing his mother to die—but it was making him reckless. He had warrior's blood, and she sensed he wanted nothing more than to lose himself in battle. The thought of losing him was unbearable.

Where are you, Ter?

But no answer came to her. Like the rest of the Sisterhood, Delores excepted, she had lost her sight. Was the Goddess truly gone? Somehow the thought of a future without the Cybele was more terrifying than Yaldabaoth's unmaking.

A hand grabbed her. A face appeared out of the fog. Insanity burned in the bloodshot eyes, in the wolfish grin. Her katana sliced through fog. The Grigori's severed arm fell to the sidewalk.

The tall, wraithlike figure kept coming.

She swept her leading left foot back and, leaning into the two-handed diagonal strike, sheared the side of the creature's face, cleaved its collar bone, lungs, ribs and lodged the blade in its sternum.

The emaciated angel collapsed. She poised, knees bent, katana gripped two-handed, blade on its side, the tip just to the left of the Grigori's head—in case it rose. It did not, but you did not simply kill Grigori. Chop it to pieces, it would knit. Burn it, it would heal. Unless you dropped a mountain on it—which would only pin not kill it—or dissolve it in acid or burn it in a fire so hot you destroyed its atomic structure, it would rise. It might take a while. Days? Weeks? She had no idea. But you didn't simply kill immortals.

Two more Grigori emerged from the fog, one from the street, the other appearing on the sidewalk mere yards away. They saw her and simultaneously charged.

Suddenly she was surrounded by duplicates of herself, as if she'd produced a dozen clones dressed as she was in camos and tactical vest with identical katanas raised for battle.

An angel appeared at her side. She pivoted, brought her weapon round, poised to strike.

The creature's eyes were bronze, its long blond hair glistened with dew. A ghostly light played about its features. There was no way it could blend into the shadows. Its hand was up.

"I've got this," the angel said. "Find Terry."

67

RED MIST

The fog was no impediment to Terry's vision. He *saw* scenes of death that would have sickened normal men, but he had seen worse, hadn't he?

Most Grigori fought with whatever came to hand: lengths of pipe, metal chairs, sewer grates. Others had learned to operate the semi-automatic weapons taken off soldiers they killed. He could not save every soldier that fell to their guerilla tactics, darting among the humans and bearing one off before his platoon mates could train their weapons. He'd decided to focus on the worst of the attacks. As he neared Times Square, a National Guard platoon turned their weapons on each other, unloading their ordinance into their own ranks.

The source of the catastrophe emanated from a darkened alcove down the street, where Samael the Destroyer set his victims' brains afire with homicidal rage. As he watched with his mind's eye the Death Angel brooding like a great carrion bird over the destruction he wrought, his own rage mounted. He welcomed the anger, felt a rising joy as it consumed him, but he resisted the compulsion to attack his fellow humans. Stroking the white pate of the raven's skull that hung from his neck, he willed himself to see through its hollow sockets; and, suddenly, he was flying with his raven flock and his mind called to them through the aether.

And they came. Whirring out of the dark, winging down from the sky, the wings of their thousands turning the night to thunder.

And Samael looked up and saw his death approaching and tried to flee. But the black-winged horde struck, flaying the flesh from his bones until he fell beneath their ravaging beaks, and they alighted upon him covering him in a writhing blanket of black feathers and their beaks rose and fell and twisted until they again took wing and all that remained of the Destroyer were a few shreds of flesh clinging to the asphalt and a fine red mist drifting in the fog.

68

VALKYRIE DOWN

Nearby, Maija and Keija battled the Two Hundred. Like storied Valkyries, they dashed out of the fog, swords flashing, dealing, if not death, then enough dismemberment to impede their victims for weeks to come.

Instead of the white attire they wore at the Sisterhood, they'd opted for black Aikido gis (both were black belts) which they'd paired with split-toed, rubber-soled Ninja Tabi boots purchased on Amazon. Black balaclavas concealed their blond manes. The result was they moved through the New York streets silently and, with the aid of the fog, invisibly.

Even their katanas were of dark, hand-forged Damascus steel so that they caught no light as they rose and fell scribing a red narrative in the fog.

Before long they caught the attention of Asmodai, who, having whetted his newly acquired weapon in human blood and ascertained its capabilities—which were impressive—delighted at the prospect of testing it against the skills of master swordsmen. Or, in this case, women. So it was that the twins found themselves facing Samael's firstborn, aptly named the Beheader.

The dark angel, his gleaming naked body streaked with gore, stepped under a streetlamp so they might see him clearly and performed an ancient dance. At first, he twirled his weapon overhead, then executed spins or flowerings more appropriate for sword or spear

300

than the two-meter-long pollaxe. Faster and faster he wove a series of figure eights and reverse flowerings, until the pole was invisible and the axe and spearhead a blur. He finished suddenly with his knees bent, feet wide in a low fighting stance, the axe blade angled forward, the spearhead low to the ground in something similar to a *Migi Gedan* katana stance where the spear could be thrust or the axe swept up or around in a deadly arc. The angel clearly knew his weapon.

Maija and Keija separated, moving slowly left and right to make it difficult for the Grigori to engage both. When they did not attack, he straightened and flipped the halberd under his arm so the axe end was behind him. But his left foot remained forward, his knees bent, and his left hand rested on the shaft so all he had to do was step back and, putting his hip into the swing, bring the axe around in a killing blow. The twins were not fooled.

"Careful," Maija whispered. It was a signal rather than a warning, and, nearly as fast as any Grigori, the sisters leapt into the fray. The edges of their katanas gleamed red as they sliced the air.

Most street fights are decided in thirty seconds, usually with a knockout or the incapacitation of one of the combatants. Real fights with bladed instruments are as swift. Mortal combat is not a choreographed series of thrusts, parries, and counter strikes back and forth with one hand behind the back for balance. It is a two-handed deadly labor, the goal of which is to stab or slice your opponent as quickly as possible and avoid injury yourself.

Maija's blade swept in a broad whistling arc aimed at Asmodai's midsection—a disemboweling if not a separating of trunk from torso stoke. But Asmodai bent like a cobra dodging a mongoose; and as Maija's blade passed, he lunged, bringing the pollaxe down one-handed as a human warrior might a war axe and cleft her from collar bone to sternum.

Maija blinked as if startled at the turn of events. Asmodai planted a foot against her chest and wrenched as Keija, screaming rage and grief, attacked. The Grigori spun, tried to raise his weapon to strike. But to his amazement, the wounded twin, expiring but still on her feet, clung to the halberd, one hand on the haft, the other grasping the spear head. Blood gushed from her hand where the blade sliced into her fingers.

Teeth gritted, muscles corded, Keija struck, her blade whistling toward his neck. The angel tried to duck but the blade caught him below the left ear and passed diagonally through his neck. Leaving a red wake, the Beheader's great hairless head rolled in the street. The torso swayed for a moment as if uncertain what to do, then toppled.

Keija dropped to her fallen sister's side, cradled her head in her lap. She wasn't dead yet, but the wound was mortal and the light in her eyes faded as she drowned in her own blood. Neither the Cybele's ministrations nor all the People's accumulated medical lore could help her.

"Oh, Maija!" Keija moaned. But her sister was dead. Her open blue eyes stared unseeing into the weltering sky.

Her lips were smiling.

69

ICE ANGEL

Several blocks away in Father Duffy Square, a flamethrower mounted on a Stryker AFV caught the angel Hemach. The angel's illusory red-and-black flames were no match for the 1800-degree inferno that reduced him to ash. It was the military's first, and perhaps only, effective strike that had a chance of keeping a Grigori from regenerating.

Seeing the danger, Semjaza turned to flee, but a second Stryker speeding into the plaza, plowing seats and tables under its eight wheels, belched fire, hurling Semjaza into the other's flame. Caught in their crossfire, he felt his flesh blackening. The pain was unlike anything he'd ever felt. He had only a moment before he shared Hemach's fate, but the master sorcerer spread his hands and pushed the flames from his body. His eyes rolled back in his head as he reached inside, down to his very core, and visualized the molecules that made up his physical body vibrating within him. He willed the vibrations to change, slowing their wavelengths, then speeding them up. Then reversing the magnetic polarity of the atoms that made up his physical body, rapidly changing the attractive power that held his atoms together into repulsion attraction repulsion attraction faster and faster alternating their magnetic polarity. The pain passed as the physical constitution of his body became something other. He grew cold, the flames bent away from him. In another minute, he emerged from the wall of flames naked, a figure of blue ice.

He clapped his hands and the flames vanished. The Strykers froze; their olive drab surfaces glistened with ice. He clapped again and the vehicles and the dead and frozen soldiers inside shattered as if they were plastic models stuck by a mallet. Shards of iced metal rained down around him.

He flexed his hands and smiled at the transformation. His flesh shone. Not with the pallor of Grigori flesh but with the luster of blue ice. He was colder than he'd ever been on Abyss—as cold as his soul would be if angels possessed souls, which they did not—only men had souls which was the immortal part of their being, while Angels, immortal in their astral flesh, had no need of a soul that plunged again and yet again into the cauldron of life. He touched his arm, his hairless face, expecting to meet unyielding firmness, but his flesh was supple. He felt no pain, only an icy power that radiated through his limbs, his fingers.

Soldiers were pouring into the Square. He met them with a wall of ice and waded in for the slaughter.

70

KASHDEJAN STRIKES A CHORD

Kashdejan and Rapture set up their gear on the roof of a nearby building. They'd lost too much time already. Because they couldn't just "borrow" Saint Vitus' speakers with the show going on, they'd stopped off at a PA rental on the way to midtown. The audio shop was closed but the lock yielded to Kashdejan's touch. The 15,000-watt array was a beast to carry but he and Carol toted one humungous speaker apiece on their shoulders and Ariel and Zak hauled the rest. They'd saved some time not bothering to tape down the cables. They wouldn't be moving around and had tossed the excess lengths to the sides.

Glancing out over the city, the Maestro saw the glows of fires and flashing lights below in the fog. Explosions and the rattle of firearms shook the night. The clock was ticking. Already he'd seen two buildings a block over vanish, replaced by older, lower structures that might have dominated midtown over a century ago. If the building they were on slid into the past, their tech wouldn't do a bit of good.

"Ariel, check the preamps' settings."

Ariel gave him the I-know-my-job-Boss look. But the settings they were using tonight were not the ones they'd use in a club. Definitely not! He wanted to get it right, and quickly.

He gave the setup a quick once-over, paying special attention to the settings on the amps. These were of his own design, the electronics supplemented with complications that accessed the astral plane. The complications, like their instruments, were fashioned from electrum, so that their instruments, tuned to astral frequencies, sounded in the astral and resonated in the physical, thereby causing rapid fluctuation in the magnetic polarity of the acoustic waves. Lower settings altered an audience's consciousness, allowing them to experience their music as it would sound if they were transported to the astral realm. Higher settings could alter the physical structure of the audience itself with devastating effect.

Ariel and Zak strapped their axes on. Carol, seated behind his kit, twirled his sticks.

Kashdejan nodded, tapped off four beats with his boot toe, and hit a heavily distorted G-flatted fifth power chord that screamed into the aether, then howled back out over the city, shaking windows and rattling teeth for miles around.

71

WELCOME SLEEP

When Talmaiel heard Rapture's dark cadences marching over the street, his heart lifted. Kashdejan had come through. The world might never see another sunrise, but tonight's battle was not yet lost.

Talmaiel peered up at the roof line barely visible through the fog. Somewhere up there, the Maestro and his band were forging the shackles that would bind the Choir.

The music was full of minor and flatted imperfect notes, a slow baroque harmonic reminiscent of a bolero, eerily melodic. Now it sped up and changed to the E Phrygian-dominant, full of dark arpeggios, a frenzy of discordant notes ascending the scale octave by octave. A mounting emotional surge alternated with darker basal notes and chords forged in the upper frets of their instruments. The cleaner notes of the Phrygian descended into a growling wind of dissonance and distortion. And still the piercing, nerve-tightening high of the neck pickup screamed over the darkness of the gain-distorted bridge. Carol's thunderous rolls sounded, indeed, as if the heavens were about to open and the deluge descend.

And now the chilling shift to the flatted fifth, or *Diabolus in Musica*, the Devil's Tritone, dropped out of the bottomless lows of the Maestro's eight-string, creating a web of dissonance that crawled over the skin like spiders. A divine furor, a frenzy at once ecstatic and maniacal, a brooding fugue, evoking madness and ecstasy.

_____

The music had its effect. All over midtown, angels looked up and faced their doom. The transformation was rapid. They had no time to run. Nor could they. Limbs grew leaden. Arms and legs froze in whatever position they were in when the music washed over them. Their chests grew stiff. Nor could they scream as vocal cords froze even as their mouths opened.

The pain that wracked them as the cells of their flesh and bone, the very corpuscles of their angelic blood, solidified was neither hot nor cold like the pain of fire or ice, but an unbearable torment that screamed through every nerve until, when it seemed as if oblivion would be mercy, the pain vanished and an alien numbness overtook them as their bodies were transmuted to insensate stone. Scattered over midtown Manhattan, Grigori statues stood frozen in attitudes of agony or hostility, as if the city were hosting a bizarre exhibit of street art.

Humans were not affected. Nor all Grigori. The music was selective. It affected only the Grigori Kashdejan willed transmuted. The shapeshifter Pahadron. Gadriel, maker of fog. Sariel, Jeqon, Penemue, and dozens more.

And Baraqiel and Baradiel, standing with Cybele's people, called down a storm of hail and lightning that, striking the stone figures, shattered them and wore them away until all that remained of the former Choir were pebbles and stony sand.

The fog lifted. The guns were silent. Amazed soldiers staggered about, poking the rubble with their boot toes.

_____

But Semjaza remained.

Just as the Sorcerer had resisted the Strykers' flames, he cast a shield about himself deflecting the wavelengths of Kashdejan's music so they passed harmlessly around him while he maintained his icy matrix. When the music ceased and the fog lifted and he saw what had become of his army, he frowned.

But his disappointment was short-lived, for he saw approaching one on whom he could vent his anger.

"You're cleverer than I thought," he said to the Grigori whose disfigured face caught the lamplight.

Talmaiel pulled back his hood, let his adversary see him clearly. "Obviously not as clever as you," he said coming closer. "No matter. It's over. Your mission was doomed from the start. Now look at the damage." He waved a hand over the rubble of the diminished.

"Perhaps. But you will not see the end. Or will you run from me as you ran from the Avengers when they came for us?"

By way of answer, Talmaiel rushed the Mage, tackling him around the midsection and driving him against the building behind him. Semjaza did not struggle to free himself but pulled Talmaiel closer, locking him in an icy embrace.

"You thought Abyss was cold." Semjaza laughed. "I'll show you cold."

Icy tendrils burrowed into the Shining One's bones; his lungs ached from breathing the chill that radiated off the Mage like a nimbus of deepest winter. He struggled but his limbs were not responding. Moths of panic beat in his chest as he realized his mistake.

The pain was as bad as what wracked his body when the girl, Delores, set him afire. Worse. Given time, his burned flesh would heal, but Semjaza was draining his life force. Was this his end? To perish ingloriously in his enemy's arms, unable to strike a blow? The injustice stung.

The pain passed, the numbness deepened. He no longer felt the Sorcerer's embrace, no longer felt anything but the cold. Even gravity left him so that he seemed to float in an icy fog. His thoughts strayed as consciousness faded. Fragments of his life flitted before his eyes. It was a long life and the relics encompassed millennia.

Blue Mediterranean waters washing a pebbled beach.

Aged Falerian wine from Octavius' casks.

Viennese *cafés*. The Paris opera.

Unleashing his bow as his chariot thundered across the plains of Babylonia alongside Sargon's finest.

Driving a phalanx of warriors through a horde of Cybele's howling Korybantes in the rugged Pindos.

The salt smell of the sea as his trireme bore down on the Greeks at Salamis.

And so on through the centuries, pleasure and peril, bitter and sweet, but all of it sweet because the memories were his and he had lived them.

Words from Kashdejan's song came to him, the Grigori's harsh voice evoking powerful emotion.

Welcome Sleep

My soul to keep.

As we plunge into the deep.

A vague throb of excitement stirred within him. Was this what it was like to fall asleep? Would he dream?

His limbs were ponderous, the desire to sleep irresistible, yet something was keeping him from slumber. A ripple of annoyance drew his gaze skyward. It was the youth. Richard Scott. Somewhere. Watching.

72
"DO IT!"

From the vantage of his lofty aerie, Rick watched the battle unfold. Saw the devastation wrought by the Grigori and the heroism—and sacrifice—of Earth's defenders.

Now he watched Talmaiel dying in Semjaza's embrace.

The remains of immortals littered the streets like so much rubble. What mattered one more? Earth was dying. Mortals and immortals would perish together. He saw no way to stop what Yaldabaoth had begun.

Still…

He was torn. He owed Talmaiel no allegiance. They were enemies. The monster was responsible for Wally's death. Did standing on the same side out of necessity make them comrades?

He remembered Wally's broken body lying in the weeds atop Crystal Mountain, his open eyes reflecting starlight. He hadn't looked serene or at peace. He'd just looked dead, the pain he'd suffered etched on his face.

But the Shining One had shown his allegiance. Not to him but to Earth. It was no small thing to watch the passing of an immortal. Even in the face of universal oblivion.

But what could he do?

He recalled Paracelsus' words: *The invisible forces acting in the visible body are very powerful and may be guided by the imagination and compelled by the will.*

Dee's pedantic tones replaced Paracelsus': *Imagination is the astral tool with which the magus manipulates elementary matter and alters the underlying sidereal forces of the ethereal world.*

But how?

The imaginatio.

And da Silva, trying to teach him what he didn't want to learn: *Visualize. See the log float into the air. It's weightless, hollow, a balloon filled with helium.*

Were they not talking about the same thing? Imagination relied on sensual imagery—sight, smell, hearing, feeling, taste. To visualize was to imagine.

And the Goddess in his delirium: *Will is needed to focus desire and turn it into a creative act.*

Will, desire, imagination…

Visualize.

He gazed into the Aleph. Worlds upon worlds receding into the infinite. The infinite proceeding from the finite.

The Sphere, the ALL MIRROR, speeding the light of emanation from above into the lower realms and reflecting the light of evolutionary consciousness back into the Pleroma, was a *lens!* A lens that amplified the desire impulse guided by will!

Imagination…

Will…

Visualize!

Far away, yet as if he were in the next room seen through a pane of glass, Talmaiel was a fading shadow in Semjaza's arms. The Grigori's pale eyes stared into his, as if the Fallen One saw him clearly. As he watched, the angel's ruined lips mouthed, "Do it!" And Rick saw what he must do.

Focusing his desire into a laser beam of will, he dipped into the wellspring of his imagination and hurled earthward a great blinding bolt of lightning.

———

The light that shot out of the sky over the eastern seaboard was seen by millions. How could they avoid it? The brilliance was in such sharp contrast with the unnatural darkness. Those looking up, seeking the source of the roar that shook the earth beneath their feet, were temporarily blinded.

Seeing the light and knowing it was for him, Talmaiel smiled.

Semjaza, seeing the smile and sensing something was wrong, looked up. His eyes widened.

Then Talmaiel and Semjaza erupted in a sun-hot explosion of mutual annihilation.

When survivors could see again, they found only a crater.

73
A PLAGUE OF DEMONS

Only Azazel remained.

Rick, gazing down from the Aleph, saw the demon glaring defiantly at the sky.

No longer did the creature wear Bellarmino's countenance but stood in the blood-drenched street in all his awful glory. His face was as red as his cardinal's robe, his robe stained a deeper crimson. He had been busy. Chaos and carnage were his elements.

As if he knew he was being watched, he smiled. His white teeth gleamed in his long red face.

Rick's anger boiled. Destroying Semjaza had been for the good of the world. With Azazel, it was personal.

Two hundred lashes.

In the morning you will burn.

His fist curled and his lips compressed into a thin grim line as he remembered the pain of the scourge and the flames licking his feet.

No lightning bolt for Azazel! The creature would look into his eyes when his destruction came!

He summoned the Merkaba.

The Merkaba vanished when Rick emerged from the inverted, counter-rotating tetrahedrons. He felt its presence, waiting in the wings as it were, just beyond the veil that separated the physical from the ethereal.

He recognized the wedge-shaped tower behind the demon. The iconic One Times Square from which the glittering ball dropped every New Year's Eve. He had watched its descent with his family on a cold winter's night when he was eight, standing in the throng gazing up open-mouthed as the ball dropped and the roar of thousands counting off the seconds to the New Year rang in his ear. Miraculously, despite numerous holes, the giant animated screen facing Times Square survived. Two gigantic blue whales swam in a slow spiral vertically up the tower as if seeking in the sky safety from the carnage below.

Azazel stood before the gaping windows of the Walgreens that occupied the ground floor. His hands were by his sides. He appeared to be waiting to see what Rick would do.

"I thought you were no wizard," the demon mocked. "Yet again, you fall from the sky!" There was no humor in his voice, only a growling anger.

Rick did not answer the angel as he strode through the wreckage but watched the creature's hands and kept an eye out for minions, human or otherwise, waiting to pounce.

Burned and bullet-ridden cars were everywhere. And bodies—citizens, soldiers...the rubble of former angels beneath his feet. The surrounding storefronts were windowless; jagged shards hung precariously in their frames. Holes of all calibers from small arms and cannons desecrated the tourist mecca. He'd seen such pictures in movies and on the news clips of war-torn Lebanon, Iraq, and Afghanistan, but he'd never thought to see such devastation in Manhattan. He kicked aside what might have been a stone ear and stopped.

Now that he faced the demon, he had no plan. He couldn't just launch into Azazel, fists flailing. He'd seen how that worked out with Talmaiel—and Azazel was massive compared to the Shining One.

As if sensing his hesitation, Azazel raised his hands.

At first, it seemed that chaos had chosen this moment to claim the building, and he thought maybe time would save him the trouble and take Azazel along with the structure. But the building itself wasn't vanishing—instead, a great hole—a tunnel to elsewhere—was opening in the façade. The gaping Walgreens windows and a section of the billboard above vanished, replaced by swirling darkness.

Streetlamps exploded. Sparks showered from the traffic lights at the intersection. All over midtown lights extinguished. Half the city plunged into a blackout.

In the purple twilight, Azazel spread his arms wide, as if inviting him to fight.

Again, he was mistaken. The Sorcerer was summoning something from the turbulence at his back.

A winged creature streaked from the portal. All sharp angles and glistening like an oil slick. And another. And another.

He ducked the first attack, but the edge of a wing struck his face, opening a gash in his cheek. Reflexively, he flung up a hand and the second creature slid to one side as if he'd raised an invisible shield. But now other creatures, as black and angular as the winged oil slicks, appeared. Their loping gait reminded him of the Tindalosi, and he experienced a moment of soul-shriveling terror. But as they neared, he saw they were not the hounds but spider-legged monstrosities that scuttled across sidewalks and leapt cars almost as quickly as the winged creatures flew. Black and featureless, as if they were silhouettes cut from shadow, they reminded him of the Nephilim, and he again recalled the creature that attacked him the night he found the desiccated corpse of the girl who had hid in the bathtub. The great misshapen skull, the scything talons, the eyes as black as its shadow flesh radiating hungry malevolence.

The memory flashed through his head in the second before the monsters struck. Again, totally reflexively, because he had no time to react otherwise and no idea what else to do but protect himself, he threw up his hands to ward off the attacking beasts that leapt through the air. This time, instead of deflecting to either side as if they had run into a force field, they stopped and hung in midair as if caught in a stop-action photo.

He clenched his teeth and smacked his hands together. The creatures exploded like Christmas ornaments. Shadow shards rained to the street, disappeared. Perhaps it was his imagination, but a primal howl of rage seemed to ring in his inner ear.

The winged attackers returned. When they were almost on him, he did the same for them.

But Azazel wheeled his arms and the void was filled with violent kinetic motion as more creatures erupted into the physical plane. Rick shielded himself as before, arms flailing, hands grasping, flinging, shoving the Rorschach inkblot monstrosities left and right and grinding them into carbon dust whenever he could. They kept coming, but then, as if seeing they could not reach him, they flashed past and disappeared into the night.

Within seconds screams echoed through Manhattan's canyons.

———————

People were dying. A windstorm of demons was loosed upon the world.

Azazel stood with his back to the whorling darkness. Rick's first thought was to hurl him into the portal and hope that he could close it. But Azazel would be lord over demons there. And though that infernal world would soon pass—as would all the planes of Yaldabaoth's devising—he would, in effect, be fulfilling Yaldabaoth's promise. That was reward, not punishment. The monster deserved worse.

Far worse.

Azazel raised his hand as if to summon another plague of demons. Though he stood beyond reach, Rick reached out as if to grab it. Azazel looked at his hand suspended above his head.

...*who harnesses the power, the potency, of desire and bends it to his will...*

A solution was forming.

...*transform desire by focusing it into a laser beam of intent...*

His desire was to punish Azazel.

Imagination is the astral tool with which the magus manipulates elementary matter and alters the underlying sidereal forces of the ethereal world.

But how?

The imaginatio.

Rick imagined crushing Azazel as he had destroyed several demons. But he could not see Azazel's face. He remembered Bellarmino watching with sadistic pleasure as his tormentor applied the scourge. He wanted to see Azazel's face as he—

An image came to him. Something he had seen as he gazed into the Aleph. A smiling child reaching up and encompassing the moon between thumb and forefinger.

Visualize…

He released Azazel's hand and shifted his own so that, from his vantage in the middle of Broadway, he saw the demon wedged between his fingers. He squeezed and the demon cried out. Raging, Azazel pushed upward with both hands as if a great weight had fallen on him and was driving him down.

Rick increased the pressure, pinching Azazel between thumb and forefinger. The harder he squeezed, the harder the demon pushed against the invisible pressure over his head until Rick's hand ached and Azazel's resistance threatened to break his hold. Redoubling his efforts, he envisioned crushing the angel until he popped like a mosquito.

Sweat ran down his face. His hand shook. He forgot to breathe. And still he pressed. And Azazel began to give.

Two hundred lashes.

The heat of the flames…

He switched to both hands and visualized Azazel's bones cracking and his body crumpling, growing smaller and smaller as lungs enfolded heart until the very corpuscles and cellular composition collapsed and the demon was compressed into a singularity, a miniature black hole, no bigger than a flea egg.

And even now the demon's transformation was not complete. As Rick continued to press—veins in his temples bulging, his face grimacing with the effort, his eyes squinting with concentration— photons, electrons, quarks, gluons boiled off the quantum singularity too small to maintain stability. Its entropy plummeted as it neared its thermodynamic equilibrium until—energy particles evaporated—all that remained was a single massive Planck-sized particle, a quantum object so dense it sank into the earth under its own weight until coming to rest in the planet's core where it would lodge as long as the earth survived.

74

THE VANISHING WORLD

The struggle was not over.

As Rick watched, exhausted, One Times Square shed its mantle of giant LED displays and its sleek marble cladding and reverted to its original terracotta and limestone façade. The sign above the entrance to the narrow gray stone structure of yesteryear advertised "The New York Times." Then the air shimmered like a heat mirage and One Times Square was replaced by a nine-story hotel. The circular logo on the roof advertised "The Papst."

Down the block a billboard advertising Camels and featuring a smoking man wearing a Fedora and puffing smoke rings over the street replaced the ABC Studio's digital displays.

Traffic lights vanished. Ornate turn-of-the-century wrought-iron streetlamps replaced modern ones. Ancient cars from the early twentieth century shared the cobblestone road with horse-drawn carriages.

He had failed! Time was fleeting. Entropy wreaking havoc as the arrow of time sped backward toward the singularity of the beginning. The world was vanishing. The bruised sky alternately dark, light, dark, light as time hurtled the earth and everyone in it back through cycling days.

The past is written; the future is an open book.

Only it wasn't. The book was closing fast.

Tempus fugit.

He closed his eyes and filled his mind with a vision of Fergi. He saw her as the Sibyl, sitting on her marble, lion-armed throne, eyes glaring, lips compressed to a thin line as she spoke between her teeth, her voice chilling, not Fergi's but that of some otherworldly being inhabiting her body, commanding her tongue.

Become Eternity…

But to become Eternity, he would have to be eternal. And if he, born of this world, were eternal, the world would not be ending. Clearly, he'd failed!

Then she was sleeping next to him in the bed they'd shared so briefly (not the Sibyl but *his* Fergi—as much as she would ever allow herself to belong to anyone but herself), the autumn splendor of her hair a sunset cloud on her pillow; the curve of her neck, her bare shoulder pale in the moonlight falling through the window.

And he saw her by the river the day they'd gone to Mud Island and she'd taken off her boots and waded in the model of the Mississippi, her white feet leaving wakes in the clear water as a rare delicious smile parted her lips, a smile that reached her eyes, and seemed—or so he remembered hoping—fixed on him…before he ruined it all and chased the smile off her face by telling her he loved her.

And now he saw her by the door to her room at the Sisterhood, dressed in a white gown, the newly acquired silver streak in her hair making her look older, wiser, telling him, "I love you, Richard Scott." And never mind she'd added, "But I've made my choice," and chose not to return to him but remain with the Sisterhood.

I have my work and you have yours.

There was love there—despite the paths they'd taken.

Believe that nothing is impossible…

But he knew his limits. He'd accomplished more than he ever thought possible, but he was not immortal, and as for changing the course of time, he might as well stand at the shore and command the tide to cease.

He opened his eyes and knew he had to see her before the end—before it was all swept away.

A horse-drawn omnibus passed before him. The horses' shod hooves clattered on the cobblestones and the iron-bound wooden wheels rumbled and squealed on the rails that ran down the middle of the street. Frightened faces gazed from the windows. The horses whinnied and balked. The driver shook the reins and hurried them on.

When the bus passed, he saw Grace standing across the intersection in front of a cigar store. The awning advertised Robert Burns Cigars. The second-floor windows, like all the upstairs windows of the buildings down the block, were hidden behind billboards advertising Broadway shows ("The Moth and the Flame playing at the Lyceum Theatre," "The Castle Square Opera Co.") alongside ads for beer and whiskey and hatters and household products. Grace's blood-stained clothes went from red to black as night succeeded day and gas lamps came on.

He summoned the Merkaba, not the green that had emanated from Hermes Pillar and transported him to Yaldabaoth's Aleph, but the blue of the ten sapphires of Raziel's Book. The light chariot appeared in the air above the street. Its inverted tetrahedrons counter-rotating at such a speed they blurred the air, its whir drowning out the noise of iron wheels and shod hooves.

He extended his hand and the chariot vanished. The ten stones glittering in his palm as if with their own cobalt fire were cool against his skin. The last time he'd held them they'd been embedded in the surface of the whorled, auger-shell-shaped device Wally had called a psychotronic generator. Arraigned in three columns, four stones in the central, three on either side, they formed the Tree of Life, the Sephiroth. The Jacob's Ladder that connected the Above with the Below, Kether with Malkuth. They were so small, yet, together, capable of generating cosmic power. It was said they contained the wisdom of the universe. Following Wally's death and Talmaiel's banishment, he'd wanted nothing to do with generators or Kabbalah or da Silva's teachings. Now he wished he'd been granted the time to learn to read them, to master their power. Maybe then… But such was not to be.

Tempus fugit!

He closed his fingers over the cool crystals—and squeezed, willing the world right again, day following night, the past flowing into the future, spring following winter. He shut his eyes as he did so. But when he opened them, the omnibus was receding and the dark sky boiled like a festering wound.

Grace still stood before the cigar store, watching him. He nodded to her. She nodded back.

He tossed the stones into the air where they formed the Tree. The twenty-two paths lit up connecting stone to stone, plane to plane, from Kether, Crown, to lowly Malkuth, the doomed physical world. Above, below.

The stones began to spin, altering their formation to become the familiar light chariot, two inverted tetrahedrons, one pointing up, the other down, whirling in opposite directions. Faster now, humming like a top. A wind blew off them, flinging the grit of the street in his face.

He stepped forward. The light vehicle received him, lifted him above the ancient, tarred roofs and vanished.

75

GATEWAY

The Merkaba set him down on the ledge outside Sibyl's cave. Avernus far below was a cauldron of ghostly mist. Save for the plop of bubbling mud, the night was eerily quiet. There were no bird calls, no buzz of insects. As before, the oppressive humidity instantly soaked his clothes and the sulfurous fumes burned his eyes.

Entering, he wrinkled his nose at the sickly sweet, decaying-flowers smell the cavern exuded like some fetid corpse-breath. He knew the way, and this time neither fear nor numinous awe slowed him as he made his way toward the torch-lit chamber beyond the tall trapezoidal doorway.

On her throne of white marble, hands resting on the carven lions' heads, the Sibyl (Fergi) sat as he had left her. How long had she remained thus? Days? His jaw clenched with anger at Cybele for making her a vessel for the ancient crone. He understood the Sisterhood had a duty to perform and Fergi was committed to fulfilling her part

I have my work and you have yours.

but it hurt to see her used like this.

She said nothing, just stared, her face unsmiling, as if waiting for him to ask his question.

What was the point? It was over. Cybele was gone, banished to who-knows-where. There was no advice the Sibyl could give that would save a world past saving.

The vapors rising from fissures in the cavern floor were making him dizzy. It occurred to him that the fumes were instrumental in keeping Fergi sedate while the ancient creature inhabited her.

Without speaking, he stepped up to the throne, gathered Fergi in his arms, and bore her out of the cavern. She neither fought nor resisted but remained ridged as if she still sat on her throne. His heart sank as he realized how much weight she had lost.

Outside, he lowered her to her feet. She swayed and leaned against him. He held her, listening to her breathing until it became even. The air reeked, but out of the cavern's lotus fumes, she seemed to relax. Her rigidity softened. She drew back, confusion in her eyes, like someone waking in an unfamiliar place and not remembering how she had gotten there.

"Rick?"

She touched his face. Her fingers were cold. He took her hands in his and rubbed them. "I'm here."

Her lips parted, her eyes clearing as memory returned. She shivered.

"The Sibyl..."

"It's okay. She's gone. You're here."

"Did we...?" Her eyes were searching, but the unnatural sky could not hide the truth.

"No." It was all he could say. More would be too much for either of them to bear.

She nodded and her gaze grew distant as if she were considering the enormity of their failure: the end of the world and everything man had ever accomplished and all he might yet accomplish, and beyond their world the universe itself, all creation—gone, vanished, as if it had never been! The slate wiped clean!

Her eyes teared. Besides his mom, Fergi was the strongest woman he'd ever known. Seeing the anguish welling beneath her furrowed brows was the last straw, the nail in his heart. His failure to reverse Yaldabaoth's unmaking was doubly agonizing, if not for the world, then for her.

"Rick, I'm—"

He touched a finger to her lips. "Shhh, don't say it. The past doesn't matter. All we have is this moment." He shook his head. He felt like crying himself.

She nodded, understanding. She leaned against him. She was nearly as tall as him and his cheek rested against her temple. Burying his nose in her hair, he closed his eyes and breathed her scent. Holding her, he felt no sense of fear standing on oblivion's shore, no urgency to find closure, only a peace he'd thought lost forever.

His fingers caressed the thick curls at the back of her head while his lips brushed her ear.

When he opened his eyes, they stood on the shore of another lake. It was surely not Avernus: birds wheeled overhead, the air was fresh as clean linen, a scent of salt blew in from the nearby sea, and the sky, paling to dawn, was moonless. Shimmering in the cobalt blue above the opposite rim, a tiny skein of stars hung just above the trees.

"Look" he whispered.

Her gaze followed his pointing finger. "The Sisters," she said.

"Beltane," he said. "In ancient times, the Pleiades rising above the eastern horizon just before dawn heralded the beginning of spring. The season of life and light." The irony that the world should end in spring was not lost on him.

She touched his face, her dark eyes searching. He didn't move for fear she would take the hand away. Was that the barest trace of a smile lifting the corner of her mouth?

"You've changed, Rick."

He had to smile at that. Though the Nemorenses no longer resided in his head, their memories—their collective knowledge—remained: vast aisles of dusty tomes he had yet to crack.

But her gaze slid past him, her eyes widened, and it was her turn to point and say, "Look."

Gone was the Sibyl's cave, the moist rock, the mist, and the sulfurous fumes. The grotto from which they had emerged had vanished utterly. In its place was a high wall built of blocks of volcanic tuff stone set into the cliff face like the rock-cut tombs of Antalya or the temples of Abu Simbel only on a lesser scale—a simple façade of cut blocks set into rock and, in its midst, a tall timber door.

The door itself bore the Crown of the Triple Goddess—two outward-facing crescents bookending a circle: the moon, old, new, and full, carved into the ancient oak.

She's here!

Despite what Yaldabaoth said, he felt Her presence. Not the earthly incarnation who tormented him with conflicting emotions of reluctant reverence and infuriating lust, but a presence ineffably greater, as far removed from Cybele as the Goddess was above him.

The Crown began to glow and grew brighter until it seemed a silvery radiance in the shape of the triune moon floated in the air before the door. As he watched, spellbound, the emblem expanded and the outward-facing crescents of the new and old moons folded inward over the full moon, the inner curves of their crescents forming the almond shape of the *vesica piscis*. He recognized the figure—the mandorla, the gateway, the cosmic portal, the intersection between the human and the divine.

The incarnated Goddess he knew as Cybele was merely an intimation of HER! The Aeon Sophia! Mother of the Demiurge, who had created the universe in which he and Fergi and all mankind and earth and moon and planets and sun and galaxy and all the galaxies beyond existed. And all of it no more than grains of sand in the palm of infinity to the Aeons and the Luminous Source.

Despite his reluctance to do the Goddess' bidding, to be Her pawn

You are my knight.

or, for that matter, to serve as Her Priest—he could not help trembling. Dizzy with the vastness of the concepts that assailed his mind, he stood before the portal as if buffeted by a cosmic wind.

Fergi's hand slipped into his. The contact of her warm flesh grounded him. She wore the white gown of the Sisterhood and the silver streak in her forelocks lent her an atmosphere of solemnity, but the green flecks in her eyes were sparkling and an unexpected dimple graced the corner of her mouth.

Fergi—*his Fergi!*—yet smiling as the cynical Delores Ferguson he knew would never have allowed herself—took his arm and they entered.

76
SEX MAGIC

The octagonal chamber seemed vast, the walls appearing far off as if an echo might take days to carry thence and back again, the vaulted dome leagues above and filled with the light of emanation as the Divine Sophia poured down Her love onto and into the vessels that were the creations of Her creation.

It was all an optical illusion, some trick of astral vision, because the eight couples, of whom he and Fergi were one, stood in an intimate circle around the Goddess, who sat naked on Her throne, facing eight directions at once.

Through eight arched windows mounted high in the walls, the light of eight full moons fell on eight beds radiating outward from the Goddess like spokes in a wheel. That it was impossible for the moon to shine from eight directions at once or for Her to face eight directions did not disturb Rick. He had accepted, upon entering the Nymphaeum, that he and Fergi had been transported to some place that bowed to other laws than Earth's material plane.

Nor did the fact that he and Fergi, as well as the other seven couples, were naked cause him concern. For once, desperate to succeed where he had failed and embracing what seemed man's final hope, he was putting his faith in the Goddess' hands. For, though the shimmering vision of the Goddess seemed only partially present, as if the spiritual realm was manifesting in the physical, he understood the

328

unadulterated light of the spirit realm was far more real than the shadows of ephemeral Malkuth.

Fergi still held his hand, for which he was grateful. He drew strength from her strong grip, her unwavering sense of purpose. He stole a glance at her. It was true she had grown thinner, her face and waist tightened, but her hips and breasts were full and her flawless skin glowing in the moonlight inflamed him.

At a nod from the Goddess, the women drew their men onto the beds. These were not sumptuous down-filled mattresses covered in Oriental silks, but soft pallets dressed in flaxen linen.

He slid his hand along her flank. She was always so pale, her skin like milk. A Pre-Raphaelite might have painted her as the Moon Goddess.

Luna.

Her hand slid between them, grasped him. His erection, already swollen, grew painfully hard. It had been so long. He felt himself swooning. Then he was enveloped in her warmth and they were moving as one.

He smelled her arousal. A deep heady primal sea scent and he pulled her tighter. Her nipples were hard against his chest, her stomach python-taut against him. He kissed her throat and she moaned, a deep guttural sound of pleasure and desire. Her hands clasped his back and he was on the cusp of laughing with joy at the strength of her, but her leg wrapped around his and pulled him deeper and he groaned against her throat.

As the sacred orgia approached its climax and the eight-fold presence of the Divine Sophia presided over the Ceremony of the Winged Serpent, a shimmering silvery-blue light snaked across the floor and climbed the walls, illuminating the lovers in its shifting, pale iridescence. And when the lovers shuddered to a crescendo of release, the pulsing Kundalini light flared and, for a moment, enveloped the room in a blinding blue-white radiance before it exploded out through the oculus in the dome's peak, pierced the clouds, and, penetrating the veil between the planes, traversed the supernal realms. Amplified as it passed through the two-sided mirror of the Astral plane, the light sped through the Mental plane where the three-sided prismatic mirror removed more of the shadow and the purified light rushed on to the Spirit realm where the All-mirror of the Aleph augmented it a million-fold and hurled it back down the cosmic ladder till it burst upon the physical universe in a light not seen since the creation. And burrowing through the atmosphere of the small blue planet, the rarified light touched off a chain reaction among the Earth's sacred stones.

The Black Stone of Mecca.

London's Cleopatra's Needle and its Manhattan sibling.

The meteorite stone that once stood in the Temple of Artemis, now housed in a Mediterranean Millionaire's private collection.

The Delphic Omphalos, the navel stone of the Temple of Apollo.

Stonehenge's Neolithic blue stones and the greater stone circle at Avebury.

The Standing Stones of Stenness and Orkney's Ring of Brodigar.

Lia Fáil, the coronation stone of ancient Tara.

The thousands of menhir or man stones studding the planes and hills of Europe.

The deer stones of Mongolia and the Korean dolmens and Scandinavian henges.

And the great crystal deposits of the world—the rich diamond mines of Africa and an undiscovered source in Antarctica, Columbia and Afghanistan's emerald mines, Kashmir and Mogok's treasury of sapphires, the vast quartz crystal deposits of Arkansas and Brazil.

The Pillar of Hermes pulsed green fire.

Gazing inland, the giant Moai of Easter Island woke.

Deep beneath the Atlantic's gray waters, lost Atlantis' prismatic Firestones, so long absent from the sun and lying like so many dead batteries on the ocean's floor, throbbed to life.

And as the sapphiric radiance rose from stone and spire and spread through the atmosphere englobing Earth, cities rent by conflicting timelines were restored. Floods receded, fires extinguished. Collapsed towers reared and shattered cups flew from floor to table becoming whole again. Space-time healed, and up and down history, people ventured out and found their world resurrected, their skies refreshed, their neighbors returned. Many wondered if they had dreamed it all—

the descent into chaos and the ravening demons. And they might have convinced themselves, but for the fact they'd shared the same dream.

77
THE FIRE OF LOVE

The brook spoke to him. *This way! Follow me!* it seemed to say. He followed along its wildflower-sprinkled bank. The bright splash of water over smooth pebbles and the occasional bird call accompanied him. The forest's dense canopy made of the sunlight a dappled tapestry so that he alternately walked in shade or golden beams. Tangled underbrush sometimes drove him from the water's edge but the stream's insistent babble and the occasional glimpse of sunlight on its rippling surface led him back to its brink.

Rick was no longer on the physical plane. He could see through his hands as if they were as insubstantial as smoke, though they were not. And he knew he could pass through boles of trees if he so willed, and gravity would not restrain him if he chose to levitate. But he preferred to walk. He had some thinking to do before he reached his goal.

He came to a pool where the stream eddied and silver minnows darted over the brown sand.

This way! Follow me! The brook insisted.

"In a minute," he said and took a seat on a lichen-covered rock. Ignoring him, the minnows continued to dart through the sun-silvered water, turning like starlings when they neared the bank.

He could still feel Fergi warm in his arms. Her scent was fresh in his nostrils. The world was healed. And he had been a part of it, he and Fergi. The memory took his breath away.

But the joy was not without sadness. Cities had risen from ruins, but the dead did not wake. Grace and John and Her people were back in Hendricks, where Maija and seven others had been laid to rest alongside those who had fallen in last year's battle. The attrition of war had taken a toll on the little hamlet. He hoped there would be no more battles on his watch.

And Fergi? Did he love her? Moody as the moon and apt to heed the Sisterhood's call at a moment's notice?

He remembered finding one of her tee shirts in the hamper after she left and pressing it to his face to capture her scent. He'd slept on her pillow where the python coils of her hair had lain.

The sky might rain frogs or the earth fall into the abyss at any moment, but his feelings for Delores Ferguson were constant.

And what of himself, Richard Scott, son of Frank and Jenny, mortal yet possessing Grigori blood? A victim of heredity and a Goddess' kiss? What was to become of him?

He was certainly not going to lock himself up in the Aleph and become caretaker to the multiverse! He'd left that job in the capable hands of da Silva and his fellow Nemorenses. It was governance by committee, but they were smart enough to figure what to do in a crisis. And with the Merkaba on call, they were never far away.

Outside the Aleph, standing on the great plain that might have been a plateau of chromium steel or a field of grass depending on his desire, surrounded by the platoon of brass golems that housed the minds or essences of Her priests, he'd given da Silva his decision.

"You saw Her? Not the incarnation, but the Divine Sophia?" da Silva asked.

On the Spiritual Plane of the Aleph, words were accompanied by thought-impressions more emotional and color-nuanced than language-based, and the Priest's tone was at once hushed, excited, reverential, and jealous, tinged with pink and green.

Nothing like conversing on the Spiritual Plane to get in touch with a person's honest feelings. Duplicity was an artifact of shadow and as such could not withstand the pure light of the Spiritual world. Da Silva's words were accompanied by emotionally charged impressions of magnificence, grandeur, mystery, awe, and love—one great heartthrob that blossomed from the mind that was the essence of Reginaldo Balthazar Tavares da Silva. Rick knew exactly what he meant, and his own thoughts mirrored the sentiments he felt radiating from the minds and figurative hearts of the host.

These men had spent long lifetimes serving the incarnated Goddess and knew the original only by legend and faith, while he, a novice — and an unwilling one at that—had gazed upon the unearthly splendor of the Aeon Herself.

"I don't know what I saw," he said to lessen their disappointment, but they saw through the brown fog of his hedging.

"The pupil outstrips the master," da Silva conceded, and Rick, despite his best effort to suppress emotion, felt the swelling of pride. A burst of blue sky accompanied by numinous joy.

Telling Reginald he was leaving him in charge of the Aleph, he saw a mental image of the Priest blowing out his cheeks. "Ay, Dios! Well, it beats rotting in the Châtelet! If I'm to be in charge, then the future will definitely have to be a happier place!"

He certainly hoped so.

And what of his quest?

Find the Philosopher's Stone.

Had he found it? He believed he had.

The Stone is the path, the path the journey.

…the Stone is nothing less than the attainment of complete self-awareness and of the higher consciousness.

The Stone is a metaphor for transformation.

The Stone is the journey connecting what lies below to what is above.

And what had he found at the end of his journey?

One startling revelation he'd discovered was one did not complete the Great Work alone.

Sol, Luna.

Sun, Moon.

Man, Woman.

The union of male and female.

Conjunctio…

The Marriage of Sol and Luna!

Make of the man and woman a circle.

334

Man and woman together *were* the mirror of eternity, reflecting the divine emanation back onto the upward path of evolution. He'd gotten that much right, for Earth without humankind, without the consciousness of man to evolve, was just a place. But man and woman *together* were so much more!

The material of the Stone was nothing less than Sol and Luna, Man and Woman. Without the seed of both, neither life nor consciousness can generate or evolve.

He thought of all the alchemists who had labored in isolation over the centuries and who had never completed the Great Work.

He smiled, for he knew the answer, knew in his heart of hearts he had it right. The *lapis philosophorum* was not a red powder hidden in an old abbey nor a formula in an antique book.

He recalled Bruno, the passionate defrocked friar so full of life, waving his arms as he declaimed, yet doomed to the Inquisition's flames in the end.

Thoughts must break free of the shadow world and soar in the light. What is required is a divine frenzy, a heroic enthusiasm, a kind of madness that poets and artists seek from muses. That is the Philosophic Fire, which is the Fire of Love. Not animal love which is the lower aspect of Venus, but the higher aspect which is Divine Love.

…the Fire of Love…

Love! Not the Hallmark-card platitude Fergi so contemptuously abhorred, nor the loin-inflaming, hormone-driven Darwinian lust of reproduction, the biological imperative, but divine, fiery Love!

Love was the Philosopher's Stone. The quintessence of the *lapis philosophorum*. The culmination of the *Magnus Opus*. The fruit of the hermetic quest.

As if she stood beside him, whispering in his ear, he heard Fergi's voice reminding him of what she said that night he visited her at the Sibylline Sisterhood before his battle with Talmaiel.

I love you, Richard Scott. But I've made my choice. I have my work and you have yours.

And he remembered how he'd realized love was a fundamental force, like gravity or electromagnetism, as natural as rain and as essential as breath. Love, profound and necessary. Perhaps the primary force that drove the multiverse, for gravity and electromagnetism and the strong force and the weak were servants of creation, part and parcel with the machinery that kept the multiverse running, while Love enshrined in the Divine emanation was the very dynamo that powered creation. The desire of the One to become Two. So that the profound aloneness and torpidity of the Eternal exploded into a whirlwind of autogenesis, of multiplicity.

He took it all in...the material planes and the astral above, the multiverse he'd witnessed in the Aleph and all the higher worlds beyond soaring to the Eternal...the Eternal mirrored in man. Was the hand that forged man and star moved by Love? If so, there was hope.

A woodpecker drumming in a nearby tree broke his revelry.

The minnows still darted in the shallows.

This way! Follow me! the stream insisted.

Rick rose and followed.

He knew he was close when he saw the anemones, columbines, and violets spring back unblemished following his passage.

78

THE ENDLESS KNOT

She was waiting by the fountain when he came up the walk, pea stone crunching beneath his Vans. In Her white gown and golden sandals, She looked as She had the first time he met Her, in the Memphis flea market. Green-eyed and fiery haired with skin like alabaster, She was morning to Fergi's evening—which was strange for a being whose power waxed greatest under a full moon.

That She was an earthly incarnation and not the undiminished Goddess Herself, he was grateful. He had no idea how he would handle a face-to-face with the supernatural being he'd beheld in the Nymphaeum.

A few of the Sisters were about, walking the garden paths, one reading a book in an arbor. Some of the younger ladies wore shorts and sneakers. The elders wore the ubiquitous white gowns. *Sign of the times,* he thought.

The garden was a cornucopia of colors and scents. Tulips and daffodils of every hue filled nearby beds. Flowering trees and banks of rosebushes and azaleas provided avenues of reds and whites and pinks. Elsewhere, white cascades of bridalwreath were underplanted with pansies and pink sweet peas. Beyond the winding walks pine trees towered where the forest began. The combined scents wafting on the summery air were almost as intoxicating as the gardenia-laden scent of Her perfume. Close by, the white, ivy-clad, many-gabled house rose against the azure sky.

337

This was no earthly garden but a paradise of eternal spring where every petal, every blade of grass, every leaf was perfect. Nowhere was there a sign of fading leaf or wilting flower.

The fountain babbled much as the brook, only it seemed to playfully mock him. *Watch out! Watch out!* it said. He was only too happy to take its advice: his last meeting with Cybele was a life-changing event. Wary of getting too close, he involuntarily wiped a knuckle across his lips, remembering the sting of Her kiss.

She laughed. As always, Her laughter was as bright as the sunshine, as playful and spontaneous as the sparkling fountain.

"My knight returns," She said and, to his surprise, lightly lifted Her gown and curtsied. While the curtsy was perfectly executed, one sandaled foot behind the other and Her back elegantly erect, She did not lower Her eyes but met his gaze with an impish smile.

Impish? Hardly. As ever, She combined the attributes of regal goddess and seductive nymphet. He felt the bewitching pull of sexual attraction She cast around Her like an aura and knew he was wise to keep his distance.

"No kiss for me today, young Sir?"

He started to excuse himself, but She—or Her progenitor—*had* helped save Creation. Unsure of the wisdom of offending a Goddess, he compromised by taking a half step forward and kissing Her hand. "My Lady."

Her dimples deepened.

"Rik-art," She used the old High-German pronunciation of his name, "what will you do now? Will you rule Earth from Olympus?"

Talmaiel's parting words before the light chariot carried him to Abyss came back to him: *The world is yours, Richard Scott. Make of it what you will.*

"Apotheosis implies death," he said, "and I believe I've earned the right to pursue my life as I see fit." He considered paraphrasing Milton's Satan, "Better to rule on Earth than serve in Heaven," but thought better of it. He didn't want to rule anywhere. While it was obvious his old life would never be the same and he'd accepted his obligation to protect the world, he could serve mankind as well from the earthly plane as from the spiritual. Better, on Earth he had his ear to the ground and his eye on the horizon. "No, I'll go back to work. Just want a normal life."

"Normal?" She lifted a brow. "You're hardly that. But you're a good man, Richard Scott."

"I don't know about that."

"I do."

He hesitated. He had to ask. "I couldn't help wondering…"

She still smiled but Her lips were closed now, the dimples softened. With the dusting of freckles across Her nose, She looked almost human, if such a thing were possible, but the light picked up the gold flecks in Her green eyes and left no doubt he gazed upon an immortal.

"She whom you knew as Cybele is an incarnation of my true self," She said. "Just as I am. No matter how many universes Yaldabaoth created—or you, Richard—there will always be a Cybele, a Sophia, a Diana, an Astarte to watch over it. I am multitudes. I'm sure you, of all people, understand."

Remembering seeing himself replicated into infinity in his twin's eyes, he nodded.

Gazing into Cybele's eyes was like staring into the sun: it was disorienting and made his eyes water. He turned his attention to the house, found the upstairs window to the left of the porticoed entrance.

"We'll keep her room for her," She said, following his gaze.

He met Her eyes. "Well, I just wanted to pay my respects and thank you for your help. And to see where we stand."

"Where we've always stood. You are my knight and my Priest, and at the same time you are your own man. I have every faith you will always do what is necessary." Her smile broadened. "It's your nature. But before you go."

She reached behind Her neck and, unclasping the silver chain that hung about Her throat, withdrew Her talisman. The pentangle. The endless knot. The five-pointed star woven from a single strand of electrum shimmered like a rainbow in the sunlight. He remembered how the crystal She'd given him in the flea market burned against his chest when he faced the Nephilim and imagined Her pentangle would do no less, nor would it be any less powerful if used against the legions of darkness.

He raised a hand to object. "No thanks," he said. "I can't take your pentangle." What he wanted to say was *I don't want to wear your brand*.

"Nonsense. The planes are fraught with danger. Perhaps one day my talisman will protect you on your journeys."

His apprehension doubled as She stepped closer and fastened the clasp behind his neck.

Her perfume made him dizzy, and he gazed at the blue sky to avoid falling into the pools of Her eyes. She didn't step back but put Her hands on his shoulders, as if testing his strength. His heart raced at Her closeness. He had willpower—he'd proven that in battle, but no man resists the Goddess.

She leaned toward him and he feared the worst. He closed his eyes.

But She merely kissed him lightly on the cheek and released him.

"Go, Richard Scott, with my blessing."

His ears burned and he hardly felt the ground under his feet as he turned and walked back toward the forest. Her parting words followed him like two notes from a crystal chime, "My knight!"

79

PERKS

Fergi was leaning against the car when he emerged from the woods into the bright sunlight feeling like True Thomas stepping back into human realms after a sojourn in Elfland. Despite the day's warmth, she wore a black tee shirt and black skinny jeans. The jeans were old and faded and hugged her hips like a Ferrari taking a curve. The vintage Doc Martens were shiny new. Her arms were folded under her breasts and she watched him with a half-mocking smile that let him know she thought Cybele had kissed him. Despite himself, he felt embarrassed, and annoyed because she made him feel embarrassed, but it beat missing her. He was under no illusion that life with Fergi was going to be a bed of roses...at least not without the occasional thorn. They were both too stubborn and independent-minded not to have their differences, but where there was fire there was light.

"How'd it go?"

"She gave me the day off. Where do you want to go?"

"Someplace quiet. Lake. Desert. Don't really care."

She flicked her head and he watched her fiery auburn hair ripple in the sun. He was amazed how the silver streak increased the loadstone pull he felt for this woman. She was as much a mystery to him as when they first met. But the uncertainty was gone, and that was a good thing. For the moment at least, the ground under his feet felt firm. The sky was cloudless, the breeze laden only with the scent of clover and wildflowers.

He pulled the pentangle from under his tee shirt. Despite the warmth of the day and its having lain against his flesh while he returned through the forest, the electrum was cool in his hand. "She gave me a gift." The talisman flashed in the sunlight. "You okay with it?"

She shrugged. "If the past is any indication..." She let the implication hang.

She had a point. Most people's problems, however horrible—war, accident, the IRS—derived from earthly sources. The terrors he seemed to attract hailed from entirely different planes. He tucked the talisman back inside his shirt.

He opened the passenger door and Fergi slipped into the T-Bird's sleek leather interior.

His first thought had been to replace the Batmobile, the 1960 model he and his dad spent a summer rebuilding and which he had lost after his doppelgänger gave the interior a bloodbath, with an identical model. Instead, he'd chosen the 1963, the one he'd always wanted. If the 1960 with the fins was the Batmobile, the '63, dubbed the Bullet Bird, with its missile silhouette and rocket taillights, was an interplanetary yacht right off the cover of a '60s science fiction magazine. He'd chosen the Bird in Rangoon red with white soft-top. Other than a few upgrades, like a state-of-the-art 3D sound system and some alterations to the analog clock, including da Silva's trademark space-time tourbillon, the Bird was stock. Right out of a Sixties showroom. Literally.

He slid into the driver's seat, lifted the straw fedora from the dashboard, settled it on his head, and turned the key in the ignition. The 390 V-8 rumbled to life. He slipped on his Wayfarers and punched the button to lower the ragtop, letting the sunlight flood the gorgeous red interior.

He smiled into the rearview, admiring the hat, then put the Bird in drive. If he was going to be a magician, he might as well enjoy the perks.

ABOUT THE AUTHOR

Garrett Boatman is the author of *Stage Fright*: (originally published by Onyx 1988, reissued by Valancourt Books as part of Paperbacks from Hell 2020), *Floaters, A Victorian Zombie Adventure*: (Crystal Lake Publishing 2021), *Night's Plutonian Shore, The Clocks of Midnight*, and *The Mirror of Eternity*: (Macabre Ink 2023).

Garrett's stories have appeared in *The Valancourt Book of Horror Stories, Savage Realms, Penumbra*, and *Weird House Magazine*, among others.

Garrett's obsession with horror began with his grandmother's *Bloody Bones* bedtime stories.

Later, a steady diet of Chiller Theatre and horror novels left him with a burning desire to contribute to the madness. Garrett lives in coastal North Carolina with his wife Roberta and their rescue mutt Brisa.

FOR MORE MADNESS

Visit Garrett at www.garrettboatmanauthor.com.

Hugs to everyone who leaves reviews.

Curious about other Crossroad Press books? Stop by our website:
http://crossroadpress.com
We offer quality writing
in digital, audio, and print formats.

Subscribe to our newsletter on the website homepage and receive a
free eBook.